NEVER GROW OLD

NEVER GROW OLD

The Novel of Gilgamesh

BRIAN TRENT

iUniverse, Inc.
New York Lincoln Shanghai

NEVER GROW OLD
The Novel of Gilgamesh

Copyright © 2007 by Brian Trent

All rights reserved. No part of this book may be used or reproduced by any means, graphic, electronic, or mechanical, including photocopying, recording, taping or by any information storage retrieval system without the written permission of the publisher except in the case of brief quotations embodied in critical articles and reviews.

iUniverse books may be ordered through booksellers or by contacting:

iUniverse
2021 Pine Lake Road, Suite 100
Lincoln, NE 68512
www.iuniverse.com
1-800-Authors (1-800-288-4677)

This is a work of fiction. All of the characters, names, incidents, organizations, and dialogue in this novel are either the products of the author's imagination or are used fictitiously.

ISBN: 978-0-595-42983-7 (pbk)
ISBN: 978-0-595-87324-1 (ebk)

Printed in the United States of America

The thief stopped to catch his breath, and to allow the pain from his twisted knee to subside. Concealed in the green forest, the sweet smells of pine, cedar, and moist earth met his gasps for air. Crickets chirped in the moss at his feet, and monkeys chattered gleefully in the branches above, but he could no longer hear his pursuers. For that, he sighed a deep relief.

He leaned against a thick cedar tree to steal a brief rest. His pursuers had followed him for the better part of an hour now, and only his leap into the forest valley had saved him from receiving a flurry of arrows in his back. His jump had been a desperate one, and very nearly suicidal. From a cliff's ragged edge he had dropped into a cushion of vegetation, breaking his fall and allowing him to spring up from the bushes and bound away into the primeval wilderness. Certainly, the men who trailed him would not dare to follow this amazing leap.

Still, his pursuers were Hittites, and as such they were as proud as they were bloodthirsty. They would not return to their encampment eager to admit failure, that a lone thief had walked off with an Annunaki statue and gone unpunished. For them, it was beyond religiosity; they would tail him for the rest of the day on bloodlust alone.

The thief gulped more air and held it, listening to his heartbeat count off the seconds. Above, no horses running, no clanging of metal weapons, no angry shouting.

Perhaps they knew other ways into the valley. Perhaps even now they were leading their mounts down a narrow path and would again come galloping after him, only this time there would be no miraculous escape. He shivered at the thought, knowing that Hittites were infamous for their love of torture.

Stepping away from the tree, the thief considered his options. Directly above him, two monkeys shrieked and startled his heart.

He didn't know this wilderness, except that it was called the Cedar Forest. A day ago he had followed the Euphrates River upstream, to where he picked up the trail of the Hittite band. Once they had gone to sleep (except for one lookout), he sprinted into camp and grabbed the satchel containing the sacred statue. The pursuit began at once.

That was an hour ago, and despite the ease in which he had snatched their loot, his plan had hit an unexpected snag. He had expected to vanish into the night, losing the group the way he had evaded capture countless times. These Hittites were different. Satchel in hand, the thief had been spotted by their lookout. A shout of alarm! The slumbering warriors leaping to their feet like cats, jumping on their horses, and hunting him through brush and bramble. Now night's cover had fled.

An hour of running. Still, the Euphrates River wound somewhere through this forest, and his innate sense of direction told him it was probably very close. He remembered where he had broken from the riverbank, how the water stayed a northward course with only the gentlest of bends into wilderness. It couldn't be far, and certainly lay away from the cliffs where his pursuers remained. All he needed to do was find it.

Tightening the cord on the leather satchel which held the treasure, he ran deeper into the woods, weaving his passage so as to not leave a direct trail for the Hittites to follow. His boots crushed moss and snapped twigs as he ran. The overhead monkeys cursed wordlessly at him.

Where to sell the statue was a question which loomed next in his mind, now that his anxiety over capture was fading. The closest city was Emar, but a much better price could be secured downstream where the Annunaki were revered. Kish, then, might drive a welcome bargain. Babylon might do one better, but the thief knew he wasn't very popular among the Babylonians. Kish it would be then, and if the market price for his booty was half of what he expected, he might just be able to winter there, in high style, as well.

Not fifteen minutes later his heart lifted when he heard the sound of rushing water, and he chanced to smile at this turn of fate. He pictured the five Hittite horsemen, clad in their patterned kilts and copper helmets, making their way down into the valley only to find his tracks evaporate by the river. The thief was an excellent swimmer and might even be able to find a log to ride the way downstream.

That thought nearly stopped him in mid-run. He stumbled, twisted his knee again, and cursed with new pain. He frowned.

The image of a fallen log filled his mind, unbidden and suddenly fearful. He didn't know why, but the image excited a nervousness that defied explanation. His palms became slippery with sweat.

A fallen tree? he wondered. Why is a fallen tree in this forest cause for anxiety?

From deep within his head, an old childhood rhyme began to emerge. It was one of those songs that all children in Sumer learned growing up. The lyrics were dusty and he strained to accurately recall them:

> *Forest dark and forest deep*
> *Has wood to build and beasts to eat*

There was more to it, the thief was certain. He rubbed his swollen knee, looked back to try and locate some evidence that the Hittites were still in pursuit.

The gallop of horses! Clashing bronze! Again he imagined the would-be assault, and again he saw that he was *not* being pursued. Instead of relieving him this time, it bothered him. Why wouldn't they follow him into the valley? They were five men on horseback, and they knew this country better than he did. Why would they keep out of the Cedar Forest?

That was it! It clicked like a sword fitting into its sheath. The Cedar Forest, an expanse of primordial wilderness, held more wood than any other forest in all of Mesopotamia. The Euphrates River cleaved it, but no axe of man was ever wielded against its trees. Man never went into the Cedar Forest.

The rhyme completed in his head.

Yet he who goes where Cedar's found
Humbaba always hunts him down.

Chills broke out across the thief's neck, and he felt a sweep of childhood terror. He was a rogue, and as such had learned to make the wilderness his home, yet there had been a time when he had dwelled within the walls of a settlement. People in cities feared the forest, and not without reason, since the wildlands held wild beasts. Perhaps the city-dwellers had once seen wolves, or baboons, or snakes, and in their nightmares they concocted worse monsters … peopling the distant lands with slavering horrors. They made up rhymes of scary creatures to keep children obedient. In his years as a rogue, the thief had encountered many animals … but no monsters.

There was no Humbaba. It was a story, like all the others.

The river wasn't far off now. The thief could hear its strong currents and its impact on riverbed rocks. He could almost taste the moisture. Yet his anxiety festered and crackled silently along his spine.

The crickets had gone silent.

Not just the crickets but the monkeys, too; their pestering chatter was absent. The forest was suddenly a terrible vacuum in which the thief could hear his own thin breathing and thundering heartbeat.

Out of defiance, he forced himself to run again. The trees gazed darkly at him, wooden bodies encircling him in a menacing thicket. Their leafy canopies eclipsed the morning.

The thief hoisted himself up a small, rancid slope crawling with beetles. He looked ahead and smiled.

The waters of the Euphrates were golden and beautiful, and the relief they brought him was like a thick wool blanket trampling out his icy fear. He allowed himself to think of Kish again, and started wondering what city pleasures he would partake in once he got there. He would laugh and tell people, "Yes, I wandered about the Cedar Forest! It's beautiful, if a little dark and lonely! But there are no monsters there! There is no *Humbaba!*"

The fear returned, black and heavy on the back of his mind. He shivered despite the warmth of the day.

As a child the story of Humbaba had often haunted his dreams. *Don't go outside at night! Humbaba will get you!* He remembered waking in the night screaming, having barely escaped a shapeless nightmare that, while never revealing its details, had surely been that hideous giant of the children's rhyme:

> *Forest dark and forest deep*
> *Has wood to build and beasts to eat—*

It had been years since he'd thought of it, and he was ashamed at the power it still held over him. He gazed at the rushing Euphrates, and reminded himself that he was no longer a child.

> *Yet he who goes where Cedar's found—*

He wiped away his sweat-dappled brow and fled the security of the woods for the muddy riverbank—

> *Humbaba always hunts him down.*

He had taken a single step into the open when something large and very heavy crushed the foliage behind him. Branches snapped and rained down to the forest floor. The thief saw a massive shadow out of the corner of his eye, tall and terrible, moving rapidly at him.

> *Humbaba always hunts him down.*

Into the river! he thought in terror, his heart banging wildly in the cavity of his chest. He ran, slipped as his knee gave out, pushed himself to the riverbank. Huge footsteps thundered along the ground. Huge footsteps stopped abruptly.

The thief was scrambling up the slope which dipped into the river when he heard the roar. It exploded from behind him like a torrential flood, like a deafening wall of water slamming into a cliff-side. The air vibrated, the grass shook, and suddenly, the thief could not move.

He stared helplessly at the crest of the slope. His muscles were locked in a terrible paralysis. His pulse skipped.

The trumpeting roar died, yet the forest paraded its ghastly echo.

Sweat splashed into the thief's eyes. Inwardly, he screamed.

The ground jumped as the footsteps resumed. A shadow fell across the slope.

Move! the thief shrieked.

The footsteps thundered behind him. A beetle raced across his chest and became entangled in his hair.

Abruptly, the thief's legs sprang to action. He pushed off the crest of the slope.

In mid-jump something grabbed him by his cloak. He jerked like a caught fish, screaming wordlessly into the quiet forest. The hidden animals perked up their ears, quivered silently, and listened to the useless pounding of his fists against the thing that held him.

His shrill screams grew into high-pitched agony as, from the feet up, he was eaten alive.

TABLET I

GILGAMESH

CHAPTER I
THE BANDIT LEADER MEETS A GOD

It was a cool red darkness in the Temple of the Sun, and Ninsun, high priestess of Shamash, gave a soft cry of pleasure as she spun through the smoke-filled altar room. The incense bowls glowed like volcanic pits in the floor, exuding pungent mist that turned the younger, droning priestesses into strange shadows. The glazed wall-carvings seemed to dance with her by gloomy fires.

Ninsun twirled, her lips chanting the sacred prayers that required no concentration from her anymore. She knew them, as surely as knowing every wrinkle on her sun-ruined face. The elegant language poured from her mouth, climbed the fervent chorus, swelled fat from feasting on their adoring voices. She tried not to enjoy the ritual too much. The intercourse of shadow and glowing reflective bowls made her feel youthful as if Time's merciless hand was forced to peel her elderly, silver-haired frame off her soul as a snake might molt, and suddenly she would peer at her reflection to find the eighteen-year-old beauty she had been when she first married, or twenty-two when she birthed her only child ...

Eleven other priestesses danced with her, their eyes awash in red firelight, their teeth a flash of white. The unified chant had a low, disorienting effect, vibrating against their ears, mixing dizziness with the vigorous elation of calling to the silent god who awaited rebirth. Ninsun cast a glance at the temple wall. A narrow slit-window threw the thinnest rays of gloom onto the wall. Only minutes now, until Shamash peeked his golden head from the mountains and set the black sky alight.

In her youth Ninsun had been a striking Sumerian girl, with dark olive skin fitted to her high cheekbones, nose, and chin. Her black curls were now bleached to silver-white, and the god she worshiped had cracked her skin like a dried mud basin. Her eyes burned like red coins in the vaporous temple, however. Her tongue appeared kitten-like, licking her lips.

Above her, the lamb thrashed once in its bondage. A suspension harness held it above the circular, stained altar stone.

Ninsun whirled orgiastically, her elderly body possessed. Yes! The god's power moved through her, spinning her, breathing on her open palms as she placed them flat against the lamb's warm skin. Its heart thudded fiercely in its body. Life! Raw life! She felt ribs bulging beneath the soft exterior in terrified exhalations.

"*Shamash!*" the priestesses ululated.

Ninsun didn't look away, even as the wall behind her lit with the first illumination of the day. A copper knife glittered, passed from hand to outstretched hand. The chanting was a wall of sound which deformed, shifted, and unfolded like invisible wings.

Ninsun's hand closed on the cold metal handle. She spun around once, the weapon aloft in her hand so that the blade glittered and sang in the day's first illumination.

"Give my son a glorious victory!" she demanded, dizzy with the presence of the daybringer. "Protect, guide, and defend him this day!"

The priestesses screamed.

The lamb screamed.

Ninsun brought the knife across the white throat with a shriek of ecstasy. The animal's fear-stricken heartbeat shot the blood into her face, emptying fast upon the altar stone which had been carved in imitation of the sun's radiance. As the lamb's life ebbed away, Ninsun motioned with her hands for this precious gift of life to rise, rise up, soar like a leaf on summer's breeze, to be snatched into Shamash's golden hands.

"Take this gift!" she demanded of her celestial patron. "Give my son triumph!"

At that same moment west of Uruk's Temple of the Sun, a caravan train wound slowly through a narrow valley overlooked by bushy trees and granite boulders.

Nedu's hands were entwined with the leather reins of the head caravan, tense with the uncertainty of a man who had never before worked with horses. The four pale brown animals trotted with tedium, pulling the car, their heads low, while Nedu used the shoulder of his grey tunic to wipe sweat off his sunburnt forehead. His own hands were as cracked as the straps of dead skin he clenched, and with the new sun making the sand steam around his vehicle, Nedu grinned morbidly at the prophecy.

Nedu was First Councilman to King Gilgamesh of Uruk. At fifty-three, he was a sprightly creature. His white hair receded to the midpoint of his fleshy crown, but from there it flowed in woolen wisps over his ears and back of his skull. He warily eyed the forest path and road curling around a green bend.

Even the trees were sweating! he noted. The sunlight speared his watchful eyes. The spoked caravan wheels crunched small stones under their listless rotation. It made him think of the grain mills back home. And predictably, this thought made his stomach growl for food.

Was it so strange to be thinking of Uruk's feasts when death was so near? Nedu shrugged the thought, telling himself that if he survived this day he'd indulge like never before at the upcoming New Year's Festival. His thoughts broke into two veins that wrestled violently with each other. He knew the bandits who had been attacking Uruk's trade routes were probably stalking him right now, but he preferred the memory of the Festival's baked breads, dipping sauces, roast venison, salted pork, fowl! And the beers, which arrived in oak caskets from the merchant roads for the occasion! Every city produced its own unique collection of beers. Nedu wanted to sample good Kish contraband once more.

He sighed and glanced over his shoulder. Eight more vehicles followed him, winding through the valley trail like white-backed tortoises. Cloth covered their bulging cargo, crisscrossed with rope, and the drivers of each looked as weary and frightened as he felt. Bow-wielding guards strode anxiously alongside each vehicle. They looked so young.

"This is insane," he muttered.

Yet such travel was necessary. Food supplies, gold, maps, spices, sculpture, and crates of other goods passed between peace-time cities. Like pollinating bees, caravans nourished the kingdoms they traveled to by providing treasures their own lands did not have. As such, caravans were lucrative business. Not only would their products be sold to the last crate, but there was a lot of room for enterprising. Maps? Intelligence reports (true or false, it didn't matter) on other cities? Correspondence? Sure, the caravan could provide all that, for very reasonable prices …

But Nedu was a councilman, not a merchant. He had lived all of his fifty-three years within the safe boundaries of Uruk. He advised. He debated. He did *not* travel.

For four months, bandits had been hitting travelers along the West Road. In that time five caravans had been hit, plundered, all riders and guards massacred. If the dark, cold, and wild animals did not discourage travel enough, murderous bandits had tipped the scales so far that trade along the West Road was drying up like a stream in a drought.

"I'm not a merchant," Nedu said, as if stating it would ward off the impending massacre. He was not a soldier either.

The caravan wheels hit a bump in the road. Nedu's heart jumped.

Arrows sprang out of the forest.

He actually saw the first one fly by his head, the blue-feathered shaft rotating a full turn as it hissed by. It buried halfway through his accompanying guard's jaw.

The next arrow landed with a hammer-like *thunk!* in Nedu's chest. It nearly pitched him off his seat, and his hands, knotted in the reins, were all that kept him from a backwards crash into the caravan's cloth. A third arrow struck the hindquarters of one of his horses. The animal squealed and began a dance of agony.

From the forest, concealed horsemen burst forth with yells of battle-lust. Bowstrings snapping, they poured down the valley as the caravan guards leapt for safety. Two more men fell dead, impaled neatly by wooden shafts.

Nedu's wounded horse was screaming with terror, kicking and stamping about as the black riders swooped into the valley, swords held high. From behind the caravan wheels, guards returned fire. Their missiles rained into the bush, which then replied with new volleys of blue-feathered arrows to cover the oncoming horsemen. Horns glinted from helmets, their bodies rippled with black feathers and fur.

Nedu remained silent but not motionless. His mare's frantic thrashing was pulling the reins and shaking him back and forth, until finally he untangled his hands and allowed himself to roll into the dirt. The mare felt the release and tried to bolt, wrenching the entire vehicle forward. Nedu dared not open his eyes. But he could hear the attackers thundering into the valley; his boyhood memories of soldiering in Uruk's army filled his mind and he remembered the hand of a stern mentor, shoving his head into the dirt, to listen for the rumble of enemy feet.

The horsemen flew alongside the caravans, bows tossed aside in favor of bronze swords. Perhaps their minds filled with hunger as they passed the swollen caravan covers, wondering what delicious bounty was copiously stored beneath concealment. What gold! What weapons! What foods to fill a starving stomach, to be enjoyed on a free mountaintop with firelight and songs of this day of easy victory!

And even as the horsemen's lust fueled their efforts to kill everyone protecting the unknowable loot, the caravan covers suddenly fell away from each train, and from the humid, cramped compartments hidden defenders sprang into the riders.

Man and beast entangled, bronze split the sinews and soft bellies of both. The horsemen panicked, attempted a desperate swerve-off, as they found themselves surrounded by terrible Urukian warriors. Fighters from the first caravan had already come up behind them to block their escape, and the bandits were suddenly in the midst of a screaming fray. The only escape was to ride back uphill, toward the forests where their compatriot archers scrambled to load more arrows to their bows.

The bandit leader was proudly distinguished by his horned headdress and skull-mask faceplate, splashed with ram's blood to imitate the demons that had frightened him as a boy. He was the first to steer away from the ambush, astonished at how badly he had miscalculated this siege. But the gods had writ his destiny, so the surviving compatriots would sing that night. A particularly tall Urukian man charged him, leapt, grabbing him by one of his helmet's horns. The bandit was twisted off his horse and broke his nose in the dirt.

The tall Urukian, clad in grey kilt, blue leather armor, and matching greaves wasted no time in facing his next opponents. Two horsemen riding side-by-side, swinging their swords atop steeds at full gallop, rushed him. The Urukian did not dash aside, nor leap to the safety of the caravans. Those who witnessed it amid the battle chaos gaped as he raced straight at the enraged duo and jumped *into* them, sword and spiked shield outstretched to each. The sword skewered the right horseman's breast and buried to the hilt, plucking him off his mount so the horse ran on without him. The shield's thorn pierced the opposite steed's eye; beast and man went down together in an eruption of dust and noise. When it had cleared, the blue warrior had already decapitated the remaining rider.

The rest was massacre. Swords clashed, men fell crippled and dying to the withered earth. A new volley of arrows streaming from the woods was quickly countered by retaliatory fire from Uruk's master archers, and at last the enemy archers retreated, realizing the gods did not favor them this day. They vanished into the wilderness, following secret trails to the hidden bandit camp where, at least, wives of the fallen dead were now available for tonight's plunder.

In the valley, the blue-armored Urukian approached the fallen bandit leader.

Nedu, hearing the sudden quiet, lifted his head to witness the final spectacle.

The Urukian's black locks writhed in the wind, a gold crown encircling his head. His long woven beard made a black point against his armor.

"King Gilgamesh," the bandit whispered.

"Remove your helmet," Gilgamesh commanded. The man slid the horned, antlered helm from his head.

"What gods do you pray to?" Gilgamesh asked.

"Marduk," the man whispered. The defending party gathered round.

"So do I," Gilgamesh said, and then he lopped the man's head from his shoulders.

He hadn't killed a man since he was twelve years old.

But hiding beneath the caravan tarp, Gilgamesh had suddenly relived it. Awakening in oily blackness, feeling a chill draft coming in from the windows, a sense of *wrongness* to the air, afraid to sit up in bed because *the door was open*—though he locked it every night—and the quiet padding of multiple assassin feet near his bed proved this was no dream. He couldn't forget the pained, heavy thudding of his heart as he felt for the cold handle of his mother's sacrificial dagger beneath his pillow. The memory retained its fangs. Eight years later, it was still biting him.

And today the biting had happened in the midst of battle, even. In the moment when he charged the two riders, his fear had crackled like water splashed onto a blacksmith's anvil. The sheer size of the foam-mouthed horses, their thunderous gallop, flaring nostrils, the riders with swords raised for slaughter! A god-king should never self-doubt, and Gilgamesh muttered a hasty prayer for forgiveness to Marduk.

The caravan's warriors looked happy enough, though. Their young faces flushed red as they looted the bodies. They joked amongst each other—soldier humor—intoxicated with their survival.

"You are no warrior, Nedu," Gilgamesh told his councilman.

"I know," Nedu said, rubbing his fingers across his chest where the now-discarded wooden chest-plate had saved him. The razor-sharp flint arrowhead had, in fact, pierced through to his skin and drew a small, bloody hole.

Gilgamesh looked at the wound and lost some color. It looked alarmingly like a maggot-hole.

"I'm fine, sire," Nedu said. He knew he was no warrior. He was thin as a marsh reed, his hands frail and still shaking from the battle. But he was First Councilman to the king, and in this capacity he had asked to accompany Gilgamesh on the journey to vanquish the West Road marauders.

Gilgamesh was a figure of a very different sort. Standing six feet tall—fully a foot taller than the average, he was the twenty-year-old god-king of Uruk. His broad shoulders and muscular frame befitted his divine heritage. The deep olive skin that spoke of Sumerian stock stretched tightly over a smooth forehead, high cheekbones like twin plateaus, a fine nose, and cleft chin, all positioned atop a trunk-like neck. It fulfilled the physical mold of his father at that same age; had they been contemporaries in their primes, people would have sworn they were brothers born at the same hour.

"Leave the enemy bodies," Gilgamesh told the men as they finished their looting. He looked out to the hill from where the marauders had come, wondering to what hive the escaped archers were returning. He frowned, his eyes distant and impatient.

Nedu pointed to the black tattoos on the visible portion of the marauders' flesh. "Assyrians. I know of no other people who paint themselves so extensively."

"Probably Assyrian militia," Gilgamesh concurred. "Defectors in search of better payroll than their kingdoms could provide. How many did we lose?"

Nedu had the information ready. "We've lost six men, my Lord. Taken out by archers."

"Load their bodies on the caravan flats. They will walk the Fire Road to Ereshkigal."

"How does my Lord feel about the day's victory?"

"I feel we should be returning to Uruk," Gilgamesh said evasively. "Hopefully it's not too late."

"Sire?"

"I want to watch someone die, Nedu."

CHAPTER 2
URUK

Long ago the city of Uruk had been two separate towns built by the Euphrates River and divided from each other by a great canal. Eventually the earliest king of Uruk had stitched the two towns together with dazzling bridges of lapis and stone, rendering the canal a unifying wellspring.

The surrounding countryside was threaded by irrigated streams, turning the earth green and yellow with wheat and barley. Tiny flecks moved across the woven landscape—men and women laborers who toiled in the fields daily, planting and harvesting as the season demanded to keep Uruk's swelling population—at the astronomical count of 70,000 souls according to the last census—well-fed.

The rich fields sprawled out at the base of Uruk's most notable feature, that being the city walls. Commissioned by Gilgamesh himself and half-completed, they wrapped around Uruk in a nearly perfect circle of baked mud-bricks rising as high as eight men standing atop each other's shoulders. Once completed, the wall would stand twice that height, with a width half that in thickness. Even the northern city of Babylon could not boast such a formidable defense. Many cities dotted the great Fertile Crescent valley, but each was only as good as it could ward off attackers. Just as locusts came in black clouds to descend on farmers' fields, so too did the human threat of invasion come from every direction. To the far north, Hittites; to the east and west, Assyrians; and from the south unnamed thugs rumored to prey on the river barges where the Euphrates was at its narrowest points. A ferocious cast of savage people inhabited the valley. The only certainty was that one day they would come. Gilgamesh, as Fifth King of one of the oldest cities in the world, wanted his domain ready for that day.

The city walls had four gates, each built of bronze bars that crisscrossed like giant spider-webs. The sun was setting as the victorious caravan returned to Uruk, and in the dying light the black gates looked truly spun by a monstrous arachnid.

The Western Road led to its cardinal gate that was flanked by immense guard towers taller than the walls by half. As Gilgamesh walked in full view of the tower guards, he sounded his cattle-horn. The note was low and long, and it told the guards not only that the king had returned, but that his homecoming was in triumph. The tower guards called down for the gates to be opened, and then they too sounded a flourish of trumpets. In this way, news of the victory spread to every resident.

The Western Road was clear of raiders!

King Gilgamesh has achieved a glorious triumph!

"Tomorrow there will be no work," Gilgamesh said as he thought of it, passing the rows of brick-workers. The air smelled of fresh mud and straw, and bricks were laid out neatly like little bread loaves baking in the sun. Workers glistened, brown and muscular, and bowed deeply to their king.

The caravan neared the interior Gate of Ishtar, a blue-lacquered structure with a tall arching ceiling and golden lions emblazoned on the walls. Gilgamesh saw the growing crowd of citizens waiting inside. He stepped out of line and told the caravan to proceed without him.

Nedu was appalled. "My Lord! The people must see you! You've earned their love on this day!"

"You lead the caravan," Gilgamesh told him. "I have a more pressing duty right now."

"My Lord, walk out into the streets and let the people see you. For too long you are invisible to them. By the gods, give them this! Give yourself this!"

Gilgamesh was not impressed with the councilman's speech. He waved the caravan through with troubled and haunted eyes. Reluctantly, Nedu turned away and was the first to pass through the blue gate. The crowd, seeing Gilgamesh turn away, yelled to an even higher pitch, but the king walked off and crossed the south-eastern parcel of the brick fields.

"Where is the king going?" a man in the crowd shouted, a gift of turnips—intended for the king—in his hands.

"He will be back for tonight's festivities," Nedu assured him. Then he shook his head, thinking of the dreadful duty that Gilgamesh had gone off to perform.

Dumuzi, former king of Uruk, had been dying for a week. His prison was in the highest room of the city's South Tower. A manic, zigzagging staircase was the only way to reach it. Below was the tower courtyard, blanketed in deep shadow after the sun had passed over the tower. A labyrinth of basalt statues made for the only way to reach the stairs, each cut into the figure of a frightful *pazuzu* demon, vaguely bird-like.

Gilgamesh stepped now onto this courtyard and hesitated, watching the circuitous path of carven monsters.

"Reveal yourselves, by order of your Lord!"

His voice rang hollowly through the labyrinth. The courtyard had been empty, but now there was movement throughout the maze. Seven black-robed, silver-masked creatures had emerged from the hidden recesses behind certain basalt statues with silent immediacy. Their bodies were hidden by black robes that fell straight like folded wasp wings.

Gilgamesh strode past them, making his way to the tower. The guards moved aside for him but otherwise were as still as before and when he reached the stairs and began its ascent, he glanced back to find them dissolved again, vanished into their lairs. They were the guardians of the South Tower, imbued with the right to kill, unquestioningly, anyone who dared entry. As such, these guards were nicknamed the *saghulhaza*, a reference to the ghastly doorkeepers of the underworld and a grim joke that to approach them was to be guaranteed a permanent trip there. More popularly among Uruk's citizens, they were called simply the Death Lords. None were better trained with swords, stealth, or speed. Terrible things they were, yet necessary. The transition from Dumuzi to Gilgamesh had been a death-clouded chapter of the city's history. Even dying, Dumuzi could be a threat, and the *saghulhaza* were to prevent any escape or attempts at liberation.

At the top of the stairs a single wooden door waited. Gilgamesh pounded on it until Dumuzi's attendant opened it from within.

Before he could ask her the condition of the former king, Gilgamesh was struck with a pungent stink. He looked beyond her and saw a chamber littered with rags that stank of sweat and medicines. An oil-lantern burned slowly on a stone bureau, spewing scented perfumes that tried—unsuccessfully—to blanket the tangy stench of death. A black curtain hung in the center of the room.

Gilgamesh strode past the woman and pulled aside the curtain.

Dumuzi was curled up on a mattress, his body white, emaciated, and his flesh sunken against the bones. Even though Gilgamesh knew Dumuzi was near death, he hadn't expected to see the former king of Uruk so … frail. The man's eyes were closed, and his chest heaved as he wheezed.

Gilgamesh hesitated, wondering if he should leave.

He turned to the attendant, noticing the pitcher of water in her hand. "Leave the water and go." The attendant hurriedly set the pitcher on Dumuzi's bedside table, and fled the room. Gilgamesh grasped a chair that lay within reach and noisily dragged it across the stone floor to set it down before the old man's bed. Dumuzi was startled awake.

"So you still live?" Gilgamesh observed.

Dumuzi's eyes glimmered in the semi-darkness as he regarded Gilgamesh's sun-burnt youthfulness. "You look good, my Lord. As healthy as the sun, strong as an ox."

Glaring, Gilgamesh leaned forward. "Speak frankly, Dumuzi. I have no time for false flattery."

"I need some water first."

"It's right there," Gilgamesh said, pointing to the pitcher. "You can bring it to your own lips."

"Even your father had respect for the dying."

"I am not my father. I'll not be your servant even in these twilight moments."

Dumuzi looked to the water pitcher as if calculating the effort required to grasp it and bring it to himself. He looked away, apparently defeated by the mathematical total.

"I'll be dead before morning," Dumuzi said brokenly. "This morning I had my servant draw open the shades so I could see my last sunrise. Shamash's bright face falls toward far-distant Egypt. I know, as surely as any man has knowledge, that I shall never see it rise again."

"Death brings even you poetry!" Gilgamesh snapped. "But if you want pity—"

"No, Gilgamesh. I would never ask you for pity. I know I would get none."

"Soon, Dumuzi, much feasting will begin. The bandits preying upon the Western Road have been vanquished; I killed their leader myself. Uruk's streets will swell with celebration. Of course, these are things you'll not see." He paused, looked sideways at the old man. "Why did you send for me this morning?"

"I wanted to see if you hate me still, after all these years. I can see my answer in your eyes."

Gilgamesh stood and turned to leave.

"When your father died you were just a boy!" Dumuzi said frantically, forcing himself to sit up with the last ebbs of his strength. "I took his place because you weren't ready, and Uruk needed a leader—"

"And when I *was* of age?" Gilgamesh challenged, turning back, the veins on his forehead bulging with hate. "Do you remember that?"

"I know what I did was wrong in the eyes of gods and men, Gilgamesh. My life recedes like the tide. I ask you for forgiveness. *That* is why I sent for you."

"I was twelve years old," Gilgamesh said. "I was sleeping in the palace you had claimed since the death of my father. I heard footsteps in my bedroom, clacking gently on the floor. I remember counting them, the way my father had taught me to see with my ears. Three men in my room! In the dead of night."

Wrinkles of sorrow furrowed Dumuzi's forehead.

"Three men," Gilgamesh continued, "who had come into my room that night, at your orders, to kill me!"

"I'm sorry."

"*You were my father's trusted friend!*" Gilgamesh screamed. "How did his spirit look upon you that night? You who sent men to kill his only son! While his mother slept *two rooms away!*"

Dumuzi held the gaze helplessly.

"I should have killed you when I took the throne," Gilgamesh hissed. "It was my mother who persuaded me to let you live."

"I know."

"And now you are dying, *finally*, and the kingdom of Uruk is rid of your treachery once and for all!"

"All kings have treachery attached to them!" Dumuzi pleaded. "Do you know the sins of Uruk in the past, before the enlightened days of your father? Do you know how King Enmerkar destroyed the nation of Aratta in the south? How he butchered every man, woman, and child? No one is guiltless! But I only wish to apologize, and to thank you for letting me live."

"Thank my mother. Had it not been for her, your bones would have made nests for vultures by now." He grinned icily at Dumuzi. "They may yet."

"Am I to be deprived of a proper funeral?"

"You'll never know my decision."

"At the least, Gilgamesh, I tried to be a good ruler of these people."

"And I don't?"

Dumuzi heard the desperation in Gilgamesh's voice. "I will tell you now what no one else will, least of all your willing councilmen."

"Advice from a usurper?" Gilgamesh turned away again and approached the curtain, gripped its edge with one hand, but hesitated. "Give me your parting wisdom with your dying breath, Dumuzi."

"Each day the men of the city labor at the wall you have assigned to them," Dumuzi said, speaking quickly as if he feared the imminent swipe of death's scythe. "These men are scorched by the sun and their muscles ache them. You show them no mercy, so that it seems in the great city of Uruk all are slaves to the whim of their master."

"Is there more?"

"Each night you lie with a different woman, I hear. Unwed daughters, sometimes even new wives on their wedding nights, share your bed. This does not inspire love for you, Gilgamesh. And surely you've had children with many of them. Would you have the next generation of Uruk be comprised of your progeny alone, fatherless and abandoned?"

Gilgamesh was silent. He looked back at the old man and remembered the way he had looked eight years earlier, clad in royal purple robes. A god-king, glimmering and bearded! The passage of less than a decade had rendered him this dying, feeble thing. A passerby who knew nothing of Uruk might have fancied him a destitute beggar, a prisoner of war, a derelict. Who could ever believe that a royal kilt had once dressed that frame?

And the stench was grotesque. Like rot. Gilgamesh's stomach twisted as he pictured the dark floor gyrating with worms, maggots, dung beetles.

"You have it in you to be a great ruler," Dumuzi continued. "But for now, you are a bully to your people. They are a crop that you harvest without planting, and one day when you need them most, you will wake to find a barren field."

"Good night, Dumuzi," Gilgamesh said, pulling the curtain back. "Save your speeches for my father when you meet him." He stepped through and let the curtain fall. Dumuzi disappeared behind the dark cloth.

CHAPTER 3
OUTSIDER

In the pine-sweet forest that carpeted the hills above Uruk, Enkidu pressed his ear to the ground and listened to the heartbeat of a dying animal.

Evening had closed itself over the valley like two great raven wings, and the forest was black save for the splintered rays of a crescent moon's silver light. In this shadow-drenched domain, Enkidu could not see the animal. But when he pressed himself to the cool earth so that the pine needles tickled his face, he could hear a weak thudding heartbeat. He crept forward a few more steps and froze, listening.

An animal moaned painfully.

Enkidu's ears bristled. At night with only a feeble moon to guide him, ears and nose were far more reliable than eyes.

The forests of the lower valley were ancient. Legends told of days when the Fertile Crescent was buried beneath a great sea. When those waters dried up, they left rich silt-beds in which the first trees took root and spread, finding continued nourishment from the Euphrates River. The trees exuded a fresh scent of life and, by day, seemed a green painting against the lifeless desert mountains around them. With the lush foliage came a variety of animals who sought their cool shade and watery roots.

The wounded animal cried again, a bleating that rose to a sharp pitch. Probably the creature was afraid to cry out lest it attract predators. Pain was forcing it to betray its location.

Ever alert, Enkidu parted the vegetation with his hands and plunged deeper into the blackness. Then as he took another step he felt no ground beneath his foot. He drew back. Again he pressed himself to the earth, his lengthy, matted hair falling greasily into his face and, when he thrust his hand down, he discovered a gaping pit in the forest floor.

It was the third pit he had found during the night, and this one was positioned well, interrupting a game-trail. Likely it had been covered with branches and grass, but now it was a black mouth in the shadows, and something had been swallowed by it.

Enkidu sucked in the air through his wide nostrils and smelled blood. Salty animal blood, permeated with fear. Deeper smells, too … the viscous juices of innards splayed open by wounds. There could be no doubt now: this pit was of the most severe kind, with a bottom that was lined with sharp spears and wooden teeth. Enkidu had seen such things. In his childhood, spent in the northernmost reaches of the valley, he had fallen, twice, into pit-traps. Neither had been this deadly but the experiences had made him wise to the world.

Months ago he had migrated to the south, and he was learning that southern forests were also littered with these savage death-traps. He grumbled in irritation, not happy with this discovery at all.

There was nothing he could do for the antelope; it would die. Backing off slowly, however, Enkidu immediately felt a second heartbeat. There was another animal, also trapped nearby.

The second animal was twenty yards from the pit. It had wandered into a wooden trap-box, its legs tripping a cord causing a door to fall behind it. These traps, too, were fairly common up north.

As Enkidu drew near the cage the imprisoned antelope kicked its legs with renewed vigor. But Enkidu reached in between the bars and gently stroked the creature along its black nose. At first it trembled beneath his touch. He petted it for long moments until it relaxed. He had never met a beast he couldn't make peace with.

Once it was calmed, Enkidu gripped two of the wooden bars and cracked them free of the box. The animal jumped, startled. Enkidu grabbed two more bars, snapped them off, and firmly seized the animal by its front feet.

The moment he had eased the beast from its trap it dashed into the woods. Enkidu only gave the creature a slap on its backside to direct it away from the pit-strewn area.

Then he turned to regard the box.

Enkidu knew that the people who had made the trap would easily repair it if left as is. More drastic measures were needed.

Lifting the box up, Enkidu threw it into a nearby tree. It exploded from the impact.

Pleased, he slipped off into the shadows making his usual detour to the forest's edge to look down at the city in the valley. Throughout his migration, he often strayed to the forest edge to marvel at the valley cities. This one, below him now, was the most unique yet. A wall encircled it, with great towers positioned in each direction.

The city was usually dark at night, but this time it surprised him. Tiny fires were moving throughout the streets like uncoiling serpents. The sounds of many feet, the sonorous voices of flutes, the pounding of drums, and the blare of horns rang out in a disorienting mixture of noise.

Enkidu was more curious than afraid. What was happening down there? He tried counting the fires but gave up. It was as if the stars had dropped down from the sky and were dancing about the solid ground, gleeful about some turn of the heavens.

For a month now Enkidu had been haunting the woods near this particular settlement in northern Sumer, and by now he knew the routine of the inhabitants. Each day the people who lived there made lots of noise … building that wall, sending hunters into the woods and fishermen along the river. But by night, he snuck to the wall and climbed it. He liked to sit there, unseen by the tower guards, and peer down into the city to spy its narrow streets and rows of mud-brick homes.

Tonight he wouldn't dare to approach. A horsefly landed on Enkidu's hand; he brushed it away before it could bite and slunk off into the forest, chewing his lip thoughtfully.

In the streets of Uruk, the feast was in such a full swing that the streets throbbed with bodies. The day had seen victory—the roads were safer, the king victorious in battle like his father before him—and if legends were true that the gods had flooded the earth because the clamor of mankind deprived them of sleep, then a new deluge was due.

Gilgamesh was in the center of the celebration though his heart was far off, in a cold place that this party could not warm. He sat on a gem-encrusted chair on a raised platform in the Avenue of the Gods, and dancers, fire-jugglers, swordsmen, musicians, and contortionists entertained the gathered crowds in this sea of humanity. Merchants hugged the roadside to peddle their wares.

Gilgamesh let his eyes explore the bustling avenue as he drank deeply from his cattle-horn goblet. His tongue licked the gold rim. The thousands of writhing bodies disturbed him, as if they were monster ants that had filled the avenue. Eyes glittered red by the fire-light of torch-posts.

"King Gilgamesh!" Silver plates were brought to him, heaped with cubes of venison and goat cheese, olives topped with cream, strips of lamb, dates plucked from the banks of the Euphrates, breads painted with honey. He pawed the offerings, bringing many to his mouth, chewing, swallowing, his thoughts growing more haunted.

"King Gilgamesh! The jugglers of Sippar!" And from the crowd came three men with monkey skulls, tossing them high into the air in an undulating, impossible pattern of balance and timing, the skulls staring at him in hollow horror, orange by firelight, spinning in shadow.

Gilgamesh held out his goblet for refilling.

"Lord Gilgamesh!" A troop of dancing girls approached and bowed. Cat-eyed and sleek, this parade of unblemished flesh began their gyrations and strutting, and the king licked his lips. He stood, pointed, and retreated from the revelry to the palace while the selected girl followed behind.

All eyes watched as the king as he retired to the palace. There were even cheers and a hasty song to his prowess in battle and lust, that put men and baboons to shame!

In the palace bedchamber, Gilgamesh stripped of his fine linens. The dancing girl entered and knelt, waiting for his approach. On the animal skins of his bed, Gilgamesh lay her down. His hands moved swiftly, undoing the knotty ribbons of her gown. Her clothes dropped away, her young breasts round and nubile. Soft skin met his fingers. He sucked at one nipple greedily while she squirmed, not with the practiced motions of an Ishtar whore but from the way his beard was tickling her. The bed-sheets were cool beneath her little back, and when he penetrated her it was like sliding his shaft into the hottest, smoothest oil.

"May I ask a question, my Lord?" she said when they were done.

Gilgamesh paused in stroking her back. "Yes."

"Do baboons take pleasure often?"

"Pardon?"

"I heard people saying tonight that baboons take pleasure more than any other animal," she said.

Gilgamesh bit his lip and resumed stroking her. His raking fingernails sent volleys of pleasurable chills up her spine.

"Yes," he replied sheepishly. "I'm told they do."

"That feels nice," the girl murmured dreamily, delighted at the way she had pleased this god-king. She thought of how she would tell the other girls of his moans, his crying out at the Final Moment, at the way his shaft filled her and throbbed as he unleashed his seed (so the older women of the harem had explained to her earlier that day.) She wondered if he wanted his seed to root within her.

Gilgamesh ran his fingers through her hair, mesmerized by the sight and feel of her thick locks sliding between his fingers. He sniffed the hot tangy concupiscence that enveloped them both. Their copulation had been wonderful; nonetheless, he felt strange. The sweaty climax had reminded him of his brief cry while killing the two riders.

The thunder of hooves, the thunder of his heart, the thunder of his fear.

Lightning flashed from the balcony.

The king rose. He strode naked to the balcony and hesitated there, ignoring the bustling revelry of the street below. He challenged the sky with his hard eyes. Real thunder rolled out like heavy wheels on hard earth. The sky blinked in spectral blue.

Stars ... no clouds ... and thunder? Gilgamesh bristled at the ominous sign. Was the storm from Ishtar? Was She displeased?

Gilgamesh looked warily to the goddess' ziggurat. Built of three gigantic brick levels one atop the other in gradually smaller sizes, it was a man-made mountain of terraces connected by rows of stairs. The Ishtar Temple crowned the very top.

Ishtar was the patron goddess of Uruk. The deities dwelt in the sky, but they could be lured to Earth if mankind built a fragrant and pleasing enough flower.

When Uruk had first been built by the original king, Meskiaggaseir, it had been devoid of anything as colossal as a ziggurat. But then the shamans of that age had urged him to construct a great house to attract divine favor. And Ishtar, wrathful goddess of love, had seen it and flown down to reside there. Every New Year Festival, She walked the Avenue of the Gods with Gilgamesh beside Her.

But why would Ishtar be displeased?

Perhaps She wasn't. Perhaps some other god, like Her father Anu who ruled the sky, was making His displeasure known. After all, wasn't Anu the patron of Dumuzi?

Gilgamesh sighed. There was the answer. Dumuzi has just died and his patron god Anu was letting the world know it.

"My Lord," the dancing girl called to him from the bed. Her eyes grew large as they watched him at the balcony, his long hair shifting in the slight breeze, his muscular back forming a fascinating terrain. "May I please you again?"

Gilgamesh could not see the South Tower from this balcony, but his thoughts fled to that stench-filled chamber where Dumuzi had just expired. Yes, he was dead. It was the only explanation for cloudless lightning. The thunder wasn't fierce, but neither was it welcome. Low and simmering, hissing its unhappiness but exuding no punishing wrath. Gilgamesh nodded, satisfied with his interpretation of the events. Anu is upset, he thought. I'll sacrifice a bull to Him tomorrow.

He turned to the girl who watched him eagerly from the bed.

She smiled, captivated by his dark intensity. She decided just then that she wanted his seed to take root. It might not happen with one coupling. Additional Final Moments improved the chances. Sore as she was, she was determined to bear more friction to her portals. She wanted a divine child.

"You can go if you want," Gilgamesh told her.

The girl blinked. "You don't want me here?"

"You're not my prisoner," he clarified, hearing Dumuzi's words in his head. "You have pleased me mightily. If you wish to leave, you may."

The girl blinked again, and said as if to herself, "You selected me tonight." In a sudden rush of fear and confusion, she leapt from the bed and seized his hands, kneeling, crying, "Please, let me stay, my Lord! I'll try better to please you, my Lord! I promise! Let me stay, I beg you!"

"You can stay," Gilgamesh told her. "I was only offering to let you go, to tell you that I am not forcing you to remain." Dumuzi's words shimmered like river-stones in the gloom. He could tell from her eyes that she still feared she had given offense. She was kneading the flesh of his hands with fearful intensity.

The awkward silence was oppressive. "Would you like to walk out to the balcony?"

The girl nodded anxiously. One tear spilled, and he wiped it away and kissed her cheek. Naked, he slipped his arm around her waist and guided her to the balcony.

The King's Chamber had a lovely starkness to it. The floor was white and glossy, semi-reflective of anything that stood upon it. A blue cloth veil was all that separated it from the balcony.

The night was cool and the girl drew closer to him for warmth as they stood outside and looked down at the canal and the parading city. He felt her hardened nipples against his flesh.

"The moon looks so close," the girl gaped.

It does, Gilgamesh thought. A man might shoot an arrow into it.

"What's beyond the city, my Lord?" she asked, with renewed hope that he might offer his seed once more.

"Cities dot the river valley," Gilgamesh said. "Smaller towns cluster alongside the Euphrates, dependant on it for rich soil, drinking water, and fish."

"And beyond the valley?"

"Assyria lies northward, and then the land of the Hittites beyond them; I couldn't tell you which people are worse. Beyond the Hittites is the North Sea. To the south, the Euphrates joins with the Tigris River, close to where they're born at the Mouth of the Rivers. To the west is a huge desert, stretching for untold miles. Deep inside it is a kingdom called Egypt, ruled by a man named Khufu."

The girl giggled at the odd name. "And to the east?"

"The Red Deserts," Gilgamesh said. "Homes to barbarians and monsters."

She chanced to touch his thigh. "Does the king ever travel to those places?"

"The king has no reason to." A strange chill rippled across his body, starting at the base of his neck and crackling down the length of his spine like branches of a cold tree.

For a hideous moment, he grew frightened that the gods would suddenly thrust him out into the world, without friend or family, and that he would lose all he cared for.

Then he, too, would die like Dumuzi ... alone and without a friend in the entire universe.

The girl's hand crept up and touched his fleshy tool. Gentle, feathery-soft strokes wrought the desired result. "You never wish to travel and see those lands?"

"No."

"Never?"

"Never," Gilgamesh said with some force. He gently slung his arm around her waist and turned her toward him. "I wish to have you again."

CHAPTER 4
THE BODY IN THE RIVER

Shamash, the fiery sun god who careened over the valley bringing the gift of day, died in the west each night, leaving behind a blue shadowland while Gilgamesh slept alongside the girl, while the celebration melted, while the forest creature named Enkidu slept in the womb of a rotting tree.

And then, four hours before the reborn sun, trouble came to Uruk.

It was an unlikely night for trouble, given the pleasure of the people—the ecstasy when they heard their king had declared a full day free of labor. Yet in the cold pre-dawn hours an insidious catalyst was about to make itself known.

The carrier was none other than a most ordinary fisherman. As Lord Gilgamesh had been battling raiders out on the Western Road, the fisherman had been casting his net into the golden Euphrates. As always, he offered prayers to his personal goddess, Nammu the Birth-Giver, and promised to throw back the first ten fish he caught. The river was a dangerous, unpredictable entity that could bring as much suffering as fortune; for this reason, the fisherman also promised Tiamat the primordial dragon that an eleventh fish would also be discarded to honor Her as well.

Yet it wasn't a fish he netted. About the same time that Gilgamesh had decapitated the bandit leader, the fisherman hauled in his net shocked to discover something heavy in his woven web. He dragged it onto the slippery shoreline. It stank of rot. The lumpish, swollen thing in his net was far too strange to be any natural river creature. At first he thought it was a hippopotamus torn apart by crocodiles, and it was with horror that he saw the netted thing was clothed in shredded leather armor.

A body, yet one so water-logged and mutilated that it was barely recognizable as being of the human family. The legs were gone ... *chewed off*, it seemed. The body was missing everything below the ribs. Frightened, the fishermen prodded the carcass carefully, for despite his anxiety at netting a dead man he harbored some hope that gold might yet be waiting in the man's pockets. Gold was no use to the dead, and neither would their spirits miss it in the netherworld of Ereshkigal.

What he found was better than gold, and he thanked both goddesses for this remarkable gift.

Now, in the bone-chilling pre-dawn, the fishermen left his house and his sleeping wife behind, and headed to the great ziggurat, the Temple of Ishtar, to make good on his discovery.

For the priestesses of Ishtar could be bought—for a short time—by men who had gold to spend.

The fisherman's heart stuttered anxiously as he ascended the ziggurat stairs. It was like climbing into heaven. The stairs were long, slanted at an austere angle, and they appeared to link directly with the star-dappled sky. He found himself remembering the call of female flesh, its fresh smell, and the wondrous landscape of a young body. His withered, scarred hands ached to caress a feline priestess.

"These stairs go on forever," he muttered, but the goal at the top could have beckoned him, siren-like, up another *three ziggurats* if required. As a young man he had been here before with enough gold for a single supple priestess. His discovery in the river might buy him *ten* priestesses if he wished. Perhaps he might be able to afford the goddess Herself! That latter thought elicited a horrible dread, and fearing Ishtar's wrath he dropped to his knees and asked the divine light of Ishtar—brightest in the sky and positioned slightly below and to the left of the moon, to forgive an old man who loved Her.

He was closing in on the third and final tier—the landing that supported the temple itself—when he heard the tinkle of chimes, laughter, and glassware. He reached the third tier and set sights on the crowning temple. Built of pale bricks and decorated with bas reliefs of serpents and dragons in coiled combat, the sight of the temple brought a surging rush of emotion to his heart. Suddenly he was young again! His friends, now dead, were beside him! And they were laughing at a joke he could not remember now ...

The entrance of the temple was narrow, flanked the entrance were twin fires that burned from bronze tripod-trays.

Two pale figures emerged from the opening. Priestesses with skin like milk, dressed in transparent gowns and silver jewelry. A dream! the fisherman thought in strange panic. This could only be a dream and he would awaken any moment, with his tiresome wife snoring beside him ...

"Good evening, mortal," one of the women said. They came to his side. Took hold of his arms. Escorted him inside.

I *am* dreaming, he thought. But as he passed through the vaulted entrance he smelled incense and spices.

"You have money for the goddess?" one of the women asked him.

Nodding, feeling small, the old man retrieved a coiled bracket of silver. It was the standard money of Uruk, worth a month of fishing and selling at the market. Quickly, he thought of other things he could buy with the silver. Clothes, meat, gifts for his brother's children, a dress for his brother's wife. But those were things that would wear out, be eaten, and be forgotten. What was the price for rejuvenation? How much did it cost to taste what it was to be young again, even if such a gift would last a fleeting hour of pleasure?

He handed the silver over. Besides, he thought, with what I discovered in the river, I can buy the silver back ... and much, much more.

The entrance opened up into a spacious room. The walls glinted with gold. Glazed bricks of lapis lazuli formed exotic diagrams and pictures.

And women filled the room. They reclined on soft fur rugs or lazily sprawled by the side of wine fountains to drink of the intoxicating nectar. A young man emerged from a hallway, escorted by another priestess. The fisherman watched him as he strolled by lazily, drunkenly, intoxicated from wine and flesh. Laughing, the young man sprawled out suddenly on a rug and let the priestess nuzzle his neck.

The priestess beside the fisherman spoke suddenly: "Choose any girl you like." He blinked and looked away from the young man.

"I'd like you," the fisherman said as he forced his mouth to work. "Please."

The priestess nodded. Without another word, she guided him down the hall where the young man had come from.

She took him to a room lined with blue and red rugs; animal furs dipped in brilliant dyes.

"I haven't been here in so long," the fisherman said, feeling a need to be honest. The women pulled off her top garment and let it crumple to the floor.

"Ishtar is pleased to see you back, then," she said as she stepped to him. He looked at the swelling tips of her breasts.

"Is Ishtar here?" he asked.

"She's always here." Sensing his awkwardness, she began kissing his neck, light and quick like the dancing of a butterfly.

Yes! he thought in exaltation. In this place age doesn't matter! Here, I become a young man again!

He found himself remembering an old fable about a plant that could make people young forever. As the priestess' lips lingered over his stubbly neck, he recalled the tale of a man who had survived the Flood, how the gods had then blessed him with a flower found only in heaven's garden. He strained to remember its name.

The priestess began undoing the ties of the man's ragged skirt. Just before her velvet hand touched his shaft, he remembered.

Never Grow Old. The plant was called *Never Grow Old.*

A smile came to his lips. Could immortality feel any greater than—

"Ahhh," the fisherman gasped. The rest of the old fable, and everything else, was lost as he took his pleasure with her on the soft furs.

"You said Ishtar is here even now?" the fisherman asked. He lay naked, spent but craving a little more time with her.

The priestess nodded. She was already slipping into her thin, scaly gown once again.

"I found something today," the fisherman said. "While I was fishing, I found something the temple might wish to have."

Might wish to *buy*, he thought. Silver bought the priestesses, but temples had been known to purchase from ordinary men objects of great significance. In ancient times even peasants could become rich, were they lucky enough to stumble upon a rare treasure and offer that find to a lucrative temple.

The fisherman reached into his bag and his fingers touched cold metal. He peeled the satchel away from it and lifted it up for her to see.

It was a statue, the size of two open hands. Roughly humanoid, with two arms and legs, the figure was cast of an unknown dark metal decorated with precious stones. The eyes were sapphires, large and taking up most of the face. The mouth was a leering grin, the neck beaded with flecks of gold, the exposed heart a larger sapphire. Ancient symbols, unreadable to the fisherman's eyes, tattooed the back and legs and belly of the grotesque being. It was neither hack-work of a second-rate smith, nor the average treasure to be found in a palace or nobleman's home. It was a sacred object boasting power and age.

The priestess snatched it from his hands. Her eyes went to the heart, and for a long while she was unable to look away from that blue stone. Then she looked up, and with the hungriest expression the fisherman had ever seen on anyone, she whispered a most peculiar word:

"*Annunaki?*"

"What?"

"Wait here," she told him in a strangely edged voice. "I will ask Ishtar."

The fisherman looked at the statue in her hands. "I can't let it go. Not unless I come with you."

She laughed harshly and savagely. "You *will* stay here!" She departed the room so fast she seemed to have flown away.

The fisherman watched her go, fearful that he would never see the statue again.

Gradually, his tensions dissipated. The priestess was not a robber. She would be back to offer him a lavish sum. Riches! he thought, and imagined the eulogy at his death: A fisherman who one day became a noble, having delivered a sacred statue to the great Ishtar Temple in Uruk!

He had just closed his eyes, his body resting against the furs, when dark shapes flooded the chamber and devoured him with capes and chains.

CHAPTER 5
REVELATIONS

Morning came to the valley with red clouds. Gilgamesh awoke at first light, roused the young dancing girl and made love to her again. The palace servants entered and paid the couple no mind; as the girl moaned softly beneath Gilgamesh's thrusts, they set down a silver tray of dates, a pitcher of beer, and a pitcher of water, and then left as soundlessly as they had come. Gilgamesh climaxed fervently, and then turned his hungry attention to the breakfast.

He had taken one bite when Nedu flew through the veils of the chamber's doorway and halted before the king's bed. He paid no mind to the naked girl who feasted beside him.

"Dumuzi died last night," Nedu said at once. Gilgamesh, bare-chested and still sweaty from sex, nodded solemnly and drank some water from the pitcher.

The chamber veils moved again. Gilgamesh's mother, Ninsun the Priestess, clad in robes the color of sea-glass, joined the councilman by the bedside.

"Good morning, mother," the king said.

"The gods smiled on your victory yesterday," she replied, delighted that he had returned from that venture unharmed. The full report of the attack had reached her before all others; there were devotees of Shamash in the king's company. She had heard of his fanatical attack against two horsemen simultaneously.

"Shamash saw all," he said.

"Good. Then you will remain safely in Uruk until you have a royal child?"

The dancing girl froze. Gilgamesh dismissed her, and she grabbed her clothes, fleeing the bedchamber nude.

"A queen is necessary first, mother."

"Then obtain one."

The king drew a fig into his mouth, chewing, and fixing his mother with a challenging stare. He realized the wisdom of begetting a royal child; Uruk would be thrown into chaos if there was no established line.

"Sire?" Nedu ventured. "About Dumuzi…"

"My ears are not clogged, Nedu."

"Of course."

On the third fig, Gilgamesh felt a sickness spread in his stomach, like the bubbling of putrid water in a quagmire. "When did you hear of Dumuzi's passing?"

"His servant informed me this morning." Nedu replied.

The walls of the bedroom were a vibrant blue in the early light from the balcony; Gilgamesh found it easy to imagine that the palace had been cast underwater and that any moment a school of brightly colored fish would swim in from one room to the next.

To his mother, Gilgamesh smiled. "It is a good morning after all, mother! The sun shines, we are alive, and the usurper is dead."

She smiled. How many times had she desired to string Dumuzi up in a harness like a sacrificial lamb, and cut his throat for the altar stone to drink!

Ninsun's prestige was older than her royalty. As a young girl freshly initiated into the priesthood of Shamash, she impressed her order through demonstrations of dream-reading. Word of her talent leaked to the streets, and the phrase "to bring your dreams before Ninsun" soon became an axiom chanted even beyond the borders of Uruk. The Temple of Shamash did not gather coin through the sale of flesh; indeed, the dictates of the order forbid such practices among their ranks. The Order of the Sun appealed to people's desire for truth and prophecy, and this drove in funds. Ninsun single-handedly made Shamash a wealthy business.

Those were the days of the Second King of the city, Lord Enmerkar, Slayer of Aratta in his youth and now an aged, withering king with no heirs. His own seers had been unable to procure him the answer to his childless condition. When he heard people tell of Ninsun's gifts, he summoned her to the palace that, one day, would become her home. And there, in the audience chamber, he told her of his dilemma.

Ninsun listened and responded at once. He would never sire a child, she told him. He was an elderly man whose loins could no longer bear fruit. If he wished to know the reasons for this curse, then he need only look back to the very triumph which had brought him glory: the destruction of the kingdom of Aratta. Gods had been offended by this act; Enmerkar's punishment was the extinction of his line.

This augury brought gasps and cries of outrage from the king's viziers, but Enmerkar absorbed it quietly, perhaps with a sense of resignation, and asked if there was more to tell.

There was. Ninsun said that although he would never sire a child, he could yet have a son to succeed him.

At this the elderly Enmerkar stroked his beard and said, "Priestess Ninsun, tell me how an old man may have a son?"

"Think back to the destruction of Aratta," she replied, "and a son will make himself known to your thoughts."

And then Enmerkar smiled, for he understood her at once. During the war the king had come to love the accomplished soldier-general Lugalbanda, himself a living legend of many adventures in the wilderness. Like Ninsun, Lugalbanda was a celebrity among the residents, beloved by noble and peasant alike. *He* would be the son that Enmerkar could never produce himself. *He* would inherit the kingdom of Uruk.

The king had smiled mightily. "And you will be his wife, Priestess Ninsun! I declare it."

So it was that Ninsun became Queen and Lugalbanda was appointed Third King. The two were holy in the eyes of the populace, endeared to the common man and woman like no other king before or since. On each wedding anniversary, Ninsun could expect to find gifts of bread, spice, and honey-cakes at the palace door from admirers. And when Ninsun lost her husband to sudden illness, her mourning was echoed by the people. Many credited Ninsun's powerful hold on the people's hearts as the reason why she and her newborn son were spared when Dumuzi the Usurper captured the throne.

Ninsun smiled now, and it was as if the glowing incense bowls, fires, and smoke still undulated in her eyes. "Yes. And you and I must make an offering, to see his spirit reaches Ereshkigal."

"Never." Gilgamesh clawed into the nearest fruit.

Ninsun seated herself beside him and touched his arm. "His soul must be sent off with the proper rights or it will haunt us. You must remember, too; he is the man who allowed you and I to live upon his seizure of the throne. He cared for the city and treated the people fairly. He was flawed, but not evil, Gilgamesh."

Gilgamesh sighed deeply, offended by her words but not willing to argue. He bit into another fruit, but memories suddenly bit into him. *Twelve years old. A draft of air disturbing the sheets that covered him. Footsteps. The fearful pounding of his heart as he counted the men by sound. The sound of a sword emerging from its scabbard...*

Shhhhhhnk!

It was a sound both ugly and beautiful. Metal, a sacred flesh of the gods, tamer of earth and slayer of men.

In those dreadful moments, the young prince found himself wondering who it was who had been sent to kill him. Which man of the palace had been appointed to that honor? Was it someone who had smiled at him during daylight hours? Someone who had patted him affectionately on the head? Or was it a hired assassin from the taverns in town, promised shiny coins in return for slicing a child's throat?

"I will make no offering to Dumuzi," Gilgamesh told his mother.

Ninsun's hand sprang out and snatched his hair. "*Yes you will.* We will send away his ghost or it will trouble us forever."

"I fear no ghosts."

"*You will do as I say, regardless!*"

A servant walked by the doorway, glancing in quickly, and walked away.

Gilgamesh firmly unpried her fingers from his lock of hair. Her wrist was like a dried twig in his grip. "Just be thankful I don't feed his body to vultures, *Priestess.*"

Lugalbanda's early death had created a crisis in Uruk as the City Council debated over what to do. Gilgamesh the Child was too young to rule on his own, even though the northern city of Babylon boasted the precedent of allowing boy-kings to rule. Finally it was Babylon's example that was followed, and Gilgamesh was elevated to kingship at the tender age of seven. Yet an hour after that decision, Dumuzi, military advisor among the city council, pulled a murderous coup along with a supporting faction.

It had been a wild gamble, yet Dumuzi seemed to have won. In those evil days the citizens had rioted over the takeover, recalling their love for Lugalbanda and Ninsun. Yet Dumuzi proved a cunning serpent. He showered his loudest opponents with land, title, wheat, and gold. Those who scoffed at his bribes disappeared in the night.

Ninsun's renown made her immune to assassination, lest Dumuzi offend both gods and men and bring about his own destruction. Consequently he allowed her and her son to live in the palace—under constant guard, perhaps, but alive. Years passed. The fire of rebellion died through lack of fuel.

Five years later Gilgamesh was emerging out of boyhood. His soft features began to replicate his father's visage. People who saw this whispered that Lugalbanda's royal blood was rising to retake the throne. Dumuzi, realizing this himself, attempted to spite fate by sending three assassins to kill the boy.

Yet foolishly Dumuzi had forgotten that Gilgamesh was the son of a godking. As the nearest assassin neared the bed, the boy sprang up and buried a concealed dagger in his eye. Then he seized the man's sword and dispatched the other two. The bodies were thrown to the palace's *mushussu* dragons.

Nedu broke the silence with a polite clearing of his throat. "Lord Gilgamesh, might I ask what should be done with the *saghulhaza* now that the Southern Tower is empty?"

Gilgamesh glowered at him, not appreciating the subject change.

"Of all the weights on my mind, they are the very lightest," he replied curtly. "Keep them paid as always, and fed; I'm sure we'll find other uses for them soon enough."

"Other uses?"

"Yes, yes. We shall have to find some other use for them."

Ninsun read the councilman's concerns as swiftly as she had interpreted dreams in her youth. "I believe what the councilman means, my son, is that the *saghulhaza* are tools. How will you use them?"

Gilgamesh sighed again. "Nothing malign, I assure you. I was simply saying that they were not foremost in my mind right now." He frowned, stumbled over a shadowy thought. "What uses did they hold before my reign?"

Ninsun's face darkened, and Gilgamesh distilled from her haunted eyes the machinations of the Death Lords during the reign of Dumuzi.

"And before the Usurper?"

Ninsun's eyes brightened. "Your father had no use for them other than to provide protection to important cargo. Enmerkar used them as personal bodyguards."

"And the First King?" Just how far back did the Order of the Death Lords go?

"No one knows," she said. "But the *saghulhaza* is an ancient order, and they were here when Uruk was built. Uruk is not the oldest of cities. Even in the days of the Great Wanderings, there were cities like Shuruppak, Eridu, and Aratta ... names that were old even then, and nomads still stumble upon the ruins of nameless, forgotten powers that passed while most men hunted animals with their bare hands. Much of what we have today is only the incarnation of older forms and structures."

Gilgamesh let his mother's words wash away his black mood; for a moment he was a child again, sitting by the palace pools and anxious to go for a dip, but forced to wait until he had recited his lessons of history and culture that his mother, his self-appointed teacher, had assigned him to learn. His fingers recalled the feel of the smooth clay tablets on which these lessons would be waiting for him; the wedge-marks of the Sumerian language he had needed to memorize. He could still remember which lessons he could expect on which days of the week: Day One was alphabet, Two was Gods, Three was history, Four was customs and traditions, Five was song, and Six was Duty. Until the lessons were completed, there was no dipping in the pool.

The memory was fond—despite the tedious homework, it was one of the few times when the young prince could forget the palpable tension in the palace under Dumuzi's dominant rule—and it brought a small smile to the king's face. "Yes, Shuruppak and Aratta and Eridu. Of course, I remember ... or else I shall be banned from the pools!"

Ninsun smiled warmly. "And no honey-cakes for any boy who fails his lessons."

The smile was still on Gilgamesh's face when he realized that Nedu was still there. The councilman coughed.

"If you have no use for me, my Lord, I would be off—"

"I have no more use for you," Gilgamesh told him. "At least, for now."

Nedu made a hasty exit.

"You like him," Ninsun observed.

"Nedu is utterly worthless in battle. And pig piss tastes better than the beer he makes." Gilgamesh realized his anger was gone. "Leave me a moment while I dress."

Ninsun bowed, and slipped through the beaded curtain. Gilgamesh sighed as he dressed into a light purple tunic. Then he took the pitcher of sweet-water and met his mother outside on the high steps of the azure-lacquered courtyard. There, he found Ninsun looking out over the city; the elevation of the palace afforded a wide view of Uruk's dusty, colorful streets and the limestone Avenue of the Gods that ran through the center of it all, parallel to the blue canal. In the distance was the wall, with workers laboring at it like industrious ants.

"It will be beautiful when finished," Ninsun said.

"As always, you know my mind mother."

"I love you always."

Gilgamesh held her hand. Again it seemed such a frail, skeletal thing. How could a person's skin be so warm, yet her hand be so fragile? She looked so old, all of a sudden.

Old age was wisdom in a silver basket, the old Sumerian saying went.

Perhaps. But a weak and worn basket at that.

"I love you too, mother," he said, gently squeezing her hand.

Beyond the walls of Uruk, two hunters went into the forest to see how their traps had fared in the night.

They were a father and a son and were all the family they had. The boy's mother had died in childbirth, and the father himself had lost his extended family through dual blows of plague and war. Now they had only each other, and like two lonely spirits in a world devoid of life, both recognized how essential it was to cherish their bond while it remained.

The father was named Gizzida, and he was a wiry man in his late forties. His body was so lean that he seemed a figure of bone embellished with tight muscles. He had thin eyes and a hooked nose, brought to prominence by the pointed chin beneath his diminutive mouth. His hands were rough, arms steady, and his twenty years as a hunter had honed a considerable skill in the trade. As was the duty of a father, he intended to pass his knowledge on to his son before he died.

Gudea was his son, a strapping youth of thirteen years. He had his father's slight build, yet his face was softer, more like his mother's, and he had eyes more given to wonder than his father's weariness.

It was mid-morning when Gizzida found the pit he had covered the night before, and even from a distance he could see that the sheet of twigs and leaves was now a gaping hole. The sight brought joy to his heart.

"Something fell through indeed!" Gizzida exclaimed, nearing the pit and looking down into it. At the earthy bottom, an antelope lay dead, impaled on three pikes.

Gizzida wiped away the sweat of anxiety that had built up on his forehead. Uruk produced massive amounts of wheat and barley, keeping the enormous population well-fed. Meat was prized by the nobles who could afford it, and their purchases kept Gizzida and his son in good health and on a good plot of land. The trouble was that Uruk had many hunters competing over a limited space in the woods. Each had an understanding of whose territory belonged to who, but competition for available game was tight and often brutal. The antelope would provide steaks for many; it would drive a good price.

"How's the other trap?" Gizzida shouted absently to his son as he stooped, ready to climb down into the pit along the notches he had dug in the sides of the hole.

No reply came from his son.

Frowning, Gizzida called out again for him. His voice was absorbed by the forest. Again, no reply.

"Gudea!" he yelled a third time. Birds chirped and squawked in reply.

He was beginning to get a sick feeling in his stomach when suddenly an answering voice shot back to him: "Father! I'm here! Come quickly!"

Gizzida's fear washed away as he hurried to where they had left the box-trap. But once there, he gasped. The trap was wrecked. Wooden splinters littered the forest floor, and four of its planks had been deliberately snapped off, arrayed neatly on the pine-needle ground.

"What could do this?" Gudea asked helplessly.

Gizzida didn't reply. He stared at the wooden wreckage.

"No animal did this," Gudea pronounced, testing out the weight of certainty. "Look at this tree! The splinters, the dent ... it looks like the cage was *thrown* into it!"

Touching the ruptured bark, Gizzida nodded. "Thrown, yes. But first the bars were ripped out." He pointed to the four planks on the ground, too neatly discarded to have landed there from the explosion.

"Another hunter?"

"Probably," Gizzida said. It was hardly unprecedented for one hunter to sabotage competition. The punishment for this was death, but you had to catch them in the act and bring witnesses to Uruk's judges.

But …

Something wasn't right. The cage seemed to have been destroyed with one throw; Gizzida could find no evidence of repeated batterings. To the best of his eyes, there was only one point of impact. But who had that kind of strength?

Gudea, running his fingers over the tree bark, came to the same conclusion. "Whoever did this had the strength of a baboon!"

"Pick up the pieces and put them in our bag. Only what you think is useable."

"Are we going to tell the magistrate?"

"Hurry up now," Gizzida said. "And no, I think we should handle this ourselves. I'll confront the local hunters." He turned and walked back to the pit to haul the dead animal out and tie its feet to the pole he had brought.

The violence of the vandalism troubled him more than the mystery of how it had come to be vandalized. Gizzida shuddered and finished tying the animal for retrieval.

The smashed cage.

Who … or what … had that kind of strength?

CHAPTER 6
SHAMHAT

When sunrise was at mid-day, Gilgamesh presided over the City Council, held as always in the ornate audience chamber of the palace's north-side. In that cavernous room decorated in bas reliefs of monsters, gods, and floods, he sat on a white throne one step above the people who had come to plead their ultimate legal appeals to the king.

Like many cities in Sumer, laws—and the penalties for breaking them—were taken quite seriously, with cases presided over by a panel of judges. A scribe sat in the courtroom's corner, recording onto clay tablets the names of all principals and witnesses, their social classes (for there were three social classes in Uruk and legal penalties varied depending on which bracket a person belonged to) and the nature of their complaint. Anyone could submit a complaint; they could also appeal their decisions to a higher court. As god on Earth, Lord Gilgamesh represented the final level of these appeals.

Much to his surprise, he discovered that he enjoyed presiding over the different cases. This satisfaction derived not so much from the power of his divine authority, but rather from the rare opportunity it gave him. Most often, a king was cut off from his people, entombed in his luxurious sepulcher while the citizens labored at their daily toils. Council tore down that wall and allowed him to see into the hearts of those who came to stand before him.

The morning had begun quite ordinary. A woman being sold by her husband in payment of a debt charged that there was no debt, and that her husband had invented it so he could remarry. She also brought forth the charge that the man had shown impiety toward the gods on several occasions during their marriage; this latter and much more serious charge was dismissed for want of witnesses, but as the husband could not produce witnesses to the debt (they had testified at the lower court, but were strangely reluctant to enter the king's audience chamber; after all, if false testimony was uncovered at the king's level of appeals, they could lose their tongues) Gilgamesh overruled the sale of his wife and then decreed she held the right to divorce him and gain a third of his worth. That was followed by the usual quarrels, from slaves to merchants to patricians, and often combinations of all three.

Gilgamesh enjoyed it. While words could be polished and honed into witchery and spell-craft, the wordless expressions of the body were like a clear pond through which he would examine the truth of their souls. His study started with the eyes, then the whole of the face, the posture, the presence (or absence) of fidgeting, the type of stance (from feet, knees, and shoulders,) and even the way they listened when he interrupted them and asked a question. How did they react to questions? How quickly, or slowly, were they were to answer? Ninsun had told him as a boy, "Be sure to look into the eyes of your people, Gilgamesh. In a gaze you may find truths which the tongue may never speak." There was also a Sumerian expression, learned by schoolchildren:

> *All beasts chatter as they can*
> *But truth lies in the eyes of man*

At the very least, Council broke up the tedium of the week in the way a battle might. Besides, it felt good to sharpen his tools of perception.

Gilgamesh was in the midst of listening to the arguments of two merchants—one accusing the other of vandalizing his shop wares—when the doors opened and an Ishtar priestess entered. She lithely moved through the crowd, approaching the king without fear of public complaint.

"Lord Gilgamesh," she said, parting the two merchants. "Ishtar requests your presence at Her temple."

A shocked murmur passed through the crowd. Even the court scribe, in the midst of pressing letters into his clay tablet, glanced up from his work, awed.

The Goddess Ishtar was known to dwell in the Great Ziggurat. Every New Year Festival, she emerged and walked the Avenue of the Gods with the king. On any other day, she was neither seen nor heard.

Gilgamesh recovered from his speechlessness. "Does She?"

The priestess nodded. Her white tunic came down to her ankles, pale bare arms revealed by the sleeveless top, and a golden amulet of her patron deity strapped to her chest. She sported a trim gold circlet around her forehead that disappeared into her raven-black hair.

"What does Ishtar seek me for?"

"I'm sure She'll tell you."

Gilgamesh felt a flicker of anger at the evasive comment. "I asked you the nature of the matter, priestess."

"The Annunaki," she said, comfortably holding his gaze. "I will say nothing more than that."

Gilgamesh let his eyes pass from Nedu to his mother. Nedu seemed perplexed by this summoning but not intimidated or awed by it; perhaps these kinds of summonings had occurred in years prior. Ninsun, however, was openly scowling, and she did not look at her son but instead kept her gaze trained on the priestess. The priestess, feeling this scrutiny, shifted her gaze to Ninsun, and a contest of gazes began between two servants of two very different gods.

"Then I will see her now," Gilgamesh said, ending the contest. "Priestess, tell the goddess I am coming."

"She knows that already," the priestess answered slyly. "I am to escort you there at once."

❦ ❦ ❦

Enkidu awoke to the feel of a bee tickling his ear; he batted it away and pulled himself out of the tree's split trunk to stretch his limbs. He breathed deeply, smelling all the forest, and yawned.

Enkidu slunk to a stream he had found the day before, stooped to dip his chin, and guzzled down the water. He drank until he was sated, leaned back on the muddy shore, and slapped his belly, content. His tawny stomach growled low. Before he set his mind to the task of securing breakfast, though, he afforded himself a moment to reflect on last night's strange dream.

Enkidu rarely dreamt, and when he did they were of ordinary things. He often dreamt of hunting, or at times he dreamt of being hunted by things he never quite glimpsed. In other dreams he explored strange forests, tracked game, or followed the sounds of a river. Yet his nightly visions could be terrifying too. Dead friends and family might visit him, only to reveal that maggots were squirming in their mouths and eyes …

His recent dream was altogether different. Instead of being grounded on a forest floor, or rocky slope, or spongy marsh, or stinging sand, he found himself standing on no ground at all. He was gliding, wingless but gliding, while the green crests of trees rushed beneath his feet and the wind blew his knotted hair away from his grinning, strong-boned face. Enkidu had laughed at the joy of this elated experience, so strange and impossible. From his flying vantage point he had seen rivers curling through woods and mountain peaks glistening as white gold. He had become as a wisp of cloud, or as a floating tendril of mist that wreathed the trees like gossamer garland.

How strange! Enkidu's stomach growled again; he crept downriver where birds hopped about, meaty and inviting. They pecked at the mud as he approached, a rock finding its way into his hand. Closer now. The birds fought over a worm, pulling the long ribbon-like body from the ground, snapping it out of its hiding hole.

Enkidu's hand was a blur. White feathers burst off the selected prey as the rock hit it squarely. The other birds flapped off. Enkidu's target flopped once on the ground, wings folded up, and lay motionless forever.

He thanked the forest before eating the animal, and once he had devoured it down to its warm bones he searched the riverbank for a worn stone to place where he had killed the bird. It was a ritual he had learned as a child, when the tribe elders taught him how to hunt with rock, bone, wood, and hand.

Yet as he searched up along the muddy banks of the river, he realized something was wrong. The scent of the forest, here by the water-side, had changed with a shift in the wind, and he breathed it in and held the new scent in his lungs.

Something had died in terror.

Whatever it was, *wherever* it was, fear permeated its rotten body. Unnerved, Enkidu squatted by the water and breathed slow and deep. A renewed breeze blew off the river. He smelled it again. He bounded forward, and saw a dozen birds pecking at a swollen lump that had washed up on the banks.

The birds scattered as he approached, squawking in irritation when he rolled the lump over.

A body. A human body.

It was purple with decay, and the water-logged flesh displayed horrid lacerations. Its head, legs, and entire lower section was missing. Its clothes were tattered from untold miles of watery travel, picked at by fish and birds and reptiles. And fear saturated it, detectable to Enkidu's nose even amid this putrid stage of decay. The scent was so strong he felt that if he were to squeeze the dead man, the fear itself would come bleeding out of the swollen flesh.

And then Enkidu felt the hairs on his body shoot straight up. His blood ran cold.

The birds continued squawking around him, oblivious to his discovery.

Just to be sure, Enkidu leaned close to the headless corpse and sniffed. There were many smells on the body, some heavier than others. Fear, water, decay.

His mouth ran dry.

Fear.

One of the agitated birds pecked at his leg.

Water. Decay.

Enkidu shuddered. The faint smell lingered in his nose.

Humbaba.

Gilgamesh and Ninsun crossed the Avenue of the Gods and walked silently to the ziggurat, trailed at a respectful distance by the Ishtar priestess who had introduced herself as Shamhat. Only gods could precede a god-king of Uruk.

The Great Ziggurat loomed ahead, threatening the sun as they neared its pyramidal shadow.

"A matter of the Annunaki?" he asked his mother. "When have The Twelve been a concern of Uruk?"

Ninsun's brow clouded with suspicion. "Never."

Gilgamesh pondered the vague summoning. The Annunaki were obscure, strange gods of no importance to Uruk. There were twelve of them. They were cultish beings even amid the gods themselves.

Ninsun's sandaled feet stopped before the shadow. "I go no further."

"You won't come with me?"

"I wait with Shamash outside, you know that."

"But—"

"Ishtar has my respect, but not my love."

Gilgamesh grinned at her. "You need not be fearful. I am here for business only, mother."

Ninsun smiled, and placed her hand on his shoulder affectionately. "You may do as you wish, of course. I won't press you for details." As she looked at him she saw her husband's ghost in his features. The doppelganger was striking; when Gilgamesh turned in profile, she felt her breath sapped away. "Just remember that a great king is governed by his mind and heart," she added, "and not by anything under his kilt."

He burst out laughing. "I don't think Ishtar called me here to seduce me."

"If She did, be *very polite* in your refusal."

The snake-like seductresses of Ishtar's House might be fitting to the Goddess of Love, but the practice was unsavory to Ninsun's sensibilities. Shamash brought warmth to the earth, light to the day, order to the heavens. Ishtar brought conflict wrapped in love's dress.

Ninsun kissed her son quickly on the cheek and turned away as Shamhat caught up with him. Together they ascended the stairs.

If the ziggurat was a gloomy mountain at night, then by daylight it was a pyramid of gold. From the crowning Temple of Ishtar at its top to the terraces draped with veins of vegetation, it sparkled like something created before the Flood, in the days when the world was pure and crystal in its beauty, untarnished by fear or failing.

"Tell me why I have been summoned to the Temple," Gilgamesh asked the priestess as they climbed.

"There is a thief who came here to lay with me. He paid in silver but carried something else, an object no peasant fisherman's hands should ever have touched."

"This object ... might it be an Annunaki *statue*?"

"It is, just that," the woman said, her white teeth appearing like tiny serrated daggers behind her smiling lips.

"And the statue has been given to the goddess' care, I presume?"

"She has placed it back among the stars, Mighty Lord."

"Among the stars?"

"The statues of the Annunaki belong to the domain of heaven, my king."

"There are twelve of these statues."

"There are twelve."

"And have they all been returned to the stars now?"

At this Shamhat's eyes glittered, and though her face was cast somewhat downward so she could watch her steps, Gilgamesh caught the sparkle of suspicion nonetheless.

She didn't answer right away, but before he could press her she said, "There are ten, Ishtar has told me, that have been returned to the stars, ever since her arrival in Uruk."

"And this is the eleventh, then? Or is it the tenth?"

"The eleventh," she said softly.

Gilgamesh tilted his head up and saw the temple appearing over the horizon of the top-most tier. He doubted very much that eleven Annunaki statues had been taken up "to the stars," particularly when this ziggurat was so immense that it could hide a small district inside its brick body, were it to be hollow. And if a district, why not eleven statues, each small enough to be carried, apparently, if a fisherman had it on his person the night before? Returning a statue "to the stars" sounded suspiciously like deceit, intended to throw treasure-seekers off the scent. The eleven Annunaki were certainly still on the Earth, tucked away in the ziggurat's subterranean depths.

Yet a sudden twinge of fear accompanied his thoughts, and he found himself muttering a prayer of forgiveness for his skepticism. Now it was Shamhat who took notice of Gilgamesh's quiet chant, and he stopped when he saw her interest. Impiety toward the patron goddess, indeed while climbing the very steps of Her House, was a frightful sin. Gilgamesh shivered, finished the prayer in his mind, and ignored Shamhat's lurid stare. After all, he had meant no blasphemy. The Annunaki were said to be priceless relics, forged in some distant time by a people whose name was lost in the shrouds of history. That a goddess should want them was no surprise; that She should be so eager to deliver them into heaven, and not keep them to add to the luster of Her earth-bound House for a little while ... *this* was the matter that Gilgamesh questioned.

"I take it you seldom come down into the city," Gilgamesh said lightly, "I should think this trek of stairs would discourage your feet."

"It apparently discourages *yours*. I have never seen you enter the Temple, though you walk with the goddess each New Year's Festival and take Her hand like a devoted servant."

Taken aback, shamed slightly by this observation, Gilgamesh managed a smile and said, "Your words cut, but they are true. I should like to remedy that. Perhaps, even, to see you, Shamhat."

She looked at him with the most malevolent smirk he had ever seen, as if she were secretly some cobra of shapeshifting talents that could assume human appearance but never wholly discard its inner nature.

"If His Highness wants me, he may take me as his mood strikes him. Yet even for the Lord of the City, I am not without price."

They reached the top tier and Gilgamesh looked at the landing, with the small temple flanked by bronze tripods. Shamhat stood aside for Gilgamesh to enter the dark mouth. She closed in behind him.

Gilgamesh looked at the lavish room cast in gold and sporting reliefs of undulating forms, both cosmic and fleshy. There were animal-skin rugs on the floors.

Down one of these hallways was a grimmer room done in stone. It was here that Shamhat stopped, pointed to the far wall where the accused thief was hung.

The fisherman looked ghastly, chained to the wall of the temple so that his arms were high above his head. His face was stained with fresh abrasions, as if rough sandstone had been used on his cheeks and the flesh had been scrubbed away, leaving two crusted lakes of bloody underskin in their place. His eyes swiveled open at the sound of their approach, and they were glassy portals of fear.

Gilgamesh frowned, seeing the man's desperate plight. "How long has he been chained like this?"

"Since last night."

"And the wounds I see? Were these present before he laid with you?"

The question was designed to throw her off-guard. Gilgamesh saw at once that it succeeded in this aim. Shamhat's lustful eyes lost their confidence. She scowled but did not reply.

"You were asked a question, and I plainly see you have two ears. Answer me! Were his wounds received here, or elsewhere?"

"I believe they were received here," Shamhat said testily, though she trembled at the suggestion of his wrath.

"Your belief is irrelevant. What did you see?"

"I saw my own hand rubbing the flesh from his face. By command of the goddess, until he became cooperative."

Gilgamesh neared the fisherman and looked into his face. The man's skin was rough with grey stubble, and had the seared blush of the sun burned into his forehead and cheeks. Age had thinned his face so that his skin was like a parchment stretched tightly over the bones, giving him the look of a living skull. His eyes were sunken, a further prelude to the approach of death.

His eyes.

Gilgamesh stared into the man's gaze, holding it with penetrating intensity. They were watery, brown, liquid eyes with wrinkles webbing from their corners. The eyes didn't look away, but they widened in a silent protestation of innocence. In their own wordless language, they cried: *I am innocent, dear king. Please, believe in me in my desperation. By the gods, I have committed no crime!*

"Where did you get the statue?" Gilgamesh asked in a hard voice.

"I netted a body," the fisherman said miserably. "I pulled it ashore, and searched it, and I found the statue. I did not take—"

"Where is that body now?"

"I threw it back into the river."

"Why?"

"I do not know," the fisherman replied sadly.

Gilgamesh looked to the priestess.

"A convenient excuse, my Lord," she said.

"The body was without a head!" the fishermen yelled suddenly.

"Even more convenient," the priestess added.

Gilgamesh stroked his beard, thinking. Seeing a moment of opportunity, Shamhat said, "Mighty Gilgamesh, if this thief found the eleventh Annunaki, he may know where the twelfth one is! These items are the rightful property of the goddess, and Uruk would certainly have Ishtar's eternal appreciation and love should they be safely returned to Her."

Gilgamesh let the priestess' voice bounce off him. Addressing the fisherman again, he said, "Do you know who I am?"

The fisherman nodded weakly. "You are King Gilgamesh, My Lord."

"Do you know the penalty for lying?"

"I am not lying!" The strength of his voice was terrible, the protestation of a damned soul who had nothing to lose but scream the truth.

"Why did you throw the body back into the river?"

"I feared being called a murderer."

Gilgamesh turned to the priestess. "Let him go," he said.

The priestess looked as if she had been hit with icy water. "What?"

"Again, this peculiar problem with your ears, Shamhat." He smiled at the fisherman. "I believe you. Go on your way."

The relief in the fisherman's eyes was immediate; new tears, this time of gratitude, streamed down his face. Gilgamesh turned away and began to leave the temple.

"This is an outrage!" the priestess bellowed, giving chase after him. "You do not have the right—"

Gilgamesh spun around so fast that the priestess nearly collided with his chest. "I am the lord of this city! I have every right under the sun and moon! If your ears are so useless, I'll have them sliced off!"

From the gloomy corridor behind him came a sudden voice: "Release him, Shamhat. Do as your king told you."

Gilgamesh turned and saw Ishtar approaching him like a pale specter. He froze, rigid with uncertainty.

Ishtar was an eerie, stunning vision. Her flesh was silver-white—gemlike and deathly. Her sable hair flowed thickly down to Her waist. Her gown was equally otherworldly, comprised of links of different metals and jewels so that it shivered in a dozen different hues. Her upright breasts were faintly visible through the meshed garment.

Gilgamesh stared. Tiny lights seemed to dance in his vision. The air thickened as if with invisible fibers. Gilgamesh shook his head, but the sensation persisted until it was nearly unbearable. He was suffocating.

"Goddess Ishtar," he whispered.

Tall She stood, eyes outlined in kohl that exaggerated their almond shape. Her lips were of bronze. She reached a hand out to him, showcasing nails like thin silver pins … the hand he had taken every New Year Festival. And Her body … barely clothed, hairless, supple and radiant.

Ishtar stared. "What does the king know of the Annunaki statues?"

Fighting his disorientation, Gilgamesh said, "They were crafted long ago by the hands of an unknown race. They total twelve, and each differs from the other because their sets of eyes and hearts are cut from unique jewels; some have the eyes and heart of ruby, others of amber. As to their purpose I know not, unless they exist simply to commemorate the Annunaki."

"They serve other purpose than that. But just as a wheel and carriage together make a chariot, the Annunaki need to be brought together to fulfill their function."

"And so you have returned eleven of them to heaven?"

Ishtar's eyes flashed, and there was an annoyance in them that made Gilgamesh brace for some supernatural assault. Then the fury faded. "I see Shamhat has fed you things only my order is privileged to know."

At once, Shamhat cried out and threw herself at Ishtar's feet, wrapping her arms around the goddess' ankles. "Forgive me, my Goddess! Forgive me, I beg you!"

Ishtar ran Her fingers through the girl's hair, and Shamhat sat up, still kneeling, to plead with her eyes for mercy.

"You are forgiven, Shamhat."

"Yes, my Goddess," the priestess said, and smiled happily. Looking at the scene, Gilgamesh felt that this was not the first time Shamhat had so submissively dropped to her knees before Ishtar.

As if reading his mind, Ishtar glanced at him with a curious, sideways tilt of Her head.

"King Gilgamesh, you will take Shamhat with you and seek the body this fisherman describes. The fisherman—" she looked at the chained prisoner. "He will be released, though he shall take you to this spot."

Gifted with an unfailing sense of smell, Enkidu had no doubts about his discovery. The mutilated corpse had been killed by Humbaba, Terror of the North. Then the body had fallen, or had been thrown, into the river, and the downstream currents had carried it like a warning to all men.

Months of southward traveling had separated Enkidu from the northern region, yet distance had not dulled his memory. He could hear his mother's voice warning him as a child: "Stay away from the Cedar Forest, Enkidu. Stay away from Humbaba. The Forest is his lair, and we are never to disturb him." Yet once the entire tribe had been forced to detour through a corner of that very forest … a horrible night. The woods reeked of his musk, and of other smells. Death smells. The Tribe Elder, with a face like a gnarled tree knob, sniffed the air and declared, "Humbaba has killed something large today."

Yes he has, Enkidu thought in grim reply. He backed away from the body, hastily washed his hands in the river, and retreated to consider his options in the shade of trees.

He had been on the move steadily for one year, leaving behind the northern forests where he had been born. How he longed to see those lands again! He remembered every hill and valley of his childhood there. But those days were lost. His tribe had perished on a black night one year ago. Enkidu was all that remained.

His tribe was his family—six adults and one child. On a moonless night, they had been hiking through a narrow valley that cut like a chasm between two stony mountains when a roaring thunder sounded ahead of them. Then the waters came, a white-headed serpent flying at them from the darkness. Having strayed far ahead of his tribe, Enkidu saw the waters coming and instinctively sprang off the path onto a slab of stone at the feet of the mountain. With horror he watched the water rush by him and devour his family—six adults and one child, gone! His lifelong troop of companions in the world, whisked away like leaves driven before the wind.

Even as the flood filled the ravine, Enkidu had given desperate chase hoping to rescue tribe members. He found two bodies when the waters subsided. The first was the Tribe Elder, his grey-haired head broken open on the rocks.

The second was his mother.

Crying out, Enkidu had scooped her up and carried her out of the valley. He set her down on a bed of leaves and cradled her, and his heart lifted when she stirred.

Yet she too had been killed by the flood—just not as immediate as her brothers and sisters. With her final breaths she smiled weakly at him and said, "You have grown so strong, Enkidu. You make me very proud."

Sobbing, Enkidu had pleaded with her not to die, but all she offered in response was a command for him to continue seeking others of their kind, as the tribe had done unsuccessfully ever since his birth. "Seek them if they can be found," she said, "And if you are the last, my son, then do whatever you must to live well." Enkidu clutched her the whole night, hoping somehow that he would awaken in the morning and it all would be a dream: the thunderous waters, the screaming, the death … he would awaken to find the seven tribe members alive and smiling.

One year now, and driven by her dying words he had headed south seeking evidence of other tribes; their footprints, droppings, perhaps the momentous sight of them. Each day he awoke to new loneliness.

The world was changing. How many times had he heard that sentiment as a child, eavesdropping on the adults as they sat around a fire and talked of ancient times? The world was changing.

No, Enkidu thought. The world has already changed. In a flash of flood, the last tribe had vanished and he alone moved as a shadow among a new people he could not understand.

Could not?

The thought jarred him. He wiped away his tears—the memory of his mother's death always made him cry—and rebuked himself for his fatalism. What could he *not* understand? He knew every tree in the Fertile Crescent. He knew each plant, animal, river, rock, and mountain as if a map had burned itself on his mind. He knew what roots to eat if he was sick. He could hunt anything, and unlike the city-dwelling humans he did not need traps to do it.

The humans. How many times had the Tribe Elder talked of *them*, speculating on their great mystery beneath the quietly burning stars? And aside from an abandoned human city he had once seen as a child, when had any members of his tribe dared to venture near one?

Enkidu's eyes settled on Uruk's mighty walls, and he glared as if challenging them to battle.

The humans were a puzzle. An enigma which, the Tribe Elder said, were best alone. But now, Enkidu was the one alone.

"Do whatever you must to live well," he heard his mother say in memory, and he shivered suddenly, for the voice was so loud it tickled his ears. He imagined turning and seeing her standing beside him. He imagined her next words: *I was only sleeping after the flood, Enkidu! I was not dead! I was sleeping peacefully ...*

You are not sleeping mother, he replied.

Not as long as I hold you in my mind.

Daylight was failing; already the shadows were lengthening. With nightfall the city would be dark. Under cover of that darkness, Enkidu thought, he would penetrate the city and see what he could. He already knew how to scale their walls without being seen by their tower guards.

The time has come, Enkidu thought in fierce determination, for the mystery to end.

TABLET II

ENKIDU

CHAPTER 7
RUMOR IN THE MARKET

Nedu crossed the noisy marketplace square and was suddenly swallowed by the shouting, swearing, sweaty crowd. It was as if he had wandered into a ruptured ant-mound, and now all the drones bustled shoulder-to-shoulder until there was barely room to breathe. He pushed through the quivering wall of bodies and sighed a great relief when he had reached a pocket of air on the outskirts of the market's heart. Yet still came the sounds of customers haggling with smiling merchants who crouched in the dust to peddle their wares. Had Nedu been blind, he would have found no problem in navigating the marketplace by sound alone.

Nedu rested by the market's central fountain, a towering sculpture cut in the shape of a scaly sea-beast spewing water from its yawning maw. There, he regained some strength and wondered if he was making the most of his day.

Two hours had passed since Gilgamesh had left the council at the beckoning of Ishtar's priestess. There were no meetings now; evening was a while off. Nedu felt acute anxiety that he was wasting precious time. It was a familiar sensation. It was a feeling that grew heavier on his mind with each passing year.

"My time is my own now," Nedu said quietly, not worrying that anyone would hear him in this din. He finished the thought in his head: My agenda is a blank clay tablet, devoid of responsibilities. Do something for yourself Nedu!

So he walked by the marketplace arches, where tendrils of ivy interwove the frame and flowers blossomed like colorful eyes at their feet. The tapestry of vegetation had been instituted during Lugalbanda's reign as part of a city-wide beautification effort. For all his military brilliance, the previous king Enmerkar knew little of simple pleasures to present to the citizen's eye. Lugalbanda had the true soul of a warrior-poet—that rare type of man whose passion for life did not falter during times of peace. He was more of a citizen's king. As for Dumuzi…

Do I miss Dumuzi?

The question found an immediate answer: No. There was little to miss about a man who had unjustly claimed the throne, silenced his critics through violence, and then tried to kill the rightful prince. Besides, Dumuzi had been "dead" for a long time anyway—an invisible issue who mattered only when the yearly budget was drawn up and payment of the South Tower guards was discussed.

A woman carrying a reed basket full of wheat, eggs, and bright linens nearly collided with him. Nedu jumped aside, silently cursing, and then turned his attention to a second question that occurred to him.

Will I miss Gilgamesh?

It was a silly query. He knew he wouldn't live to see Gilgamesh's passing. Another five, ten, twenty years, and Nedu would die, while Gilgamesh would still be a healthy man in the prime of his strength. The real question, then, was: Will Gilgamesh miss me? There was no way to tell; Nedu liked to think that when he passed, there would be a vacuum difficult to fill. Yet he knew the raw truth of things. He was a councilman, not a king, and in the end not a soul on Earth would miss him. His two daughters would for a time, and so would his wife, but his wife would not survive him by many years and his daughters would soon be married off.

It was a grim scenario to be contemplating on such a vibrant day, and Nedu felt a morbid giddiness spring up inside him, demanding further prodding. It was only natural to wonder at his mortality. Young people rarely did, and why should they? It was the elderly who stood at the end of life's road. Sumerians might consider old age to be silver baskets of wisdom, but before death all wisdom ultimately failed.

Nonetheless, Nedu had resolved to make a request to the gods when the time of his own death was at hand. It was a request so strange that his two daughters openly laughed at him when he confided it. Embarrassed, Nedu decided then to keep it to himself.

When death neared for him, Nedu intended to ask the gods for a special sight that would allow him to see into the future, to see what would become of mighty Uruk. Who would rule it in its final days? What would it look like? He didn't think it such a bizarre request. After all, the gods would have no reason to balk at lifting the heart of a dying man with a glimpse of things to come.

Nedu plunged into another pocket of activity in the marketplace. Fresh meats, newly skinned, hung from posts for city nobles to inspect and haggle with the hunters for a price. Wheat, furs, oils, charms, fish, and cheap trinkets lay on myriad rugs and tables. Nedu glanced at the displays, brushing away overzealous merchants. Disappointed, Nedu picked a brown-skinned merchant and tapped him on the shoulder.

The man looked at him, all sparkling eyes and toothless grin. His skin was beaded with sweat, wrinkled from too much smiling and too much squinting. Seeing Nedu, he nodded and spoke in a quick, galloping pace.

"And what can I do for you today, councilman?"

"Where's the younger boy, the merchant from Babylon? He was with you last month."

"Ah," the man said. "He died of a scorpion-bite two weeks ago."

Nedu blinked. Considered the news. Blinked again.

"I'm sorry to hear that," he said finally.

"I know. Terrible, really. But perhaps I can do something for you?"

"I told that boy I was looking for some Kishian mead."

"Ah!" the merchant said finally. "I remember now."

"Good."

The merchant slapped Nedu on the shoulder. It was a friendly, playful gesture, but it nearly knocked Nedu into the dirt. "There've been a few holdups with obtaining it."

"Yes, yes, yes," Nedu said dismissively, having heard enough merchant-talk in his life to know that they always held the upper hand. "Just get it for me, and you can name your price."

The merchant's smile grew.

"So long as it is reasonable," Nedu warned. "I'll not shell out my life's savings."

"Of course!"

"I'm sorry for the young boy's death."

"So am I," the merchant said, looking appropriately crestfallen. "But I'll get you what you're looking for, councilman. Rest assured!"

"Thank you." Nedu turned away.

"Of course, there may be some political issues that could delay a speedy purchase," the merchant added as if in afterthought.

Nedu sighed, turned back, and said, "What political issues?"

"The word is spreading in Kish, and all along the Euphrates, up north."

"What?"

"I hate to be the one to tell you, but—"

"What?"

"It seems that Uruk may not be a kingdom for long," the merchant said with a sympathetic smile. "Word is that Uruk is in its final year of life, about to be swallowed up a larger fish in the valley pond."

After the fisherman had been treated of his wounds and declared fit enough to take the king and priestess to where he had found the body, Gilgamesh found himself at the river's edge staring at the flaxen water, no body in sight.

The fisherman panicked, sputtering excuses as he hobbled along the riverside searching for signs of the corpse. "Here is where I netted him," he said. "Here is where I threw it back." The fear in his voice was palpable—the nightmare of new torture in the ziggurat haunting his eyes.

"You are free of the temple," Gilgamesh told him. "Unless you perpetrate some new crime, you shall remain a free man."

Further downriver they walked, for a mile until they came to a sharp bend in the Euphrates.

"The body may have sunk to the river's bottom," the fisherman said. "I could trawl with my net for it."

"Or it could have drifted downstream, to the Mouth of the Rivers," Gilgamesh said thoughtfully, looking to where the great Euphrates cut across the green land beyond Uruk and disappeared into the purple horizon.

"Or it may only have existed in the mind of this thief," Shamhat said unhappily.

"A man who finds something that has no clear owner—and a dead body in the river would certainly fall into that category—is not a thief," Gilgamesh told her.

They trekked along the smooth riverbanks, and Gilgamesh was beginning to think of abandoning the quest when suddenly he saw a gathering of birds on the muddy slope ahead. A lumpish thing, washed up at the river's bend, proved the object of the scavengers' attention.

"There it is!" the fisherman exclaimed.

The priestess' eyes simmered upon this find, as if boring holes into the dead man who had once carried the sacred statue.

"The clothes are northern," Gilgamesh observed, drawing near and scattering the birds by his presence. "I should say Assyrian by the colors of the tunic." He lifted one of the soggy, cold arms and examined it, then checked the other. Ignoring the stench, he ripped open the tunic and looked at the bloated chest. "No tattoos, however. It is in the manner of all Assyrian warriors to paint themselves for all to see. You rummaged through his pockets, true?"

The fisherman nodded, somewhat shamefully.

"And you found nothing else?"

"Just the statue in his bag, slung tightly round his shoulder."

Before Gilgamesh could think of another query to pose, he noticed how the corpse's ribs up-thrust against the soft flesh. He had been looking for some sign of the ethnicity of the corpse, but now he found himself drawn to the manner of death. Shattered ribs on both sides. Legs missing, arms limp with shattered bones, head gone.

Maggots. Worms in the flesh.

Gilgamesh shivered and felt bile in his mouth. It was such an irrational fear. Since childhood, the fear of maggots and other corpse-eaters had plagued him. At seven years old, he had once found a dead bird and picked it up ... only to discover it was wriggling with white worms *and they had gotten onto his hands.*

Gilgamesh stepped back. "There," he said, pointing. A blue-black symbol was tattooed at the base of the man's spine, where the leather armor ended above the dreadful dismemberment. The mark was small and simple, but the artistry of design was indicative of the north, and Gilgamesh had heard of only one culture that practiced such brandings upon the spine's base, pressed into the flesh of all infants as proof of citizenship and heritage.

"He is from Nineveh," Gilgamesh said, pleased at his resolution of the mystery. He spat and turned away from the corpse. "I've seen marks like that before on merchants and ambassadors from that ruby city."

"Nineveh is by the *Tigris* River," Shamhat said.

"Where he went after his birth are things his corpse doesn't tell. But all citizens of Nineveh are very proud of their heritage, and only the lowliest of their caste go without branding. The mark tells of his bloodline and the status of his family." Gilgamesh could not read the symbols, and likely there was no one in Uruk who would be familiar with a particular family crest from so far off. "It follows that this man discovered the Annunaki somewhere in the north then, and presumably near the Euphrates." Yet what had happened to him after that? Gilgamesh wondered. How had the man been so pulverized?

Shamhat nodded, bowed. "Ishtar thanks you, for all the help you have given Her."

"I am at the Goddess' service," the king replied. Shamhat walked off.

Watching her go, Gilgamesh said to the fisherman in a quiet tone, "And now I will help you, fisherman, by committing some advice to your safe-keeping. Go back to your family. Explain your wounds however you will. But I would advise you to never again seek your pleasure at the Temple of Ishtar."

"Your advice is more divine than she, Lord Gilgamesh," the old man said, sharing in the king's view of the departing priestess.

CHAPTER 8
CONFRONTATION

Returning to the palace, Gilgamesh was intercepted by the pale and shaking figure of Councilman Nedu. He didn't notice the councilman's mood right away, as his thoughts swirled over the mystery of the corpse he had seen, and he reflexively asked Nedu why he wasn't home with his family.

As soon as the councilman spoke, Gilgamesh felt pierced by a volley of arrows.

"Call the High Council," Gilgamesh said at once.

"I already have," Nedu panted. "They are awaiting you, My Lord."

In the Council Chamber where hours ago had gathered droves of citizens anxious to state their cases, now five solemn men stood round the throne in a half-ring, like game pieces in an Egyptian game of Senet, ready to be called on. Gilgamesh sat, grappling with a nervous energy that possessed his body and made him want to pace around the chamber.

The High Council consisted of Uruk's most esteemed officials, men who were masters of their chosen field. Tirigan the Trade Advisor, with a smooth bald head and a long chin-beard. Rimush the Foreign Minister, dark as a shadow, and like Tirigan fluent in all human speech. Kazallu the fat City Engineer oversaw all physical infrastructure of Uruk. One-eyed Zariqu the Religious Minister handled religious squabbles, issues, and worked with Kazallu on the maintenance of Uruk's temples. And then there was Ibi-Sin, Military Advisor to three kings including Gilgamesh.

He summoned Ibi-Sin first, and did not delay in posing the dreaded question: "How prepared are we to resist Agga of Kish?"

Ibi-Sin was stout and fierce, shorter than average height by several inches. As if to make up for his stature, the man presented to the world an angry countenance with hard eyes like onyx set in a scowling mask.

"We are unready, My Lord," he stated flatly.

"And why is that?"

"Uruk boasts the world's greatest population of *masons*, Lord Gilgamesh. Their time in toiling at the walls is time better spent in up-keeping our militia. While we have been adding levels of bricks, Agga has been adding soldiers to his army."

"You state this like a gripe. It is for the very defense of Uruk that I have ordered the walls built."

"And yet walls are not warriors," the Military Advisor protested. "It is a point that I reluctantly remind you has been made before, by me. Uruk's soldiers have traded in their swords for trowels."

To Rimush the Foreign Minister, Gilgamesh said, "What do you think of the news that Councilman Nedu brings us? A rumor peddled by a gossipy merchant? When in its long history has Kish ever shown hostility to Uruk?"

Rimush rubbed his black, freckled forehead. "King Gilgamesh, we are all acquainted with how a city's character transforms with each new ruler. King Enmeenbaragisi brought to Kish open trade. Agga brings to it the chariots of war and the promise of glory."

The Mesopotamian valley was a great flower whose verdant scent had attracted people like so many bees to settle down and build cities. The invention of the city allowed for food to be harvested *en masse*, precious metals to be mined, livestock raised, crafts produced, and all the fruits of civilization sown and harvested. Yet it came with a price. A prosperous city was seen as a shining treasure chest, a cornucopia to be pillaged and ransacked by those strong enough to do it. As a result, cities built walls and defenses. To overcome those defenses, stronger weapons were fashioned. The pattern was as tireless as the course of the sun through each ripening day.

In time certain cities had earned fierce reputations as plunderers of their neighbors. The very name of Assyria could strike terror in even the most seasoned warrior's heart. The northern Hittite tribes were held equally vicious ... even the Far-Distant Egyptians feared them. And Uruk herself, in the time of Enmerkar, had thrived on battle like a vampiric spirit.

The city of Kish, however, had been a quiet player in the contests of Mesopotamia. For seven decades it had been ruled by Enmeenbaragisi, an accomplished general who ruled shrewdly but peaceably. Agga was the man's only surviving son—himself a general of great renown. Agga's ten-year-reign had already seen four wars, whose concluding chapters had resulted in yearly tributes from three surrounding states and the genocide of the Hanite kingdom to the south-east.

Uruk was not the Hanites. It boasted the largest populace in the world. Its history was old, its reputation fearful. Only a fool would select it as a target for invasion or a simple villa to be bullied into submission. Agga was no fool.

"He is a man of ambition," maintained the councilman.

Gilgamesh shook his head. "We have spies in Kish. Their military is nominal. No plans of southern conquest have ever crossed Agga's table."

"And spies are such a trustworthy lot," Ibi-Sin countered, his face purple-red with frustration. "My Lord, I submit that we have received disinformation over the past few years. I have collected reports of vast training drills in the deserts east of Kish. The gold from their tributes could hire a mercenary army three times as large as our own!"

Gilgamesh felt himself reeling from this news; his attention had been so tightly focused on Uruk that this threat from Kish sprang at him like a deadly north-blowing plague. "Uruk will not fall, not under my reign, not under any reign," Gilgamesh declared, a seed of determination taking root in his desperation, growing, flowering, and bearing the fruits of rage. "Ibi-Sin, as of this hour you are to reorganize our militia. Work on the wall will cease. The funds will go into new weapons' production. The masons will become warriors, and their abilities will be a reflection on you."

Ibi-Sin bowed, visibly anxious to begin. Yet Gilgamesh could not resist one more question.

"But what of the wall we have built thus far?" he said.

"As is, Lord Gilgamesh, it will provide formidable defense. Yet a walled city without warriors is only a great egg waiting to be cracked. Split up the labor force, and put half of them into building an army. Archers, mostly, to take advantage of the wall. But we must have presence of warriors, My Lord. And we must do this soon."

As soon as the black flower of evening blossomed, Enkidu emerged from the forest and made for the eastern side of Uruk's walls. They were tall but not sheer, and he managed to find hand- and foot-holds in the creases of mortar between the bricks. When he reached the top, he perched like a living gargoyle to contemplate the sleeping city below him.

In weeks past he had gone this far. He had scaled the manmade barrier and looked down at the city. Now he resolved to go the few steps further, to plunge down the other side of the wall and face whatever lay there. For a moment Enkidu was flooded with fear and doubt. But then he thought of all he had faced in his young life. Traps, wolves, and flood-waters had not felled him. He would not turn away from this enigma called man.

Yet no sooner had the thought passed through his mind like a fluttering lunar moth than he saw two figures walking the perimeter of the wall, swiftly approaching where he crouched. The sight startled him. There were never humans patrolling the wall itself.

They were closing in on him fast, yet didn't seem to have seen him. Their conversation was relaxed, their heads turned out to the shadowy wilderness and the first stars in the melancholy sky.

Enkidu bounded away from them, retreating along the lip of the wall where a cone of shadow lay behind an unlit streetlamp. With the dexterity of a monkey he found hand-holds on the wall's inner side, and he scuttled down just as the men passed by where he had been. He caught whispers of their speech, unknowable and alien to his ears. He wondered if they were discussing the placement of forest traps.

Couldn't humans climb?

With ease, Enkidu penetrated their city. He stuck to the shadows, and upon arriving at the inner Gate of Ishtar he simply climbed over it. The moonlight was dim, flooding the brickyard with an anemic light on clusters of adobe huts.

Enkidu breathed deeply. He smelled humanity.

The city walls, it seemed, did more than protect this city: They prevented the wind from washing away the stink of so many people living so close.

Enkidu could smell spoiled food thrown out, urine and feces, and traces of other bodily secretions. It was disorienting, but then came a smell Enkidu was familiar with. It was the excrement of an animal, a horse, and it was nearby. Enkidu crept forward to the nearest of the homes, and he stopped at its walls. He touched the stonework wonderingly.

Who were these creatures who shaped rock as if it were silt? Who were they who had erected the towering walls, dug the roads crisscrossing the heart of this city, and made the very water of the river obey their whims?

The smell of the horse rescued him from an all-out panic. Enkidu prowled to the home's stables, and he melted into the shadows within.

The horse was there, leaning its massive head over the stable door. It whinnied sharply, recoiling from him. Enkidu was unconcerned, and he let the creature smell him. He hummed pleasantly, patiently waiting until the animal's curiosity compelled it to investigate him. He stroked its neck.

And then the door to the stable flew open and a young boy entered, and Enkidu jumped back, startled at the intrusion, but not nearly as startled as the boy was.

For a moment he froze with uncertainty, mired in the conflict of fighting or fleeing his unwary assailant. His paralysis was not shared by the boy, however, who cried out and brandished an axe, swinging wildly.

Enkidu ducked and fled the wrong way, finding himself trapped between the axe-bearing youth and the end of the stables. He turned and saw the young boy screaming, the weapon glinting in his hands. Enkidu attempted to run by him but the boy swung again, and all Enkidu could do to avoid the whirring blade was to fall back into the dirt and scramble back to the stable where the horse snorted frightfully.

"Father!" the boy cried in words foreign to Enkidu's ears.

Enkidu didn't need to know what the words were; he understood this human was shouting a warning cry to bring others. In panic, he wondered how he'd gotten into this predicament.

The door of the stable flew open again and an older man, thin as all humans were so thin, came forward with a short blade in his hand. The man's eyes grew wide when he saw Enkidu.

"Gudea!" he cried. "Back away! Back away from it!"

But Gudea, encouraged by his success thus far with cornering the beastly intruder, was spurred into making a gutsier move. Realizing that the furry, squat-bodied creature was in the grips of terror, Gudea saw his chance to make a kill. He raised the axe high above his head, screamed a prayer to Marduk, and charged at the beast.

Enkidu's reflexes were far, far quicker. He ducked the axe, hearing it embed into the stable wall. Instantly, he grasped the boy by the front of his tunic and lifted him into the air.

Gizzida's surprise evaporated as he watched his only son in the terrible grip of this hairy man-beast. Enraged as only a father can be at the threat of harm to his only child, he let out a roar and sprang to his son, his dagger held flat and aimed for the monster's pinkish abdomen.

Enkidu saw the man rushing him, and he tossed the boy into the stable doors. They cracked inward, and Gudea bounced off of them just as the horse, terrified beyond control now, charged the damaged doors and broke free.

Gizzida plunged his dagger at Enkidu. The creature *charged into the attack*, avoided the strike, and head-butt the old man squarely in the pit of his stomach. The air exploded from Gizzida's lungs and he hit the dirt, legs rolling over his head, and lay still as the horse dashed out of the stables into the street beyond.

"Father!" Gudea screamed.

In a show of concern, Enkidu bent down to the unconscious man. Seeing this, Gudea jumped for Enkidu's throat, hands hooked to strangle. Enkidu caught him in mid-leap, and he drew the boy close to his face, snarled in mock anger to frighten him, and said, "*NO, Enkidu gor anta!*" Only the *No* was a human word; it was all of the human language that Enkidu's Tribe Elder had known. *No* was a word often used by humans to discourage or threaten. Enkidu figured that both uses would apply in this instance.

Whether it was the word *No*, or the sound of the man-beast talking, Gudea went rigid and silent, his eyes as large as snake eggs.

Enkidu threw him against the stable doors again, less violently this time. The doors, already cracked, folded in and Gudea hit the straw.

Yet the boy wouldn't stay down, figuring his beloved father killed by this animal, and so he rolled back to his feet and found his axe. He burst from the pen swinging.

The creature was gone.

CHAPTER 9
A STRANGE TALE

Uruk's spies had been dispatched in the middle of the night like hornets from an anxious hive, and under cover of darkness, clad in merchant livery or the weather-beaten tunics of bandits, they seeped into the valley forest seeking information. Villages awaited them, and trade route cross-roads. Nedu's merchant friend had heard the rumor of brewing war from the region north of Uruk, in some villages outside of Kish. Urukian spies made quickly for that sweet region with all speed.

And in the daybreak following the battle between two hunters and a mythical forest beast, Gilgamesh paid visit to Nedu's merchant friend, held in a guarded room of the palace.

"Your tongue didn't slip," Gilgamesh told the man when he entered with Nedu. "You mentioned this to my councilman quite deliberately."

The merchant bowed low. "I may have felt some duty, My Lord. Though I am no citizen of your godly kingdom, you did grant me trade rights extending to Uruk's south-eastern borders. I know also you would reward a faithful man for this information."

"And torture endlessly the man who fed me lies."

The merchant's wide face lost a little color. "I have nothing to fear. What I speak is true."

"I've sent men to follow up on these 'truths,'" Gilgamesh advised him.

"Come spring, Agga's army will be standing outside your door. You will know it for a truth, then."

Nedu scowled. "And he intends to turn Uruk into a vassal tributary?"

"He intends to destroy you and sack your city. You specifically will die, Gilgamesh, and in your place he will instate a puppet governor. The lesson will carry into the south like the fear of a plague. From Uruk, Agga would then have the whole south of Sumer as his picking fields. You are the greatest strength here. If you fell, your neighboring kingdoms would kiss Agga's feet—"

Gilgamesh's bearded face hardened with skepticism. "And do you hate Agga so much, that you'd betray these plans to his enemy?"

The merchant shook his head. "I don't love or hate any king, mighty Gilgamesh. Uruk's plunder would go to Agga's royal court. I'm not permitted to trade there."

Nedu nodded. "So it benefits you to have Uruk as a trading port."

"Rather than as a ruin? Yes."

Gilgamesh exited, with Nedu on his heels. "He shall be moved to the South Tower," the king said in the hallway. "Until his story is verified."

"Yes, sire."

At the other end of the hall, one-eyed Zariqu the Religious Minister spotted the king and rushed forth. "Mighty Gilgamesh? You sent for me?"

The king's frantic thoughts swirled like fireflies; he felt the sudden need for release, sexual or through violence. "Bring word to Ishtar that Agga is threatening Uruk. Ask Her if She wishes our city to fall to invasion."

Zariqu nodded happily. "I will, My Lord. At once." He hurried away.

Nedu could sense Gilgamesh's dangerous emotional state. "Have you eaten, sire?"

"No."

"Perhaps you should—"

"I am presiding over the City Council today," Gilgamesh said, telling himself that he'd select two women for his bed tonight instead of a solitary companion.

Nedu followed him as Gilgamesh moved off again like a caged tiger. "Is that wise, sire?"

"Ibi-Sin is organizing our defense. Our spies have been unleashed. There's nothing for me to do right now, and I *need* something to do."

"But last Council was—"

"Unusual, yes. The headless corpse. But that's not likely to be repeated." Gilgamesh silently mouthed a prayer to Marduk that today would bring him simplistic legal cases, enough to distract him yet not rile him. "It will be fine, Nedu."

"May I accompany you today, My Lord?"

"To make sure I don't order some delinquent taxpayer an execution?"

"Yes," Nedu admitted.

"Come along, then."

As Gilgamesh seated himself, the guards brought forward his first (and as it would turn out, only) case of the day. Two men, one old and one young, both dressed in the green tunics of hunters. The men knelt. Gilgamesh sized them up, gleaning only that they were certainly a father and son.

"A *lahmu* attacked us last night!" the young boy said stoutly. By the reaction of his father, it was clear this was not the opening line they had decided on.

Quickly, the father interjected: "My Lord, the boy speaks true. In the blackest hours of night he was returning an axe to our stable when the beast attacked. I heard his cry, I seized my dagger, and saw this thing with my own eyes."

A long silence flooded the chamber. Even the other citizens, anxious for their turn of speaking with the king, were stricken dumb at this news.

When Gilgamesh recovered from his initial shock, he could find only two words worthy of being spoken: "A ... *lahmu*?"

"For one week, we have known that a strange folk was prowling your Majesty's woods," the old man continued, "ever since one of our cages was pulverized. It was my first thought that other hunters had been responsible, so fierce is the competition for sellable meat. But the sheer strength of the damage made me wonder. Not long after, my son began noticing strange tracks along the muddy banks of the river. I saw these prints too. I—"

Gilgamesh held up his hand for the man to be silent. He looked at Nedu.

"A *lahmu*?" Gilgamesh repeated.

"Majesty," the old man persisted, "I swear that I witnessed this creature, that I battled with it, not six hours ago!"

The strength of conviction swelled in the man's voice; Gilgamesh could not ignore it. Could it be, though? His astonishment blossomed into fascination. "Go on."

The hunters related all they could tell of the bizarre incident. Their tale wound to a conclusion, and they waited with eager eyes for the king's wisdom.

Gilgamesh shifted in his seat uncomfortably. "What kind of assistance are you seeking?"

The older hunter, who had introduced himself as Gizzida, blinked. "My Lord, this beast has violated the sanctity of your mighty city. Put men in the forest and rid our lands of this creature."

"A *lahmu*," Gilgamesh said again, pronouncing the word and measuring out its strangeness. He wondered how long it had been since he had spoken those syllables. As a child, the name had come up in his studies on history, and he now dusted off those memories and retrieved what pieces of disused information he could find.

Lahmu. An ancient folk who lived far out on the borders of mankind. They were not exactly beasts, but neither were they recognizable as a tribe of people. Stories of their race came from oral legends passed down through generations, and from merchants whose routes took them through less habited areas of the Earth. Some mothers used these stories as warnings to keep children from straying too far into the dangerous wilderness, though there were many more frightening creatures of legend than *lahmu* to select when seeking to intimidate a child into obedience.

Nedu had lost his startled expression; the councilman looked vaguely disinterested now, and when he met Gilgamesh's gaze he shrugged. "It is not entirely unheard of."

"It is for me," Gilgamesh said, feeling no shame in admitting his lack of knowledge on the subject.

Nedu realized by the king's tone that he needed to follow up his statement with example. "During your father's march to Aratta, some soldiers spotted shadowy, hopping beasts in the forest alongside the route, watching them pass from afar. The soothsayers declared them to be *lahmu*, that they represented a good omen, a blessing from Mamu, that the expedition would turn out well. Which of course it did."

"Are the *lahmu* known to attack men?"

"Not in any story I've heard."

Gilgamesh looked back to Gizzida. "You bring a strange tale, hunter."

Gizzida nodded, bowed, remained silent. He had said all.

"And you are sure that this was no man?"

"I pledge my very life that what attacked us today was as my father described it!" the young boy exclaimed. "Not a man or beast, but something in between. A *lahmu*, my Lord, that by his presence brings the old stories to life!"

"What is your name?"

"Gudea," the boy said.

"And do you truly, Gudea, pledge your *life* on this?"

Gudea's face flickered in anxiety. "It was a *lahmu*, My Lord. Yes, upon my life."

"Return to your home then," Gilgamesh told them. "And I will look into the matter at once."

When they had left, Gilgamesh jumped out of his throne like a fish leaping from water. He glared around the room in exasperation, realized that the chamber still had people waiting to plead their cases. "Go home! All of you! King Gilgamesh will not hear your cases today! Leave at once!"

A minute elapsed. The hall was empty.

"Sire?" Nedu asked cautiously.

"Go, Nedu, with messages for the High Council. Are you prepared to hear all this? Is your memory as strong as ever?"

"Yes."

"Wonderful! Seek word from Ibi-Sin, and bring back reports of the new training! Follow up on Zariqu's mission. And as for the *lahmu* prowling our city streets at night ..." Gilgamesh shook his head. "I assign *you* this noble task!"

"Me?"

"Select five or six men, and have them report each day on their progress of capturing the *lahmu*. I will pay them well if they bring me the creature alive. I will pay them double, if they can capture the invisible Anzu bird! And I will relinquish my throne to the man who fetches me the Bull of Heaven on a spit!"

Gilgamesh stormed out of the chamber, and burst into the open courtyard behind the palace like a bird desperate to escape on a strong wind.

He found his mother sitting in a corner of the small Kullab courtyard, built on an artificial rise of earth so that it overlooked the palace. Behind her the domed Temple of Shamash rose like a stone mushroom. A modest structure, not a tenth of the size of Ishtar's inspiring monument, the House of Shamash was nevertheless older by at least a generation. Its original incarnation had been a simple sun altar built by the settlers of Uruk, and by command of the First King that altar had grown into an ivory-enameled temple.

Ninsun looked like a wizened oracle sitting on the limestone courtyard. A colorful cloth spread on the floor before her, decorated with hymns to the sun god.

Gilgamesh walked past her and leaned against the courtyard rail, his face thrust out fiercely to the city like a carven angel of wrath. "I feel as if the gods are laughing at me," he said. And he told her about the rumored massing of Agga's troops, the headless body by the river, and the report of a temperamental *lahmu*.

This last piece of news brought a smile to Ninsun's face. "Did you know that during your father's march to Aratta—"

"I heard," Gilgamesh said sharply. Then he winced at his tone. "Forgive me, mother. I feel like the sky is caving in on me. Was father ever confronted with chaos like this?"

"No," Ninsun admitted. "Which isn't to say his reign was without challenge. Each king opens a new chapter. He can never know what lies ahead of him."

"General Agga," Gilgamesh said, and conjured up a memory of seeing the white walls of Kish thrusting up from the northern horizon like teeth. "At what point did it occur to him that Uruk would make for a welcome target? What hunger would drive him to split asunder an ancient friendship such as stood between our two cities?"

"You said yourself that it may only be a rumor."

"His treatment of other cities is no rumor," Gilgamesh replied. "Yet I confess it never crossed my mind that he might wield sword against his southern neighbors."

Ninsun folded up her cloth. "As for the matter of the headless corpse, I shouldn't think it would bother you anymore. It isn't as if he will be seeking you out, to inquire where his head might have drifted to."

"Given my recent kingly challenges, I shouldn't be so surprised if that did transpire," he said. He glanced at his mother.

Just then the sun came out from the clouds, and illuminated her in an eerily grim way. Though she was a priestess of Shamash, the illusion the sun cast about her was not flattering. In the white light she seemed a *very* elderly figure, with liver-spots on her hands and a face carved by lines, with crow's feet forming at the corners of her eyes. And suddenly, Gilgamesh realized this was no illusion. The sun was not veiling her in deceit, but showing how she really looked, and Gilgamesh's heart dropped. When had she gotten to be so old? When had the hands of Time slipped into her bedroom and worked its vile artistry, pressing wrinkles into her skin like lines on wet clay? And her grey and brittle hair … why was Time in so much a hurry to bleach away her color and render her an aged, weak creature?

Ninsun saw his expression of sorrow. "What is it?"

"Just the realization that I am a man and not a child," Gilgamesh lied. "I cannot flee to your counsel whenever the unexpected marches through the doors of council."

"Yes, you can," she laughed.

Still, to distract himself, Gilgamesh decided he would select three women that night to be brought into his bed.

CHAPTER 10
MUSIC

When Enkidu came to rest in the little forest cove he used as a lair, he slumped against the nearest tree and slammed his hands against it in frustration. His legs, weakened by all the running and climbing endured in the past few hours, could no longer support him. He sat on the leafy ground and wondered how everything had gone awry.

It was nothing *I* did, he thought. I attacked no one. I stole nothing. I only wished to understand the city.

He wondered if humans were so different from other animals. Most predatory beasts, after all, had a sense of territory and they would defend it savagely.

The human city was quite obviously a well-marked territory. Lions sprayed urine to establish their boundaries. Humans used rock.

So then, were humans predators? Enkidu scratched his head as he pondered the possibility. Yes, he decided. Humans were predators. And since then they were predators, they had acted as all predators did when their territory was invaded.

Enkidu felt himself drifting off to sleep, and he could not summon the will to fight it. The nagging realization that sleeping during the day, especially so close to the city, could be dangerous did not change his mind.

"I'm sorry father," Gudea said finally, desperate to shatter the silence that had enveloped them ever since leaving the palace. It was more than uncomfortable; his father seemed semi-comatose. Gudea's adolescent assurance wilted in the face of this grim mood.

Gizzida nodded, or perhaps it looked like he nodded when in fact his neck had only faltered for a second, under the weight of all that the king had said.

Gudea felt tears springing in his eyes. "Father?" he said, and his voice cracked. "I should have listened to you in the palace! Please look at me and tell me we're not doomed!"

"No one can say if we're doomed or not."

"Give me some hope then! What if the king does not find this creature! What if I scared it off and it will never return, and the king will look and look and never find it! Will he think we're lying?"

"Probably."

"Then what will happen?"

"It depends on the mood of King Gilgamesh."

Gudea's face became as severe as jagged stone, as he wrestled with the fate of his social class; the mood of the monarch could determine if he lived or died.

"However," said his father, "The matter is done."

"Done? Are we fated to whatever fancy strikes our oppressor?"

"Oppressor?"

"Yes, oppressor!" Gudea cried. "The king who has made a city of slaves who work at the wall without rest, day and night! The king who sleeps with any woman he pleases, be she married or widowed! The king who …" He stopped, seeing his father's expression of rage. "What, father?"

Gizzida pointed to the earth. "Get to your knees and pray for forgiveness!"

"But what I speak is true!"

Gizzida didn't need to repeat himself. His furious eyes were all his brash son needed to realize he had overstepped the bounds of decency and respect.

Gudea knelt. As he whispered a prayer of forgiveness to Shamash the Sun God, his father watched him coldly.

When he had finished, his father asked, "Where did you hear all that?"

"What do you mean, father?"

"All the charges you made against our king. Where did you hear them?"

Gudea blushed in helpless confusion. "People talk. In the tavern, in the street. At the market when I was selling those pelts last month." He held his hands out desperately. "Father, please don't be mad. You always said truth was better than lies. I spoke only the truth!"

"You judge the man without thinking things through. His parents were noble beings. His father died while Gilgamesh was only a boy. The reign of King Dumuzi was terrifying. By your age, Gilgamesh was nearly murdered in the palace by the former king's assassins. It was not so long ago."

Gudea still felt insolent, but he bit his lip and nodded.

"I have lived through the reigns of three kings, Gudea, and I do not believe our rulers are gods. They are mortal men, though you are never, *never* to repeat this sentiment publicly. No, I tell you this because I mean you to realize that mortals make mistakes, but they also make wonderful music."

"Music?"

Gizzida sat down, aware suddenly of how weak his knees were and how much his joints were in pain from the day's excitement. "Do you remember when your mother would tell you stories?"

Gudea's anger resurfaced momentarily. "Yes. Yes, of course I do."

"Do you remember when she told you the story of the music of the gods?"

"No" Gudea admitted.

"There is a story older than the Flood, and your mother's family was heir to it, passing it like a sacred torch from the old to the young. It told how the gods used to make music, and from that music came the Earth and all that dwell here."

"I don't remember that."

"Well, I like to think of a man's actions in life as a kind of music. Bad actions produce discordant themes that stay like a residue around the man who produced them. The positive actions, of course, are a symphony that moves others to good things, like the invisible strings that pull the tide."

"So what manner of musician is Gilgamesh then?"

"I think he is still learning to play," Gizzida said. "So I will not speak ill of him. We don't know what music he was exposed to growing up. But I know there was strife in that palace. Remember that when Gilgamesh was your age, he was living in the fear of Dumuzi."

Gudea was not impressed. "How does this help us, father? The king must find the *lahmu*!"

"Then we must help him find it. Sleep first, Gudea. Then awake with a clear mind and heart. We are hunters. The *lahmu* is not a divine creature. It is a beast that leaves tracks. And I don't believe the thing will go far."

CHAPTER 11
SONG

The next morning changed the history of Uruk forever.

As even the mightiest wave begins with a small ripple, the city's transformation began with seemingly insignificant and unrelated factors.

One was a woman, who went to the River Euphrates to fill her pitcher with fresh water.

Another was a pre-dawn meeting between Nedu and a team of hunters.

A third was the frenetic commands of Military Advisor Ibi-Sin, who took charge of the city's laborers before the first sliver of sunrise, yelling, pointing, commanding them to make the rapid shift from masons to warriors.

The final piece was Enkidu. While the woman went down to the river with her pitcher, while Nedu dispatched the hunters into the forest to scour for traces of the intruder, and while Ibi-Sin spat manic orders, Enkidu was sleeping in the gash of a rotten tree.

Every morning for two years, Uruk would awaken with the clatter of masonry. Ten thousand hands churning the chalky clay pits, slapping the muddy mixture into wooden molds, clapping the glistening bricks onto the sun-baking ground, lifting the dried blocks and passing them, hand to hand, to the wall where new fingers would push them into place.

Now, that curious music had ceased. The animals of the surrounding woods were gripped by its strange absence.

As sunrise brightened the half-made walls, a new chorus of sound ascended from this human hive. Feet stomped the earth in unified thunder. Metallic weapons collided in discordant vibrations, shields slammed into shields like the locking of ram horns, and men grunted under their new burden. By midday, the hammer of blacksmiths had joined the fray.

Enkidu sprang awake to this new clamor. It was the noisy fruit of Ibi-Sin, but Enkidu knew nothing of this man or the nature of human warfare. He crawled to the edge of the forest and stared at Uruk's walls with newfound fear.

I've disturbed a hornet's nest, he thought.

It was time to move on. Enkidu felt an unaccountable sadness as he realized it. There would be new lands to the south, strange and unknowable, with their own cities and forests. The only comfort would be the great river he had followed from the north. Like a beautiful friend, it was his one constant.

"We will be our own tribe!" he told the river. "You are my only friend!"

Enkidu pounded his chest to stave off the painful feelings in his heart. He was a nomad. Nomads called the entire world their home, and it was foolish to grow fond of any one patch in such a vast universe.

Enkidu's stomach twisted and grumbled. Yes, he answered. I will eat once more from this forest, and then I will leave.

He went in search of food, even as unseen hunters discovered his tracks and began to close in on him. Enkidu shambled through the woods and his ears bristled at the sounds of soldiers running through military drills. When the quiet voice of a brook reached his ears, its promise of juicy frogs lured him into a lightless glen.

Then he heard a woman's singing.

Lilting through the forest, the soothing melody was haunting and perfect. He had never heard the songs of people. The notes undulated and danced, remaining high and anguished, as if Enkidu's own heart had found voice through this invisible crier.

He hesitated.

Run! he told himself. The humans are setting a new trap, and this was made with you in mind. They know how lonely you are! Run!

He did run. Straight at the source of the sound.

His muscular body crashed through branches and bramble, without his customary stealth. He moved with the strength of a bull, irrational and enraged, his confusion and anger and sorrow finally coalescing into blind rage. He didn't know what he'd do once he reached the hidden songmaster. Strangle her, frighten her, break this bewitchment that taunted his spirit.

It was most unusual for Enkidu to be so careless with his movements. And the noise he made was heard by the hidden hunters, the men who were that very moment turning away from the tree where he had been sleeping. Enkidu ran, and the hunters followed.

When he bounded into the brook-fractured glen, he came upon the sight of a lone woman, as pale and fragile as a dragonfly's wings. Her song caught in her throat, her eyes grew wide.

Enkidu halted abruptly at the feet of the brook, regarding the human who stood two meters away. A pitcher was in her hand, its slender neck eerily like her own.

The woman, a priestess of the Temple of Ishtar named Shamhat, watched him steadily.

Enkidu gazed at her, mesmerized, his impulses twitching.

"Did Ishtar send you to test me?"

His fascination with her loveliness was buried beneath the sweeping reality of her lack of fear. Every time Enkidu encountered people, they flew into mad panic. Now, for once, was a meeting like that of two birds by a pond ... the tranquil acceptance despite being of different color and breed.

The woman held her vase out toward him. Enkidu's feet remained as tree roots. But he recognized this attempt to communicate and, wishing to forestall any seed of panic, mimicked her intent by cupping the brook's water into his hands and outstretching them to her.

The woman laughed.

It was a cheerful sound, stilling Enkidu's heart.

"Did you like my singing? Is that what brought you here? Would you like me to sing again?"

Enkidu dared not move. Her gibbering words meant nothing to him but he was encouraged by this strange progress. Maybe he could get her to understand that he hadn't meant to attack anyone. Maybe ...

She tilted her head back and began a new song.

It whirled and cascaded, a melody so beautiful that Enkidu's heart was gripped by a bronze vice. She smiled as she sang. He sat down on the banks of the stream and listened as a dog might to the sound of its master's voice.

The song ended. Shamhat laughed again.

"Would you like to belong to me, creature?"

Enkidu swallowed anxiously. From behind him, shadows formed a half-circle. Enkidu's ears bristled from the sounds of Ibi-Sin's military drill.

Shamhat saw the hunters and understood at once what was happening. It came together in her mind like mosaic tiles.

"Another song, then?" Shamhat began a new melody.

And then the hunters attacked.

TABLET III

THE WALLS AND THE WILDS

CHAPTER 12
LEGEND

Rimush crossed his arms and steeled for argument. "Perhaps we should extend a greeting to King Agga."

The statement drifted in the air like a tendril of incense smoke, uncurling, wavering high above everyone's heads. Gilgamesh and the High Council all seemed to be watching these invisible antics.

And then Ibi-Sin shattered this truce of solitude: "You have the brains of a goat!"

A kiss of silence, followed by an explosion of verbal battle.

"It's called sifting for intelligence!" Rimush charged above the din, "We find out if he's still at Kish! What his disposition is! We need not reveal anything!"

"Or perhaps we should reveal it," Kazallu offered, "to discourage—"

Ibi-Sin erupted in a string of curses, his face beet-red and fists clenched. The ruckus was largely held by the Military Advisor against the others, though one-eyed Zariqu was leaning toward his side, saying that the gods might see an attempt at communication with an aggressor as a sign of weakness.

Gilgamesh twisted his woven beard, sighing. The voices soared into indecipherable belligerence, when he suddenly heard a smaller clash of voices in the chamber just beyond the hall's door.

"Silence!" Gilgamesh roared.

The babble evaporated, and all faces turned toward him expectantly. He rose from his throne and craned his ear to the door. Again came the storm of yelling voices, growing closer.

Incensed and already in a foul mood, Gilgamesh flung open the door and stared at the vast connecting hall. At the far end, shadows increased as many men approached. Their voices, at least those he could discern, swung into clarity. Some were cursing, others flagrantly jovial, but all were involved in a rapid chattering of directions:

"Hold it steady!"

"Watch it! Tie the end tighter!"

"—thing is as strong as ten men!"

"Five, by my reckoning!"

"—trying to bite through the leather! Watch yourself!"

"Hurry!"

"Watch out for his Majesty's walls! Keep the bag level, by the gods! You're letting it lean on your end!"

"—it gets loose it'll tear down the palace!"

A group of hunters, headed by Nedu and the old man Gizzida, were working their way down the hallway, a large sack held between them. The sack was bulging and twisting, pulsing with constrained violence that curiously reminded the king of the face of Ibi-Sin; primal rage thinly imprisoned behind a worn exterior.

"My Lord!" Nedu cried, his white hair shooting out like pale spikes in every direction.

Could it be that the fabled creature had been caught? *Already?*

The councilmen filed behind Gilgamesh. Ibi-Sin's neck turned purple and he sputtered angrily, "Have madmen infiltrated the palace?"

The hunters spied Gilgamesh, and reflexively started to drop to their knees. The moment the swollen underside of the sack touched the palace floor, however, the unseen quarry bucked with renewed energy, and suddenly an arm thrust from the mouth of the bag. The man responsible for holding that end shrieked, and beat at the clawing appendage until it retreated. They lifted the bag again, and one of the men, grinning and sweating, said, "Lord Gilgamesh, by your decree we were to capture the beast and bring him here! What orders shall we next receive?"

Gilgamesh didn't respond at once; his mind was still replaying the sight of that reddish, hairy, muscular arm sprouting from the bag's mouth. In that instant, all doubt of Gizzida and Gudea's story vanished. Both were there; Gizzida looked exhausted, but the boy flushed fever-crimson with triumph.

"My Lord?" said dark-faced Rimush thoughtfully. "What exactly have these men caught?"

"We'll see for ourselves, no?" Gilgamesh called to the hunters. "Bring it in here, and set the sack down. Then we'll have it unveiled!"

Gilgamesh stood aside as the hunters filed past. The captured entity had stopped flailing; since its arm had been beaten back, the creature had been as motionless as death. The hunters stopped in the center of the chamber.

Ibi-Sin cried, "My Lord, is it your will to release that devil in here?"

"You may leave if you have not the courage to stay," Gilgamesh said, but as the hunters set the bag down and backed off, he ordered them to draw their weapons and remain ringed around the sack.

The bag did not move now that it was released. The mouth was turned away, facing the wall. The leather conformed loosely to a man-like form.

"He did not come easily, I would estimate." Gilgamesh came to stand with the hunters, noting the fresh bruises and abrasions on their hands, arms, and faces. "Is he now afraid to come out?"

"We exhausted him," the young hunter-boy said proudly.

"Come out!" Gilgamesh commanded to the captured beast. "You have seen fit to trounce about our hunting grounds, setting free our game! Come now, and face the lord of this domain!"

Whether understanding his words, or responding to his tone of authority, there was a slow renewal of movement from the bag. The outlined figure melted, reformed, shifted into obscure shapes. The mouth came loosened, and stretched like a womb giving birth to some vile new creation.

Gilgamesh felt his breathing stop. The council gasped, Nedu flying to the king's side.

A hand, pink and finely formed, emerged from the mouth. It gripped the lining and hesitated. There were dirty, but perfectly formed nails, on the tips of those fingers.

Gilgamesh's stomach dropped at this sight, so different from the furry limb he had glimpsed moments ago. This hand was not that of a beast at all. It was that rare tool of man, five-fingered with rough nails, that was now showing itself. The sight so astonished him that he wondered if it had been trick of the light, or a furry sleeve, that had caused his initial certainty that an animal had been brought to the palace.

"The wretched thing is a shape-changer!" Ibi-Sin shouted.

The hand clung to the bag's lining with evident fear, perhaps expecting that it would be beaten back as it had been in the hallway.

"Come out!" Gilgamesh shouted again.

At the sound of his voice, a head covered with long, matted locks appeared next. The hair was coarse, with chips of forest leaves and crud entangled in its length. It might have been a headdress of some kind, in the manner that the smooth-shaven scalps of far-distant Egypt were said to wear removable hair for fashion or comfort.

Another hand appeared next while the first held fast to the lining. This hand, too, was pink, but it was attached to a long arm like that seen in the hall—coated with trailing reddish hairs—and the surrounding hunters tensed, angling their weapons into more lethal poses.

The first hand moved now, peeling back the leather. The head upturned to peer over the bag's horizon. Its gaze settled on King Gilgamesh.

The moment Gilgamesh saw the eyes of the creature, he wondered again if this was just a man, merely wild and untamed. They were brown eyes, and they stared with all the fear of a man facing imminent execution. But then Gilgamesh saw the nose below, and it was a wide, flattish nose unlike that of a Sumerian, or Babylonian, or Semite, Elamite … unlike any race known in the valley or beyond it. Below the nose was a wide mouth, with large flat teeth. A square chin. Small ears, mostly hidden in the matted hair. And something else, an oddness about the skull that Gilgamesh couldn't immediately place. It was disproportionate somehow, too low in the forehead resulting in thick accretions over the eyes. The back of the head was like a swollen bag of rocks.

"A *lahmu*?" Rimush cried.

"Kill it or set it free," Ibi-Sin insisted. "We must not keep that thing in here! They are strong beyond measure!"

Gilgamesh moved before anyone could stop him. In four strides he was standing directly before creature.

To Enkidu's eyes, the giant man who towered above him was a thrilling, fascinating, frightening sight. That this man was the ruler of his strange tribe was something Enkidu understood at once, the knowledge arriving with unaccountable certainty. Enkidu also understood, in much the same way, that he was in danger.

I will not allow them to hurt me further, he thought. *If they let me leave, I shall run to the forest and never return.*

Gilgamesh held its gaze. Perhaps it was the fear of Agga's reputed invasion, or the fear he had suffered under Dumuzi's reign, or even the realization of how twilight his mother had become, but Gilgamesh felt a sinister anger toward the captured quarry as if it was responsible for all things recently endured.

This was the fabled creature of legend? This was the *lahmu*-hero of the old epics, this creature that cowered like a dog before him?

"*You're* the great beast of the wilderness?" he accused. "The one who fights with old men and a young boy, yet grovels at my feet so abjectly?"

The words were gibberish. Enkidu could only hear the outraged tone.

His Tribe Elder had known many human words. If only that old being with his face like a gnarled tree knob were here now!

"Nothing to say?" Gilgamesh challenged. Fueled by the beast's visible fear, he took another step and snatched it by a clump of hair.

Enkidu's face changed.

A dark scowl bled into its features, its lips peeled back to show those flat teeth, and the eyes, that had been bursting with fear, now turned into twin radiant pools of wrath. Quite suddenly, the harmless *lahmu* had become an enraged animal, and—quite suddenly—Gilgamesh felt his arrogance pulled out from under him like a rug.

Before Gilgamesh could blink, Enkidu sprang up and lifted Gilgamesh off the floor with a two-handed shove. Gilgamesh flew into the air, hitting the floor and sliding. At the same instant, the beast drew onto all fours, looking more ape-like than ever, and scampered for the doorway. The guards darted in with their swords.

"Stop!" Gilgamesh commanded, and they recoiled from stabbing the *lahmu* dead. Enkidu blinked at the shiny bronze blades surrounding him.

The king tore off his royal cloak.

"Shut the door!"

The guards, refusing to turn their backs on the *lahmu*, backed up and pulled the door closed. Suddenly they were scattering as Enkidu charged them, throwing his shoulder into the barrier. The oak stayed firm.

Gilgamesh grunted. Galvanized by desperation, he sprang at the creature and tackled its furry flank. Together they fell aside from the door. Enkidu twisted in his grip while they rolled on the tiles. Wrestling was a common boyhood sport in Mesopotamia, and Gilgamesh had studied fervently under the tutelage of trainers. This beast, though shorter and squatter than him, was unlike any opponent he'd sparred with. He managed to land a single punch to its head before it tore free of his grip and bolted where the Council was most thickly congregated. At the sight of this hairy beast barreling down on them, they disbanded like white birds in every direction.

Gilgamesh stayed where he was, waiting for Enkidu to realize there was no exit from this room except through the door.

"*Lahmu!*" the king cried, and when the creature didn't respond—too busy with running around the perimeter of the room to look for a way out—Gilgamesh unlocked the door and swung it open. The moment the metal hinges creaked, Enkidu, far on the opposite side of the room, stopped so suddenly his feet nearly kicked out from under him. He looked at the door.

"If you want, *this* is the way!" Gilgamesh challenged. He pulled the door shut again. "Before you go through this door, you must go through *this* door!" Gilgamesh drove a fist into his own chest.

Enkidu knew a challenge when he saw it; it was no different in his old tribe. This tall human ruler had echoed the *lahmu* method of challenge eerily well, even down to the pounding of the chest to signal a melee.

Very well, Enkidu thought. He snorted his acceptance.

With a guttural grunt, Enkidu sprang forward. He crossed the council chamber in three incredible seconds and collided with Gilgamesh. The force of the impact was stunning ... as was the *second* impact when the king's back crashed into, and through, the oak door. The breath was knocked from his lungs as the door caved in; Enkidu cast aside the fallen king and smashed his fists into the breached door to widen the gap.

Enkidu had one leg through when he felt a clasping grip around his other one; he looked back to see Gilgamesh's powerful arms rippling as he pulled back on Enkidu's leg, wrenching him from his escape. Enkidu was dragged back into the room. He shoved against Gilgamesh. The king growled and charged much as Enkidu had done. Their new collision brought screams from the councilmen, and suddenly both king and beast broke completely through the shattered door to spill into the hallway beyond.

Renewed shrieks, this time from the palace slaves who had, a moment ago, gathered near the door to hear the inexplicable commotion within, rang wildly in the hall. Enkidu saw the long hallway in front of him and knew that this was his moment of escape, but pure rage held him there, and he was determined to stand and fight as never before. Enkidu and Gilgamesh grappled. The councilmen rushed and crowded the jagged doorway to watch as their king wrestled and pummeled the monster.

Rapid punches landed on Enkidu's head and jaw. He took them, then scooped Gilgamesh up, and charged for the next set of doors.

Gilgamesh frantically rained his fists down on the creature, but could not discourage this newest charge ... and the eastern doors were *bronze*.

The air rushed by him, the creature's charge was relentless. Desperately, Gilgamesh hooked his hands into the creature's thick neck, but finding it as immovable as a tree-trunk, he switched to punching the creature in the center of its throat. That did the trick; the *lahmu's* eyes went wide, bulging as if in hemorrhage, and he released Gilgamesh with a light throw that nevertheless slammed the king into the bronze doors. At the sound of his impact, the door actually opened, swung open by guards. The result was that Gilgamesh, already slumped against the metal, fell into the next room.

"Sire!" they cried, then scattered as Enkidu leapt *over* him and made for the last set of doors that would secure his freedom. But his legs tangled in Gilgamesh's grasp. He fell face-first to the floor. Gilgamesh staggered to his feet and punched the creature's ribs, back, and neck. He attempted a hasty headlock and was rewarded by Enkidu's teeth burying into his arm.

Gilgamesh bit back, his own teeth clamping down on Enkidu's shoulder.

Palace guards closed in at last on the melee. Enkidu saw his imminent death glinting in their short swords. With one final act of strength, he broke free of the king and leg-tackled three guards at once. They collapsed, and he was through their defense, stumbling for the line of merchant carts that protected the last doors.

Gilgamesh slammed into him from behind. Enkidu was shoved into the carts. The king, bloodied and bruised and garbed in shredded clothes, stumbled over the spilling foodstuffs. Two carts keeled over and emptied their wares onto beast and man alike.

Depleted of strength and motivated by pure vendetta now, Gilgamesh looked for the beast but found instead a creature whose hair was caked in white flour. The sight startled him so much that he recoiled. As he did the creature lost its rage and stared back in shock. Gilgamesh realized that he, too, was covered in flour.

The guards waited anxiously, their weapons ready for a fatal intervention. Nedu staggered into the room and gaped.

Be it the sight of the fearsome *lahmu* covered in flour like a clumsy child, or a recognition of his own foolishness, Gilgamesh chanced a laugh. And be it the sight of the proud human ruler messier than a hog in the mud, or mere reciprocation to the long-lost sound of laughter, Enkidu felt a rise of pleasure in himself, and he laughed too.

The encircling crowd was agog. No experience in their lives had ever prepared them for what they now beheld. The sound of their king's laughter, however, evoked a shattering of tension. *Gilgamesh is human!* they would report to their families and friends. *He wrestled with a beast, and then he started laughing! We heard the king laugh!* Only then would their talk turn to the other remarkable thing, the *lahmu*, creature of the wild, sharing his deep mirth with a smile of flat teeth.

For Gilgamesh, he sat there amid the destruction for a long moment, laughing until tears were in his eyes. When he did stand it was to extend a hand to the creature who shared the flour with him. The *lahmu* grasped his hand, firmly and painfully, and rose.

"Come," Gilgamesh said to his former assailant, and flour blew from his beard as he spoke. "We must get you cleaned up!"

Gently taking the *lahmu* by the arm, he hobbled out of the palace and headed to the courtyard fountain, where he rinsed the grain and blood from his body.

Enkidu followed suit, rinsing his shaggy body as he would in the river. He shook his locks dry the way a dog would, throwing water in every direction and earning a collective gasp from the onlookers.

Gilgamesh's tunic ripped away entirely in the water, so that he stood, barechested, with only the skirt-like piece covering his waist. He saw Nedu come forward.

The old man looked as fascinated as a little boy. Gilgamesh laughed anew.

"My Lord?" the Councilman inquired. He glanced warily to the saturated ape-thing sharing the fountain with him.

"Do they have a language, Nedu?" asked the king.

"The way cattle snort at each other, perhaps. I really don't know, my Lord." From behind him, the rest of the council arrived and formed a line of unbelieving faces.

"Nedu seems to think that you have no gift of language," Gilgamesh told the creature. It regarded him attentively.

Gilgamesh touched his own chest, gently now, in contrast to his ferocious and unthinking challenge of minutes earlier. "I am known as Gilgamesh. That is my name. Gilgamesh."

The *lahmu* blinked, looking from Gilgamesh's eyes to where he was touching his chest.

"Gilgamesh," the king repeated.

The *lahmu* smiled. He touched his own chest.

In a voice that seemed to come from far back in his throat came his reply: "Enkidu."

CHAPTER 13
IN THE BELLY OF THE ZIGGURAT

Over the next three days, Gilgamesh saw to it that Enkidu was introduced to the joys of civilization.

He would later wonder why the *lahmu* fascinated him so. When he questioned his own motivations, he felt it was largely to atone for his monstrous behavior the day they had met. After all, such a creature was a wonderful rarity in the world! To fight it like some thug was beneath a king. It brought hot shame to his face.

Gilgamesh fancied, too, that his fascination lay rooted in pure curiosity. The *lahmu* was a citizen of the wild, hailing from a nationless world which Gilgamesh only glimpsed in his defense of the Western Road. The *lahmu* born from the womb of legend was now guest in his palace. Curiosity pupated into obsession.

The three days were individual, episodic adventures. On the first day Gilgamesh had the creature bathed in the public fountain again, this time with a full staff of palace slaves to make certain the beast was thoroughly cleansed of his rank wilderness smell. Then he was dried off, the coat of soft hairs that sprouted from his body looking strangely lustrous, in the way that a lion's coat possesses a golden majesty. It was long hair, reddish, streaming from his arms, back, chest, and legs, as well as the thick mass that erupted, more darkly, from his head. His beard, too, fell into curling waves as majestic as any royal beard.

"Good gods!" Gilgamesh gaped when he saw the transformation. The wilderness beast had enjoyed its bath of scented oils, golden combs grooming its body, and now dressed in a blue linen robe from the king's own wardrobe.

Enkidu had never worn clothes. He could only liken it to the plumage of birds he had seen, the strange colors and soothing fabrics cladding his body ... and not uncomfortably. Enkidu marveled at the feather-soft feel of these strange coverings. He held out his hands and watched how the bright sleeves rolled up his swollen forearms. The fabric tickled him pleasantly, and when he saw his own image in a palace mirror, he gasped so loudly that the servants fled in fright, though Gilgamesh roared with laughter.

That first night, his mother chastised him for the whole business.

"When will you be through toying and playing with this *pet?*" she asked him. "There are far more important tasks at hand! Send the creature back to the forest, Gilgamesh!"

Was it a pet? Gilgamesh bristled at her words. It was amusing to see the beast dressed as a man, sure. But no cruelty lay in that amusement. The expression on the beast's face moved him to delight, akin to the pleasure an adult gets when sharing in a child's first taste of honey, or the feel of brushed cotton around a tired body, or the sight of a fish popping up from a river to swallow a slow-to-move dragonfly. Gilgamesh could not deny his feelings were founded in affection.

All this passed over his face. Ninsun sighed, her lips summoning a motherly tenderness, and she touched his hand.

"Never mind," she said, and looked dubiously at the guest bedroom door behind which the new resident slept. Snoring. Loudly.

On the second day, Gilgamesh had the creature escorted down to the palace dining hall. Gilgamesh made certain that his guest had sampled steamed robin's eggs, seasoned bread, roast fowl, porridge, honey-dipped berries, and of course, beer. This latter item was not to the creature's liking at all. Enkidu spit it out messily until, seemingly embarrassed, he gave Gilgamesh a questioning, wide-eyed stare. Gilgamesh's gentle smile was all the indication needed that no offense had been given.

"You'll make the creature sick," Nedu complained when he entered at the feast's conclusion. "Fancy that you were its guest in the woods, and it sat you down for a royal breakfast of grubs, raw pig, and leaves! Would your stomach not scold you mercilessly?"

But the beast showed no signs of sour indigestion, and whatever Gilgamesh brought before it, it ate.

Afterwards, Gilgamesh took the creature on a full tour of the city. He was warned to bring guards, but he declined and discovered that they were not necessary. Together they walked the grids of Uruk, gathering stares.

That night, Gilgamesh had the creature brought back to the guest room, while he talked at length with Nedu.

"It broke one of your ribs, sire," the councilman said.

Gilgamesh shrugged, conscious of the tight band across his side the royal physician had fitted him with earlier that day. "Never mind that! Why can no one tell me where they first came from? Do they have cities? If they do, where? What happened to—"

"There aren't many *lahmu* left," Nedu interrupted softly. "That much I know. They are a forsaken people."

Gilgamesh stared down the end of the hall, where his father's statue watched him. It was rendered in stone and covered with an outer skin of beaten metal, so that the dead king glimmered like oil in the lamplight.

"You must find out who has further knowledge of the *lahmu*," Gilgamesh said absently, beholding his father's image.

"I shall, my Lord. And what of King Agga?"

Gilgamesh looked away from the statue in surprise. "Agga?" He pronounced the name like it was a foreign word, infinitely more alien than the entity slumbering in the guestroom. "Uruk boasts the finest defensive wall in the world, even in its uncompleted stage. Ibi-Sin trains our men for war. And meanwhile we have no reports that Agga is marching out to conquer us."

Nedu had been thinking about that, too. "It is possible that our merchant friend was misinformed—"

"Yet it was time Uruk's military was strengthened, regardless."

Nedu nodded. He wondered how accurate their intelligence reports were. Was it possible, if Agga's troops were secretly on the move, that *every* single spy could have been paid off or killed? How crafty was Agga?

"I want Enkidu to be taught our language," Gilgamesh said.

Nedu withheld his sigh. "Yes, My Lord."

"Starting tomorrow."

"Of course."

Gilgamesh retired from the hallway to his own bedchamber … empty tonight, without dancing girl or priestess or feminine pedestrian awaiting him. As he reached the doorway, though, he turned back to Nedu.

"Yes, sire?"

"Send word to our river fleet, Nedu. I want ships sent up the Euphrates. Have them anchor at regular intervals, within sight of each other. Agga may not bother with a landward expedition. He may be moving his men secretly by ship to our doorstep. And I want us ready for that eventuality."

Nedu straightened. "Certainly."

Deep within the secret bowels of the Great Ziggurat, it was always night.

And like the night, constellations glittered along the stone corridors and secret chambers, a row of torches dancing to the dank underworld draft that pranced about the structure's labyrinth.

Shamhat descended a chilly stairway, gleeful as always in the knowledge that while the outside world was run by mortals and mortal kings (for she didn't believe any Urukian lord was a god) there was another universe, a hidden one, inside the protective womb of the ziggurat. No one in the city realized the ziggurat was hollow. Ishtar and Her priestesses lurked in hives where all the luxuries of civilization were stored. A maze of subterrestial passages like tentacles into the under-dark; an underground city constructed at the dawn of Uruk's existence!

She found Ishtar in the Goddess' Chamber. It was here Ishtar slept, and bathed, and ate in stillness with Her priestesses. Shamhat's eyes lingered at the sight of the goddess' bed, visible through curtains of blue veils. She longed to be invited there again.

Four priestesses tended to Ishtar, painting Her sleek body with gold dyes that dripped warmly over Her skin. Ishtar's face was already painted, and She looked out from this mask of gold to Shamhat. The priestesses dipped their brushes in the bowls of dye at Her feet, dabbing color at an uncovered naval. The first stroke left a glittering trail—like a divine scar above Her belly button. Though the New Year's Festival was three months away, Ishtar liked to let Her disciples paint Her every so often. The few times She allowed herself to be publicly seen, She dressed a thin layer onto Her body … such as the last time King Gilgamesh came to the temple above.

"What is it?" Ishtar asked, eyes piercing Shamhat.

Shamhat sat down by the goddess' feet. "The city is abuzz with news of the *lahmu*."

"The king has found a new friend, it would seem." Ishtar nodded disinterestedly.

"The beast is certainly ugly! Yet there's a charisma to him, when he was looking at me by the stream. He was …" She blushed. "He was quite enchanted by my singing."

"You're so proud of your ability to soothe animals, are you?"

Shamhat's blush of pride reddened to humiliation.

"What else do my people speak of?"

"Agga of Kish."

"No invading army will ever conquer Uruk while I sit as its patron goddess."

"You'll strike his army down?"

"I'll let loose the Bull of Heaven," Ishtar said, and Her attendants froze, hearing this.

The Bull of Heaven was a divine creature of cosmic ferocity. A single stamp of its hoof could open the ground up and swallow men by the hundreds. Its breath was poison, its roar apocalypse. The mere threat of the Bull of Heaven being unleashed upon the world crackled the air like a thunderstorm.

Ishtar stretched backwards, back arching and ribs jutting out to give better access to Her painters.

For several minutes Shamhat waited, wondering if the goddess would offer some measure of attention tonight. But at last, reading Her mood, Shamhat begged to be excused and fled the chamber.

As she went, however, she let herself hesitate by the two rooms which always seduced her with mystery. The first was the Heaven Gate, a massive wood-and-bronze double door locked with an incredible copper bolt. The priestesses were free to explore their underworld home, but the Heaven Gate was forbidden. Never was anyone to unlock the bolt. Daily sacrifices of food were delivered into the room through chutes from high floors. Shamhat herself often supervised the offerings, which needed to be blessed before cast into the narrow shafts of stone feeding the chamber.

What lay inside? The mystery tortured Shamhat. Sometimes when making sacrifices, she felt the temple shake. Other times she heard the grunts of a monstrous force within the chamber. Ishtar explained that a magnificent animal, a beast of the gods, lay within. It was to be worshiped, offered sacrifices, prayed to. Never disturbed.

Shamhat paced the stairs and hesitated before the second intriguing room. It was the Secret Altar, built of brick and encased in gold. Upon its opulent shelf, the eleven Annunaki statues were set like game pieces. They were lined up, six in the back row and five in the front, with the newest member occupying the center position of this foremost row. The statues looked like living creatures to Shamhat, their gemstone eyes catching the torch-light and appearing to dance and blink.

For all Shamhat's life, there had only been ten statues. Ever since the eleventh one was found in the clutches of that fisherman thief, Ishtar seemed possessed of special energy and insistence. Each statue was identical—about eight inches high, and with eyes and exposed hearts boasting a specific gemstone. Thus the first in line had eyes of emerald, and a matching green heart; the next glared with ruby eyes and a corresponding heart. Sapphire, gold, silver, pearl, amber, diamond, opal, onyx, and lapis lazuli. Eleven statues.

One was missing, one needed be found.

Where was the twelfth statue? Of what precious stone was its eyes and heart? Ishtar spoke of them frequently, saying all twelve needed to be returned to the stars. She never elaborated on what would happen once their rightful place was reestablished.

At least, not directly. But Shamhat made an awful discovery once. A year ago, Ishtar had drunk deeply of sacrificial wine and had taken Shamhat to Her bed. The wine had fogged the goddess' head, and loosened the goddess' lips, and She had spoken of an Annunaki map leading to treasure. Shamhat immediately understood this was a deep secret the goddess had spilled unwittingly. Terror seized her; she knew to never reveal what she'd heard. There were two pitiful creatures deeper in the ziggurat who suffered daily tortures at Ishtar's hands ... for the past five years now. Shamhat didn't know what those girls had done, but instinctively felt the same fate would be applied if Ishtar knew the Annunaki's secret had even partially slipped.

It was late. Shamhat retired to her bedchamber alone, undressing, slid her nude body beneath the furry animal-skin blanket.

Shamhat blew out her bedside lantern. The blanket tickled her face. In the blackness, Shamhat wondered if Enkidu would feel similar.

CHAPTER 14
SEASHELLS AND FLOWERS

"I thought you said they couldn't speak," Gilgamesh asked Nedu, as Enkidu stooped to sniff the flowers potted along the courtyard's rail. The outer pool steamed beneath the sun in a wave of golden knives.

Three weeks had passed as effortlessly as days. Business had resumed as usual in the king's life; the City Councils, supervision of Ibi-Sin's drills, and daily command of the city. Gilgamesh looked forward to the hours spent with

Enkidu, though, and found an alleviation of fear just by being in the creature's presence.

Nedu watched Enkidu creep from one potted flower to the next. "I truly don't know."

Enkidu gently grasped a plant with stiff leaves and pink petals. He gave a quizzical look to Gilgamesh.

"Flower," the king said.

Enkidu grunted. He leaned over the rail at the lower level's pools when suddenly he tensed, powerful shoulder muscles bunching. Below, the palace's *mushussu* dragons had congregated directly beneath the rail where he leaned. Two very large specimens, almost twenty-one feet in length, swiveled their heads. Black tongues flicked, tasting the air. Their orange head-crests quivered.

"They can't reach us here," Gilgamesh said.

Enkidu didn't look away from them. The largest specimen hissed and propped two front feet against the wall as if intending to climb. Enkidu's body hair puffed up.

Since the marketplace battle, the rudiments of conversation had been laid like careful bricks between Gilgamesh and his fascinating friend. Essential conjugations like "I want" or "you want," "I hungry" and "You hungry" had been established. The names for a couple dozen items, from flowers to stones, had been handily memorized by the *lahmu*.

By now, all of Uruk knew of Enkidu. The fight in the marketplace, not to mention the sight of him taking tours with the king, was an amazed gossip that reached all ears. Guards, merchants, farmers, hilt-dressers, everyone was whispering of who had seen the strange new beast for himself.

Enkidu eyed the dragons warily. He had met their breed before, around lakes deep in the northern forests of Assyria. They were disgusting, inexcusably vicious animals. Enkidu retained a terrible childhood memory of the Tribe Elder crouching with him in a tree, pointing down at a pack of dragons converging on an adult bear guarding a cave. The bear's defiant roars did nothing to divert the dragons; they stalked forward with unsettling effectiveness, two dragons in the lead padding at the bear, then splitting around it to attack from opposing angles. While the bear batted at one, then the other, four other dragons plunged forward eagerly. A bite here, a bite there. Bloody legs, throaty yelps of pain. The bear killed two dragons, as ever more teeth cut through its fur and muscle. And still they kept coming. A dragon slithered past into the cave. This latter action put the bear into a frenzied panic, and it went after the invader. Back turned, the dragons chomped down, hanging by their fangs like scaly leeches while their quarry thrashed and roared. One last bellow of agony. The bear collapsed and didn't move. Then came the hissing of the dragons as they fought over pecking rights to the corpse … and to the cubs cowering in the cave.

He didn't wonder why Gilgamesh would keep such monsters. In fact, he was beginning to get a firmer sense of these humans. They liked to collect things, sort of like the way his mother liked to collect seashells. Humans went into the wilderness and grabbed flowers, animals, birds, beehives, and brought them back to their own lairs. Even *mushussu* dragons.

Mushussu, he thought. The word was the same in his own language; he wondered if it was because it sounded like the angry hissing of the creatures themselves.

"Enkidu," Gilgamesh called. "Hungry?"

"No hungry," he replied.

His keeper resumed talking with the old man. Enkidu casually hopped away from them, to test how far Gilgamesh would let him go. Was he free to leave? he wondered. For nearly a month now, he had been treated better than any Tribe Elder. An everlasting supply of food in exotic variety. Soothing plumage to adorn his body. The most comfortable place to sleep he had ever known, if somewhat lonely … he had awakened several times, longing for the sounds of his tribe's omnipresent snores.

Enkidu reached the end of the courtyard. One level down, adjacent to the dragon pool, he saw Ninsun.

His keeper's mother. Gilgamesh was clearly the ruler of this gigantic tribe; Ninsun also commanded deference from the city-dwellers. But Enkidu's sharpened nose caught the warm, moist odor of their skin; a slight musk that Ninsun's floral oils failed to conceal. Humanity had a stench anyway but here—between the king and his mother—there was similar odor.

Glancing back to Gilgamesh, Enkidu saw that the king was now talking with the angry man who also held great authority over people; this man shouted incessantly, turned purple-red so that the cords on his neck went taut, and directed the young men into a strange, unified arrangement of bodies with swords and shields. It was the most bizarre thing Enkidu had ever seen; he couldn't even guess the purpose.

But Gilgamesh was distracted, and so Enkidu decided to test the bounds of his imprisonment even further. He slid over the rail, feet dangling above Ninsun. She was crouching on the floor, her hands pressed to the tiles. Her eyes were closed and she was mumbling. Dreaming?

He held to the rail with one hand, judging the short distance as he would a tree branch. Then he jumped.

Ninsun's eyes snapped open as he landed near her. In that instant, he realized how foolish this impulse had been. Screams! Human panic! Another fight with Gilgamesh, this time to certain death, for terrifying his mother.

Is that what I'm trying to accomplish? he wondered.

"Good morning, Enkidu."

He recoiled, bracing for a delayed reaction. Ninsun sat perfectly still, watching him.

"Did you come to join in my prayers?"

Feeling dubious, Enkidu swallowed and sorted through the words he knew. His strangely disproportionate head tilted on its nonexistent neck.

"Hungry?" he asked.

"No."

He sweated and paced before her staring eyes. Stupid! he cursed himself. Then he caught sight of more potted flowers on these rails.

His mother had loved two things—seashells and flowers. He had buried her with both, in a shallow pit dug with his hands and a jagged stone. The shells she always carried on her, pierced with gazelle tendon so it could hang round her neck. The flood had snatched this trinket away, but he found it, half-buried in mud about a mile from her body. This, along with blue and yellow petals such as she adored, went into the ground with her as he sang the *lahmu* death hymn alone.

Now Enkidu went to the potted flowers above Ninsun. His fingers closed on two stalks. He lifted them free of the soil.

"My mother always liked flowers. Perhaps all mothers do."

Clearly she didn't understand his explanation when he gave them to her, but her smile was tremendously reassuring. She accepted the gift and said silken words that sounded how honey might. Not quite as beautiful as the song he'd heard that day in the woods. But lovely, wonderful, and affectionate nonetheless.

He climbed back up to the higher deck, feeling her eyes on him.

"Enkidu!" Gilgamesh was walking over to him.

"Enkidu hungry," he replied.

True or not, this always seemed to make the king happy, and he clapped his guest on the shoulder. "We eat. Let us eat!" Then he hesitated, seeing the tears in Enkidu's eyes. "Are you all right?"

By way of answer, Enkidu looked up to the sun until his eyes moistened anew.

CHAPTER 15
THE FIRE ROAD OF ERESHKIGAL

Two months.

Uruk awaited the New Year Festival, now lurking a mere three days hence.

From Kish and elsewhere in the valley, spies crawled into markets, taverns, shipyards, villages, public festivities, even the homes of nobility. They posed as merchants and bards, musicians and rogues. Prodding, questioning, then meeting others of their station to exchange rope knotted in secret code, their findings circulated back to Uruk's domain.

The drums of war were silent.

King Agga had at last produced a son. This brought his litter to eight; a long-awaited male heir to join his sisters in the royal family of Kish. This news found its way to Uruk by spies and then to Ninsun's ears, where she cursed and performed three special sacrifices to Shamash—a lamb, a goat, and a bull—letting the golden daybringer drink well of their hot blood so that he would grant her next prayer: *Give my son a wife worthy of his seed!*

"Gilgamesh does have heirs," Nedu told her when they watched their king in the practice ring with his wrestling mentor.

"With whores and commoners," Ninsun observed. She waited as the king collided again with his sparring partner. The practice ring lay in a cedar gazebo surrounded by the canal, providing merciful shade from both sun and the gleaming water. Gilgamesh sweated, bare-chested and panting, and planted his feet firmly on the dirt-covered floor to shove a shield against his grinning opponent. All he accomplished was to slide further back, losing ground.

His opponent was Gimil-Sin, a bald warrior outmatching the king in both height and bulk. With his crooked eye, lumpish nose, and yellow teeth filed down into shark-like fangs, Gimil-Sin looked like an *ugallu* demon, leaping straight off a carving of other monsters. He was also bare-chested, his legs bulging as he pushed Gilgamesh inches backwards, the dirt sliding around this contest of will and muscle.

"Give in, My Lord!" Gimil-Sin said smoothly. There was no exertion in his breath.

Gilgamesh grimaced, knowing (or hoping) that the confident voice was designed to demoralize him. He slid further, heels almost touching the gazebo wall now. His shield groaned, its inner concavity already cracked by the repeated battering of the hour-long practice. Over its edge, he caught glimpse of his mentor's savage, razor teeth as discolored as a corpse's smile.

A swift spin of his body and the tension was shattered; he sidestepped the unrelenting force of his opponent, turning his shoulder inward as Gimil-Sin went careening forward.

But the crafty wrestling mentor had anticipated the move. Even as he lunged for the walls, his free right arm hooked the king by his torso. Gilgamesh's feet went up, Gimil-Sin propped a foot against the wall with the king in one arm like hefting a child, and then he dropped his quarry against the ground, following up by landing his bulk atop him. Only then did he let his exhaustion show in a wide, desperate smile.

"May the gods curse you!" Gilgamesh said with a laugh, tapping the ground to submit. Gimil-Sin stood and helped the king stand.

"They already do!" his opponent said. "By refusing me any halfway decent challenge in a fight!"

By way of answering, Gilgamesh went to grapple him again … the shields discarded like old tortoise shells. Gimil-Sin hopped backwards, as Gilgamesh leapt and caught one of his legs; the wrestler dragged the king around the ring to the amusement of Nedu. Even Ninsun cracked a smile, shaking her head.

"All right," she yelled. "You are beaten!"

"Indeed," Gilgamesh said, laughing again. When he had dusted himself off and slapped the dirt from his beard, he dismissed his mentor. He embraced his mother warmly.

"You need a royal son," she told him, ignoring the dirt he'd gotten onto her garments.

"I heard the two of you talking."

They left the gazebo, striding into the warm air. Gilgamesh felt his knees stinging from where he'd been dragged, but somehow that added to his swelling heart. The strange joy of life rapidly coursed through him; an awareness of blood, heartbeat, flushed skin, moist air, faultless sun, and fellow humanity. He was shocked by it. Is this what poets feel? he wondered. Remember the sixth day of my childhood education! The study of song! Poetry's exotic brevity, the majesty of words themselves, had thrilled him in youth. With the passage of a haunted adolescence, murder, the purging of Dumuzi's supporters, the usurper's exile to the South Tower, and the subsequent years of indulgence had caused him to forget his joy of the poetic arts. Now it rushed upon him just as a pleasant and forgotten scent revives old loves.

When Enkidu greeted them at the doors of the palace, Gilgamesh felt overwhelmed.

"My friend," he said, and to his mother added, "I will not leave Uruk without a rightful heir, mother. But today is no day for such discussion."

She frowned, not pleased. "Tomorrow then. Good afternoon, Enkidu."

The *lahmu's* smile was all teeth. "Good afternoon, mother."

When Nedu and Ninsun had gone, Enkidu accompanied Gilgamesh on a lazy walk of the palace grounds. Enkidu maintained the habit of crouching while walking, like a hunchback's gait. It made his lengthy arms seem even longer.

"The festival is in three days," Gilgamesh told him.

Enkidu said nothing. He'd been hearing about this festival for weeks now. Something about it frightened him.

"It will be great fun. The entire city …" The king trailed off. "Do the *lahmu* have cities?"

"No cities."

"Where do they live then?"

"Forest, sometimes."

Hearing him speak was still unusual; the words appeared to start off as an animal's grumble far back in his throat, only to be hastily dressed in civilized formulations by reluctant lips.

"What about other times?"

Enkidu's forehead wrinkled as he searched for the sounds to explain. He wanted to explain that the *lahmu* were all dead, that Gilgamesh walked beside the last of the tribes; therefore, the only place where the *lahmu* lived was in fact a city. But he knew the king was inquiring on the past. Tethered as it was to painful memories, the discussion pained him. Finally, he gave up and simply pointed to the mountains beyond the city walls. Blue-grey in the distance and wreathed in golden sunlight.

Gilgamesh appreciated the mountains for a moment. "Those mountains, specifically?"

"Mountains," Enkidu said flatly.

Gilgamesh lingered a while, locked as if in trance by the sight of the jagged peaks that erupted from the hazy gum-line of the earth. It was the edge of his world, grander than Uruk's walls and just as protective. Without even setting eyes on the unknown terrain beyond them he acutely felt the chilly isolation of those distant regions. He recalled the girl who had shared his bed on the night Dumuzi died, and how she questioned him so innocently about the world beyond the valley.

I could learn much from Enkidu, he thought.

It was this thought that prompted Gilgamesh's decision to go *outside*, into the forest, with Enkidu.

Since his capture, Enkidu hadn't been permitted to leave the city. Yet during the next hour, that changed; both left the city to prowl the tree-studded wilderness. Gilgamesh felt a momentary flicker of worry marring his otherwise heartfelt mood, that Enkidu might realize how easy an escape into the woods would be. He could bound away. Gilgamesh had no prayer of catching him.

And suddenly, Enkidu *did* move.

His arm flew out, striking the king in the chest.

The pain wasn't as great as the anguish caused by the attack. But why should I be surprised? I've captured the creature! Imprisoned him! Of course he wants to return to the wilds!

Gilgamesh stumbled back, lacking the will to defend himself. Enkidu, however, hadn't moved again. His body was as rigid as stone, hairy arm like a tree-limb draped in shaggy moss.

"What is it?" the king asked.

Enkidu pointed to the earth. "Bad ground."

"I don't … what do you mean?" Leaves, twigs, and earth littered the forest floor.

Then he saw it. Gently pushing Enkidu's arm aside, Gilgamesh approached, crouched, and pressed his hand against the ground. There was too much give to his push, the twigs bending far below the level of the ground. Finally, as Gilgamesh added pressure, some of the twigs snapped and went spilling down the hole they were covering. Leaves slid after them.

"A trapping pit," the king said. He saw the severe expression on Enkidu's face. "You could fall into these."

Enkidu grunted, neither an affirmation nor rebuttal. "Enkidu fall."

"You fell into these before?"

"Animals fall."

"That's the purpose of the traps. We need their meat."

Enkidu' discontent did not leave his face. He tried several times to say something, gave up, started again, and finally dismissed all effort. It was not until they had hiked down to the river that, drinking water from his cupped hands, he tried to put into words his objection to the traps.

"Animals die, but no stones put there," he said.

"No stones?"

Enkidu plunged his hand into the river, dislodging a large pebble. He rinsed off the mud from its smooth exterior, placed it in Gilgamesh's hand.

"Stones put near animals," he said insistently.

Gilgamesh stared at the shiny red rock. "Are you saying that we should be burying the animals that we kill? Covering their bodies with stones?"

Enkidu's arm moved so fast Gilgamesh didn't even have time to jump; Enkidu's hand shot out, grabbing and crushing the dragonfly. He opened his palm, displaying the crumpled green insect.

Then he lifted the insect to his mouth and ate it.

Gilgamesh would have laughed had it not been for Enkidu's deathly seriousness about this enigmatic affair. Suppressing his mirth for fear of offending him, he brought his own hand to his mouth in imitation, and to cover up the smirk that wanted to form.

With his other hand, Enkidu placed the river-stone on the ground, almost exactly below where he had snatched and crushed the creature.

"Animal die, stone put near animal," Enkidu whispered.

A breeze came off the water, spirit-like through their hair and beards.

"I understand," the king replied, his humor gone.

Later that evening, as Gilgamesh walked his friend back to the upper hallway where their bedchambers were and passed the statue of King Lugalbanda. It was a solemn thing, standing in the corner of the hallway like a watch-guard of immense proportions, stately yet cold in its ceremonial blandness. A full three meters of carven alabaster, its helm nearly scraped the ceiling. Exaggerated curls of a kingly beard, eyebrows joining over the nose, hands at his sides with the thumbs pointing outward. His smooth, egg-shell-like eyes were large but without pupil or iris.

Affable. Generous. Wise. Gregarious. Many descriptions from a hundred mouths. For Gilgamesh, these words were meaningless as he confronted his own recollections. He had been too young to form any opinions; his memories seemed more of dream-substance than reality. His father was a warm man, that Gilgamesh remembered. He remembered being held in his father's arms. He remembered a rough hand being gentle, touching his face as one touches an object of great fondness.

Enkidu stopped before the statue.

"That is my father," Gilgamesh told him. Before the stone's blind gaze he made the sign of mourning; touching his forehead, lips, and chest with light pressure, in the Sumerian manner of honoring the dead.

Enkidu noticed Gilgamesh's subtle hand motions. "What … that?"

"It's something we do in honor of those lost to us. A ritual for remembrance."

Enkidu frowned; he wondered if he resembled the Tribe Elder's knobby face. He mimicked Gilgamesh, touching his forehead, lips and chest. The imitation, while correct in its mechanics, looked clumsy and discourteous.

"Slower," the king said.

"Why do you do this?

"For the very reason you place stones on the spots where animals have died. To remember them, to honor them. We touch the head to remember the person we've lost, the lips to honor their words and lament for conversations that can no longer be had, and the chest ... here, in the center of the chest, is where the soul is rooted." He saw from Enkidu's child-like, questioning eyes. "Then the soul retires to the Underworld and walks the Fire Road of Ereshkigal."

This concept proved impossible to get across to Enkidu, and the king soon gave up on it. He himself didn't care for it. The Underworld was a land of wraiths and shades, where the echo of the living rang eternally in ghostly shadow. If life was a bright shaft of sun illuminating a sapling tree, then the Underworld was the shadow that sprang out from behind the tree. Black, moving with all the speed of a shadow on a listless afternoon, it was a place where memories gathered like dust, and whenever a shade moved about this dust was shaken from its shoulders, and a little more of its former self was lost forever.

Perhaps, then, the statue of Lugalbanda was accurate and telling, Gilgamesh thought grimly. The affable and wise ruler, Third King of Uruk, now dissolved of his lifeblood, as cold as stone, with no more passion to bring a grin to his lips or make those eyes flicker with care.

Gilgamesh sighed. "It is not a happy place."

Enkidu seemed to see the troubled train of images in the king's eyes. It was a look he had caught in his own eyes, reflected in water, when he thought of the tribesmen he had lost.

"What of the *lahmu*?" Gilgamesh asked suddenly. "What lies after life for your people, Enkidu?"

"The Earth," he said, and then he touched the foot of Lugalbanda in a weird show of affection. "*Lahmu* go back to the earth."

CHAPTER 16
FESTIVAL

Gilgamesh would ask himself in later months how, if Enkidu was any typical example of the *lahmu* race, he could ever have been thought of as an animal by the people in the Fertile Crescent. His initial, unshaven appearance had been frightening; Gilgamesh recalled how the sight of Enkidu's arms had alone been enough to deem him a beast. Yet men of all known races had body hair, some thicker and more prevalent than others. And if the *lahmu* were a shy, secretive band, so too were many peoples up and down the Two Rivers' length; forgotten hill-people and mountain-dwellers, the descendants of displaced races, scavengers holing up in cliff-sides. The outsiders. And yet were these people considered to be animals? Even the most aloof noble had to admit that outsiders were of the same family of Man.

Other times, however, a barrier sprang up like a great drawbridge and could not be lowered to let even the tiniest glimmer of mutual understanding through.

The New Year's Festival was one such example.

"Why is this difficult to grasp?" Gilgamesh asked him while trying to get him ready for the evening's first celebration. Four palace servants were tending to Enkidu in his quarters, fitting custom-made arm bracelets and medallion-studded necklaces to his bulky body as Gilgamesh, who had only stopped in to check up on his progress, now paced in the room with the challenge of explaining the holiday to him.

"Master Enkidu, please hold still," a servant complained as Enkidu kept twisting to follow his friend around the room. Seeing this, Gilgamesh ceased his pacing.

"Spring follows winter," Enkidu protested. "Then summer becomes winter. Then again! Always happens! What is New Year Festival, then?"

"It's another year!" Gilgamesh said, exasperated.

Enkidu's nostrils flared in agitation. "Always spring come. So always have New Year Festival?"

"Yes!"

Enkidu shook his head. "Morning you always wake up. Do you celebrate waking up?"

Gilgamesh put his face in his hands. Through his clasped fingers, he said, "No, but my friend you are missing the point."

The New Year's Festival was not a holiday; it was *the* holiday. Twelve days of ritualized joy and preparation in which each level of society united. It began always on the new moon nearest the autumnal equinox; work ceased, hearths emptied their old ashes, the public fountain was blessed by a priest and priestess of every temple and acolytes oversaw the bathing of all residents. The cult of Ishtar, ironically, lost much traffic during this countdown to the longest day of the year; it was Shamash who saw the greatest adoration in daily prayer and sacrifice.

As the festival progressed, though, the cult of Marduk swelled in visibility. The same throng who chanted to Shamash by day now eagerly cheered to nightly reenactments of how Marduk summoned the bravery to challenge the

Chaos Dragon Tiamat and her army of monsters. Bald and glistening in oil, Marduk priests clad in bright costumes brought the favorite tale alive; the crowd responded with the appropriate yells, hisses, and chants. Every schoolchild knew the tale: Scaly Tiamat brings fear and death to the world, while all the gods cower in fear of her vast bulk. Marduk, alone of the deities, summons the courage to face her. The battle shakes the stars! Marduk lands a killing blow! Tiamat roars! From her corpse, Marduk carves the heavens and the earth.

Enkidu blinked, at first bewildered, at last bored. He didn't understand the parade of strange forms; the enrapt glitter of audience eyes was grimly amusing.

Eight days into the festival, he was no longer amused. He was terrified.

It started on the pavilion where Gilgamesh had presided during the celebratory hours following his triumph over the West Road bandits. The king sat on his gilded chair, his mother nearby, the High Council seated comfortably, while an ocean of bodies pulsed, swarmed, and bulged around them. Then came the tide of foods. Bird eggs, fowl, an edible forest of sweet fruits, mountains of bread and dipping sauces, fish and wild boar, eggs, great basins of beer and mead.

The panic began in Enkidu's stomach.

Dancers arrived like strange fish popping up from the streets, led by streams of priestesses droning prayers. Everywhere Enkidu looked he saw greasy mouths, the white-saber flash of a woman's smile, the roar of male laughter. He tried concentrating on one group at one table, but the maelstrom of distraction prevented this, and he couldn't easily ignore everything else that was happening. Gilgamesh had seen it all before; to Enkidu, it was a nightmare. Jugglers spinning monkey skulls. Fire-breathers, contortionists, bards ... and then came the musicians, adding more noise to the already gibbering crowd. Enkidu dropped his goblet, reeling in panic. These are not my people! he cried inwardly. They are devils!

In the din, no one saw or heard his franticness; even Gilgamesh was clapping to the sight of dancing girls strutting their bodies like oiled serpents. At this latest show, Enkidu's loins stirred helplessly. He squeezed his eyes shut, shocked that he would find them enticing; these writhing creatures weren't anything like Shamhat's lilting melody that had first ensnared him. He turned his head, opened his eyes. Two dead boars met his gaze, accusing him silently from silver platters.

Enkidu's open-mouthed horror was too much to bear. He screamed.

Gilgamesh leapt up, saw his stricken face, and spoke quickly. Guards parted the crowd; an instant later the king and guest were moving down a thin aisle into the quiet palace.

"My friend, what is it?" the king cried.

For a moment, Enkidu forgot the language he had learned. All he could manage was a nod of his head and a rapid snort of air. Had his tribe heard such a sound, they would have understood at once: *Enkidu wishes to be left alone. We will leave him alone, then.*

Though Gilgamesh was not privy to Enkidu's language, he perceived the meaning. He drew back several steps. "Would you like water?"

Enkidu found his voice; the strange human words latched back onto his thoughts like pollen caught in tall grasses. "Too much noise," he said with difficulty. Then he looked into his Gilgamesh's eyes and saw the depth of empathy there. It moved him. "Enkidu sorry, my friend. This place not like forest."

The forest!

Dusky, frightening, glum, lonely. But sane! Oh! Trees exuding their moist scent! The damp soil! The wind! When was the last time he had heard the lilting notes of wind?

Gilgamesh watched this pass over Enkidu's troubled face. In that moment, he too heard the muffled crowd with different ears. The talking and laughing and singing and music and the trickle of wine and the clatter of plates … Gilgamesh also felt the beginnings of suffocation. He shook it off.

"People enjoy sound. A lost man lets his voice ring out across the earth, and if an answering cry is heard he knows he is not alone. For people, there is comfort in that. We like to know others are near. We don't enjoy being isolated from one another."

The word was something Enkidu had not heard. "What?"

"Alone," Gilgamesh clarified.

Enkidu considered that. "*Lahmu* not like being alone. But we not make so much noise!"

Gilgamesh grinned. "In the Epic of Creation, the gods created man but then regretted it because, as it turned out, people were so noisy. The sounds of dozens of cities rose up and assailed their ears. The gods couldn't sleep. Couldn't think."

"Enkidu understand this very well."

"So the gods set out to silence us."

"How?"

"They unleashed a Flood upon the world's face." Gilgamesh imagined the valley filling with water like an immense drinking basin.

"Gods made flood?" Enkidu's voice was hollow.

"That's what the stories say. Are you all right?"

"When this happen?"

"Very long ago. Before cities. Before warlords. They allowed one man to survive it. His name was Utnapishtim. When the gods saw what they'd done, they regretted it and recreated the human race. For surviving, Utnapishtim was given a gift."

"What gift?"

"Immortal life."

"Gods sound ... not nice, my friend."

"Are you feeling better?"

Enkidu nodded.

"Shall we return to the festival?"

He nodded again. "Just, no more music tonight?"

"I'll dismiss them at once," Gilgamesh replied sincerely. Enkidu stopped him as they reached the door, looking sheepish.

"And, maybe people talk quieter for a while?"

The king laughed. "You have my word they will comply."

Enkidu met Ishtar four days later.

On the pavilion, surrounded again. Enkidu stood to Gilgamesh's right, Ninsun to his left. Foods and dancers and reenactments had constituted most of the day. The evening was as silent as if a new flood, invisible but just as deadly, had swept life from the city streets.

Torch-posts lit until the Avenue of the Gods blazed from palace to ziggurat. As Enkidu looked, a contingent of females approached from this latter structure.

"The priestesses of Ishtar," Gilgamesh explained.

Ninsun sighed, her sharp eyes watching their approach. They each bore scented jars while the head of their column, Shamhat herself, bore a golden standard depicting the Eyes of Ishtar above the sun, ziggurat, and city. Ninsun's tongue pushed against her teeth, disgusted with the blasphemy of lessening the sun god's importance to this parade of flesh.

"Her," Enkidu gasped.

Gilgamesh rose, bowed before the standard, and recited a prayer. Enkidu watched, astonished to his powerful friend kneeling subserviently before these women. The king then rose to take the standard. He walked the length of the Avenue of the Gods followed by his entourage. The crowd knelt as he passed them by.

The ziggurat drew near. It glowed defiantly against the night. Tripods crackled on its steps, and Enkidu could see more priestesses fanning out from the high temple's mouth. At last, a shimmering golden figure emerged from the temple and waited.

"He cannot climb the steps with you," Shamhat said, when the king had already started the ascent and Enkidu began to follow. She looked at Enkidu apologetically.

The king nodded. "Enkidu, wait here."

"Yes," Enkidu said. He coolly held Shamhat's gaze.

Just as Dumuzi had, as Lugalbanda, as Enmerkar, as Meskiaggaseir before them, King Gilgamesh climbed the ziggurat steps to the top tier, to the high temple, where Ishtar waited. Her skin glistened in gold. Gilgamesh felt his head grow heavy, senses fogged. He knelt. He offered the standard to Her.

Ishtar stood above him, a living statue marbled by flickering illumination. In contrast, Her eyes were very white; Enkidu could see them from the ziggurat base.

Ishtar passed the standard to Her priestesses. She extended a hand to the king; he accepted it, heart thundering. He stared at Her painted feet.

"State yourself before Heaven," Ishtar spoke.

"Gilgamesh, son of Ninsun and Lord Lugalbanda. Ruler of Uruk."

"The old year dies," Ishtar spoke quietly.

He repeated the words, the same every year.

"The new year hatches."

His lips moved, as they had the year before.

The same mantra was sure to follow, shuffling from the vaults of his memory, shaking dust, reminding him how Ishtar would next ask what kind of ruler he'd been, and had he honored the gods, protected the city, built great monuments to the glory of Uruk. Everything ritualized, without variation, and punctuated by the same recitations of prayer.

Ishtar's metallic lips parted.

Gilgamesh watched for his chance to reply.

"King Agga has just entered your lands," She said.

The new year had begun.

CHAPTER 17
INVASION

The High Council squawked in panic around him, but Ibi-Sin looked serene as he rattled off details of Agga's invasion. Gilgamesh wondered if the man was drugged. His words spilled like a tranquil poem, his face relaxed, and his eyes were scrubbed of their typical rage. He ticked off numbers on his fingertips.

"Eight thousand troops, with three chariot divisions," the old hawk recited. "Their rear-guard are transporting massive baggage-cars. We're meant to believe these are the king's luxuries and his royal family's belongings; of course, that isn't the case at all."

Nedu looked stricken. "What then?"

"Ladders, and siege equipment. Battering rams."

Gilgamesh fingered his beard, taking a cue from his Military Advisor's demeanor. He finally understood the calm; the anxiety of waiting was over. Agga was here, his soldiers were advancing a day from Uruk. It was time for battle.

"Why didn't our scout ships report this?"

Ibi-Sin cracked his knuckles. "Because Agga was crafty. He smuggled his army into trading vessels which we had no right to board. Eventually, the sheer number of ships compelled our people to forge a blockade. So Agga bought them."

The king's eyes grew. "What?"

"He bought our scouts like a child purchasing beads." Anger finally infected Ibi-Sin's voice. "Another ship was set alight, the crew killed."

Gilgamesh stood and turned to Ninsun. So often she exuded confidence in Uruk's divine favor! Now her lips were tightly set. Her eyes swam in fear. She looked her age, shriveled and vulnerable. He pictured her head cracked open, her grey hair separated around a yawning red wound. In this vision, birds pecked flesh from her corpse.

Ibi-Sin was still talking. Rimush interrupted him and the council burst into squawking argument again. Gilgamesh watched them with a peculiarly detached sensation. Morbid visions swirled through his mind. Tirigan the Trade Advisor, an axe embedded in his smooth head; fat Kazallu cut off at the knees, screaming as Kishian dogs savaged him; Rimush, one-eyed Zariqu, Ibi-Sin, each piled atop the other like logs for burning.

The worms of rot wriggling beneath corpse-flesh. Maggots chewing their putrid way through human organs. The stench of Dumuzi's dying in the South Tower.

That's where Agga will put me, Gilgamesh thought. Under guard of the puppet governor he'll install here. My mother will die. My father's statue will be disfigured. Enkidu ... they'll put him in a cage and parade him through Kish as pet of the deposed king!

"On a forced march they'll be here by morning," Ibi-Sin explained. He frowned, seeing the strange look on the king's face.

Gilgamesh turned to Zariqu. "Will Ishtar help?"

"I pleaded our case last night after the festival. She says this is your test, My Lord."

"Convenient," Ninsun spat.

But Gilgamesh smiled. Taking Zariqu by the arm, he steered the man toward the door, speaking in the friendliest tone. "Then express my gratitude to Her, for reminding me that the mortals of the city will accomplish what a goddess dare not! Thank Her! I have the priestess of Shamash at my side, the god Marduk in my heart, and the young men of Uruk manning the wall that I conceived! We don't require Ishtar's help ... though I appreciate Her offer."

"I dare not say these things!" Zariqu shouted.

Gilgamesh pitched him through the doorway. "You will, or I'll have your other eye for dinner." The king motioned to Nedu. "Go see that he repeats these words *exactly*."

Nedu scurried out. The High Council watched him go.

One by one, their gazes returned to their king.

"Prepare for battle," Gilgamesh said.

Uruk's army rolled out to the outer court and formed into rows. Arrows were stuffed into quivers. Scouts sounded horns, and beyond them came the Kishian army like locusts, beating their metal wings and shaking the earth with their march.

Agga was immediately obvious, standing tall in his gem-encrusted chariot. A squat man, bearded, with an amber-colored helm. The army stopped short of archer range. The valley plain was darkened and brightened at the same time; the morning sun glinted off the soldiers, standards, and chariots while swamping their feet in black shadow.

Gilgamesh stood on the wall with Enkidu beside him. They were both wrapped in simple garments, to appear as little more than scouts to calculating Kishian eyes. Now wasn't the time to reveal the defending lord; despite the novelty of cities, dramatic timing was a principle warlords had grasped long ago. There had always been cityless marauders who painted their faces blue, sported horned helms, and hung firebrands from their beards to better ape the demons of the netherworld.

Enkidu was, like Ibi-Sin, strangely calm after Gilgamesh explained what was happening. "Why he hate you?"

Gilgamesh looked on the inner side of the wall, to where his troops were gathered. They watched him anxiously. "He wants this city. He wants power." To the men, he made a vulgar joke about other big things small Agga wanted, and the nervous soldiers erupted into laughter. It was a healthy release of their tensions, and the laughter would strike into enemy morale ... especially since they believed a mere scout was tearing into their illustrious king so effectively. Gilgamesh continued jibing, raising more laughter, while his friend gazed upon the invader's army.

To Enkidu, the horrifying sight brought a strange calming acceptance. He understood now why his people were doomed to die off. Never had there been *lahmu* numbers like this. Never had such unified discipline been imposed on any tribe. Humans had mastered a secret unknown to the rest of the world. When they saw a beast and their stomachs growled in hunger, they looked beyond it to the whole herd. If one tree could yield materials for shelter, so would an entire forest.

And even that wasn't enough. The incredible city of Gilgamesh had caught another man's eye. Now Agga's tribe was here. Gilgamesh's tribe waited to defend. Someone would live, another would not.

Gilgamesh's hand touched Enkidu's broad shoulder. "This is hardly your fight. You may return to the palace."

"I stay."

The king shook his head. "You're not trained for war, Enkidu. Much death is coming."

Enkidu snorted derisively. "Enkidu see more death than you, *King* Gilgamesh."

The sarcasm in the statement was so astonishing that Gilgamesh was speechless for several seconds. But then Enkidu smiled. Hunched, bulky, neckless, that smile puffed out his cheeks and made his eyes merry.

"My Lord," a scout on the wall said. "Agga sends an emissary to the walls."

The two friends turned. A single chariot was drawing near.

"That Agga?" Enkidu peered skeptically.

"His messenger. Come to discuss terms of surrender."

"You want me go talk Agga?"

Gilgamesh stopped, moved by the sincerity in Enkidu's voice. Is that how you people resolve conflicts? he wondered. Do you walk out to meet with neighboring clans armed only with words, and do your border conflicts or aggressive assault evaporate like the morning mist? No. Gilgamesh could not believe that any such innocence existed, not even in the *lahmu*. The world was a brutal gauntlet that did not bend to the will of innocence. In fact, the world didn't bend at all; the world flatly *was*, and everything that walked or crawled or flew in its heartless grasp had to bend to *it*. Two hungry beasts, meeting in a desolate and empty plain where the only food is each other, cannot talk out their shared case of starvation. The stronger beast, or the one with the deadlier claw by skill or luck, makes his kill, eats the flesh of his opponent … and lives another day. Gilgamesh's thoughts raced back to the argument he had had with Enkidu over the New Year Festival, and he recalled Enkidu's downplay of that whole affair:

"Morning you always wake up. Do you celebrate waking up?"

Perhaps we should, Gilgamesh thought. Surely there is triumph in surviving to another day!

The idea of talking out problems with Agga the Conqueror was not merely silly; it was dangerous. It would make for a bitter tale of failure sung as a warning to idealistic youths, of how Uruk's Fifth King went out to talk peace with a man hungry for war and enslavement. And if Enkidu did the talking, it would be more than folly; bards would rouse audiences into ceaseless hilarity at the retelling of the *animal* who sued for peace with Agga of Kish.

But then another thought flared across Gilgamesh's anxieties, and this was a different interpretation to Enkidu's words. He looked upon his friend with renewed respect. He drew him close.

"Actually, I have a better idea."

The North Gate opened, just enough to allow a single horseman to gallop out and meet Agga's emissary. But then, to the astonished bewilderment of all, he rode past the Kishian emissary. Halfway to the line of Kish's army he stopped, dismounted.

A chuckle passed through the Kishian ranks.

"I am authorized to entreat only with King Agga," Uruk's rider shouted.

The slighted Kishian emissary drew his chariot around, but Agga was already coming forth, on foot, surrounded by six shield-bearing guards should Uruk's archers violate the terms of entreatment. The horseman patiently awaited him.

Stout-bodied Agga smiled, his woven beard tickling his teeth. Uruk wished to sue for terms! Or perhaps issue a threat? Agga studied the mighty Urukian walls and calculated once more the effort needed to breach them. The Kishian troops had sailed for many days and then force-marched to Uruk … they were hungry for a fight. Agga counted on it.

"I seek King Agga of Kish," the rider repeated.

"You look upon him!" Agga bellowed. He stretched his arms to showcase the army and added, "See my hands, my body, my size!" His army roared and beat their shields.

The rider was a very young man, not yet fourteen, but he made no reaction this boisterous display or vulgar humor. He serenely waited for the clamor to fade. Then: "I speak for Gilgamesh the Mighty, son of Lugalbanda and ruler of Uruk."

Agga stroked his beard. "I might ask how mighty is Gilgamesh. He seems more to me like a tortoise cowering within his shell."

"Gilgamesh the Mighty asks if you are blind. Uruk's boundary stones are set in plain sight, proving this land belongs to her alone."

Agga grinned. "Then why is a Kishian army here? Tell your king that the North Road and all these territories are *mine*, and when I lead my army through your gates so too will Uruk be *mine*. And bear this message as well: Any Urukians may now defect and join my ranks. By doing so their wives and mothers will be spared … though all others will be shelled out to my men. That goes for you as well, fair emissary."

But the Lord of Kish didn't know that the youth he addressed was without family, that all had perished by disease and age. Uruk was his family, Gilgamesh the only father he needed to love and serve.

The boy said, "I see. You'd have me return to my fearless king and report that General Agga has come so far to barter for bodies like a meat merchant?"

Agga's eyes boiled in his pitted face. He struck the boy, shoving aside his own guards to better reach him. His hand clasped around the youth's delicate neck and he shoved it into the dirt.

"A meat merchant? Consider me a butcher!"

He barked a command and his bodyguards seized the messenger, bent his head, and drew their swords.

Uruk's North Gate parted again.

The invaders from Kish watched a very tall man, clad in ice-blue armor, advancing like a titan through the very Gates of Heaven themselves. Behind him followed two men, red-faced Ibi-Sin and an unknown man garbed entirely in black, with a faceplate obscuring even his visage. This latter figure was short, but inspired no one in Agga's front line to jibe about height; the black armor, the covered face, and the bulky presence of the man who wore it conjured inexplicable fear in their hearts. The Gate remained open, soldiers clogging its mouth. For the first time, the two armies beheld each other across the distance.

Gilgamesh strode fearlessly toward the enemy king and his six bodyguards, quickly calculating his chances. Outnumbered two-to-one, with the rest of the Kishian militia a running distance away. If things turned sour his survival was in serious doubt. If the army lunged they'd place themselves into bowshot from the walls, but that would not save him or his two companions.

Still coming, he thundered, "I am Gilgamesh the Mighty, ruler of Uruk and son of Lugalbanda! I sent a man out to speak with General Agga, but now I see how he treats the rules of engagement! Is he such a coward?"

The bodyguards fanned out protectively before their king. He knew they'd be the best warriors of Kish. Their stance, the quality of their swords, their coordination were seamless. If Agga gave the word ...

Gilgamesh drew his sword regardless, determined to see this play to the end. He halted a few paces away. Ibi-Sin also drew his sword, the sinews in his arms bulging. For an elderly hawk, he retained surprising agility and presence; below his kilt, his legs positioned into a classic fighting stance. The concealed warrior also stopped shy of actual attack.

This latter figure arrested the attention of Agga's bodyguards. They saw no weapon in his hands, nor shield. But they plainly observed the reddish hair sprouting from between the patch-and-stitch seams in his armor.

"Lord Gilgamesh," Agga said uneasily. He stepped out from behind his protectors, sword still in its scabbard, but didn't stray far. His spies in Uruk had prepared him for Gilgamesh's preternatural height and physique; nonetheless, the king cut an intimidating vision. Garbed in his armor and kilt, the crown pressed against his shoulder-length hair, he seemed the carven image of a god-hero sprung to life from dusty temple walls. The king of Kish wondered how much strength Gilgamesh could put into a killing stroke.

He recognized Ibi-Sin, too. The old monster had visited Kish during Agga's youth as part of an embassy during Lugalbanda's reign. Craggier now but no less dangerous, he would be a formidable adversary.

"Explain yourself!" Gilgamesh said. "You steal your men from their wives, force them on this march while the New Year Festival goes on without them! They spend it in the belly of boats! Why?"

Agga's mind worked swiftly. He hadn't expected the king to come out from the protective walls. This war could be over in a blink if he made the correct play. Gilgamesh and Ibi-Sin, against six highly trained warriors ...

But no. There was the unknown *second* companion of Gilgamesh, too. Agga considered the warrior's concealing faceplate, the overflowing hair spilling out from the armor seams like red fire ...

Surely not!

Strange tales had escaped Uruk lately, brought to Agga by spies and informants. He had laughed them off, so bizarre had they sounded.

He squinted again at the unknown warrior.

Surely not.

Agga tugged on the end of his beard. "The terms are simple, Gilgamesh. Uruk will submit to my authority, to be part of—"

"Then come take her!" Gilgamesh cried with a wild laugh. "Fly over her walls! Wield your battering rams against her gates! Then fight your way through the great Urukian army whose numbers are plucked from a population *twice* that of Kish! But perhaps the gods are with you! Perhaps you'll defeat my *first* army! Will you have stomach to face my *second*?"

With a flourish, Gilgamesh turned to the black-clad warrior and said, "General Enkidu, make yourself known!"

The helmet came off and Agga's bodyguards recoiled with gasps. The unveiled creature was all reddish hair, a protruding jaw like outthrust rock, and a deformed head too low in the front, too high in the back. Dark eyes glowered at the bodyguards from beneath accreted hoods. Its fists beat the its chest armor and when it hopped forward, Agga and his guards retreated again. Gilgamesh tried not to gape at his friend's terrifying aura; Enkidu looked neither human nor animal, nor even a hybrid of both; he seemed a *pazuzu* demon risen from hell. Enkidu beat his chest again, and then roared.

An answering roar came from the walls of Uruk.

Agga's jaw dropped as he sighted some two hundred black-clad monsters hopping frenetically upon the city walls.

"General Enkidu leads the *lahmu* contingent of Uruk's defenders," Gilgamesh declared, "And they are far hungrier for battle than you or I can ever know! *Enkidu dol u-gallu! Eresh ka zul!*" With that Enkidu sprang forward several paces, and the bodyguards broke and drew in.

Cursing, Agga sprinted to his army and screamed the battle command. His soldiers charged a few paces and stopped awkwardly, the second row crashing into the first.

For Gilgamesh's alien ululation was more than a command to Enkidu; it was meant for the creatures of Uruk herself. And from the gate came his answer. A steady stream of hunched soldiers, black-tarred and manic, poured from the wall's orifice. To say they assembled themselves into ranks would be false; they pooled into a spreading body of lunacy the way oil might fill a basin. They beat at their armor. They hopped grotesquely. They pounded their shields. And kept coming, straight at Kish's army.

Gilgamesh raised a hand, and from the wall rushed a black wave of arrows.

The Kishian army imploded.

From the beasts bearing upon them and the death from the sky, the ranks disintegrated and scattered like wind-driven sand. More arrows hissed, and were answered with screams. Agga himself looked like he was becoming unhinged, his eyes glowing with panic as he watched the ape-soldiers and the archers.

"*Unleash the Anzu Birds!*" Gilgamesh roared.

Agga fled from this last ghastly threat, and the frontline caved in completely, the darkness of the ranks torn asunder like a great cloth ripped by spectral claws. The Kishian lord leapt into his jeweled chariot.

Gilgamesh held up one fist and the rest of Uruk's army came, thundering out in chariots ahead of speedy hoplites.

Gilgamesh led the charge straight into the remnant heart. He struck cleanly on his left and right, felling fleeing warriors as he galloped ever deeper, penetrating into the disbanding thickness of Agga's army. He spotted the general's royal chariot wheeling round him, drawn by two horses, and he caught Agga's pained but resolute expression. The man did not intend to flee right away. Whether to save face, or out of true faith in his own divinity, Agga was careening into the Uruk army and circling his way to Gilgamesh, even as his troops fled around him. And as he came, he swatted at the nearest troops of Uruk's militia.

"Agga!" Gilgamesh cried, his long hair trailing in the wind. "*If you seek me, here I am!*"

Agga's severe countenance hardened and he cracked his whip. His horses spurred on, crazed with terror or possessed by their implacable master. Gilgamesh ran to meet him.

Around the two warriors a great rift had formed, and a wall of bodies—both defenders and invaders—stood by to witness the suicidal spectacle.

"Upon the gods, I smite thee!" Agga screamed, his face flushed crimson as he came. Gilgamesh leapt aside, avoiding the head-on collision by inches of his kilt, and he struck out both shield and sword, simultaneously. The shield caught Agga's blade, while the sword took the invading king in the belly, splitting his armor like an arrow through tree bark.

Agga didn't even yell out. His body capitulated backwards, flying out of his chariot as his horses—now free of will—ran off wildly into the crowd of militia, still tethered to the carriage. Agga's body slammed into the dust.

Gilgamesh approached slowly, staring openly at the wound on his opponent. The Kishian army had scattered and now watched, seeing they were no longer being pursued.

"What gods to you pray to, Agga?"

Agga regarded his vanquisher. From his dirt-caked beard, he spat. "I'll take you to them!" His jab was wild; Gilgamesh easily sidestepped the blow and batted the blade away. His sword kissed Agga's throat.

"What gods, Agga?"

Agga looked at his own reflection on the blade. In the polished bronze, he saw every day spent with his family; the newborn son so recently born; his palace; his bee-filled gardens; his favorite concubine Beletseri who knew skills which entirely conquered him in bed. When Agga swallowed, his throat pressed deeper against the edge. "I pray to them all, Gilgamesh."

Gilgamesh's face hardened. "My god is Marduk. You are beaten, your army shattered as you shattered the ancient friendship between Uruk and Kish. Our fathers graciously upheld that friendship! Do you have children, Agga?"

Agga's sweaty face glared. "Take my life, Gilgamesh."

"You just had a son. He will grow up without a father … if you refuse to take my sword and swear your submission." With that, Gilgamesh jabbed his blade into the earth. "Grab the metal, Agga, or outstretch your neck. I leave this choice to you."

Agga clasped his hands around the blade. Without hesitation.

"Swear before all that you will return to Kish, and abandon this foolish dream of belligerence. Swear you will become Uruk's ally in trade and intelligence against those enemies greater than us both, the Assyrians and Hittites who mass like locusts in northern Babylonia to destroy all we hold sacred. Swear all this!"

The King of Kish obliged. He watched as Gilgamesh wrenched his sword free, slicing Agga's palm and chopping digits as he did.

"Remember how I gave you the gift of life this day! Our war is over. The new year has begun."

"You should not have let him live, my Lord," Nedu said.

"Because he will return to Kish with eight fingers and a wounded belly, and stew in bitterness, and return one day bent on Uruk's destruction?" Gilgamesh asked. "Or that he will plant seeds of hatred in the minds of his son?"

"Those are my very arguments."

Gilgamesh continued to watch the Kishians retreat into the horizon. Even the dead bodies were gone, retrieved by his allowance to walk the Fire Road of Ereshkigal in Kish. The saturated grass stank of carnage, littered by overturned chariots, slain horses, and weapons discarded in the first moments of flight.

Ibi-Sin turned from the retreating enemy and nodded at his king. His sword, kilt, and face were splattered by gore; his eyes shone as if through a red mask. "Nedu is right, my Lord."

"The possibilities are of equal strength in both directions."

The Military Advisor sighed, shrugged, and sheathed his sword. He walked over to the nearest chariot and righted it. Surely to add to his private collection of war trophies, Gilgamesh thought in amusement.

Nedu couldn't let the subject drop so easily. "Sire? Why let him live?"

"I looked into his eyes. I saw there a man who wanted to live."

"All men want to live."

"Some men want glory or power more than they want life. Agga wanted to go back to his family. He was defeated. I believe his dream of subjugation will die. Yes, I think this day's victory will remain as an echo over the valley, for many years to come."

Returning to the city, Gilgamesh walked openly among his overjoyed soldiers. He pronounced twelve new days of celebration, and the thunder of joyful voices made him wish, curiously, that he was simply one of them, not a ruler but a soldier, to dine alongside them, drink from goblets, and compete for womanly affections. Possessed by this whim, he dismissed his bodyguards and strode into their fray. When he walked toward the public baths, the crowd moved with him like extensions of his body.

At the public baths, Enkidu met Gilgamesh and the men. They were so delighted to see him that they rushed to embrace him, hoisting him above them. Enkidu grinned. When the soldiers returned him to the ground, he playfully hoisted them up … three at a time.

Later that night, they shared wine on the deck above the dragon pools.

"People will sing of this for a thousand years," he said. "How Gilgamesh and Enkidu repelled Agga of Kish! They will remember! A man and a *lahmu* …" His voice trailed off as his tongue seemed to reject his last word.

Not a *lahmu*. Not a man.

A *friend*.

"What can I do for you? You can have anything you want! A woman? Do you want a woman to share your bed? They will come of their own desire, my friend! Listen! The city is singing about you! They will willingly warm your sheets!"

Enkidu considered this offer with a mix of fear and confusion. That he felt the impulse to mate, especially with so much female flesh about him in the palace, was undeniable. Humans were a strange lot, so thin and forceful. What would he do with a human woman? Among the tribes, a woman made the sign of sexual willingness; the male responded. From what he'd seen at the New Year Festival, the only signs were oiled, strutting bodies. True, he could learn these signals easily as their language, but there was something else, more insidious, about the thought of lying with a woman. From *lahmu* womb he had sprung, and so to a human womb would he go? He remembered the distant sight of the city, encircled by its walls, and he imagined it as an enormous womb swallowing him, a reverse birth taking Enkidu into a new land so strange as to be incomprehensible.

But then he saw it differently. The Earth would never resurrect his clan. Neither would the river pour life into his mother's buried carcass. The *lahmu* were dying, one and all, like a year winding to its close. Like a clay tablet still wet, the final word of the *lahmu* story was being pressed into final permanence, and that word was Enkidu.

Gilgamesh drew close, concerned by his friend's silence. "What do you want? Please, tell me." An unwelcome thought formed, and Gilgamesh struggled with panic-tinged fear. "Do you want to return to the woods? Is that it?" His voice wavered. "Do you want me to release you?"

Enkidu stared deeply at Gilgamesh. "You are my friend," he said. "But Enkidu wishes to go to forest again."

"Then you are released, Enkidu."

As soon as the words came out the panic overtook him. He realized how empty things would be with his newfound friend gone. He saw the future days as covered by a grey veil. He saw himself alone, far more alone in a city than he had ever feared could be found in the wilderness.

I am the king of Uruk! he thought desperately. I can order him to stay, and bar the gates, and he will have no choice but to remain! In time he will come to accept this new life! He will realize I saved him from the hostile wilds.

The thought came and fled without stirring him to action; he only stared helplessly at Enkidu and repeated, "You are released, my friend. I will open the gates for you … in the morning … and the people will watch you go."

And then will you forget me? Or will you tell the remainder of your people about the days when an evil human king captured you, had you brought to his court in a bag, and tried to make you into one of his own people?

Enkidu frowned.

"You can go, Enkidu," Gilgamesh repeated. "I would ask only that you stay one more night in our company. That is my command … if you don't mind abiding by it."

Enkidu shook his head as if the king were unbearably thick-headed. "Gilgamesh not understand."

"Why?"

"Enkidu wish to go to forest when Enkidu wants. But not stay. Not be alone." He looked at the bearded, smiling, strange, arrogant, fierce, courageous, foolish, wonderful face of the king. "Enkidu like Uruk. Uruk has Enkidu's only friend."

TABLET IV

SIDURI

CHAPTER 18
THE TALE FROM THE NORTH

Not all cities survive.

At the southern end of the Fertile Crescent where the Euphrates and Tigris Rivers come together, ruins jut from the wet green country like exposed bones. Boundary stones worn to shapeless nubs are found by children playing in the brush. Where the two rivers link to the southern sea—the place locals call the Mouth of the Rivers—memory lingers of an empire which held sway there. Many tribes were drawn to the music of its halls, its sea-nourished gardens, and the pleasures of a bountiful land. But the king of Aratta angered the north, and one day an army arrived like metallic locusts to plunder, murder, and destroy. They left just as swiftly. Flames died, smoke cleared, rains scrubbed away the scent of death ... and people built villages over the ruins by the shoreline.

On the loneliest stretch of beach, in the safety of her tavern, Siduri gripped the yellow-feathered end of the arrow and hesitated, the swell of panic starting in her heart. The shaft had pierced the man's thigh several inches above his knee. Its flint tip protruded fully through the other side. The meatiest part of his leg had been skewered.

Siduri only knew that the man's name was Oros, that he claimed to come from the north (though his accent lacked the musical elegance of the northerners ... in fact, he spoke with a truly foreign pronunciation that stirred unkind memories in Siduri's mind.) Oros was bronze-skinned and heavy-bellied, but otherwise not fat. He had the musculature of a mercenary, the sinewy arms for fighting and chiseled legs for fleeing. Two arrows had caught him; one in the shoulder, and this one in the thigh.

"Hold him," Siduri commanded, and her two hunter friends exerted more weight to keep Oros' arms pinned.

Siduri's olive-toned skin flushed darkly, and she wiped sweat from her brow. She was a splendid specimen of a twenty-one-year-old girl, though her beauty was lacquered with the hardened quality of polished oak. Behind her lowered lashes, green eyes flashed like emerald swords. Siduri had been many things in her short life; a runaway, a slave, a warrior, a medicine-woman ...

and her eyes had always mirrored the passion of a soul that hotly embraced whatever task lay before her.

That task, right now, was how to pull the arrow out without causing the blood fountain to gush. There were several such fountains in the human body; the leg held a large one. If the arrow had pierced it, then wrenching the shaft free might start a hemorrhage.

A Mouth of Rivers, she thought grimly.

Siduri let her fingers relax on the feathered shaft. She plucked a bronze knife from the table and brought its serrated teeth to an inch below the flinthead. She began to saw through the wood.

Oros moaned softly, his teeth clenched.

A sharp, demanding knock came to her tavern door.

Reflexively, Oros sat up and jerked his wounded leg, ready to dash. The movement sent new pain coursing up his leg and he choked down the rise of vomit, spat, and lay back down. His honey-colored eyes looked desperately to Siduri.

"No one will harm you in here," she told him. She resumed sawing, and an instant later the flint arrowhead clattered to the floorboards. "I give you my word."

"Siduri!" The voice was sharp, rugged and nasal.

"Give me a moment!"

"We know the criminal is in there! Give him to us, or we'll get him!"

Oros looked desperately around for his sword, but it had been taken from him. That was the rule. There were no weapons allowed in Siduri's tavern, unless they were her own. A huge woven basket sat in the corner of the tavern. Oros' saber, along with the bows, quivers, and arrows belonging to the hunters, sat safely within it.

"Lie down Oros!" Siduri barked, and to the hunters she repeated the necessity of holding him still. They obliged, but watched the tavern door. Six men stood behind it, hollering and pounding.

Then the tavern door swung open.

Her fingers moved like dexterous spiders. In one instant, the knife was in her blood-spattered hands; in the next, it was embedded in the narrow, three-inch width of the opened door. The intruder froze, his eyes like white eggs in their sockets. He backed away and drew the door shut; with the blade stuck in the wood, though, it wouldn't close completely.

Siduri whispered a blanket prayer to the full pantheon, knowing that some gods craved blood, hoping that the others would overrule these appetites. She pulled the shaft cleanly from the muscle.

Oros cried out. Heavy-bellied, blackish droplets trickled down his thigh.

Siduri watched the wound. It was weeping, but not in the gush of the blood fountain.

She pressed a foul-smelling rag against the wound and told the hunters to press it there, stalling the blood. The rag was soaked in sacred oils … strong enough, she hoped, to drive away the disease spirits that loved to sneak into open wounds and rot the flesh.

"Siduri!" The men outside again.

She finally went to the door again. She pulled her dagger from the wood and stepped outside.

No effort was made by the men to disguise their fear. They had heard stories of Siduri from their warlord Cyaxares. Many stories, some fanciful while others mundane, but one unquestionable rule: Siduri's tavern was a neutral place. None could enter it without her permission.

The man who had, in fact, pushed the door open moments ago recovered himself. He didn't like the look of the blood over her hands and the incredible greenness of her eyes.

"That man is a trespasser on the lands of Lord Cyaxares," he said.

"He is under my care for the moment," Siduri answered.

"There is no point in treating a man who will be dead soon."

A second bronze dagger appeared in Siduri's other hand. It was simple sleight-of-hand learned from two elderly healers she'd studied under long ago, but the six men were unnerved by it.

There aren't six men, Siduri told herself. There is only one.

She stared hard at the leader of this cutthroat group.

"Leave my tavern or become a corpse," she said.

The man managed a weak grin, his hand on the hilt of his sword. "My apologies, Siduri." He turned and the others went with him. When they were back on their horses, he turned to her and added, "Please tell him we'll be waiting when he leaves."

She shut the door and bolted it.

The hunters told her what they knew. Oros and four companions had passed through Cyaxares' land and encountered his border guards. A spat of some kind erupted. There was a chase … into the village and along the shoreline. More of Cyaxares' thugs had joined the rout and shot arrows into them. Three men were killed before Oros managed to stumble to her doorway, knock, and be pulled inside as more shafts whistled past where he had been standing.

Siduri listened calmly, wrapping a bandage around Oros' leg and thanking the hunters. She fetched a cup of bitter herbs and brought it to her guest's brown, parched lips.

He drank greedily and smacked his lips when she took it away.

"Thanks."

"That will make you sleep."

"I welcome it."

"What happened?"

Oros' smile faltered. "We were hunting north of here. There was an argument with that camel dung. He and his friends outnumbered us."

"Your accent isn't local."

"I'm originally from Avaris."

"In *Egypt*?"

Oros nodded. "But I migrated northwest along the Tigris. I met up with most of my companions in Nippur. That city is a vassal of King Agga, and I joined Agga's southward campaign last month."

How strange to hear the stories of the north! Local tensions had dominated Siduri's world lately. She had almost forgotten there was a world beyond the Mouth of the Rivers … the exotic cities travelers spoke of. Oh! how she wanted to see the Babylons and Uruks and Ninevehs, or the western cities of Egypt's hallowed lands—Memphis, Giza, Karnak. She had been many things in her life, but now it seemed the meager pacings of a scorpion, confined to one tiny portion of the universe.

Not wanting to tax Oros with too many questions, she nonetheless encouraged a few morsels of information before sleep claimed him. He spoke of Agga's secret river invasion. Sleeping in cramped quarters, always sunless, the stench, the paltry meals, with promise of good pay from Uruk's plunder the only delight he could look forward to.

"When Agga was defeated, I defected with my companions," he said.

Siduri perked up. "Who defeated him?"

"King Gilgamesh of Uruk, and the *lahmu* captain-general Enkidu."

Wind rattled the meshed windows; Siduri's time-honed instincts forced her to glance and make sure it was *only* the wind, but she never completely let her gaze leave Oros' face.

"Would you repeat that?"

He obliged.

"The *lahmu captain-general*?" She couldn't keep the astonishment out of her voice.

"You should have seen it."

"You did?"

Oros related the miracle that had passed before his eyes. He had been on the right flank, part of a mixed contingent of mercenaries and conscripts, when Gilgamesh emerged from the city walls. The man had nearly been within bow-shot; Oros remembered the ribbons in his beard, and the unusual blue-stained armor. Two men had accompanied him, with the seemingly least impressive of them soon revealed to be a wildman of legend.

Then came the massacre, as Gilgamesh took deadly advantage of the surprise.

Siduri listened, enrapt, like a young child by a campfire.

"And there were other *lahmu* as well?"

"Hopping up and down like monkeys on the walls, then streaming out of the gates. Gilgamesh obviously forged some alliance with demons. At least, no one will ever bother him again."

Siduri shook her head in strange glee. Through all her life's adventures (if that was the word, she thought deprecatingly) there had been one constant joy. Stories, gathered from travelers, gleaned from carved images, plucked from the mouths of the drunk in her tavern, captured in song. Most childhoods are tethered to one location; perhaps because of Siduri's life, she thought of the world as a place to be explored.

But I do like one location, she thought. The fantasy of travel is not reconcilable to the reality.

She had heard of Gilgamesh, because many tales surrounding his rise to Urukian kingship drifted like pollen spread by messenger bees. Here was a god-prince whose rightful claim on the throne had been waylaid by Dumuzi the Usurper. For years the prince was forced to live as a slave to the conqueror, being his cup-bearer, never allowed far from his sight. Then Dumuzi was told in a dream that the boy would soon plot to overthrow him; to avert this fate, the usurper sent the kingdom's greatest assassins after him on three different nights. It was here the boy's divine heritage radiated, for he dispatched the assassins each night and then called upon the people to back his claim to the throne. Thunder cracked the firmament, Gilgamesh was crowned by Shamash the Sun God and Marduk the Slayer, and his first act was to handily toss Dumuzi into the underworld where the *saghulhaza* guarded against any escape.

Siduri knew most stories were simply that; tales invented to win coin or favor, and to assign creative explanation to things unknown. This lesson impressed itself on her when she was a diminutive thirteen-year-old working with two old healers. One night the nearest village had been overcome by western raiders; those who weren't killed outright were close to death. There was a young boy, arrow-shot in the neck but still alive, crying. The old healers wanted to remove the arrow, but the village priest of Baal insisted sacrifice must be conducted first; Baal's appetite for blood needed to be sated.

At first, Siduri had been frightened by the words of the priest. A demonic tentacled entity, hovering close but invisible, licking its lips for a taste of human blood … the image of Baal terrified her. Yet she knew about the blood fountains of the body. If the arrow hadn't struck the wellspring—and it looked like it hadn't—then the god's appetite be damned.

The healers had caved to the demands, however. The Baal priest found someone in the village (whom Siduri now suspected was an old rival) and had him sacrificed. The arrow was pulled. The boy lived.

Oros asked for more water and she passed it to him, lost in thought. Then she put him to bed, blew out the lantern, and drew the door shut. He would be safe here.

At the end of four days, he was well enough to purchase a camel from the hunters and make for the woods. They found his body hanging from a tree the following day, stuck with yellow-feathered arrows.

CHAPTER 19
URSHANABI
THE FISHERMAN

For most of the time, Siduri lived alone in her wooden tavern by the Mouth of the Rivers' bleak seashore. Travelers came and went sporadically. The hunters of the region laid claim to the tavern, strictly as a way of extending their protection. Their homes and families formed a crescent around the tavern; Lord Cyaxares' borders were above in hilly country. His forces habitually entered the villages, though. And he himself had visited Siduri several times.

The two factions had been at odds long before Siduri arrived to settle here. She had been a hunter then; formidable with any bladed weapon. Half the time her band hunted animals; the other half, they tracked and killed people who were causing mischief to the region. It was a way of life that had largely evaporated up north, as the kingdoms of Uruk, Babylon, Kish, and Nineveh were able to suppress, incorporate, or destroy most threats to the general peace. Here in the south, the hand of Aratta no longer held sway.

The evening after Oros was found dead, Siduri walked down to the beach and sat upon its mud. The water lapped quietly near her toes, whispering secrets from its foam. There were plenty of fish in the depths, but now Siduri imagined the gulf was utterly empty. One of her earliest memories was of a shoreline of this very gulf further southeast. Even then, the shoreline captivated her with its perverse promise of loneliness.

The gulf's waters were like melted copper as the sun set. She stared, thinking of dead Oros. His death wasn't any of her concern. He had paid for his cabin, the food and water. She had saved his life. Cyaxares had taken it. Everyone in these parts did only what they could.

Nonetheless, Siduri indulged a childish habit as she sat there, the tide kissing her toes. She quietly related everything she knew about Oros. The beach was her only audience, and she told the water to remember him.

Yesssssssssssssssssssss, it seemed to reply.

Siduri felt renewed pangs of loneliness. Memories of healers and prophets encountered passed through her mind, with their honeyed words offering explanations of life. For Siduri, life was simply about heat and cold.

The softly undulating water broke around a murky shape. A boat, surely that of Urshanabi the fisherman. He was a young boy of fifteen, orphaned except for a sister, and able to meet her needs because of the gulf. He was an attractive boy, leanly muscled, with friendly eyes and an eager smile.

The water rushing over her toes was refreshing. She closed her eyes and listened to the sea's heartbeat. Urshanabi's oars dipped gently into the water.

Siduri's own parents had been fishermen. One of eleven siblings in a tiny village, little Siduri worked the land, too. They were successful. Between the crops and fishing, they earned a surplus to sell at the sea-front market. Her playtime was spent among the reeds with frogs and birds.

A motley assortment of people thrived there. Friendly, affectionate, and possessed of the warmth which only a small village can achieve, they toiled together and helped each other when seasonal floodwaters came. Even the neighboring villages that carpeted the bountiful horizon in cheerful nests were agreeable. Open to air and traveler alike.

And the travelers! Little Siduri learned the names of many tribes, gods, and lands. Brightly painted Egyptians, bearded scholars from Eridu, brooding Canaanite priests! She looked forward to the market because there was always something new there. One day she gaped at a family of tattooed Assyrians. Shortly after, she saw a bizarre entourage of men from a land called Harappa far across the northern sea … men with pleasant high voices and lean bodies. Siduri could still remember her mother, tucking her in one night, saying, "My lovely daughter! What a gift life is! Who knows what new people may come from what Far Shore, as you grow up?"

A year later, new people did arrive. They arrived with swords and spears. They left a land of blood and enslavement.

The latter fate had befallen Siduri and two of her sisters; the rest of the family was either slain or sold off to different masters. Siduri shared the beds of two gruff, swarthy warriors for a year. One night her older, favorite sister was murdered in front of her when one of their masters grew insanely angry … at what, Siduri never discovered. She only remembered awakening to a din of angry voices, and then her sister was being dragged from her bed by her master. The flash of a copper dagger. The red yawn of a cut throat. The dark stain on the tent rug.

Siduri escaped the following week when the two warriors were off riding. She couldn't convince her other sister to come. Since the night of the murder, that sister had ceased speaking entirely. Like a dog, then, she could be commanded about. Siduri at first tried to use this to her advantage, ordering the poor girl to leave with her. But it was no use. The girl's terror at disobeying her masters was absolute, and it was Siduri alone who fled into the sparse wilderness with a waterskin clutched against her chest.

The next few years were like a caravan train of friends and men. She attached herself to a troop of merchants for a time guarded by strong, good-natured warriors. One took her as a wife, gave her a child who died the instant it was born. When he was killed in battle against raiders the following month, Siduri picked up and left.

Again the wilderness. Again the lonely excursion into strange and exotic parts. She discovered the power of spells … not true magic, but the power that came from people apt to believe such things. She would chant and tear at her hair if cornered, and spit dire predictions of disease and death. Sometimes her act drove off her attackers. Sometimes it didn't.

That was when she met the two old healers, a man and woman. They took her in and taught her the magics of healing. They were repositories of great knowledge, passed along through many many generations … to such an extent that many believed they were immortal beings. She healed the wounded for two years.

Then their traveling camp was taken prisoner by raiders. The old healers were killed, and Siduri (who had grown into a sleek, beautiful creature) was claimed by one of the marauders.

It was then that Siduri learned her healing arts could be put to more drastic use. The first night during coitus, Siduri clasped her hands over his mouth in the darkness of the bushes, pretending to be possessed by ecstatic fever arising from his sexual skills. When he screamed as she bit into his neck's blood fountain, it was muffled.

Rather than run off again (a futile effort with these raiders ... they were preternaturally gifted trackers) she strolled to the center of their camp. The warriors sitting around the fire gasped at her gore-spattered face. She held her victim's sword, related the details of her kill, and expressed her desire to ride as one of them. Siduri had expected laughter and there was some ... though not as much as she'd thought. To the first man who laughed, she challenged him to a death-match. It was her first time holding a sword, but despite her opponent being fatter, he was an accomplished swordsman. He picked up an unburnt log from the fire, advanced on her, and the duel began to the merriment of the raider camp. The fat raider never intended to kill her. He toyed with her while she swung wildly. He tapped her bottom with the wood when she missed. Finally he clubbed her to the ground.

But no one raped her. The camp's leader, a powerfully, one-eyed Nubian swordmaster named Taharqa, helped her stand. He admired her spirit. He promised to teach her to fight. She became part of their band for one year, murdering with them, riding into strange forests, taking part in plunder. Then she left them and formed her own band of vigilantes and hunters. But it wasn't the last time she saw Taharqa's band, nor the Nubian swordmaster himself.

At eighteen, Siduri's party discovered an area of four villages near the Mouth of the Rivers. They wintered there. They enjoyed the serenity of the location and people.

In the spring, Taharqa's group attacked. Siduri's band retaliated.

She still remembered her horror when she saw it was them. The fattish warrior who had fended her off with a log of wood was still there, as well. Little with them had changed.

Recovering, Siduri rode against them. Taharqa sent the fat man forward and Siduri cut his belly open at the first pass. While his dead body continued to ride behind her, spilling its guts and juices, Siduri made straight for Taharqa. The rest of her clan came up behind her and took on the raiders, but Taharqa and Siduri ignored all, moving toward each other. One of her compatriots tried cutting him down; Taharqa lopped the man's head off with barely an effort and advanced on Siduri. They exchanged heated words climaxing in battle. It was one of the most vivid, enduring memories of her life; recalling it even these years later still made her wrist throb the way it had while clutching her sword, parrying with him, seeing sparks fly off the metal.

But Taharqa was the better fighter, the stronger one, and the longer they fought the more Siduri came to realize that he wasn't really trying to kill her. His band was destroyed, he was surrounded. He was simply prolonging the inevitable. When she realized this, she backed off. He only watched her, his forehead beaded with sweat, his single eye accusing her. "Tiring you?" he challenged.

"Yes," she replied.

"You owe me thanks for creating you!"

Siduri rang her finger against the flat side of her sword. "It's right here. Gratitude for what you did to the villages, the people, the old healers. Come take it, Taharqa."

He threw aside his sword and walked straight into her blade. She held her wrist firm, burying it up to the hilt below his sternum. His single eye clouded over. Warm life covered her fingers. Strangely, the death made her weep.

Her group disbanded after that. The villages praised them as they left, and gave what they could as gifts. Siduri stayed behind. The only gift she asked for was local help in building her tavern here, by the shoreline. She stocked it with medicines purchased with the loot she'd collected. She went to the trading ports in the high hills and by the Mouth of the Rivers (not far, ironically, from where she had been born) and struck deals with peddlers of foodstuffs and herbs. She learned to make ale, stored it in oak containers.

Business was poor yet she knew her purpose hadn't been success. The tavern wasn't a means to money. It was a castle in which she could hide, regroup, relax … and dream. For the first time since her half-clouded childhood, Siduri had achieved a home.

Siduri hugged her knees as she watched the water. The boat drew nearer, and Urshanabi, all white teeth and hair braided in the manner of Eridu, the closest city.

"The day grows late," she shouted to him.

"The sea was kind today," he replied, and kicked at the net in his boat, where fish were piled in a silver-scaled ball. "This is the second catch!"

"Then by the gods, why aren't you home with your sister?"

He leaned so much over the edge of his little boat that the vessel actually tipped partway out of the water. The sight made her leap up with a shout, but he laughed and readjusted his weight. Catastrophe averted, he smiled. The low sunlight was fading fast, turning his face featureless surrounded by black curls shaking in the sea-breeze.

"Sorry!"

Siduri folded her arms across her breasts. "Get home!"

If she hadn't been looking at him she might never have seen the torch on the adjacent shore. A brief flicker of red against the inky shore, then gone, like a stray band of sunlight thrown from the water to alight on glistening bark.

Siduri's brow darkened. She knew it had been a torch, and now that flame had been extinguished for fear of betraying a hidden interloper. The adjacent shore bordered Cyaxares' makeshift kingdom.

"I went to talk with the Old Man," said Urshanabi, unaware of what had caught her attention.

Siduri nodded, her green eyes latched onto the forest. "Why?"

"I like to hear him talk."

Siduri looked out to the hazy, red-lit waters. She couldn't see the old man's island, but her eyes rested on the misty spot where she knew it was. "You didn't leave your boat, did you?"

"Of course not. But do you really believe there are monsters there?"

"What did the old man say when you asked him?"

"He said there are. Terrible creatures."

"Don't ever leave your boat when you talk to him."

Urshanabi shivered, laughed. "I won't. I paddled in the shallows, following him as he walked the beach. He carved a statue for me while we were talking, whittling with his knife, and made the best statue I've ever seen! In less than one hour, by the gods!"

The forest was silent on the far side of the water.

Urshanabi's heart swelled as he watched the tavern-keeper on the shoreline, her hair jostled by a strong sea breeze. He couldn't see her face very well, but he knew it well enough that his imagination placed it easily. He fancied he could see the green fire of her eyes.

"Siduri?"

"Yes?"

Marry me, he thought. Be mine forever!

"I could have the Old Man make a statue for you, if you wanted. He does them so quick. He said that long ago, he made a whole series of them, each with different gemstone eyes!"

"Make one for your sister," she said kindly.

"Good night, Siduri."

"And to you."

CHAPTER 20
PROPOSAL

At first light the knock came to her tavern door, but she had been awake an hour earlier. Fitful dreams had disturbed her sleep, and several times she arose, crouching in the narrow bedchamber to peer clandestinely through the window at the shore and stygian woods. She stared the way a tiger might, her eyes like emeralds in starlight. An hour before she heard the first whispering footsteps approaching her tavern, she was already dressed. Taharqa's killing saber was tucked carefully against her wrist.

Three men greeted her when she opened the door. They were Cyaxares' bodyguards, bearded and dressed well in kilts and furs. Their outer vests were studded with lapis.

"Siduri? Lord Cyaxares requests your presence."

She stared at them with congeniality. "Of course."

Cyaxares ruled from a cylindrical hut that crowned a tall grassy hill. Siduri had visited it before in the daylight, when its reddish wood contrasted against a bright blue sky. In these starlit morning hours, the hut looked more striking than usual. Siduri's sense of aesthetic was touched; it had rained earlier in the night, and so the hut seemed turned to glass in the starlight. The sky was unusually crisp, too, and when Siduri turned to see the greatest view in all the land—the place where the Euphrates and Tigris merged—she gasped at the sight.

"Look," she pointed.

Her escorts followed her finger. "What?"

"Where the rivers join."

An awkward silence sprouted. The heavier guard spat to break it. "Lord Cyaxares awaits you."

Siduri sighed. How could she express what the sight of the conjoined rivers inspired in her? Beneath the bright firmament, they looked like strands of quicksilver melding into a shimmering stream.

She entered the hut.

The interior was redder than the wood. Smoky incense bowls on tripods crackled, and Siduri saw the War Council kneeling before the cedar throne. Cyaxares was there, wrapped in bear-skin. A new crown was on his head—the earlier one had been blander—while this one was gold with several rubies set on its band. Nubian artistry, she had no doubt.

The rest of the chamber contained some dozen men. Each bearded, furskinned, decorated, and jackal-eyed. They were his War Council.

Cyaxares was a tall man with a woven beard and tightly cropped curls. He was from a little-known tribe called the Amadai. Nomadic, scattered as the peoples who refused to submit to cities were scattered, people who drank from meltwater marshes and stalked game in the mountains, who raided against other tribes. Outsiders.

Until now. Cyaxares had risen to leadership of his tribe through a bloody coup and he caused them to settle. The extent of his kingdom was debatable; neither the lord nor his men could read or write, and this absence of records was echoed by the absence of boundary stones too. The practice of shooting their yellow-feathered arrows into periphery trees was a poor substitute.

Yet it was these arrows that Oros had ignored, Siduri thought.

She bowed respectfully.

"The tavern-keeper herself!" Cyaxares roared in pleasure. "Siduri, why must I beg for your presence here?"

"I don't know. Why do you?"

The War Council murmured uncertainly at this response; Cyaxares slapped his knees and let loose a hearty laugh. Siduri let her eyes stray to the man standing to the right of the warlord. This man wasn't smiling, and he watched her with cold black eyes.

His name was Nergal.

Nergal was the name of the god of the underworld, the husband of Ereshkigal whose Fire Road all souls walked. But *this* Nergal was a High Priest of Ereshkigal, advisor to Warlord Cyaxares. Legends swirled about him like incense smoke: He was supposedly the mortal husband of the Goddess Ereshkigal and often walked the Fire Road ... and returned ... to the land of the living. He had familiars, imps, and various spies in the shadowlands of death. He was said to be master of several magical arts, including those regarding life and death.

"It is good to see you," Cyaxares said.

"You look healthy and strong as always."

"Have you ever been on a lion hunt?"

"No."

The warlord grinned. "Then today I will introduce you to this kingly sport!"

She said nothing. Her mind worked swiftly as it had during the chariot ride to the hut. Why had he summoned her? Surely it couldn't be about this Oros affair. He understood the rules of the village; Siduri could treat any injured in her tavern and none could interfere.

"And on the hunt," Cyaxares continued, cheeks red, "We will discuss the future of the villages."

Of course.

"I don't speak for the villages."

"But they listen to you."

Nergal licked his lips before he spoke. "The villages must be absorbed into Lord Cyaxares' domain. These demands come from Ereshkigal Herself, tavern-keeper. She wishes Cyaxares to found a kingdom here." He licked his lips again. "Divine will is not subject to debate or discussion."

Siduri smiled. "Of course not. But *I* haven't heard it from the lips of Ereshkigal." She hadn't looked away from Cyaxares, but she could feel Nergal's eyes boring into her as surely as if hot pokers were being twisted into her forehead.

Siduri wondered how much of this dream was Nergal's, or of Cyaxares himself. He was a warlord after all; a title not easily given. Nearly a thousand men were in his employ, their salaries nourished by the silver mine to the northeast and the copper mine to the south. Two neighboring tribes had been wiped out by his invasions; four others were his allies by way of negotiated marriages. He levied no taxes upon the hunter villages … yet. In this, Siduri sensed it was simply a matter of months. In fact, all he had presently done to them (aside from petty harassments from his border guards) was to lure village blacksmiths into his employ, and they were turning a helpful profit.

The hunters would object, of course. They had taken no pledges to a ruler and wanted none. Many of them had fled the northern kingdoms for want of freedom. No boundary stones here. No kingdom banners. The hunters made families among the natives and worshipped the local gods, traded with neighbors, and kept watchful eyes on their borders.

In the end, they would be eradicated by Cyaxares' men. There were sixty hunter families in the village, and perhaps as many in the eastern village across the river; though hardy, capable fighters, they would simply be overwhelmed.

Representatives of the villages had been summoned to Cyaxares' court over the years. They had politely refused allegiance.

Siduri considered what she wanted to say. "The villagers cherish their own autonomy. They've heard stories of the northern cities, how kings claim the right to lie with any woman they choose, married or not. How kings force men to labor at projects to their own vanity. Pharaoh Khufu claims to have built a pyramid! King Gilgamesh builds a wall! But we hear nothing of those who actually set these bricks into place! The ones who died! The ones who had their lives stolen to sweat and toil for another man's ambition."

Cyaxares stroked his beard thoughtfully. "Gilgamesh builds the wall to keep out invaders."

She laughed. "Gilgamesh builds the wall so the future will remember him! Sniff the air! You can gain a whiff of his ambition from here!"

Again, Cyaxares laughed. The War Council looked pleased too.

The only one not happy was Nergal. He twisted his ornate staff in his hands, fingering the carven head as if contemplating what plague to call down upon this petulant tavern-keeper. Wasn't that what he always referred to her as?

"Tavern-keeper," he said glumly, "You may giggle at your ingenuity, but the goddess is thin on patience. She strikes ghastly curses on those opposing Her holy designs."

Siduri turned slowly. Her eyes flared and danced in the torchlight. "Do you threaten me, Priest?"

"Ereshkigal threatens you."

"Until She appears in the flesh, I will deem the threat coming from you alone."

The War Council was utterly, completely riveted.

"Enough," Cyaxares said. "Day is wasting! Nergal, you are dismissed!"

The high priest bowed and left without looking back at her. Head held high, Nergal strode from the proceedings as if it were his idea … that other matters were demanding his attention, and that he couldn't be bothered with the silly relationships of mortals.

Or *was* this all the priest's idea? Siduri couldn't shake the feeling that she was watching something that had been rehearsed.

"All of you too," Cyaxares told his council. "Leave us." The men unfolded, rose, vanished through the hut doorway.

When they were alone, he smiled fondly at her.

"I would have Nergal's head if he harmed you. But you needn't worry about that."

Siduri shifted where she sat uncomfortably. "Why am I here?"

"Partly because I wished to know if the villagers would consent to being governed."

"I believe I answered that."

"But I didn't finish my question. Would they consent to becoming subjects of my kingdom if I took a wife from among them?"

Part of Siduri froze, panicking, her mind racing to ready a safe reply to what she suspected was coming next. Another part of her pressed her to answer, immediately, lest Cyaxares' crafty perception notice her shock and try to exploit it.

"Even a wife might not be enough," she said. "They would want representation in the laws that would affect them. It is a tribal custom."

Think!

He's going to ask you.

She had thought of it before, considering the advantages to being the wife of a lord. Life began in a gout of blood, pushing out a child into the blistering sun and chilly winds. Why not enjoy the benefits of a royal life? Life with Taharqa had certainly given rewards … but the physical pleasures were fleeting, the plundered gold would tarnish, and could she ignore the suffering he brought to the world even if gemstones were stitched into her eye-sockets?

The warlord drank from a cattle-horn goblet. He watched her over its rim. "And if my wife was Siduri?"

She smiled slightly. She envisioned herself like a painted Egyptian wife, basking in indulgences and perfumes while her husband ruled by crook and flail. A pleasant life, yes. She considered accepting this overture, knowing she might secure safety for the villages. They might accept it.

The warlord waved his hand.

"We'll leave these matters aside," Cyaxares said. "When you see the strength of my trade routes, your people will rush to become citizens of my court. Let us kill a lion together!"

They went out into the brightening morning and mounted his royal chariot. It was fine craftsmanship; too fine for local metalworkers. It must have been shipped downstream from Eridu or Ur.

Into the poplar-studded valley where the two rivers connected they went. Scouts sprinted ahead to locate the lion trails. Warriors on horseback trailed them and surrounded them. Cyaxares wielded a jeweled spear purchased from the same metalworker as the chariot, surely. To say the woods were black was incorrect; they were silver in the starlight, and gold too, as sunlight began a simmering blossom on the horizon.

The raw, chilly air tickled Siduri's face. She felt her heart pounding, thirsting for excitement as when she had lived *out here*, in the wilds. A rogue's morning began at once … no lazy rising from bed, no drawn baths. No comfortable breakfasts. In the wilderness you awoke and were on your feet.

Cyaxares scratched lazily at his beard. The chariot's two wheels ground listlessly beneath them. "Are you considering my offer? To be my wife?"

"I am," she said truthfully.

"And?"

"Would you even have time for me, with all your other wives?"

"I would elevate you to supreme wife."

"That might cause problems for you, with the Elamite woman you married first."

"She has a firebrand temper, true. But marrying you, I might grow displeased with her and find excuse …"

His words chilled her. She knew he didn't mean divorce; that would be too complicated. No, he merely had to accuse her of adultery and bring forth witnesses. Then she would be executed but the treaty with Elam would still hold.

"What would happen to the villagers if I accepted you?"

"You could bring their needs to me. They would join my kingdom."

She nodded.

"And you could usher them over to the worship of Ereshkigal."

Siduri struggled to keep her face emotionless. "What?"

"Divisions are the enemy of all kingdoms. Babylon worships a hundred gods! A *hundred!*" His nose wrinkled in displeasure. "Think of all those different rituals! Every neighbor divided from each other, because one worships Adad the Storm God, while another bends knee to Nammu. Yet despite this individual worship, all men go to Ereshkigal in the end. She receives them along her Fire Road. Do you know why souls languish in the afterlife?"

Siduri shook her head stiffly.

"Because they haven't embraced her. They cow to the anger of Anu, yet He abandons them at death! Or Ishtar's beauty!" Cyaxares slammed his fist into the chariot deck excitedly. "Where is She when they beg? No, Ereshkigal is the true power of the earth. She has risen me up from a leader of tribes to the greatest warlord of the south. She has my devoted allegiance, my love …" He smiled at Siduri, face vermillion with his impassioned speech. "We will marry in Her temple."

Siduri considered escaping into the poplar thickets. She hadn't known Cyaxares to be this impulsive. This …

Unstable.

She formed her next words carefully, weighing them, inspecting their angles and calculating the waves they might cause. "And if people don't worship Her?"

Cyaxares' smile turned cruel. His scalp darkened to livid scarlet. But he said nothing.

He no longer needed to.

Heart pounding, Siduri forced herself into a relaxed pose, with one arm leaning casually against the rail. A jug of wine was with them; she lifted it, filling an ornate goblet. "I would do my part to change their minds, Lord Cyaxares."

That softened him, though the accusation had not gone out of his eyes entirely. "We will make a mighty couple! Now, tell me about Atrahasis."

Siduri managed to hide her surprise in her goblet.

"Do not deceive me," he added teasingly. "You know him."

"Atrahasis the old man?" Enclosed by the cup, her voice sounded tinny and lost.

"Atrahasis the Immortal."

The last gulp of wine vanished down her throat. Still maintaining her airy veneer, the tavern-keeper tried to keep ahead of this latest subject, reading its tracks the way she might hunt an animal, guessing where they might lead. "Atrahasis is just an old man crammed full of folklore."

Cyaxares didn't share in her mirth. Up ahead, his scouts were waving a green banner to signal they'd found a trail. "People say he was born before the Flood."

"People say many things!" She forced a laugh. "Stories trickle down from the north about a *lahmu* general, of all things!"

"I've heard of Enkidu the *lahmu*. They say he's quite real."

"Immortality is less real."

"If I asked Urshanabi the fisherman, would he agree with you?"

Siduri fought hard to contain her fear. The subtle threat wavered over her head and her fingers instinctively twitched for the concealed saber in her sleeve. "No," she said. "He will tell you all about Atrahasis the Immortal! He's a boy and will want to impress a warlord like you. But these are stories! No man lives forever!"

"One does."

"And you wish to possess this gift? Even if it were possible, won't Ereshkigal be angered by someone who defies her Fire Road?"

She worried he might be offended by this question, but instead he responded congenially, as if pleased to enlighten her stupefying ignorance. "I do not seek immortality. Atrahasis is an affront to Ereshkigal, and he must be brought, forcibly, to Her gates. He must die if my kingdom is to flower."

And so it begins, Siduri thought. She wondered how she had considered, even for a moment, marrying him. Converting people to his faith by swordpoint wasn't enough. Perceived enemies would now be purged.

She had never thought Cyaxares was more dangerous than any other tribal leader. Now, the mask had shattered. A poisonous serpent lay coiled underneath.

The chariot wheels spun against soft earth, then lurched forward.

"I tell you he is simply a befuddled old man," she persisted. "Does he deserve to die if he's not immortal?"

"To know Ereshkigal sooner will be a blessing," the warlord responded, watching his scouts. He hefted his spear.

When they found the lions at last, Siduri was so possessed of anguished thoughts she could barely concentrate on the hunt. The forests here were filled with lions, as they made their own competing prides in the hilly country above the game trails and rivers. Cyaxares' scouts located a trail, and in the brightening sky pinpointed the telltale sign of a new kill; vultures drawing insidious circles above the trees. His attendant pulled hard on the reins and the chariot swung awkwardly into the brush.

There were three lions at first, resting comfortably around the crimson carcass of an antelope. A large boulder jutted behind them as a buffer against the cliff-drop. When the hunting party careened into view the wondrous, lean animals sprung up in alarm.

"Northern kings keep lions in enclosures for this sort of thing," Cyaxares told Siduri as he stood in the vehicle, spear balanced on his shoulder. The lions were green-eyed in the semi-dark. Two padded forward while the third roared in agitation.

The accompanying entourage had been on enough hunts to know the pattern. As the two nearest lions charged them, the archers fired a spray of arrows. The beasts scurried off, stuck and bleeding. Cyaxares himself leaned into the deck, watching the third pace rapidly in front of the carcass, not knowing whether to abandon it or charge these brazen intruders. Its panicked cry was thunder on Earth.

A cry for help, Siduri thought.

Cyaxares yelled for more speed. The lion's indecision ended with an impulsive flight from the cliff toward the brush. It was a move Cyaxares' men had anticipated. As it neared, the tree-line warriors jumped up, screaming, waving their spears. The lion swerved back to the kill, zigzagged, and attempted to pass the oncoming chariot.

Cyaxares leapt to Siduri's side of the vehicle and thrust the spear in a lightning-fast downward motion. Tendon and bone snapped, the javelin torn from the warlord's grip as the chariot went on. The beast gave a plaintive howl and tried dragging its paralyzed leg, streaming red where the javelin wavered in its flank.

"Turn!"

Real anxiety filled Cyaxares' face as the chariot drew a circle. Siduri understood at once; the lions were crying for help, and help was audibly crashing through the bramble to come to its mate's defense.

The male attacked the chariot before Cyaxares could retrieve his spear from the dying lioness. It burst from the woods with heart-stopping wrath. The chariot nearly tipped over from the incredible impact. Hot, rotten breath filled the chariot and Cyaxares shrieked.

Siduri fought to steady herself against the rail. The lion's head was gigantic, all mane and enraged eyes. She grabbed for her saber.

The beast was gone.

Cyaxares looked around wildly. The chariot kept going toward the lioness, pursued now by the warriors whose desperate arrow volley had saved their lord's life. Siduri drew her weapon and spotted the male, fresh arrows in his hide sticking from his flank and side. He pranced lightly up the boulder as if to announce to his mates that he had returned to deal with the human threat and then, just as quickly, he sprinted down at full gallop, charging straight at the chariot again.

He'll kill us this time, Siduri thought.

With a jubilant cry, Cyaxares plucked his spear free of the motionless lioness. He hefted it on his shoulder once again. The lion closed the distance to them. Its eyes were the hottest, most livid hate Siduri had ever seen.

"A gift from your lord!" Cyaxares screamed when the creature lunged again, and he let fly the spear.

Siduri watched the jeweled shaft spin as it flew at the beast. The lion ran on, ignoring the wide-shot spear. It pounced against the horses, taking them down in a cloud of red dust. The attendant, warlord, and tavern-keeper lurched into the deck. As if contenting itself with this kill, the lion dashed off the dead horses to disappear into the foliage as three of Cyaxares' men fired arrows after it.

The warlord's face turned purple with rage. Siduri wisely elected total silence while he went to retrieve his spear and discovered it had flown off the cliff.

When dawn fully broke they found the lion. Twelve arrows had pierced its hide. Cyaxares leapt off his chariot and plunged his sword into the creature's cold breast.

"It is dead," he proclaimed, and no one doubted his meaning.

Later a celebration of the hunt was held. Cyaxares presided over it, feasting in gluttony, drinking, brooding, and occasionally turning his face to regard the three warriors who had killed his lion.

Before evening, Siduri excused herself from his court. There was business to be done, she said. Her tavern needed her. Cyaxares barely acknowledged her. She exited his hut and saw, from the limb of a nearby tree, the three warriors' bodies swaying in a light breeze.

She ran back to her tavern. Taharqa's saber was in her hand. Only when she was safely within, door locked, did she collapse to the floor in relief and consider her options.

Two weeks later, plague struck the nearby villages.

And the villagers.

TABLET V

QUEST

CHAPTER 21
THE VARIETY
OF DRAGONS

Ninsun collapsed like a sweaty rag, crying lightly in the red shadows. The sacrificial knife felt heavy. Her priestess robe was heavy too, saturated with the life of three lambs as Shamash brightened the temple window.

Her own voice continued echoing like the complaint of a fading ghost. *"Bring my son a queen!"* The eleven droning priestesses were silenced at this climax. Such supple, youthful creatures! Ninsun despised them for a moment. Fighting to catch her breath, she pondered their faces and wondered if her quest might be fulfilled right here, among her own order. Her son's sexual tastes weren't all that particular; most of the Order of the Sun's disciples could fulfill him, while simultaneously wielding influence on the throne after Ninsun died.

The trouble was that her son was desperately driven to earn his immortality, like his father and King Enmerkar. What would future tablets say for future peoples to read? That he built a wall? It wasn't enough for him. Besides, Urukian brick-workers used unfired bricks in their constructions, as was the standard for all cities in the valley. They required constant maintenance or else they dissolved over time. The mighty wall was not a gift to the future; it was a necessity of today. Ninsun knew her son realized this. He wasn't interested in siring a royal child until his immortality had been achieved another way.

Panting, she watched the priestesses rise in the mist. One by one, she studied them. There was one, maybe two, who might make a fine wife for her boy. Of course, that meant them giving up the devotion of their god. Some would rather die than lose their place in the Order.

Ninsun licked her blood-drenched teeth. Damn everything! Her frustration even reached to the sun-god. He always came through for her! Why not now? Were more sacrifices required before he allowed Uruk's king to find a vessel worthy of his seed?

Yes, she thought. More blood might be required to win Shamash's favor. More sacrifices …

When she was done rinsing her face, she went to find Enkidu.

Instead, she found her son on his way to City Council. In the fresh daylight he looked unnervingly like her husband. That chiseled face and braided beard, cloak flapping in the high breeze like the banner on some seagoing vessel. Gilgamesh noticed her coming down the stairs from the Temple of Shamash, and he waited for her to join him.

"Blessed morning, mother," he said. They rounded the corner of the dragon pools.

Ninsun laughed, noticing the bounce in his step. "Dare I ask what you did last night?"

"I slept soundly!"

"Mm-hmm. Did she?"

"I was quite alone," he persisted.

A month had passed since the great victory over Kish. In that interim strange wonders had come into being. A flood of emissaries to Uruk bearing gifts of friendship had set the council abuzz, including an entourage from a land called Harappa across the north sea; they bore never-before-seen gifts of silk, exotic spices, and something called a Hanuman medallion for Enkidu. Uruk's citizens had changed, too. Gilgamesh walked openly among them and collected their smiles. He stopped to help an ox-cart that had tipped over, and was invited to meager lunch by the peasants whom he aided. Eating with them, joking with the husband and wife, playing with their three little children, Gilgamesh felt loved as never before. And for the first time, with the children on his knees, he considered siring a royal progeny.

"Good!" Ninsun exclaimed, her eyes aflame with fierce joy. "I will send letters to Babylon."

"What?"

"Our treaty with Babylon will hold more weight if solidified by marriage with a Babylonian noblewoman."

"Send your letters in the spring. I don't want to entertain courtship until then."

"Have you seen Enkidu?" she asked slyly.

Enkidu.

He had changed since the defeat of Kish. No longer shaggy, lustrous red hair pouring from his body. The morning after Agga's flight Enkidu ordered the palace slaves to shave him from neck to feet. Shears and scraping scissors removed the stubble as Enkidu stood, feet spread and arms held outward, to be soaped and depilated.

The transformation was astonishing. Enkidu's pale muscular body looked more dwarfish than ape-like now. He was suddenly sensitive to cold nights and the burning sun. Clothes felt like the kiss of running water against his skin.

Four weeks later and his reflection continued to transfix him; the mirror showcased a red-bearded human blinking back at him.

"Here he is!" Gilgamesh smiled.

As he rounded the corner, he saw his friend crouching on the white stone with a female guest. True enough! The king had wondered when his friend would take advantage of his newfound fame.

Ninsun stopped abruptly. Gilgamesh walked on another pace, then halted his stride.

"Shamhat," he said.

There was no mistaking the vile priestess. She was tittering at some joke, Enkidu clearly miming a story with his hands, when he spied Gilgamesh and Ninsun. His grin grew.

"Friend!" Enkidu bounded over, practically dragging along his giggling companion. "Friend, this Shamhat!"

The king glowered at the girl. "We've met, friend."

Shamhat's smile faltered. "Lord Gilgamesh."

"She sing to me," Enkidu explained.

"Does she?"

"She sing like beauty."

Enkidu felt warmed as if he'd drunk too much wine (which had happened several times in the last couple weeks.) So often he had thought about Shamhat since the day of his capture, and again when he encountered her at the New Year Festival. Yesterday the long-awaited confrontation came to pass. He was strolling about the palace grounds doing his best to imitate a human's walking stance when he caught a whiff of her scent on the air. Delighted, he trailed it like a dog until, in the royal marketplace, he found her.

For Shamhat, the initial seconds of meeting Enkidu again were terrifying. The animal had bounded through the crowd, startling her. She thought he meant to attack her until, recovering, he did an unbelievable thing. This beast she'd met in the woods suddenly smiled and bowed his head like a nobleman! And it wasn't a poor imitation! Clothed in royal fabrics, the creature had clearly been acclimated to the ways of civilization.

"Enkidu greet you happy," he had said, and she couldn't prevent laughing.

"I greet *you* happy," she replied.

Then came the next incredible thing. She had been fingering a tapestry, interested in decorating her ziggurat bedchamber. Enkidu, perceiving this, snatched and bought it, right there. It all happened so fast.

"Yours now," he told her. His teeth were so white and large they looked like alabaster cubes in his mouth.

"Thank you!"

"But you pay me," he warned. "Or I keep."

Shamhat blinked, uncertain how to interpret this rudeness.

"But you just bought it for me!"

"I bought with coin," he explained confidently. "You pay with name. Enkidu have your name?"

"Shamhat!" she cried in pleasure. "My name is Shamhat, General Enkidu!"

The rest of the afternoon had been a strange, glorious dream. The damned thing was charming! Friendly! And undeniably taken with her! When she returned to the ziggurat, cloth in hand, she deliberately avoided seeing Ishtar for fear the goddess would taunt her for enjoying such pleasures with an animal.

Gilgamesh's murderous stare didn't leave Shamhat's eyes. His mother's scowl was worse.

"Did Ishtar send you here today?" he asked.

Shamhat blushed. "I came of my own desire."

Gilgamesh studied her with thinly concealed wrath. Was Ishtar extending a threat to him by having this serpent visit Enkidu? Relations with the Cult of Ishtar had frayed after the confrontation with Kish when Ishtar failed to reply to the king's challenge. Patron goddess of the city perhaps, but what good was a deity if it abandoned you when need was most desperate? Besides, Gilgamesh had already entertained one very dangerous talk with Rimush about the possibility of modeling Uruk's religious leanings on the Babylonian model; a city of a *hundred* gods, with *no* favored cults. He envisioned a new temple devoted to the full pantheon, equal under the sky, and various city gates named to honor them. Rimush had expressed guarded optimism, hearing this idea. Marduk, Ea, Shamash, and the full host might warm to it; Ishtar, however, dwelt *in the city itself.* There was no deity more frightening to anger than the Goddess of Love and War.

Gilgamesh glanced at his mother, then again to Shamhat. "How are you, priestess?"

Shamhat chanced a nervous smile. "Quite well, sire."

"Enkidu," the king said, "Would you fetch Nedu please?"

Enkidu nodded and bounded off, hesitating only once to let his eyes smile upon Shamhat. Then he was gone.

Ninsun's mouth hung open. She had seen the look of love enough times to recognize it here.

Gilgamesh had also seen the look; his hand shot out and grabbed Shamhat by the elbow. Effortlessly, he pulled her toward him. "Why are you here today?"

"To visit General Enkidu."

"*Why?*"

"He is a gentle creature."

"And why should that interest a woman who scrapes the flesh from men's faces?"

Shamhat swallowed. "I took no pleasure in doing that. I—"

"*You took every pleasure in it*! I saw your eyes! You enjoyed it Shamhat! It moistened your portals."

Shamhat blushed deeper. "Release me."

In a ghastly move, Gilgamesh lifted her by one arm and dangled her over the rails above the dragon pool. Shamhat screamed, her legs kicking. The dragons below perked up, their orange head-crests fanning brightly.

Ninsun circled the would-be murder, enrapt.

"If you *ever* speak to me that way again, if you ever visit Enkidu without my permission, I'll chop you into pieces for the dragons. Is that understood?"

Shamhat held onto his arm wildly. She saw three dragons gathering below her. One stood on its hind legs, trying to close the distance between its fangs and her feet.

Gilgamesh felt his grip loosening. His fingers sweated and grew slippery around her arm. "Do you understand, Priestess Shamhat?"

"*Yes! Yes!*"

Gilgamesh struggled with a perverse desire to continue holding her over the edge, his fingers slipping more and more, until she fell to certain gruesome death. He often liked watching the creatures feed; boars were the preferred offering, their hind legs cut so they couldn't run. The dragons hunted with chilling determination.

His fingers slipped.

Shamhat dropped away, screaming, when his other hand closed on her wrist.

"Please, My Lord!"

Gilgamesh hoisted her back to safety. Then he shoved her to the floor.

"Leave."

She dashed from the palace. He took immense satisfaction in her fear.

A moment later, Enkidu and Nedu rounded the corner. Gilgamesh was looking at the dragons which, seeing their potential meal plucked away, lazily retreated to the banks of the pool. One got too close to the lead male. Its neck darted out, teeth biting the contender's flank. Both creatures' neck-frills fanned out in brilliant displays, but the injured one, bleeding freely, backed away and slipped into the pool. The water turned slightly purplish from the leaking wound.

"Where Shamhat?"

The king turned to his friend. Before he could reply, he saw how crestfallen Enkidu looked. Deep lines furrowed Enkidu's forehead while his eyes scoured the courtyard for her.

"Ishtar summoned her," the king said. The lie wrought the desired effect; Enkidu didn't understand human religion, and so he never persisted in questioning when confronted with one of its mysteries.

Still, he scratched his chin, looking thoughtful. "Can I summon her like Ishtar does?"

Gilgamesh blinked, caught off-guard by this statement. "Well ... if you want her." He needed say nothing else; Enkidu needed no reply. The answer was plain, and Gilgamesh's heart raced, wondering how he'd resolve this conundrum.

Ninsun intervened just them, drawing Enkidu aside, asking him to walk with her. He obliged her. He always did.

Gilgamesh watched them walk off. The sight pleased him.

Tomorrow frightened him.

"Sire?" Nedu asked. "You sent for me?"

The king nodded. "Thanks for coming so speedily."

"Yes, Majesty."

"That's all for today."

CHAPTER 22
ISHTAR'S MESSAGE TO THE KING

King Gilgamesh didn't expect to see Shamhat for a very long time. He told himself this was wishful thinking; Enkidu's infatuation would summon her soon enough, and before long she'd be occupying his bed. This was an undeniable reality, one immune to his kingly influence. Gilgamesh wondered if he could distract Enkidu with other women ... before he remembered that for weeks now, his friend had stoutly refused the flagrant advances of innumerable Urukian females.

The next day, he went with his mother to preside over city council. Shamhat was there.

He couldn't believe his eyes. The slut stood as his first legal case of the day, accompanied by a full contingent of Ishtar's whores garbed in scanty costume.

"My Lord," she started nervously. "I speak for mighty Ishtar, the—"

"Then speak!"

The priestess stuttered, positively shivering in dread. "My Lord, Ishtar has a command for Her king."

"Indeed?"

"You are to go in search of the Twelfth Annunaki statue, and return it to Her."

Gilgamesh nodded. "Of course. I shall abandon my throne, and walk the Earth like some vagabond. My hands will overturn every stone while I sift amid the sowbugs for this treasure."

Ninsun smiled, pleased with these words.

"The Goddess Ishtar knows where the Twelfth statue is."

"Then have Her fetch it!"

"She has commanded that the king of Uruk—"

"I heard you," Gilgamesh said, letting none of his true rage show on his face. The line of his mouth bent up in his beard in a show of bemusement. Enkidu might be taken with this whore, and the dalliance might be unstoppable, but this kind of impudence—ordering Gilgamesh into the wilds!—took guts, to be sure.

He said, "Ishtar makes no appearance while Uruk is under siege. Not to protect the army, nor congratulate it on victory. Suddenly She deigns to shoo me away, like the Bull of Heaven swatting at a fly? Where to?"

"The Cedar Forest."

Gilgamesh's rage submerged somewhat, overtaken by superstitious dread at the mention of the fabled northern woods. Childhood memories of monsters lurking there, of ferocious bandits, capered through his thoughts. But there was something else, the stirring of a dream. Shamhat's words excited the persistent omen that to exit Uruk would invite eternal isolation.

Then his anger resurfaced, shining glassily in his eyes though he fought to keep the smirk on his lips. Legends aside, the Cedar Forest lay to the north … at the roof of Assyria and the feet of the western sea. Ishtar might as well have sent him to the stars!

Ninsun's nails dug into his shoulder. He didn't need to look to see her reaction to this ridiculous business.

For a terrible instant he wondered if his friend was betraying him in some conspiracy. The thought squirmed through his head like a rat, biting, clawing, then scampering for cover as his deeper sensibilities came storming after it. It hid, deep in his mind, and quivered there.

"Ishtar wants me to leave my throne and go to the Cedar Forest?"

"Yes, my Lord."

"She fancies herself another Dumuzi," Ninsun whispered in his ear.

The king nodded. "My thoughts precisely." To Shamhat, he said, "Just the Cedar Forest? Not an expedition to the edge of the world where I should dance on the ragged slope blindfolded, singing Ishtar's name?"

Shamhat's piety overcame her fear. "Ishtar commands this of you!"

"I don't believe you," Gilgamesh said plainly.

The priestess reeled. "I convey Her Word! You are not permitted to disbelieve!"

Gilgamesh flew from the chair at the priestess. His speed shocked all present, and even Ninsun gaped at this feral agility. He seized her by the hair and tossed her one way, then another, where the brown locks ripped and she spilled to the floor.

"Bring your goddess here and let Her command me! Only then will I be moved, you plotting whore!"

He glanced over her shoulder and saw Ishtar.

How She had gotten into the hall, no one could later remember. Part of Gilgamesh's mind wondered at the attendant priestesses who had accompanied Shamhat, how they hid their faces behind veils. So easily could Ishtar have been disguising Herself among them! Then, with sleight-of-hand like any street thief, the veil comes away while everyone is distracted …

Ishtar's wrath was plain. Gilgamesh paled.

"*I* command you, haughty king!"

The goddess advanced on him. He dropped to his knees, but She kept walking, past him to his throne, where She sprawled out and pointed to the scribes, officials, and guards. They all knelt in a wave of bowing heads.

"I command you to leave this city and strike deep into the Cedar Forest, to the ruins of Teshub, and find the Twelfth Statue! You wanted Me here, to hear the words from My divine lips? So you have it!"

Gilgamesh quaked. Shamhat knelt beside him.

In that space of subservience of the entire hall—indeed, the entire kingdom!—Ishtar contemplated taking control for good. The temptation was there, and Ishtars before her had indulged it from time to time. Foolish! Who wanted such headaches? Councils? The day-to-day gripes of the people? And then there was the threat of assassination and usurpation for anyone who occupied the throne. Even a goddess …

The temptation passed.

"Yes, Great Ishtar," replied Gilgamesh.

"Good."

For several minutes, Ishtar remained in the throne and laughed quietly at the utter stillness. No one looked up. No one budged, though their knees surely ached. She waited, to make Her point.

Sudden footsteps clacked on the marble. All eyes went to the sound.

Priestess Ninsun rounded the throne, staring with undisguised anger at the gathering.

"There is only one backside allowed on that throne, Goddess Ishtar," she said, walking straight to the head of the crowd. "And it is not yours. Remove yourself!"

Ishtar brought a hand to her lips, to hide her nervous swallowing. "Priestess Ninsun? You'd do well to kneel before the patron goddess of this—"

"I will not bend knee before you, or any god but Shamash!" She stopped at the head of the crowd. "Remove yourself from the throne of Uruk, unless you intend to wrest control of it. And if that be your aim, I'd remind you of the South Tower!"

Ishtar's eyes widened. The priestesses gasped.

Leaning forward with the slinky malevolence of a lioness, Ishtar scowled. "Bow your head woman!"

"I shall not!"

"*Then I shall raise the dead up to eat the living!*" Ishtar shrieked, reddening like a creature sun-burnt. "I can visit any number of plagues upon this—"

"Then *do* it!" Ninsun challenged. "Unleash graves! Bring down the Bull of Heaven! But before you do, remove your *ass* from my son's throne!"

Gilgamesh's jaw dropped.

"And you!" Ninsun cried, turning to her son. "Your father knelt before Ishtar at the New Year's Festival alone! She has no more jurisdiction here than any god has in the house of another. Stand tall!" She seized him by his beard and yanked him to his feet. The most peculiar expression of mixed furor and love swirled in her eyes.

Ishtar strode toward the insolent priestess of Shamash, so mighty was her rage. But then she saw Gilgamesh's hand drop instinctively to his hilt and she halted.

Ninsun smiled at this hesitation. She made sure Ishtar saw it.

Mind racing, Ishtar said, "You want a divine spat, acolyte? Then let us dismiss these mortals! Begone!"

Figures rose on trembling knees. At that same instant, Enkidu entered the hall and froze, seeing Shamhat, the goddess, and the terrible paralysis ... the palpable dread in the room.

"Only my son can command the bodies of Uruk!" Ninsun yelled.

"Only *I* can command their souls!"

"*Then command them after they're dead!*" Ninsun hissed. Her face was so red that, by contrast, her silver hair looked truly metallic. "Lord Gilgamesh? What is *your* will?"

Gilgamesh felt the power streaming from his mother. In that instant he would not have been surprised to see the blinding face of Shamash Himself pour from her fingertips, eyes, and mouth and lay waste to all present. What have I ever done that can compare to this? he mused. Physically overpower bandits? Defeat Agga through guile and a show of clever strength? But stand up to a goddess? My mother wouldn't last a second on the battlefield armed with weapons ... but *this*, here, is what true strength is all about!

Gilgamesh swallowed and deepened his voice. "Be gone. All of you!"

The crowd departed with the silence of the walking dead. Enkidu let them walk past him, but he dared not move. Though his body was shaved of the reddish pelt which once covered him, he could feel his skin turn to gooseflesh, every sense attuned to the danger of the moment.

Ishtar stared at Ninsun as if to melt her. "You have damned yourself, woman! You think Shamash can match the wrath of Ishtar?"

Ninsun circled her, while Ishtar turned to match it. Suddenly, they were circling each other.

"Does the goddess Ishtar bleed if cut?"

Ishtar's eyes blazed. "You threaten Me, woman?!"

"I pose a question ... one that shouldn't trouble a *real* goddess!"

"And where is your beloved Shamash?"

Ninsun laughed. She pointed to the high windows, to the bright point of light in the sky.

"There my god is! You can see Him! Feel His warmth! Watch the trees and flowers drink in His radiant gift! See how He defies the night. What of yours, Ishtar? Where are your powers, if not between the legs of your priestesses?"

Shamhat's hand went to the jeweled dagger she kept in her robe. Gilgamesh saw the movement, and as Shamhat drew the weapon to slice Ninsun's throat Gilgamesh leapt at her with his fists like mallets—

"Stop!" Ishtar cried.

The king's hand came down on Shamhat's wrist, knocking the dagger with bone-cracking force. Shamhat coughed and the blood left her face. She twirled, clutching her shattered wrist, and rushed for Ishtar's protective embrace.

The goddess channeled all her anguish, fear, and rage into the only action she could take. As Shamhat drew near, Ishtar bellowed and savaged her face with a gold-nailed claw. The vision in Shamhat's left eye turned blistering white. She spun away, howling and grabbing the eye which now dribbled messily over her face, the juices splattered.

"You act without your goddess' command!" Ishtar yelled, to be heard over the din of screams. Shamhat fell pitifully to the floor, her tunic spooling around her like the petals of wilted flowers. She bowed her head to the floor, sobbing.

Enkidu gaped at the scene, his heart driven to protect the girl and yet knowing plainly that she had tried to attack Gilgamesh's mother.

Ishtar glared at Gilgamesh and his mother. She knew she had gone too far, and now her favorite priestess was suffering. The situation could still get worse; she dismissed all doubt that Gilgamesh would lop her head from its shoulders if she threatened his mother again. But how to resolve it?

"There will be a penance for this Gilgamesh," she tried.

As soon as the words left her throat, she realized her mistake. He took two steps toward her, eyes dangerously wild. "If one of Your priestesses ever threatens my mother, or my friend, or myself again, I shall—"

Ninsun spoke swiftly. "My lord! Enough!"

Ishtar held his stare. She switched to look at Ninsun. Shamhat continued to sob.

"This palace is yours, your mother has spoken truly. And you are a powerful king to stand up for it. I needed to test you." She forced a smile. "I needed to see if King Gilgamesh can do more than slay a few bandits on the road, or use his pet to thwart a war!"

The king blinked.

Ishtar's smile deepened as she saw her words finding their mark. She neared him and placed her hand on his neck. "You are mightier than your father and the kings before him. Truly divine, and with a mother of courage to earn her a special place in the heavens!" She saw the old woman's lips stir to reply, and so she added quickly, "But you Shamhat!" She spun around and looked at the miserable creature wailing at her feet. "You disobeyed your goddess! If the gods ever strike at Mighty Gilgamesh, it is for *them* to decide! Not you!"

Ishtar swallowed, feeling weak and dizzy. Forcing the act, she added, "Rise!"

If she disobeys, I'm through.

Shamhat stood on shivering legs.

"Fetch the dagger you drew!"

Tears spilled from her remaining eye. Still covering her injury, Shamhat scanned for the weapon. She stooped, grabbed it.

"Now cut your own throat."

A soft cry escaped Shamhat's mouth, but she put the blade to her neck and pressed.

"*No!*"

The voice echoed through the chamber. Enkidu stood, wide-eyed and appalled. Ishtar was taken aback by the nearness of the creature. His arms bulged, his jaw hung open and terror burned white in his face.

Torn between reestablishing her authority through ordering her compliant priestess, and the undeniable fact that she did *not* want Shamhat to die, Ishtar commanded the girl to wait.

Shamhat froze, glassy-eyed, the skin of her throat beginning to separate around the knife-edge.

Enkidu bounded forward. "No kill." Seeing Ishtar, he knelt. "Please."

Bless you, ape.

Ishtar looked testily to Gilgamesh. "I leave the decision to our king. After all, My disciple tried to attack his mother. He need only command her to die."

Gilgamesh regarded the priestess. Her single eye burned with the desperate apology of a woman hanging by life's final thread.

Kill yourself, Gilgamesh thought. His lips quivered in his beard.

"Or," Ishtar slyly interjected, "You could allow Me to punish her."

Enkidu looked plainly on his friend. Gilgamesh did not need to see the expression there. He understood what he must do.

"Punish her, but … let her live."

Ishtar snarled to Shamhat, who hobbled to her like a deformed wretch. They exited the chamber with the goddess glancing back only once to see, unquestionably, that Ninsun hadn't bought a word of it.

CHAPTER 23
A SECRET NIGHT VISIT

For the rest of the day, Enkidu was uncontainable. He paced in the hallway while Gilgamesh tried to calm him. Continually, his simian brow clouded with terrible frustration and he shouted into his friend's face, spit flying, "Why She do that? Why?"

For Gilgamesh, real fear was coursing through his veins. He didn't even have time to dwell on this divine command to go north; he was too concerned that his friend would do something really rash. He tried to offer Enkidu some wine, promising it would calm his spirits, to which Enkidu vigorously declined. "Why I want calm spirits? My anger is good! It help me make changes!"

It took more than two hours of debate and discussion for Gilgamesh to convince his friend to retire to his bedchamber and try to sleep. The king was exhausted by this ordeal; he had never seen his friend act like this.

"Make sure he stays here," Gilgamesh told the two guards he summoned to watch Enkidu's door, but he realized that if Enkidu did emerge from his bedroom, there wasn't a damn thing two or twenty guards could do to stop him.

In this, he was more right than he knew. At sundown, Enkidu didn't even bother with the door; he climbed out his room's window and stole quietly across the palace rooftop.

The stars on his back, Enkidu made straight for the ziggurat. From the palace rooftop he clambered down to the perimeter wall where guards were playing some game with wooden pieces on a board of slits and slots. It was easy to avoid them; the path to the palace was lined with palm trees and he simply went from one to the next, then bounded straight over the bronze gate and was out in the street. At the late hour, few people were about. Enkidu was able to walk straight to the ziggurat in twenty minutes.

From its bottom step, he bounded up, several stairs at a time, passing the first landing, then the second, and finally, keeping as flat as he could, he reached the third and uppermost tier where the little temple stood and incense smoked from bronze tripods.

At the entrance, Enkidu crouched and sniffed the air. There was no doubt what went on in here. Beneath the blanket of perfume and oils, the scent of sex was omnipresent. Enkidu saw shadows move in the temple doorway, and he leapt straight to the top of the temple as two men emerged, laughing crudely, and descended the ziggurat steps. One of them turned back and sang some indecipherable praise to the priestesses, and then went on his drunken way.

Enkidu watched them go. Then he closed his eyes. His sensitive ears pried into the temple, feeling out every noise like the trunk of an elephant. He could hear better than most could see in those smoky carnal chambers. And since living with the humans, the sounds weren't so alien and terrifying anymore. He could identify the sounds of goblets thrust into wine fountains, necklaces jingling as they were unclasped, the moans of throaty women, the vocal climaxes of men, the gathering of plates and knives from where they'd been carelessly thrown for washing.

An hour passed, then another. The temple grew quieter, and Enkidu drew himself down from the roof and snuck inside.

He smelled for Shamhat.

It took a few minutes, during which he prowled through the main room. Once, two bare-breasted priestesses walked past while he hid behind the fish-scaled wine fountain. Enkidu smelled them ... one was freshly post-coitus, the other menstruating. He had only known two females in his *lahmu* tribe, including his mother. The sacred blood-flow was a trait of theirs as well.

But everything with humans was exaggerated! They required food; so they dressed their eatables in exotic fashions. Clothing for their smooth hairless bodies? They wove gold threads and patterns like reptile skin into the cloth. Shelter? They built immense constructions of stone, large enough to swallow mountains. And sex? Enkidu himself was a stranger to it, aside from witnessing foxes and rabbits and lions copulating. Who knew what level of spice or dress humans used to enhance the rutting of their species?

Abruptly he caught Shamhat's scent. He dashed to the nearest corridor and found it again, stronger now, like a visible trail down the brick hallway. It was a narrow passageway. There would be no hiding if more priestesses came upon him ... but Enkidu went onward, sensing that these creatures were retiring for the night.

The halls were surprisingly drafty. Though ignorant of architecture, he nonetheless felt there should be no draft here. How could wind move so freely in these tight corridors that twisted this way and that? Enkidu's tribe had taken refuge in caves before, where the wind only bothered them if there was another exit deeper in the cavern. The ziggurat interior was so windy that it seemed there *must* be another exit somewhere, though Enkidu couldn't see one.

And there was a lurking stench here, too. Subtle, as if coming off the walls. It was the unmistakable musk of an animal.

Enkidu had never smelled anything like it. This unsettled him. He knew all the creatures of the world. This musk was bull-like, perhaps, yet more ancient and sinister. There was venom and rage in it, caged frustration, dried feces, rotten meat. What were the Ishtar priestesses keeping down here? Though he couldn't identify the musk, something stirred in his mind ... older, unknown memories of his ancestors. He couldn't tap their collected knowledge. There was simply a jabber of whispers and images. Like two quick lightning strobes. He fancied a large, four-footed snorting monster charging about a misty forest while tiny horses fled from it ... but then the image was gone. Enkidu wished the gnarly faced Elder was alive to make sense of such buried secrets. The Elder was best at explaining these mnemic moments.

Enkidu forced himself to press on. Shamhat's scent grew deeper.

She was crying.

He could hear her whispered distress below him. There were stairs and he plunged down them. The stonework was cold against his bare feet.

He came to a series of doors and knew immediately which one belonged to Shamhat. The bull-musk was very strong down here too. In some strangely unaccountable way it made him think of Gilgamesh.

"General Enkidu?" Shamhat cried, seeing him enter her room. She lowered a rag from her eyeless socket in surprise.

"Shamhat!" he whispered, coming to her. Before he realized what he was doing, he had scooped her up in his arms.

She struggled violently, and he was just thinking he had made some terrible mistake in human etiquette when suddenly he felt her kisses on his neck. Frantic, fierce.

Enkidu's body responded. He suddenly forgot about why he had come here. Was it to see if she was okay? To make certain she wasn't being tormented by Ishtar? To kidnap her? Suddenly he was kissing her. Her gown was sliding off her bare shoulders. She was naked beneath his pawing hands.

And he undressed himself, with atypical meticulousness. The kilt came away, the bracelets from his wrists, the sash over his shoulder, the tunic from his barrel-like chest. These items he piled delicately on the floor. He looked at Shamhat and seemed to breathe for the first time.

Enkidu had never copulated. The action came naturally enough. In the yellow light of an oil lantern, he explored her body with childlike fascination. Her bones were so delicate beneath this drapery of honey-brown flesh! He watched his hands sliding with the gentlest care to cup her hill-like breasts. Her pulse squirmed in her neck and he kissed that place of life. Enkidu smelled her aroma and was dizzy in its lofty fragrance.

I am human.

The thought came unbidden as he pressed his tool against her portals and slid in the first inch. Deeper he pushed, withdrawing, pushing again, until he discovered a steady rhythm that maximized the pleasure. Shamhat ground against him, smiling happily, the rag entirely gone from her bloody socket, that eye trying to close over the wound.

I am human, he thought again. Then came another epiphany, while Shamhat wrapped her arms and legs around him so tightly that he couldn't retreat if he wanted to ... and the pleasure was so intense and magical that nothing could make him:

I want to be human.

In months past he had rested an ear against Gilgamesh's door while the king bedded two, three, sometimes four women at once. He had chuckled in those furtive moments. My friend is a caged bull! he'd thought. But he's also human.

Memories of his forest hunts and chases, of pine-sweet earth, river-stones, rains and floods, of hiding in trees, of sweet adrenaline mounted, grew in power, until his eyes seemed to glow with it. When he climaxed, he couldn't suppress a cry of pleasure himself.

Fear took him then; he worried that Ishtar would awaken to find him here.

And if She does, I'll kill Her.

The orgasmic spasms were fading gently. Enkidu understood that he was now human, but so was Ishtar. She was no magical creature. In that council chamber, he had smelled Her … and it was a fleshy scent. Would a goddess possess the stink of mortality?

"My sweet Enkidu," Shamhat sang gently.

He stroked her back, marveling at how his hand had changed. Gone were the dirty nails, chipped and broken. His hand was pinkish and smooth as the creature he touched. It was like a hand belonging to someone else.

Shamhat murmured pleasantly and buried her face in his chest. Enkidu watched this, feeling wanted like never before. His pride swelled, and with it a gradual cynicism.

She had tried to kill Gilgamesh's mother.

His mind wanted to uncover some excuse. The best it could manage was that the Goddess Ishtar had commanded it … but this didn't work. Ishtar had been furious at Shamhat for that action. Thus, Shamhat had done it on her own.

Enkidu stroked her hair until she fell asleep. Then he left the chamber, the hall, the temple, and walked down the ziggurat steps a changed being. He felt he belonged more than ever to the city.

When he looked to the woods over the wall, a chilling certainty that he was now unwelcome there filled his heart.

He knocked on Gilgamesh's door.

Gilgamesh opened it at once. He was still fully dressed and looked edgy.

"We talk," Enkidu said, letting himself into the room.

Gilgamesh moved aside and closed the door. "What do you want to—"

"What Ishtar say to you?"

The king considered what was being asked. "She wants me to go north to the Cedar Forest. A magical statue is there. She wants it."

"And if we do this?"

Gilgamesh sighed. "Ishtar will be pleased."

"What is Cedar Forest?"

"A legendary woodland north of the Euphrates with trees as old as time."

Enkidu felt a creeping fear descend on him, and his scalp bristled as if by a cold wind. North? That was where he'd lost his family, and north was now a place of tombs for him. And something else, too … an old fear, chanted by red firelight by the Tribe Elder. "North forest?"

Gilgamesh nodded.

"What is cedar?"

"The gazebo near the canal is made out of cedar. A very distinctive look and smell. The Cedar Forest is called that because it's filled ..." Gilgamesh trailed off, as in the midst of his explanation he saw Enkidu turning away and walking to the other side of the lavish bedchamber.

"Enkidu!"

Enkidu glanced back with hooded eyes. "My friend, do not speak of this place."

"You said you were from the north," Gilgamesh said, crossing the distance to him. "Do you know this place, where cedar grows?"

"Humbaba is there."

"Humbaba?" Gilgamesh stopped at the word, astonished to hear it from his friend's lips. "I've never spoken that word around you. Where did you hear it?"

"Enkidu know Humbaba."

"But where did you hear the word?" When Enkidu didn't respond, Gilgamesh pressed him until it dawned on him that Enkidu was not talking about the *word* Humbaba.

"You mean Humbaba himself? You mean the *real* Humbaba?"

When Enkidu had first been captured, there had been fear in his eyes as the hunters' bag came away. The sight of Agga's army had summoned trepidation as well. But now, the king saw an unutterable terror deeper than ocean or stars. The emotion was absolute, a dark scream in his eyes. He shivered, and this shivering passed to the king.

"Enkidu!" he persisted. "Are you telling me that there really is a Humbaba?"

The stories emerged from his childhood memory. Out in the great northern woods lurked an undying beast who fed on the bones of men. His flesh was the strongest armor, immune to any sword-stroke. The old stories told of how brave and forgotten warriors had gone into the woods to destroy Humbaba, and how only one or two had escaped. The detail Gilgamesh remembered best was how the survivors had gone into the Cedar Forest as young men but emerged with hair stricken white. They muttered only about Humbaba's divine weapons, and how no sword could hack through his flesh. And his *voice* ...

Why was Enkidu's word for the creature the same as in Sumerian? Was it more than a word, then, altogether? Was it truly the creature's name?

"Enkidu," he grabbed Enkidu's arm, and his friend pulled away sharply and growled in challenge, so that Gilgamesh recoiled, hands up defensively. "Tell me about Humbaba. Please!"

With lowered head, Enkidu spoke of what he knew. Men avoided the Cedar Forest; this naturally endeared it to the *lahmu* tribe. But there was a musk on the trees, lingering in the air like rotten meat and dank fur, like moldy skulls found in forgotten corners. The Elder told tales of the Guardian of the Forest, how once the hills and mountains had crawled with others like it, but now there was only one, the progeny of rage and time, a terrible monster who claimed the entire woods as his lair.

The Elder had advised against going into the forest, despite the refuge it offered from humanity. *Any one of us, even myself, is capable of warding off two or three humans,* he had said. *Enkidu here could take ten! But twenty lahmu wouldn't dare move against Humbaba. He is not merely strong. He is insane. He lurks in a green cave, hating everything that lives. He dreams of a world filled with bones.*

But one day human hunters had picked up the trail of his tribe. Thirty humans on horseback, armed and angry, perhaps mistaking the *lahmu* trail for enemy tracks. The tribe needed to escape into the wilderness. They needed to brave Humbaba's forest.

It was decided that if Humbaba appeared, one of them would sacrifice himself so the tribe could escape. Enkidu himself volunteered. They crept quietly, barely rustling a grass blade. They took measured breaths, and cupped delicately from the river to drink. Humbaba might hear them, but might think them foxes or smaller creature hardly worth his time.

That first night, they camped high in the trees, huddling together like sacks nestled in branches. They kept watch for the terror.

It was during Enkidu's mother's watch that Humbaba came. She awakened her son with forceful prods, and he stared down the tree in time to see a massive black shape pass just below his feet. The air stank of it. The ground grumbled beneath mountainous weight. Enkidu had clutched his mother's hand and the tree bark, wondering how to wake the others where they slept in adjacent trees. Quiet, his mother said to him. Enkidu waited.

Humbaba's feet splashed into a small stream, and he stretched to a godlike height, his bestial head craned to watch the cliff-tops. The size of the monster was extraordinary. There was only the thinnest sliver of moonlight that night, fractured among the many branches. Such darkness may have saved the tribe's life. Enkidu still remembered the awful silhouette as Humbaba appeared to study the cliffs …

Then the monster roared. Enkidu felt his hair stand up all over his body. The air vibrated as if a waterfall were bursting from the cliffs, or as a storm might sunder the firmament. It was the loudest sound he had ever heard. A trumpeting blast of helpless rage turning Enkidu's muscle to stone. His ears throbbed, his heart alone moving with painful horror.

Then Humbaba was running back into the forest. Trees snapped as went. His shoulders clipped the tree on which the Elder slumbered and the bark tore whitely. Humbaba ran onward, vanishing with savage cacophony. It was as if the forest and cliffs had become his enemy, and he was battling against them, tearing apart the woods with his claws, roaring once more.

Enkidu vomited down the tree. Then he clambered down, helping his mother and the entire tribe (woken the instant of the roar) and they braved the climbing of cliffs to get out of his woods.

What had inspired Humbaba's late-night patrol along the borders of his deciduous kingdom? Enkidu didn't know. Maybe like lions he was simply marking the trees, or calling out to the unforgotten dead, or challenging the new masters of the world.

Gilgamesh was silent as a scolded child, sitting now, his arms on his knees. Enkidu also crouched, because his legs wouldn't hold him; the memory of that night made them weak. If Humbaba had glanced up and seen Enkidu's dangling foot …

He shuddered.

"He's not a man, then." Gilgamesh's initial conception, of some isolated warrior, or even a group of outcasts lurking in the woods to perpetuate Humbaba's myth, evaporated like rainwater on hot metal.

Enkidu shook his head vigorously.

"Not *lahmu*, either."

Enkidu shook his head.

"And his roar? It actually paralyzed you? How is that possible?"

"It is the flood-weapon."

Gilgamesh was stricken mute at that reply. Again, the same phraseology. It couldn't be a coincidence, for people up and down the Fertile Crescent told these same details of the legendary monster.

"What is the flood-weapon?"

Enkidu shivered, and to Gilgamesh's wondering eyes the hairs along Enkidu's neck stood out like porcupine spines. "It is the voice of Humbaba. If Gilgamesh heard voice, Gilgamesh could not move. Then, Humbaba get you. Kill you."

"What do you mean, could not mo—"

"Eat you."

The rest of Gilgamesh's words stuck in his throat like sand. "Eat … He feasts on human flesh?"

"All flesh of everything that walks, slithers, or climbs. Humbaba is hunter."

"But how does his voice prevent you from moving?"

Enkidu mulled that over, and again his hair stood rigid with fear. Three times he started to say something, only to give up. Finally, he muttered, "Enkidu can't explain."

Where did the legend enmesh with the facts?

The king stared at his friend. A slow smile formed at the corners of his mouth to bristle his beard.

Enkidu frowned. "What, my friend?"

"We're going north to find this statue for Ishtar ... and to kill Humbaba."

"No."

"Yes ..." Gilgamesh panted suddenly, seeing the glory that had eluded him so far. People sang songs of his father's adventures, of Enmerkar's triumph, up and down the Fertile Crescent, men were distinguished by immortal names which immortal deeds could be attached to. But what had he done? Build a wall? Defeated a Kishian warlord? Men had done such things before. No one had ever quested for the head of Humbaba the Terrible. At least, none had lived.

"Listen," he explained excitedly, and Enkidu could see plainly that there would be no way of talking the king out of it.

CHAPTER 24
PREPARATIONS

Ninsun's reaction was dangerously violent. She flew up from her chair, eyes wild, her hands contorted into claws meant for Ishtar's throat.

"I don't care about blasphemy! That bitch won't send my son away on some suicidal quest! Her star shines so brightly? Let her channel a ray of starlight onto the Annunaki! Let her dip down from heaven and snatch it! This reeks of treason!"

Gilgamesh and Enkidu stood side by side like scolded children. The king waited patiently for his turn to speak. The more Ninsun ranted, the dimmer that chance seemed.

"She wants to get you away so she'll move against the throne! Many people support Ishtar! Even among the military! She could rile them up into a crowd and stand at its head, her and her whores! They'll take the palace by force! One night, all of a sudden, Ishtar's dainty ass is in your throne again! Then she'll move against the council! Ibi-Sin will be the first to die. Then she'll send word that Lord Gilgamesh is out in the wilderness. Oh! I wonder how Agga will react to that news? Any city, petty warlord, hunter, would love to have *you* to ransom! Do you know where the Cedar Forest is? Between Hittite Anatolia and *Assyria!* Two of the most wretched peoples on Earth!"

She stopped to catch her breath, flush from face to neck. The wrinkles on her neck looked like blood-red gills.

Enkidu sighed. "Ninsun angry?"

She spun around. "Yes, Enkidu! Ninsun is very very *very* angry! This is madness!"

He looked at Gilgamesh. "You not go, your mother not angry."

Gilgamesh tugged anxiously on the end of his beard. "Mother, have you ever heard of the two bards who rescued a dog from a trap?"

Ninsun stared at him.

"What about the farmer who told Enmerkar the best pass to reach Aratta? Remember his name?"

Ninsun sighed forcibly, white spit flying from her lips.

"No one remembers these people because they worked in the mundane. If Enkidu and I kill Humbaba—"

"You're taking Enkidu with you, then?"

"And retrieve the Twelfth Annunaki, future kings will remember us for thousands of years. They'll commission songs about our deeds, mother!"

"You're a king of Uruk," she said bitterly, seeing plainly that his mind was made up. Enkidu would do whatever Gilgamesh wanted; she could see that too. "That alone will get you fame!"

"It isn't enough. The souls who walk the Fire Road to Ereshkigal burn up! Like wood tossed into fire! No one remembers what they loved, hoped, or feared! If they built roads or towers! I will not fall into oblivion! I refuse to be a shade hovering mutely in the afterlife! It isn't Humbaba I hate! Or even Agga of Kish! It's Ereshkigal! It's the hand of death that steals everything from us. They say that to the west, Pharaoh Khufu is building a pyramid to the stars. Why do you think? Because long after he and his family line are extinct, future generations will visit Egypt and see what he built, they'll see his name on a placard, and they'll say, 'Khufu built this.'"

"They'll say the same about Uruk's walls!"

"I want more than that! I didn't build these walls, mother! Just as Khufu didn't set the blocks of his tomb with his own hands. The men of Uruk did, like the men of Egypt. But Gilgamesh the king will sever that monster's head from his neck! I will kill Humbaba. I will bring that skull back to hang in the palace. And I will find the statue—"

"How? The Cedar Forest covers an immense area. They go as high as Hattusas and as wide to Nineveh." Ninsun strode to the windows and tore the drapes from their hangings, where the ziggurat stood like a black pyramid. She glared at the crowning temple as if to challenge Ishtar to a contest of sorcery.

Gilgamesh cursed and paced once through the room. "This command comes from Ishtar Herself. If Shamash had assigned me this task, would you be so quick to scorn it?"

Ninsun balked at this religious rebuke. "This would take you months, Gilgamesh, and would put you and all who accompanied you into horrific perils."

"Of which I'm sure you'll list them for me."

"I will do just that. Start with Kish. If word reached them that King Gilgamesh had fled the security of his walls and his ferocious *lahmu* army, do you think Agga would shrug and say, 'Good hunting, fair Gilgamesh'? He would dispatch troops to find you, or perhaps put out a price on your head while he sends his army back to Uruk, only this time, there shall be no Gilgamesh and Enkidu to defend it." She stopped, drummed his fingers on the wall, and asked, "You will be traveling by boat, I presume, for at least part of the way?"

Gilgamesh nodded.

"Then you should know that up north, where the splinter river Habur breaks away from the Euphrates, there are pirates to be found there. Uruk does not have many vessels, and even if we could boast a fleet like the Harappans, you would still need to travel quietly, with only one vessel so not to bring attention to yourself. Madness!" Ninsun shook her head in anguish.

Nedu appeared in the doorway. Gilgamesh waved him in.

"Come in, Councilman."

"You are throwing yourself onto the path of demons!" Ninsun screamed as a last effort. "You might as well take Enkidu with you on a visit to the underworld and ask the Gatekeepers for admittance to see your father!"

It was too much now, these stinging words from his mother. Gilgamesh's face reddened and he declared with all the confidence he had ever felt, "I *will* return alive! I can kill this beast and rid the world of him!" He hesitated, grinned, and added, "Make whatever sacrifices you need to. When I return I'll marry."

The altar stones of Marduk and Shamash ran deep with the gore of goats, bulls, and lambs, each tethered and massacred by swiftly working priests and priestesses over the next three days. Gilgamesh himself took part in the Marduk offering, supplanting the head priest to kill the bull they had prepared. He peered into the crimson pool beneath the lifeless animal and considered his own reflection.

Councilman Nedu, having lost the battle to dissuade his king from the task ahead, slipped easily into his role as organizer of the expedition. He rushed about like an old stork, first to the armory, then to the palace's storage vaults, onward to the shipyard, while stopping at a dozen temples along the way to instruct them all on more sacrifices. To what end? the orders asked, to which he replied evasively: The health and success of the king! Gilgamesh's departure needed to be secret.

Weapons were gathered, shields like tortoise shells, armor like the slough-off of a metallic snake. Enkidu awoke to the clatter, slipped on a robe and went out to investigate. When he reached the council room door, he pressed his ear against the wood. In that instant the door swung open, Nedu saw him, and pulled him inside.

"Good morning General," Nedu panted. "Have you ever used a sword before?"

Enkidu gaped at the arrangements going on behind the old man. "No." Armor, swords and shields were being arranged like little meals. Twenty, thirty, forty settings!

The councilman took Enkidu by the arm. "You must learn now," he said, and standing aside, Enkidu saw Ibi-Sin holding a weapon, grinning at him.

"A sword, a shield," the military advisor said, thrusting the items into Enkidu's hands. "Your appearance may have stunned Agga, but I doubt it'll work on Humbaba! Defend yourself!"

Twelve.

Twelve was the sacred number for all of Sumer. There were Twelve Tablets of Destiny seized by the monster Anzu and rescued by Ninurta. The Annunaki statues were twelve in number, as were the celestial bodies in the heavens—ten planets and the sun and moon.

The "hunting party" would consist of forty-eight people broken into four divisions of twelve. Gilgamesh himself combed through the barracks and selected forty-four of them. Each brick chamber he entered, the commanding officer bowed low and called out the soldiers. The king's heart swelled with affection, recalling the day of Agga's defeat and the way all soldiers had celebrated with their king. So he now paced up and down their ranks calling many by name, joking with them, inquiring on the health of their wives and children. The ones he selected were told they would be guarding a special caravan.

The soldiers looked at each other. Rumor had been circulating that marriage overtures to Babylon had been made. Perhaps a wife (and soon queen) had been selected and was coming to Uruk for the ceremony! Perhaps it was *her* caravan they'd be guarding!

Forty-four soldiers full of gossip reported to the palace. In the council-room, they met Nedu and were told the truth.

The king and Enkidu would comprise numbers forty-five and forty-six. From the barracks, Gilgamesh went next to an unassuming home in the hunters' square.

"He is my only son," the hunter Gizzida explained.

"How does that matter? His life with you has been meager, and when you die he'll inherit the same difficulties ... multiplied with a family of his own." The king looked to the young boy who stood watching them eagerly from the doorway. "Is there a lovely lady betrothed to you, boy?"

Gudea shook his head. There was a girl his age at the market. She was pretty and lithe, and her eyes often rested on Gudea when he stood with his father selling meats and furs. He liked her enough to conjure her in recent dreams.

At the table, Gilgamesh turned back to Gizzida. "Ishtar Herself, *in person*, commanded this quest. All who accompany me are guaranteed immortality. For those who survive, they will receive honors, gifts, and a place within the palace grounds. Your boy will be elevated to lesser noble. The laws he has lived by will be thrown aside, for those of a higher station."

Gizzida nodded weakly and rested his chin on his folded hands. There was no refusing the king, nor denying the benefits to his child should the expedition be successful.

For a terrible instant, the old man went back in time. Gudea was a troublesome six-year-old, denied dinner for knocking over the neighbors flowerpots *again*. His mother was alive, an olive-skinned woman named Nidaba, scrubbing the pots they'd used for dinner while he skinned the animals for drying. Oh! he was younger then. No aching joints, no wrinkly face battered by hardship and hard work. Not so long ago he'd been ... *everything* had been ... different.

"And if he dies out there?" Gizzida heard himself ask.

The king's heart swelled with sudden pity. "He will receive fame in death. You will be taken care of for the rest of your days."

No, the father thought. If my son dies then I'll follow him *at once*. I'll skewer my heart with a dagger to join my boy in the land of shades.

"This house," Gizzida said, "Would be honored to send forth brave Gudea in company of the king."

He saw his son smiling broadly, cheeks flushed and eyes bright. Gilgamesh rose.

"You are now part of the hunt," the king told Gudea, unbearably pleased.

For the final member of the group, the king went to his wrestling trainer Gimil-Sin. He found him at home, on Uruk's upper tier in view of the South

Tower. As always, the trainer was bare-chested, dressed in sandals and a kilt, enjoying the sun that had darkened his skin to a smoked-oak appearance. Gilgamesh wondered if he ever wore a top.

"I want you to accompany us on our quest."

Gimil-Sin touched his own sweaty chest. "Quest?"

"To the Cedar Forest."

"What's there besides cedar?"

"Immortality."

"But I don't want it."

"We're going to kill a monster."

"Ah."

"And retrieve a sacred statue for Ishtar."

Gimil-Sin chewed his lip, considering this. "Of course."

"This isn't the time for jokes."

"No?" Gimil-Sin slapped his belly and asked, "Have you ever thought of conquering all of Sumer?"

Gilgamesh's face tightened. "Are you trying to anger me this morning?"

"Am I succeeding?" Before the king could reply—and an incendiary reply it would be, the trainer knew immediately, he continued, "My Lord, since your defeat of Kish this entire region is in awe of you. We could spread our hands and capture all territories to the south without a fight. Just send emissaries, richly dressed as a Babylonian whore, with large retinues and some soldiers for good measure. Urukian influence will reach the Mouth of the Rivers."

Gilgamesh felt his good humor slipping. "Are you willfully ignoring my invitation?"

"You mean you *weren't* speaking in metaphors?" The trainer gave a wry grin and feigned surprise. "When you said we were going after a monster, I just assumed you meant Sumer and all her Cities. That would be the most *reasonable* thing, sire. Just think! Your crown bends the knees of multiple Cities, and Uruk's name is applied to an empire! A single pharaoh claims all of Egypt! Why not do the same?"

"We are going north to kill Humbaba."

"I see."

"And we'll bring back his head to mount in the palace."

"Can we capture some Anzu birds too? I've always wanted one to ride. It would be much more convenient than *walking* everywhere!"

Gilgamesh went silent. He didn't move, but the trainer suddenly perceived his outrage. Gimil-Sin's wry humor evaporated; suddenly he was on his knees, begging forgiveness.

"Stand up!" Gilgamesh gave an exasperated sigh.

Gimil-Sin obliged. His fat cheeks quivered sadly.

"Will you come or no?"

"Of course sire. I would accompany you to the edge of the world. But I should tell you ... I mean, you should know ..."

"Say it!"

"The chance that Humbaba exists is about equal to you ever beating me in a wrestling match."

"Might you have said the same about a *lahmu*?"

Gimil-Sin slapped his fat belly again. "I might have said that a king like yourself should capitalize on success and extend his influence. Humbaba doesn't scare me. Hittites do. Piss-drinking Assyrians do!" He laughed and spat over his wall, where a warm gust snatched the spittle and stole it away. "One day those corpse-eaters will invade us. You can deal them a crippling blow if your fist comes on the muscle of an entire region, and not just one City."

Gilgamesh wiped a light spread of sweat from his brow. His cheeks were burning, partly from anger at Gimil-Sin's impudence ... and partly from the ambition his words fueled. Like kindling, he envisioned this would-be conquest. Yes! It could be done! Ibi-Sin had already hinted at as much. Gilgamesh suddenly gazed beyond his trainer to the South Tower where Dumuzi had died—Dumuzi, who had once been his father's Military Advisor—and whose ambition blazed the trail to corruption and usurpation. Ibi-Sin had been instrumental in defeating Kish; but now, like Gimil-Sin, he desired more. All of the Crescent. Then Hattusha? Egypt? Harappa? The whole world?

Gilgamesh's smile, faltering into extinguishment, suddenly re-ignited. Yes! his heart cried. To go north and kill Humbaba would certainly be written into legend for a thousand years, but *to rule the Earth?* Never had any mortal wielded such power.

But no, the gods would never allow such a thing. Their tolerance for mankind's ambition surely had limits, and to see a king claim the world as his throne would bring punishments like another Flood.

So we'll build boats, Gilgamesh thought.

The wrestler read the king's thoughts as if they'd been pressed and baked into wet clay. He debated a further push; for all his playful demeanor, Gimil-Sin had thirsted for universal roads connecting all Cities ever since Agga fled like a mutilated puppy. The dream of being able to leave one's home and just walk, past boundary stones, into other lands for new wrestling opponents, strange foods and good brew, was so natural as to be inevitable. Why shouldn't Gilgamesh be the one to make it possible?

He watched Gilgamesh's face. He decided to let the idea simmer. "When do we leave to kill the monster, sire?"

"Two days. We're getting a statue for Ishtar as well."

"Ah. I guess that other group failed, then."

Gilgamesh frowned. "What other group?"

"For about two months now, I've been hearing about some group of mercenaries from Uruk who went north to fetch some treasure for Ishtar."

Panic whirled inexplicably in the king's heart. "Are you saying we're not the first people assigned to this? That's an insult. I demand you retract it."

"My humble apologies, lord. I'm certain they were only tales."

But his words had upset Gilgamesh, and now the king wondered whether there was truth in them. Ishtar wanted all the Annunaki statues; there was only one left. After so many years the eleventh one had been returned to her, and suddenly she believed she knew where the twelfth one resided. Did each Annunaki bear a clue to the origin of its brethren? Had she told that clue to simple mercenaries ... and had they gone in search of it?

Was Humbaba munching on their bones?

CHAPTER 25
THE RIVER

Two days later they set off during the lightless hours of morning, packing their belongings onto the barge bobbing on the black Euphrates. It was a strong ship, though no larger than a wealthy merchant's float and certainly lacking the luster of a kingly vehicle. Gilgamesh had seen frescoes of Egyptian barges used to navigate their Nile River. Great Pharaoh Khufu might laugh, he thought, if he could see Great King Gilgamesh aboard such an undecorated boat.

Enkidu regarded it suspiciously, pausing before he stepped aboard.

"You don't like boats?" Gilgamesh asked him.

"They safe?"

"A lot safer than swimming in crocodile-infested waters."

Enkidu looked across the river's far bank where several black shapes lay in wait of the sun; the reptiles themselves. Giving a peculiar, low-sounding grunt that Gilgamesh was learning meant his friend was reluctantly agreeing to something, Enkidu stepped aboard the ship and took a few uncertain steps around, feeling the way the floor swayed under him.

"Ah!" Gimil-Sin cried from within. "The great Enkidu!" He clapped his arms around Enkidu in a bear-hug.

"Hello," Enkidu said.

Gimil-Sin released him and sized him up. "Are you ready for adventure?"

"Enkidu here."

The wrestler threw back his head and laughed heartily, then ducked into the inner recess of the ship. Enkidu stayed close to his friend, letting the other passengers file by him into the ship's gullet. Then came a face he recognized at once.

"General Enkidu?"

The voice and face belonged to a young boy Enkidu had last seen wielding an axe at him in his father's stables. Back then, the child had worn simple, colorless garments. Now he sported a helmet with feather-designs pressed into the front, and a bronze cuirass over leather armor, a noble kilt, and a sword and shield painted in Uruk's ochre wings.

It was only for a moment, but suddenly Enkidu felt cornered again. His memory pulsated like a living thing: the tight stable, the smell of horses, the flint axe swinging at his head, and him fighting for his life.

Gudea didn't understand what was going on in Enkidu's head; he only saw the silence and conflicted emotions. Swallowing nervously, he bowed his head and pleaded forgiveness for what had transpired those months ago.

"No," Enkidu said gently. He lifted the boy's head and smiled. The expression was more frightening than encouraging—all teeth bared like gleaming alabaster pylons, eyes scrunched, nostrils wide—but his touch was tender. Gudea almost cried. Since the Kishian war, he had come to love Enkidu. He went to market now as much to see the girl he liked as to hear the latest gossip of Enkidu's exploits, strength, or feats.

Gudea managed a dreadfully nervous nod. Enkidu said, "Misunderstanding. We both different back then."

The boy blushed and retreated hastily into the ship. Several minutes later they settled into the oar-galleys and the vessel pushed out into the opening sunrise.

There was a large mattress, with colorful spreads rolled tightly at its end. There were amphoras filled with fresh water, and some with beer, and still others with oils for bathing and oils for burning. There were three barrels with salted meats, flatbreads, fish. A tapestry hung on the headboard, and in vibrant hues it showed a kaleidoscope of heroes poised in the very second of their triumphs: Four-armed Marduk was cleaving the dragon Tiamat, Enmerkar oversaw the pillage of Aratta, Ninurta was battling the Anzu and retrieving the Twelve Tablets of Destiny …

That first night the men crowded the belly of the ship, chewing noisily while Gilgamesh talked of the quest. His enthusiasm was contagious. Soon the munching jaws had stopped, eyes ceased blinking, as he related the glory Humbaba's death would guarantee.

"And then there are the rewards of Ishtar," he added. "Uruk will forever be blessed, spared from ruin or famine."

"Why She want them?" Enkidu asked absently.

"It doesn't matter. Perhaps the gods are at war again, and the Annunaki represent some pivotal advantage in that contest."

"By that argument," chanced Gudea, "Wouldn't we anger Ishtar's opponents even if we please Ishtar herself?"

Gilgamesh grinned inwardly, though his lips made no movement. The boy was truly fearless. Courage knew nothing of social station.

"Ishtar is the patron of Uruk. As Her devotees we are bound to Her commands. The other gods surely understand that. If they don't ..." He flirted with blasphemy. Considered it. Gave in. "Don't forget that I am descended from the gods as well."

Gudea seemed satisfied with that; he nodded thoughtfully. Beside him Gimil-Sin looked disinterested in the whole discussion of divine favors, and seizing on the sudden quiet he asked about the Cedar Forest and Humbaba.

"We've all heard the legends," Gilgamesh replied.

"I heard a legend once of some Nubian wrestler who was the best in the world. I met him during a match in Nineveh and bent his back in three places."

Gilgamesh nudged Enkidu, who sat hugging his shaved knees. The dim lamplight made him look very human indeed, softening the more ape-like features and lingering on the hairless cheeks, arms, bare chest.

"Tell them, my friend."

Enkidu raised his eyes and watched the gathering under his accreted brows. "Humbaba not legend. He real."

"What is he, then?" Gudea asked. "A giant? A dragon?"

Gimil-Sin said, "How tall is he? What are his weapons?"

For the next several minutes the men were Enkidu's captive audience; his sparse words fueled their imaginations. When he related how the monster had bellowed at the cliffs, the man let out a collective sigh. The boat was just dark enough, and still smelled of forest enough, to stir even the most jaded listener.

Almost.

Into this silence Gimil-Sin farted loudly. Spell broken, the hunting party exploded with laughter. Even Gilgamesh cracked a smile.

"Let Humbaba deal with *that!*" the wrestler cried.

Lively discussion dominated the rest of the night until they retired to their congested bunks. Monsters were quite real to all of them. There were soldiers whose great grandfathers had passed them stories of immense, shaggy elephants or unnamed horned creatures. There were some soldiers who had been fishermen before the Urukian military draft, and they claimed to have seen sea-devils of perplexing variety: tentacled monstrosities, serpentine ribbons, entities that blew fountains from their heads or mouths, sharks larger than the king's palace, and floating blobs that could strike a man dead with one touch. Some people had traveled further than most, and talked of cockatrices, tomb-guardians, birds that could cart off elephants in their claws, serpents with the heads of women, great ogres with a single eye in their faces.

Of Humbaba, everyone had their own idea.

"The stories say his flesh can't be pierced by any mortal weapon," someone offered.

"I've heard that as well," Gilgamesh agreed. "The same was once claimed of Tiamat. Her coils filled the universe and broke all weapons thrown against them! Her scales could thwart the heaviest rocks! Yet wasn't it Marduk's blade who cleaved her body in twain?"

He was pleased with his own analogy. His patron god surely smiled upon it, and might forgive the offense of the subtle comparison between Gilgamesh and Himself. Just to be safe, the king muttered a quick prayer, asking for His aid in the fight to come.

CHAPTER 26
THE HITTITE'S CHRONICLE

Not all that is written survives.

When Gilgamesh was ten years old living under the watchful eye of Dumuzi the Usurper, a Hittite soldier quietly chronicled the northern parts of Mesopotamia.

Most scribes pressed their writing into wet clay tablets, to be baked and stored in royal libraries or legal office vaults. The Hittite had neither the materials nor desire to haul around heavy stone records. His life was one of everlasting combat and he adored it. By the time he was twenty-seven, he had killed ninety-three men, raped seventeen wives and daughters of the slain, killed eight lions during formal hunts. He drank mixed bull's blood before every battle. During a game of Senet he'd learned from the same Semite scholar who'd taught him to read and write, he once killed his brother-in-law for cheating.

The Hittite was a writer, though. He couldn't explain why he enjoyed chronicling his exploits and travels, inking the tales on leather hide he kept rolled in a small satchel. Six years worth of writing, done by campfire between battles, or at the end of revelries as his fellow warriors slept off their drunkenness. The Hittite wasn't interested in sharing his stories. He wasn't a bard, by the gods! But late at night he enjoyed unrolling the hide to reread the tales of yesteryear. The battle in which he'd killed thirty men in one night! The gold-haired slut who howled in pleasure as they rutted! The sight of a living *mushussu* dragon sunning itself on the shores of the Lesser Zab!

History wouldn't remember the Hittite. His throat was cut by thieves one night while he slept on the edge of camp. His gold, weapons, and satchel were taken. This latter item was emptied of its contents; the inked hide meant nothing to the thieves, and they sold it cheap to a woman who used it to make boots. The words were washed away by sweat, sun, and water in the years that followed, until the boots themselves were discarded.

Gilgamesh would have enjoyed the tale of those boots.

The Hittite wrote about Kish, where the Euphrates and Tigris rivers were closest. Then north to Emar and the long stretch of lonely lands, green villas and warlord kingdoms. The Hittite also knew of the Cedar Forest and the ruins of Teshub.

History would never remember Teshub's ancient empire. Local youths grew up on tales of its loot and treasure. The Hittite was just an adolescent when several members of his own village went to those ruins to search for lost gems, gold, and fame. From the cliffs above the forest, the Hittite had been charged with guarding the camp while they went. Thirty strong men and a contingent of Phoenician women just as bold.

From his hilltop camp, the Hittite heard pitiful screams, snapping trees, and the deafening roar that paralyzed him where he sat. He remembered the hellish echo, and the permanent silence, when it was all over.

It was the one story he *didn't* write in his chronicle.

Enkidu dreamed every night of the voyage.

His sleeping mind raced through gloomy forests. Sometimes in his dreams he recognized the locales; sometimes not. Certainly these latest dreams found him in unknown deciduous pockets. And there was something invigorating about these misty woods, where daylight diffused like murky water through the vapors.

He was running on all fours in the dream. It was so freeing! He wove through the trees with effortless speed smelling mud and night flowers. There were no traps in this Dream Forest. Even the unusual trills of exotic animals from the underbrush didn't disquiet his pleasure in this place.

It didn't take long for Enkidu to realize that he wasn't alone in the woods. His family tribe scampered a short pace behind him. Enkidu led them through the twists, turns, and ravines of the Dream Forest. Mist was everywhere; trees glistened silver beneath it.

He couldn't turn his head to see them but he *knew* they were there. The certainty thudded in his chest. Six *lahmu* running after him.

Chasing him.

That's when the ghastly realization hit him. He wasn't leading his tribe; he was running from them. They lumbered after him like furry nightmares, slavering, green-eyed and *rotting*. They were all rotting corpses. Worms wriggled in place of hairy arms. Leeches sucked the putrescence from their shriveled necks.

And every night Enkidu woke from this dream sweating. He escaped to the deck, leaned against the rails, and hoped the chilly breeze would soothe him.

It never did. And he always cried.

TABLET VI

HUMBABA

CHAPTER 27
SPARRING

In warm daylight, Enkidu was fascinated by the ships they passed.

The Urukian vessel had managed a harassment free voyage up the Euphrates. At the ports of Babylon and Kish, trading vessels swayed like colorful birds while merchants frolicked on the piers. No less intriguing were the sights of the cities themselves. Gilgamesh stood beside his friend to witness Babylon's remarkable sights; blue-glazed walls adorned with golden lions, the spire-like watchtowers, and the *two* ziggurats—one like a needle jutting to the pale sky, the other like a smaller, more traditional version of the Great Ziggurat of Uruk.

When they passed Kish, Enkidu grew edgy. From the water he spied the white walls and yellow crop fields. The port was flanked by sleek military vessels with red sails. Gilgamesh watched that port silently, letting his mind wonder what Lord Agga was doing this very moment. Was he on his palace's upper deck, appreciating the fresh air with his baby son, while an unassuming "merchant" ship from Uruk glided upstream?

Gilgamesh turned away to descend the steps to the ship's hold when the galleymaster called to him.

"Trouble," the man said, pointing to a Kishian vessel pushing out from the port's gate to intercept them.

"Be calm," Gilgamesh said. He hastily sent Enkidu below deck; his friend was likely to draw unwanted attention at close range. Then he tucked his beard into his merchant rags and waited, heart pounding, for the ship to get within ear-shot.

Or bowshot.

The Kishian vessel moved millipede-like across the water, oars rapidly rising and falling. A man on its prow greeted him with an upheld hand. "From where do you hail, strangers?"

"From Ur," Gilgamesh said, smiling and squinting.

"What do you peddle?"

On deck were arrangements of woven crates; Gilgamesh hobbled to one, removed the lid, and hoisted an exquisite silver jug to his interrogator's gaze.

"Kishian markets would give you fair price. Where are you headed?"

"Emar. We hear it's an open doorway to the buyers at Hattusha."

The man laughed. "The world's full of stories! Be safe, and may the gods protect you. I might suggest again you'd find good price in Lord Agga's royal market. If you have some days to spare on your return, you could apply for a trading permit."

"I will tell my companions," Gilgamesh said. "Good day to you."

In the hold below, the men were cheering around a wrestling contest. Enkidu was bare-chested, sporting a loincloth, against the equally dressed Gimil-Sin. They looked strangely well-matched.

Gimil-Sin grimaced and struck a fist into his own chest. "Come now, Enkidu!"

Enkidu watched his opponent with amusement. He was intrigued by that chest-beating technique; the same that Gilgamesh had used in their first encounter. The same that *lahmu* always used with each other.

The king arrived just as the fight began. Gimil-Sin charged, keeping low to tackle Enkidu's legs. Enkidu took a half-step to the side, balling his muscular body up, and stopped the wrestlers charge as surely as would a stone wall. Then his arms moved. Gimil-Sin was lifted straight off the floorboards, spun through the air, and driven down in a sickeningly fast display of strength.

"You could beat an ox!" the wrestler gasped.

Enkidu smiled, unbearably pleased. He saw his friend beyond the circle of soldiers and his grin grew. He beat his chest.

"No thank you," Gilgamesh laughed. "I'll stay right here and enjoy Gimil-Sin's humiliation!"

The wrestler made some good-humored jabs at Gilgamesh's fighting style. "He spends most of it with his face in the dirt!" he told the men, licking his filed, yellowed teeth. "I'm convinced its part of a larger strategy. When his opponents see him eating the ground, they buckle. And grass, stones, bugs … they have no prayer against our king!"

The soldiers howled. Gilgamesh nodded, cheeks flush. Then he gave a signal to his friend.

Enkidu defeated the wrestler four more times for good measure.

CHAPTER 28
THE PLAGUE

Siduri had seen the boy many times playing with his four brothers. He had puffy red cheeks and a toothy smile, and he liked to climb the local fig trees like a monkey, nestling into the branches mischievously while his playmates went looking for him below.

Now he was dying. His cheeks were ruptured with running blisters that oozed yellow pus. His eyes were swollen shut, while plague pustules hatched like hideous new eyes all around them. When he cried, his mouth showed even his pink tongue afflicted so it lolled, like a piece of moldy firewood.

Siduri backed away from the sobbing boy and glanced at the village through the tent flaps. The dirt trails were littered with bodies. Birds flapped around them, tearing off flesh. A fire had begun in one hut but no one was watching; Siduri watched the glowing embers tear free of the thatched roof and drift dangerously on the wind, like fireflies.

"*Why have they punished us?*" the boy's mother screamed. She tore at her hair frantically, grasped the tunic of the nearest hunter, named Warad. "What have we done? *What?*"

Siduri studied her. She recognized her dimly from the village, mother of several children. A strong-boned, meaty woman who usually carried herself with a certain air of dignity.

The mother spotted Siduri. "Why are we being punished? Please, use your powers Siduri! Bring my children *baaack!*"

Warad tried to steady the woman, but she fell into his arms and slumped on the ground. Siduri rushed to her side and felt for a pulse. Then she nodded to the hunter and he gently dragged her to the far side of the tent. Warad wiped his brow.

"Can you heal him?" Warad said.

Siduri held up a finger for silence. The little boy was too far drugged to understand anyway; the opium put him into a very deep slumber. Siduri felt her tears rise; she choked them back and swallowed hard.

"It's not a question of healing him anymore," she explained. She waited for Warad to read her meaning.

"That's her last child."

"I know."

"He was … I had started training him …" Warad's eyes filled up. "He …"

"He would have made a good tracker," Siduri finished for him.

Warad glared through his tears at the ruined world beyond the flaps. It was the end of his universe, Siduri knew. The villages were destroyed. An old woman who carried local folklore on her tongue couldn't remember a pestilence being this deadly. It struck nearly everyone except for the few hunters who were away on extended expeditions. The other families came down with it, spread the infection, and died in the most hideous way Siduri had ever witnessed except for torture … and in some ways, this was worse.

Warad screamed. It was a terrible sound. He turned back to Siduri and nodded. Tears flew from his eyes.

"Wait outside," she said, wondering if there were two worse words she'd ever uttered in her life. Warad obliged, and she looked at the sleeping child. His pustules looked like the watchful glare of a fly.

When it was done, Siduri emerged through the flaps to stand beside Warad.

"And so we all go to Ereshkigal," the hunter said bleakly.

Siduri's face glistened with drying tears. In the midday sun, it glistened like a mask of hard glass. "I want to talk with you about that," she said. She climbed the nearest hill and looked down at the villages on one side of the valley. Then she regarded the ones on the other side. The hunter followed her gaze.

It was inconceivable for plague to strike both villages at once, she told Warad. These were not highly traveled areas. They were self-sufficient, with trade routes handled in the hills because of the old wisdom of not letting travelers see too much. To see was to covet.

"My father always said that plague demons lurked in temples or old tombs," he offered. "Could someone have found a long-buried tomb? Maybe one of Aratta's dead priests assigned a guardian to protect his body, and some local here stumbled upon it ..."

Siduri was pointing to the village well. It looked like a puckering mouth set in a grassy green face, ringed by granite lips.

Warad blinked. "You think an old tomb is under there?"

"No."

"Of course not. We've been using the well for generations."

"Have you noticed anyone unusual near the well in the days before the plague started?"

He considered that. "No."

"Trawl it," she told him. "Then tell your friends in the neighboring villages to trawl their wells too. Bring back whatever you find; don't touch it yourself. And don't drink from the wells anymore."

Warad finally understood. "You think someone placed an evil amulet in our waters."

Siduri's eyes burned like green hellfire. "Something like that."

When she lived as a marauder there had once been a village in the red lands between the Fertile Crescent and Egypt. The village had been unusually well-protected from a geographic standpoint. Built into one side of a mountain by a large oasis, with only one way to approach it across open sands, its people were a fascinating lot. They were gifted in archery and the novel defense of firing oil casks and rolling them down into invaders. Even Taharqa wanted to stay on their good side.

Siduri had visited it twice. The first time it was healthy, thriving, and powerful for an unaffiliated territory. The second time was a corpse town. The wells dried up, and rats—Siduri knew instinctively they were plague rats—were half-buried in the mud. Her companions hadn't believed her when she voiced her theory; to them, plagues were punishments from the gods. But Siduri's healer days had uncovered cause-and-effect. If an infected rat were in the water supply …

Siduri didn't tell Warad this; she waited patiently outside her field tent while he and others lowered weighted nets into the well. Behind her, unaffected villagers removed the deceased and carted them to the large, shallow grave dug yesterday.

He would have made a good tracker.

She had loved the little boy. So eager to absorb skills and knowledge. So loving. So playful. She could hear his high-pitched voice (monkey-chatter, she'd teased him) in her mind even now.

Where do plagues come from, Siduri?

The gods, she'd told him.

Then why do we worship the gods?

Because most don't send us plagues, she'd explained, impressed with his bold insight.

Which ones do?

Far off, Warad was yelling at his able-bodied companions. They drew up the nets, checked them, dropped them again.

Siduri struggled to control her emotions as the memory reverberated in her mind. She could almost feel his little hands tugging on her tunic.

Siduri? What gods bring us plague?

Ereshkigal.

I know that, he'd said. *What other ones?*

The husband of Ereshkigal.

What's his name?

"Nergal," she uttered, looking sharply to the wooded territory of Lord Cyaxares.

When Warad next drew up his net, the bloated bodies of three plague rats were contained in the mesh.

CHAPTER 29
ARRIVAL

When the vessel glided past the ports of Emar, the Euphrates hooked sharply west across low plains. It was midnight when this last boundary stone was passed. Emar was alone for many miles, and it blazed with playful torches and jaunty music in the darkness. The expedition's full complement stood on deck and watched this last city of man dwindle away, a lonely ember beset by unforgiving wilderness. The men watched it a long, long time.

That's when the panic began in King Gilgamesh. He studied the men's bearded faces while they strained for the fading music. He suddenly longed for Uruk again. The certainty that what they were doing was wrong rushed into him, filled his chest like leaden weights, and compelled him to abandon his men where they stood. He moved to the opposite rail where his eyes bore into this untamed country. No one sat in the oar galleys; the river was drawing them on. Hittite territory according to maps. Frogs trilled on the riverbanks.

Enkidu was abruptly beside him.

"We disembark there," the king said, pointing to a small bay. To steady his thoughts he recalled the map Ishtar had given him. The ruins of Teshub were almost directly north of Emar in the heart of the Cedar Forest.

An hour later, the ship was anchored just where the king commanded it.

They moved steadily into the embrace of willow trees. Double-anchored, the ship was stuffed into the tiny cove with astonishing effectiveness. Low-lying branches scraped its deck, prodded the retracted oars, and slid protectively over the ship with better camouflage than any of them had anticipated. Four men were ordered to stay behind to guard it; the temptation to include young Gudea in this number was so great that Gilgamesh's lips moved to vocalize it. He was distracted, however, by his friend's strange behavior the moment they set foot on shore.

One instant, Enkidu was beside him and the next, he was vanished.

Like a magician's sleight-of-hand, his absence was only noticed when the men began their march. Gilgamesh sprinted ahead of his men and hopped up a fallen log, looking for his friend.

"Here," Enkidu said, dropping down from the nearest tree.

Gilgamesh frowned. "We need to stay together."

Enkidu held his gaze comfortably, considerably shorter, squatter, his wide nostrils flaring as he sniffed old memories. "Humbaba's forest ahead," he said.

"Not this forest?"

Enkidu shook his head. He looked at the line of armored men pooling at the fallen log. In the crisp starlight, they made a truly majestic sight. Their armor sparkled coldly, helms reflecting the heavens as if through warped, melted-glass.

"Come, my friend."

Enkidu moved ahead quickly, his long arms swinging. It was all Gilgamesh and the men could do to keep up with him. They ran warily, seemingly perplexed by every fallen tree, boulder, stream, or owl watching them skeptically from high perches. Enkidu moved with the serenity of a man in his home turf; Gilgamesh couldn't help but chuckle.

More than once they lost sight of him.

And then they caught up with him at the edge of a rocky ridge above steep, sloping country. For twenty meters lay an open space devoid of trees. Grassy terrain that in the daylight might appear inviting looked more sinister here, like knife-blades glinting in frost, forming an unsettling gulf to a new wall of trees. The men stared grimly.

"Cedar Forest?" Gilgamesh asked.

"Humbaba's forest," Enkidu said emotionlessly.

"How do you know?"

Enkidu sniffed. "Humbaba's mark."

"You mean ... his scent?" The king smelled the air. He detected only mold, wet bark, and cedar.

"Like boundary stones," Enkidu said as the example occurred to him. "Those trees have Humbaba's scent on them."

The men shifted uneasily, hearing this. Gimil-Sin, looking like an overstuffed tortoise in his armored shell, lost his yellow-fanged grin and gazed interestedly at the wilderness.

Gilgamesh saw the pulse in his friend's neck quickening.

"You okay?"

Enkidu surveyed the woods. His meager tribe had been vulnerable while Humbaba moved below them that dreadful night. Forty-seven armed humans should have made him feel safer.

"We should not be here, my friend."

Gilgamesh's chest burned in anxiety. "We have to. Ishtar commanded us."

Ishtar is just a human woman! The words wanted to form on Enkidu's tongue. Instead, he let himself listen to the chorus of frogs and insects piping so thickly that it vibrated in his ears. Enkidu closed his eyes to listen deeper. He understood the language of the drones, buzzes, and chirps. Territorial cries as certain as boundary stones, as certain as Humbaba's scent. He heard little heartbeats, too. Monkeys slumbering in trees. Without budging, Enkidu's ears took him on a trek into the forest ahead.

He licked his dry lips. "Humbaba hate all."

"Why?"

Enkidu shrugged. He remembered the way the creature had glared at the cliff-tops and bellowed. Such incredible wrath, unfathomable, the sound of twisted madness and frustration coiled as a thousand serpents cramped in a great vessel. Pure, lunatic fury had filled the air that night. For all the monster's physical prowess, it was this madness that plagued Enkidu's nightmares.

The king motioned to Gudea. The young boy brought forth two jewel-crusted javelins.

"Take one, my friend. These were gifts I received long ago."

Enkidu absently grabbed a weapon. Gilgamesh drew in an admiring breath, for his friend cut such an entrancing picture—one man with a spear, facing the shadow-drenched lands of an ancient enemy—that he wanted to commission a poet to write it into song.

Quite suddenly, Gilgamesh laughed.

The sound shocked all the men. They turned to their king, agog.

"Do you all feel that?" Gilgamesh asked them. "In your heart? The taste of bile in your throat? Cherish it. You'll tell your children what it feels like … to have immortality in your grasp. We are Urukians! And that *animal* out there—" He pointed with his sword. "Is taking its final breaths of life. Before the sun sets tonight, I promise its head will be in a sack!"

The images sprang in his mind following these words; the names of everyone present carved into Uruk's wall for future generations to read. A Twelve Tablet Epic of how Uruk's finest went into the most primeval forest and returned with the Guardian of Ages, skull cleaned for mounting on the palace wall above the council chamber. It *would* happen. Unlike the moments before his battle with the bandits, or war with Agga, he felt certain. The gods were with him …

Gilgamesh laughed again. If there *were* gods who opposed him, they'd best stay far from the sharpness of his blade.

The soldiers smiled.

He stepped over the rocky ridge and descended the slope toward the line of cedar daring him.

It was remarkable how fast the world brightened, even before the low sun appeared. The soldiers moved rapidly on energetic feet. Monkeys chattered and squealed at this unexpected march of humanity.

Enkidu cut a spectacular figure in the morning light. He clutched the spear (which, the king noted with some irritation, he'd still not taken the time to appreciate the richness of its construction.) Gilgamesh remembered Ibi-Sin's report of how quickly Enkidu had taken to swordplay. Partly, the old advisor had said, this was due to Enkidu's tireless strength; the weight of a bronze sword was nothing to him. Once he had been shown how to do it, he'd exhibited a startling proficiency. The spear should prove even easier. His shield was slung on his back like a tortoise shell.

Before reaching the ruins, they stopped for a quick breakfast. At Gilgamesh's insistence, the meal was done in two shifts so that one group could eat while the other climbed the nearest trees and provided lookout in all directions. They'd brought enough rations for three days; their waterskins bulged, too, but there was no concern for running dry. These woods were fragrant with moisture. Streams were plentiful.

Gilgamesh tore off a piece of salted meat and hungrily devoured it. He fished in one of the other bags for the last of their bread, and scraped off the blue-green fungus with one finger before taking a bite.

"There are some fruits on those trees," Gilgamesh said, noticing the clusters of berries that decorated the sparse trees. The branches shook suddenly as a monkey scrambled along one branch, leapt to a nearby one, and perched like a miniature gargoyle to peer at Gilgamesh.

"Do you think those berries are good?"

Enkidu looked up at the tree. "Berries good."

Hearing that, Gilgamesh walked over to the tree and grasped a low-lying branch. The monkey urinated over the branch in agitation, but this suddenly rainfall didn't discourage the king. He plucked a dozen red berries before letting the branch snap back, and the monkey fought to hold on, screeching in protest.

Popping the berries into his mouth, Gilgamesh picked up his sword. He practiced a few defensive and offensive postures, feeling the weight of the weapon and adjusting his grip accordingly. He remembered the way the blade had vibrated while lancing Agga's armor.

It was Gudea who saw the ruins before anyone else. Inspired by Enkidu's effortless climb of trees earlier, he had scrambled to the highest branches beyond the feats of any of the heavier, older men. Suddenly he was shouting to his king. "My Lord! My Lord!"

"*Quietly*, Gudea!" Gilgamesh scolded.

The boy hopped down to the ground. "Ruins, sire! I saw them."

"Where?"

"Northeast some eight miles as the falcon flies."

The king nodded. "Everyone finish your meal. General Enkidu will lead our sprint."

The noise of the sprint was unsettling. Armor grating against the leather seams, swords clicking in their scabbards, shields bouncing, boots stomping, through the abyss of verdant life that engulfed them, a massive bed of vegetation and towering cedar trees packed into a sun-destroying wall. No human villages broke the forest. No trails carved their way through the valley. There were no palaces or temples. No fires burning, no smoke spiraling up to the heavens.

Monkeys followed above them across the avenues of branches; so too did the grey mist hanging like a spider-web over their heads.

Gilgamesh ran easily, his natural athletic frame handling the weight of his livery. Up ahead, Enkidu was a small shadow weaving in and out of trees. He'd hesitate, bound onto a low-lying branch, sniff the air. Gilgamesh would almost be upon him when Enkidu would vanish again. Finally the king ran into him.

Enkidu's face was solemn. He looked much more ape than man in that instance, with his extended lower jaw and his sloping forehead. His long hair, falling out of the locks which Uruk's slaves had done for him, was a matted ball of weeds. The scent of lotion in which he had bathed before leaving on this quest had long washed out of his skin; they were all rank, but Enkidu's smell was different, pungent like an exotic spice. His body hair had begun to re-emerge, too; there was nothing to shave with aboard the ship.

"Ruins," Enkidu said.

The trees here were diagonal, sagging, and bent. Interrupting their vista were the grey heads of shapeless stone columns. Curtains of ivy sagged from worn stonework, which a thousand years of storms had scrubbed of all paint, gem, and cuneiform.

How in hell are we going to find an Annunaki statue in all this? the king wondered. In all his life he'd never seen one, but Ishtar had been descriptive. A metallic idol fashioned with eyes and heart of a unique gemstone. They were priceless relics; this itself made the expedition a problem. If the statue was originally in Teshub there was no assurance it was still here. Even considering the threat that Humbaba posed …

Gilgamesh looked smugly on the surrounding trees.

In a surge of pride and arrogance, he breathed deep and considered yelling out across the forest a challenge to Humbaba. At the pivotal moment, though, he decided against it; his lungs exhaled without fuss. This would be an ideal place to battle the beast. He could see old pylons driven deep into the earth and foundations like great pits littering the semi-clearing. He didn't care how strong the fabled Humbaba was. The monster wouldn't be able to move rocks like *that*.

The soldiers had filed themselves into a serpentine column due to the thickly grown woods. They arrived on Gilgamesh's heels and panted, flush with courage.

"This is Teshub?" a soldier asked.

No one answered; no one knew for sure.

The forest had long retaken whatever city once stood there. They could see only a green tower caved in like a tree split at the mid-section, with its top half laying in defeat against wild grass. Masonry hid underneath camouflaging veils of moss and ivy. The broken tower was possibly the remains of a watch-tower, with stone teeth as rails behind which archers might steal some protection as they fired down at invaders. But as to what race of people had dwelled here, and for what aggression a watchtower had been needed here, in a land thought to be entirely uninhabited by men of any kind, Gilgamesh could not know.

Surely other men had found these ruins. Whatever loot once lay in old cellars, casks, or vaults must have been long stolen by them.

"Enkidu?" Gilgamesh called.

"Enkidu listening to Forest. Don't interrupt your search."

Commanding the party to scour the ruins, Gilgamesh himself dipped eagerly into the work. His hands scraped on stone, dug into the dirt. He silenced his doubt ... the inner voice that insisted that bandits and armies of yesteryear had surely pillaged every worthwhile item around.

And there was a smell here. Gilgamesh caught it during his scouring. A stench of fecal matter, old and new.

"What a lovely treasure!" Gimil-Sin called to the others. The tall ruins to the north were splattered with piles of black-green feces.

The air prickled the hairs on Gilgamesh's neck.

Shiny black beetles crawled in the splatter. Gilgamesh's stomach turned but he refused to back away. How many maggot eggs lay slumbering in that sickening mound? Once conceived, the image was hard to handle; he obsessively pictured little white heads crawling out of the filth. Why, the entire forest probably owed its fly population to these droppings.

Don't vomit, he pleaded. Perversely, he fancied chopping at the fecal mound to reveal entire colonies of corpse eaters, laying their tunnel-work bare, exposing their dreadful shit-cities. Tiny corridors stuffed with swollen worms.

His skin crawled. The memory of the dead bird he'd found as a child swamped his thoughts.

Maggots on his skin. Slimy little white beads ...

A sour belch came through his gritted teeth.

"Look," a soldier said, and *actually poked the droppings.* Amazingly, something metallic came to light.

Ignoring the smell, all the men leaned forward to inspect what had been found. A ring, caked with feces, ticked against the soldier's sword-tip.

Gimil-Sin lost his ironic smile. "And so we come to the fate of Ishtar's former slaves."

The king shot him a murderous glare. "Temper that blasphemy!"

"*If* it's blasphemy, sire. Look." The wrestler used a flat stone to scrape away more of the wriggling stool. Gilgamesh averted his eyes—he had to—and only looked when more rings, copper fragments, and coins had been exhumed.

The coins were Urukian.

There was no use denying it; Ishtar had sent an expedition ahead of them when She first acquired the eleventh Annunaki relic. It failed. Undeterred, She then sought royal endorsement.

An argument wafted from the men, dividing them quickly into Ishtar supporters and others who sided with Gimil-Sin's observations. Gilgamesh paled, overcome at last by the maggots and dung-dwellers on the stone, and he staggered away.

Don't vomit! You need your strength.

He swallowed several times, hard.

Enkidu was suddenly standing over him like a specter of doom, solemn-faced and grim. "You okay?"

The king nodded weakly. "Yes, my friend. Are you?"

"Humbaba is here," he said.

CHAPTER 30
DEATH

At these words the panicked circle of men turned outward. Enkidu hadn't spoken loud, but the message was heard. The men bristled with swords and shields; their pained faces alternated between the forest and the king who'd led them here.

Gilgamesh looked up at his friend. Enkidu stood on a fallen slab of granite, his arms folded across his bulging chest. "How do you know he's here?"

But Enkidu didn't reply. His senses had never ceased in their attunement to the wilderness, measuring the monkey chatter and bird-song and insect courtship. Suddenly, a presence had moved into the area. A crunching of twigs. A hush among animals. A *wrongness* to the air.

We're going to die, he thought.

Panic exploded in Gilgamesh; he suddenly thought this was all a horrid mistake, and he wanted nothing more than to be back home, listening to the mercifully tedious cases of his citizens.

"Where is he, Enkidu? From what direction do you smell him?"

Enkidu dashed from the slab to a higher, overturned column. The leap was astonishing. He glared at the forest from this modest vantage point. "Can't tell. But swords good now."

Gilgamesh addressed the men. "We're in a position of strength. Use the stones here. Go for his legs, belly, and face. Where are my archers? Get up to the highest points you can!" They hurried to comply, arrows rattling in their quivers. Gilgamesh strained to listen to the forest.

Humbaba is here.

The droning of insects flared.

Cautiously, Gilgamesh drew his javelin and leaned out from a leaning, moss-covered column, soggy twigs snapping under his boots. The way was dark before him. The trees were so thick that a large animal could be right *there*, right behind the cluster of trees and the sprouting bushes and weeds and he'd be unable to see it. Yet he strained his eyes to try and discern movement in the dimness of the forest.

We have the advantage here, he thought rapidly. *Please* gods! Let us have the advantage! In this merciful pocket of human construction amid moss and deep vegetation, where crickets chirped in their incessant chorus—

The crickets were silent.

It was then the sickening panic of Gilgamesh's worst memories fell upon him, the paralyzing fear, the dreadful calm before death. All his accomplishments seemed to evaporate. He ordered his men to spread out, but *stay within the ruins.*

Enkidu held his spear firm with both hands. He was like a statue, unmoving, part of this lost city of Teshub.

A warm, stale air met Gilgamesh's nostrils. He stood, unblinking, as he watched the foliage ahead of him. He studied the sable trees, wondering which ones were *not* trees. How crafty was Humbaba?

The forest quiet was maddening. Even the monkeys overhead had ceased their play.

Something was walking toward them.

Gilgamesh could hear it in the woods. Brush and bramble crunched below the approaching footsteps. The men turned in the same direction. The footsteps stopped in suspicion. Every man held his breath.

The footsteps resumed, and every mouth exhaled together. Enkidu crouched low, alert to the growing thunder of something large. *Very large.*

Swords, arrows, spears and shields glinted dully beneath the tree canopy, inspiring a panic-stricken image in the king's mind. He suddenly pictured these same weapons strewn about the clearing, the hands that once held them pulverized beneath mighty claws. A field of broken, bleeding bodies would remain along with these implements of civilization, while the monkeys resumed play and vultures picked clean the bones of men …

No! Gilgamesh tried to purge the image from his mind.

The men gasped.

Immediately ahead of them, a colossal shadow had walked straight into view and halted, watching them with black eyes. Gilgamesh had a momentary impression of a face like coiled intestines, a black-furred body, a protruding jaw with grey teeth. Then the apparition vanished behind the trees.

"He's a true demon!" one of the men cried.

Perhaps it was to confirm this vocal pronouncement, or simply a reaction to the sound of a human voice, but the ground began shaking, thundering, with the charging malevolent sound of footsteps running … circling them.

The men all turned as one wheel, horror-struck at the sight of the massive shape winking in and out of the trees. Enkidu looked to Gilgamesh.

"Get ready," he said.

A tree was shoved forward, its rotten base crumpling into soggy splinters, and the weeds ahead flattened, and then Humbaba burst into the clearing.

Gilgamesh opened his mouth to scream …

His mind formed lightning-quick impressions of a furry body like that of a great bear. Its legs were stalks of muscle wrapped in the same bristly pitch hair. In three seconds it had crossed half the distance to them. Upon the legs was a shaggy torso quivering with flies. Then, a barrel-shaped chest where the fur was overtaken by grey wisps over pink muscle. The rib-curvature expanded with each vast breath; the behemoth's lean stomach appeared as immoveable as granite. Alongside this repellent bulk were ropy lengths of arms, strangely disproportionate in that the upper arm was thinner than the swollen forearms, and terminated in clawed fists twice as big as a man's head. In one grip, it brandished a slender white tree-trunk … or rather, a tree whose bark had once been white but was now striated with patches of brown blood. Where a neck should have been was simply the head ... a head as large as a war chariot. A greasy mane surrounded its face of coiled wrinkles. Lubricous eyes glimmered wetly, a pug nose flared.

All this flashed through Gilgamesh's mind in an instant, but it was Humbaba's mouth that devoured his thoughts. The wrinkly, intestine-like visage was dominated by a gaping o-shaped mouth lined with discolored teeth. The stench pouring from this orifice was like open graves and half-digested meat.

Archers!

Gilgamesh couldn't hear his own voice, wondering if it had left his mouth at all, when two arrows flew by, missing wildly. The men scattered like mice. Humbaba drew up, towering and terrible but *alive*, no question of that. It surveyed the fleeing mortals and held its tree-trunk club aloft. With the fastest attack Gilgamesh had ever seen, Humbaba splattered the nearest man against the ground.

Four men on Humbaba's right side charged forth uttering screams of desperation, their swords raining down upon his hide. Humbaba batted three of them into the trees The fourth had time to drill his sword into the monster's side.

His sword broke on impact.

Impossible! Gilgamesh's thoughts were a mass of panic. He stared helplessly at the man's broken sword. Uruk's best blacksmiths had fashioned the weapons for this adventure—

—this *nightmare*

—and now they were collecting fast among the ruins. Humbaba grunted and hissed, lurching around the ruins to snatch another fleeing soldier. The man's body flailed in the monster's grip. With blinding speed, Humbaba dashed his body against the rocks and hissed, spraying a sour mist.

"Archers fire!" Gilgamesh screamed, and before the words had fully left his mouth there was a new volley of arrows raining upon the beast. They stuck into his hide and arms like pins. Humbaba thrashed and beat at his arms, snapping the shafts off. He looked wildly for the source of this new annoyance. The man whose sword had broken had fled and was crouching, like a little boy, knees drawn up and face buried in his hands, behind the security of a toppled column.

Another arrow popped out of the maze of ruins. Humbaba let it strike his chest and he lunged after the man, roaring. There was a sickening crunch of bones and armor as the archer died beneath his wildly stomping feet. Humbaba's eyes flashed with glee.

His eyes.

"Shoot his eyes!" Gilgamesh cried, and then acting on a wild surge of purpose, he took up his spear and charged. The monster was facing away from him in that instant. A wave of new arrows riddled his head and the creature turned, a mangled body in its mouth. Gilgamesh let the spear fly even as he recognized the body.

No!

Mental agony infected his arm and the spear flew wild. Nonetheless, it nearly caught the creature in the face, and Gilgamesh saw surprise register in its hideous visage. The jeweled spear whistled by its gaze and stuck in a nearby tree … too high for any man to reach it.

Humbaba's teeth crunched down on the body in his mouth. A gout of gore erupted from the shredded carcass. With a sudden shake of his head, the monster sent the deceased morsel flying into the nearest column. There it slapped hard against stone like butcher's meat. It was almost impossible to tell the corpse had once been Gimil-Sin.

Gilgamesh never saw Enkidu throw the spear. All he later remembered was the dreamlike way the weapon flew into the monster's midsection. Such incredible force! He watched the spear bury halfway, lancing the quivering, grey-covered ribs. Humbaba's mouth gaped, the head turned like a mountain facing a new horizon.

But Enkidu was already moving off, hopping from one sunken column to the very highest pylon. Pounding the stone exactly as an ape would, he cried desperately, "Humbaba hurt! Humbaba hurt! Humbaba hurt!"

Gilgamesh's mind cleared, grasping the meaning in his friend's rant. Humbaba's hurt … attack him *now!*

The king's fear melted and flowed into a new mold, hardened like blacksmith's ichor. He raced up to the beast, unaware of who remained to watch, and drew his sword. With a furious cry, his blow slashed at one knee. It was exactly like hacking into a tree, and the next thing Gilgamesh knew he was airborne, the air popping from his lungs. Ground raced under him and he was suddenly breaking through low-lying branches, snapping them as he went.

He landed hard against the forest floor and slid. It occurred to him, somewhat surreally, that his body had narrowly missed being plastered to the nearest column.

Earth-shaking thumping brought him out of his trance; the monster was running through the maze, snatching men, dashing their brains on the rocks. His club was thrown aside so he could use his hands; with terrible effectiveness, too. Gilgamesh saw the monster hunch over an enclosure to shove an arm inside, hammering that fist manically into the screaming men hidden there.

An arrow jumped out from the forest, striking Humbaba in the chest and shattering. Gilgamesh drew himself up, seeing Gudea and one other man, a soldier named Harash, standing at the tree-line. Harash was hastily fitting another arrow to his bow.

Humbaba withdrew his dripping hand from the enclosure; the shrill wails coming from it were now silent. A scampering shape among the rubble caught its attention: Enkidu. The sight of *him* brought searing madness to its eyes. The monster bounded forward; Enkidu jumped off his newest perch just in time, for Humbaba's fist crashed into it and snapped off the pylon's tip. Enkidu scrambled past another man—Gilgamesh realized it was the man who had first broken a sword against the beast, still hugging his knees, still crying—and vanished into the maze.

The monster gave an eerie bray. Lambent-eyed and obsessed with killing his escaping quarry, the creature tried unsuccessfully to clamber over the shapeless stones to cut Enkidu off. But though it could no longer see him, Humbaba's intensity—and intelligence—burned in dreadful urgency. In three strides it was finding another way into the labyrinth, stepping over column bases like a child might surmount insignificant litter. Enkidu's spear jostled from its ribs.

Gilgamesh pursued the beast again. Seeing this, Gudea, Harash, and a dozen other men came from the other direction. All were screaming, swords high. The monster shoved aside two half-sunk columns as if they were reeds. From their bases, hidden men scrambled in every direction. Humbaba ceased his pursuit of Enkidu to stomp wildly about, crushing men, throwing their bodies, repeatedly bashing heads into the masonry.

Gilgamesh's legs burned to reach the beast. If I'm a god, he thought, then now's the time to show it! The beast continued its destructive capering; there was glee in it, the king perceived. Enkidu's spear must have been driving the thing mad with pain, but it never tried to dislodge the weapon. That entire flank was red.

Harash, Gudea, a half-dozen warriors, and Gilgamesh came at the beast from all sides. The natural instinct to shrink back burned nauseatingly. Gilgamesh pumped his legs harder to reach his target.

And then Humbaba roared.

It was a blast of sound that overpowered Gilgamesh's thoughts and actions. It came like a flood, filling his ears and clouding his head and all the world seemed to stay still for that monstrous ululation. He froze in mid-run.

His hands twitched on the sword-hilt.

Sweat flowed down his stone-like legs.

He couldn't move.

It seemed like hot perspiration erupted from every pore on his face, but try as he might he could not bring himself to summon motion. But Humbaba moved, bearing down on two similarly paralyzed men and killing them with two tremendous blows from his fists. Gilgamesh couldn't see who they were.

Humbaba mangled two others. Harash was definitely one of them; the king could see the man's wiry frame being spun in mid-air, inverted, and thrust headfirst to the ground. The body was then discarded like a limp puppet.

The paralysis broke, at once, and Gilgamesh's pent up energy caused him to stumble forward. He recovered right away, though, spurred on now by sheer defiance, hatred, and the agony of knowing that just like Harash, the boy Gudea had died.

"*Humbaba!*" Gilgamesh cried, and drove one fist into his chest.

The monster saw him, sprang forward to meet him.

Before Gilgamesh could make his frenzied stab with his sword, something flew by his head like a bronze discus and smashed into the creature's face. Humbaba's head snapped back and he gave a sound that was like a surprised yelp, and in the momentary pause Gilgamesh saw that it was a shield that had been thrown, and he knew at once that it was Enkidu who had thrown it. Yet he did not stop his charge, not even at this interruption, and he looked at Humbaba's feet. Five toed, with each toe displaying a claw, but the bulging and muscular ankles were not as thickly covered in fur as the rest of him, and pink flesh was visible here where the fur was sparse. Shrieking, Gilgamesh hacked down at this seemingly tender spot and was rewarded at once. The sword splintered the ball of muscle, cut into gristle or bone, and stuck; Gilgamesh held his shield high to deflect the anticipated counterattack.

The monster attempted to smash Gilgamesh with its fist but couldn't manage the lunge. It staggered backwards several drunken paces. Its shaggy back crashed into the most peripheral ruin and it panted, chest heaving. Five new arrows from nearby soldiers jumped at the monster's face and one found its mark in the beast's right eye.

The monster howled pitiably. Blasphemous though it was to think of it as remotely human, Gilgamesh felt his hatred and fear mutate into a strange sympathy. The beast was neither god nor a demon; just an animal ... unknown to the world of men, a race of giants who ruled the wilderness. The *other things* of the predawn, which survive as misty legends only.

The sympathy vanished the instant Gilgamesh turned to see the splattered, broken bodies of dozens of men across the ruins. When he looked back to Humbaba the monster was vigilantly beholding him, blinking, bewildered.

Dumuzi, he thought.

Agga.

Death itself.

He was suddenly that little boy again in his bedchamber, his mother's sacrificial dagger in his shaking hands.

Humbaba pushed himself upright from the stone. He blinked again, squinting his remaining eye. Gilgamesh strode to him with manic calm. Popping out from the ruins came Enkidu to join him; they walked together, abreast, swords and shields in their hands.

The monster stumbled forward on one useless foot. It inhaled its vast lungs and roared again.

From various refuges came new arrows. Humbaba's roar broke; he shook his head like an immense dog trying to discard fleas. One shaggy fist snapped off the newest arrows but, in its frantic movement, nudged the shaft protruding from its eye and he screamed again. He staggered around the pile of corpses, cradling his head. New arrows fell upon it. Humbaba grabbed a fistful of the slain and tossed them as a child might throw pebbles. The bodies fell among the archers, who ducked, hid, then re-emerged only to scream, for Humbaba had next thrown a gigantic fallen tree. It smashed like a battering ram into one stony crevice; no arrows came from there again.

Gilgamesh and Enkidu's coldly murderous walk gained speed. They bounded at the monster, who saw them coming, and tried to roar again.

"*Diiiiiiiiie!*" Gilgamesh yelled hoarsely. He up-thrust his blade into the soft nether-regions of the creature's groin, hidden behind a sprouting of black fur that could have passed for a kilt. The blade vanished into this forest of hair and again Humbaba's head snapped back, screaming to the sky—a grotesque baying for mercy.

With the coldest premeditation the king had ever seen, Enkidu drove his sword into the monster's underbelly.

Humbaba seemed to have used up his vocalizations. He staggered away from his tormentors to the forest. He gave a messy cough. Gilgamesh, Enkidu, and four others followed him.

The creature swayed and fell against a tree. The tall cedar groaned from the impact. Humbaba slid off this support beam and crashed to the forest floor.

A soldier went to leap upon the creature's chest when he was grabbed in mid-jump, shaken violently, and tossed aside. The man was dead before he hit the ground.

Everyone halted at this. Gilgamesh and Enkidu circled the creature patiently, passing by its feet, rounding to its right arm (yet staying out of grasping distance.) At last they came to the head.

"Kill it," Enkidu whispered.

Humbaba glared with his remaining eye at the bearded, human warrior.

Gilgamesh crouched to look into its wrinkled, hateful, frightened face. Frightened!

Yes, the king realized. And after all, why not? The woods which terrify us are its sanctuary from the tiny men with barbed sticks and sharp thorns that have come to dominate the valley. Was there truth to the tales of battles with giants and monsters in the distant past? The epic of gods who vanquished dragons and beasts … were those gods …

Gilgamesh forced himself to complete the thought.

… simply men who had killed frightening animals, and much as we remember those things from yesteryear as preternatural devils, do we likewise celebrate the accomplishments of mortals as divine?

Humbaba hissed, spraying vermilion spittle.

Gilgamesh raised his sword.

Fear or pity, rage at all the men dead or shame at having invaded a place where they didn't belong. Perhaps it was all these things that brought the king's sword down on the neck of Humbaba the Great.

It took six hacking blows to behead him.

Five men had survived.

When Gilgamesh stumbled away from his decapitated quarry, he nearly wept when he saw Gudea among them. The boy trembled, white vomit on his lips. He couldn't look away from the fallen monster.

Even headless it was a maddening sight, and none of the survivors dared approach it. An unexpressed desire to be far away before sunset plunged them in blackness was shared among the men, though Gilgamesh knew this fear was rootless. Humbaba was dead. The Cedar Forest lay open to the axes of men, and it would be nearly three thousand years before the very last of Humbaba's race—a grotesque mother and her deformed lunatic son—would face true extinction under the iron swords of another group of bearded warriors in a land far, far to the north.

"We cannot leave until our friends are buried," Gilgamesh said. Enkidu, Gudea, and the two soldiers beside them walked off to begin digging the pit. The king tore off his cracked armor and worked alongside them.

A shallow grave was dug by nightfall. The bodies were dragged in, one by one, as Gilgamesh sang a soft prayer that ended in shameful tears.

"They will walk the fire road of Ereshkigal," Gudea whispered. Enkidu returned that instant with numerous river stones to place over them. He had also retrieved Gilgamesh's spear from the tree; his own he left sticking out of the monster's carcass.

It took four hours to track Humbaba back to his distant lair deep in the slimy marsh of the Cedar Forest's heart. They lost his tracks at the edge of those stagnant, buzzing waters, but there could be no mistaking the cave on the other side. Enkidu proposed a makeshift boat from fallen timbers, and they all went ashore to Humbaba's green asylum.

Bones they expected to find, and these they did in abundance. Remnants of snacks, arm-bones chewed and split to get at the succulent marrow. Skulls shattered like glass. Ribs and pelvis' caked with putrid rot, beetles, and marsh-scum. The stench of the cave turned all their stomachs.

Humbaba had been a collector, it seemed. Helmets were heaped in one corner of the cave, scabbards in another. The Twelfth Annunaki statue had been ignobly discarded amongst the bones of horses, and it was Gudea who found it.

"My Lord!"

Gilgamesh grinned at the boy, seeing the mystical statue with eyes and exposed heart of coral. "You and your father are now noblemen." And he tussled the boy's hair proudly. To the other soldiers, he bestowed the same honor.

Enkidu didn't share in their sudden mirth. He walked among the bones of Humbaba's cave. Gilgamesh never asked him what he saw in the back of that lair … if the bones of *lahmu* were mixed amongst the victims. The cave stank of centuries. There was no telling how long the monster had dwelt there.

As they rafted across the marsh, Enkidu broke the quietude only once. Sitting beside the sack containing their quarry's head, he stared at his friend. "Now we immortal? Because Enkidu not feel any different."

TABLET VII

THE WRATH OF ISHTAR

CHAPTER 31
BLOOD DAWN

Kazallu, city engineer for Uruk, ran the entire length of the audience hall so that his fat jiggled crazily. His wheezing breath and red face horrified the guards there, but they listened as he gasped his request. Then he collapsed against the nearest wall, sucking air like a lungfish.

When newly proclaimed Regent Ninsun finally emerged from her bedchamber a few minutes later, Kazallu pulled himself to his feet and bowed dizzily.

"What is it?" Ninsun demanded, concerned for the scarlet flush in his face.

"The *saghulhaza*," Kazallu panted.

"What of them?"

"They're missing."

Ice melted along Ninsun's spine, and suddenly the shadowy hallway seemed a treacherous place. Uruk's Death Lords were masterful warriors and assassins. No one knew their true identity behind their masks except for the king and First Councilman ...

"Where's Nedu?" she demanded.

"Sleeping, I would imagine. Or bickering with his daughters."

Ninsun dispatched a guard to rouse the councilman, and then she helped steer the engineer to the throne room. There, he slumped like a wet sack.

"Tell me everything," Ninsun said, and as she listened she realized not since Dumuzi first snatched power had she ever been so frightened.

From where she sat enthroned, Regent Ninsun shivered—her body still damp from her bath—as Nedu's lone figure crossed the empty council chamber. Night moaned against the walls' high window-slits. A regent crown dug against her forehead; Gilgamesh's own crown was tucked away in his sealed bedchamber.

The room was very cold. Day temperatures in Sumer usually soared like glass-workers' ovens, while the city's stone and mud-brick soaked in the heat to defy chilly nights. But yesterday had been cloudy with a tenebrous haze transforming Shamash into a faded discus. Subsequently the night was chillier than most, the morning even colder. Ninsun's slight body felt steeped in mountaintop ice.

Likewise, there were no torches lit in the chamber. From her bedroom, Ninsun had finished bathing and walked, unguarded, to the council chamber. She wanted it dark. She wanted no one to guess she was already awake, conducting this furtive business.

Nedu was, therefore, a black shape. Ninsun slid open some lantern light.

"Regent Ninsun?"

"Where are they, Nedu?"

Nedu's face was very white in the lamplight. "I didn't realize they were unaccounted for until Kazallu's message a few minutes ago."

Ninsun shivered again, and this time it wasn't from the chill. "I want a city-wide investigation. Let the people know what we're doing. Anyone with information may come forward and be rewarded." She groaned painfully, overcome with anxiety. "We can't simply *misplace the Death Lords!*"

"Of course, My Lady."

She gathered herself. "My son will be returning soon."

Nedu blinked. "He sent word to you?"

"Shamash sent me dreams. His ship is even now sailing down the Euphrates."

Relief crashed like ocean surf in the councilman's soul. The past few weeks had been increasingly unsettling, particularly since he couldn't discern just why he'd been feeling that way. He tried mentioning it to Ibi-Sin but the old hawk shrugged dismissively. The other council members treated his inexplicable dread in a similar fashion except for Kazallu.

It was the job of the Death Lords to be unnoticed. Unless specific business regarding the South Tower was at hand, no one really thought of them. And the annual budget had already been drawn up. Gilgamesh could think of no other use but to keep them at their posts. Next year he'd find them other work, he'd said. The war with Agga, friendship with Enkidu, the quest from Ishtar … these things had wrested the king's attention.

Nedu licked his lips. "The quest has been successful?"

Ninsun hesitated. Her dream had shown her son standing tall on the ship's prow. Strangely, there was no one else on the ship with him. The oars sat uselessly. The river alone guided the ship. She didn't know how to interpret such a strange vision.

Finally, she admitted as much. "I am not certain. The dream was … vague."

"But he is safe?"

"He is."

"Good."

"Nedu, we need to discuss Ishtar."

"What about Her?"

"Her control over Uruk has grown far too great. My son has plans to curtail Her influence. Before he left, I shared in his view that She may be playing us all for fools."

Nedu lost all color in his face. "I cannot indulge this conversation."

"You *can* and *will*. Remember that She threatened me and my son."

"The ways of gods and goddesses aren't ours to question."

"Aren't they?" Ninsun challenged. "Nedu, what if Ishtar ordered us to allow Agga's army into Uruk. Would Ibi-Sin go along with that?"

Nedu looked to his feet.

"Or if She commanded that you fall on your sword for Her?"

"I would end my life if a goddess told me to."

"What if a goddess told you to stand against Gilgamesh? Never mind how quickly my son would dispatch you?"

Nedu looked pained.

"My point is that a battle-line *can* be drawn against gods trying to harm us. If it was Shamash's pleasure I would gladly burn in His radiance, but would defy Him to save my son and city. I need to know who you stand behind."

The councilman nodded. "My Lady, I loved and served your father. Gilgamesh also has my love. These last few months especially … the way he's changed …"

"I understand." Ninsun leaned forward and took Nedu's hand, squeezing it affectionately. They might have been two elderly people in a gloomily lit tavern for that flashing instant, unburdened by the affairs of gods and kingdoms.

The priestess' next words changed all that. "Send riders up along the river to flag my son's ship and tell him what's happened. Do it now, Nedu."

He melted into the lurid darkness. She listened to his sandaled footsteps fading on the stone. Then, seeking the comfort of her temple, she stood and glanced at the window.

The sky was red.

At first she wondered if she was still dreaming. All her life she'd been so attuned to Shamash that she could conduct His rituals and sacrifices blindfolded. But now, He had emerged wrathful and swollen, like a bloodstone, wounded perhaps? What had beset Him on his nightly journey?

Ninsun immediately dropped to her knees and began the chanting she'd been practicing during her son's absence. It was a new prayer she'd written; before the quest, she'd even sought Enkidu's help with it. It had occurred to her that Shamash might be better addressed (and thus more easily pliable) if His many names were used during prayer. Ra to the Egyptians, Simige to the Hittites, and from various tribes known to Uruk's scholars, the Sun God's multiple names included Utu, Mithra, Estan, even Agni of the Harappans. To this litany she added Enkidu's input: the *lahmu* called Him Wer. Ninsun hoped her great god would be flattered if called upon by all His names.

Perhaps He was. But this morning, something was wrong.

Blood dawn.

That was the name for this kind of morning. Something ominous had transpired on Earth or in the Heavens; it didn't matter where, for both realms were sure to be affected.

CHAPTER 32
THE RETURN

Gudea dipped over the side of the ship to rinse his sword. When he righted himself, the droplets glowed like splashed silver on the blade. His black hair was newly rinsed and disarrayed.

"Why does She seek it?" Gudea asked.

The ensuing weeks aboard the ship had been difficult. Lonely, quiet, without the promised trumpets and celebration to commemorate their adventure. The return voyage had been plagued by fog and strong waters. Unhelpful winds battered them throughout the bland southern stretch from Emar. Now they were just north of Kish and Babylon.

Gilgamesh fingered the statue absently. "It matters not, boy. The Annunaki are property of the gods. Humbaba's head belongs to us, and I shall have it mounted for public viewing. Ishtar can have the statue, but that's all …"

Gudea watched him with bright eyes. "Sire?"

Gilgamesh frowned and moved to the opposite deck rails. Two horsemen had emerged from the brush there and were galloping along the banks. Suddenly one of them brandished a wavering ochre flag.

Enkidu squinted at the riders. "That Uruk flag?"

"It is. Dangerous to be flying it around here."

Gilgamesh ordered all men to one side of the oar galley. The vessel turned in the water, gliding closer to shore. Then they dropped anchor and, from shouting distance, the king spoke to the riders.

"A message, sire!" the rider replied, and fired an arrow into the vessel's side. Enkidu retrieved it; the king unfurled the short banner wound over the shaft.

Two cuneiform wedges had been pressed into cloth.

Saghulhaza.

Missing.

Gilgamesh withdrew his sword and used the edge to carve a response. Two words. Then he rewrapped the message around the arrow and had his nearest soldier shoot it into the sand. The rider opened it.

"When I arrive," the king said, "Have those two items brought to the ziggurat's feet and await me."

The rider nodded. Together with his companion, he rode back the way he'd come.

Gudea watched them go, fascinated by the secret correspondence he'd witnessed. "Is everything well, sire?"

"We will soon see," Gilgamesh said. He was surprised by how little the rider's news had shocked him. After all, he had not authorized the departure of the Death Lords. By vanishing, they were in violation of their code to Uruk's protection.

Quite suddenly, Gilgamesh knew precisely where the Death Lords had gone. He hoped, too, that he could deal with them … and with whatever was to come.

They reached Uruk on a red morning with storm clouds gathering in the eastern sky. As the sun rose it was swallowed by this malevolent storm, in chilling comparison to the Egyptian legend of the mighty serpent Apophis devouring fiery Ra.

Enkidu stood rigid on the bow of the ship, his head thrust out over the water. He sniffed deeply. "Rain will come today. Much rain and … kadru?"

"Kadru? Gilgamesh inquired.

Enkidu said apologetically, "Enkidu forget word for sky's anger."

"Thunder," Gudea said behind the king.

When they had reached the canal, the storm clouds swelled overhead like a distended tumor. This dismal daylight reflected greyly on Uruk's mud-brick wall and watchtowers. Oddly, it also enhanced the greenery of the countryside; the riverbanks exuded the most beautiful, emerald color. The crop fields wavered in softer, oceanic hues.

Councilman Nedu was waiting for him on the port pier, white-clad and small-looking with the city walls behind him. Fat Kazallu stood beside him.

"Your mother and I despaired, my Lord, until your ship unfurled its banner to tell us you lived," Nedu yelled.

"I confess I almost forgot," Gilgamesh said, and frowned when he saw how thick and bubbling the clouds looked from this angle. "It is a grim day. Unfitting for a day of triumph like this."

"You have done it then?"

"We have done both quests," Gilgamesh said. Nedu's eyes strayed to the bulging sack on the ship's deck. It was rank, wet with rot. "Did you receive my reply?"

Nedu swallowed nervously, memories of battle with the Western Road bandits flashing across his mind. He sensed another battle. The humid air was thick with it. "We did. Your instructions have been carried out, sire."

Gilgamesh threw a rope to the pier guards, who hastily began tying it round the posts. When they were in range, the king helped his companions across to the gangplank. Gilgamesh carried the bulging sack himself.

The nearest guards gaped. All of Uruk had been told of the adventure as soon as the king's ship appeared on the horizon. Criers were dispatched from the palace to every podium, wall, and pedestal with a pre-prepared statement of the mission to kill the Guardian of the North. Nothing was said of Ishtar's request; shrewdly, Gilgamesh wanted to make certain the twelfth Annunaki could be found before he made it known they'd been searching for it. The pier guards, then, knew instantly what the sack must contain.

The pier gate swung in. Priestess Shamhat stood there.

"Shamhat," Enkidu said. He embraced her immediately.

"General Enkidu!" she whispered in his ear. Her missing eye was concealed now behind a pale blue patch. "Oh! how I have missed you!"

The king waited patiently. When they had embraced again, Shamhat came before the king and knelt. So submissive! he thought in bemusement. Is it because she's in love? She wants my blessing to see Enkidu? Despite his desire to hate her, Gilgamesh found he couldn't any longer. Enkidu was clearly taken with her. Soon enough, his friend would seek royal approval to marry ... and Gilgamesh would have to grant it. At least there was one good thing; the girl would have to leave the Ishtar cult. Just as well. Looking into her single eye, Gilgamesh perceived that she wanted out.

"Rise priestess. Tell me your business."

Her eye became frightened.

"Lord Gilgamesh," she said. "Ishtar awaits you."

"Tell Her I'll come straight away," he replied. "But first ... I have wonderful gifts I must prepare for Her. An hour before sunset, I shall come to the goddess' feet."

A modest crowd gathered at the base of ziggurat when they saw their king and Enkidu arriving at the head of a caravan. Dismounting, the royal friends unveiled the tarp to reveal several smaller tarps, each covering an unknown offering to the Goddess of Love and War. People muttered of spices, gold, food or rare treasures which their ruler had prepared to the city's divine protector.

Even as the goddess appeared above them on the second tier of the Great Ziggurat, Gilgamesh made no move to reveal the treasures. He simply nodded to his friend and, together, they began climbing the stairs while numerous slaves carried the mysterious cargo behind them. Only slaves could do it; soldiers were forbidden to step foot on Ishtar's House unless coming unarmed, seeking pleasure.

Enkidu sniffed the moist air. "Rain and thunder."

Gilgamesh swallowed nervously. His heart was an anxious war-drum. "Be alert, my friend. Ishtar and I must have a talk."

In that moment Enkidu realized his friend suspected her true heritage. Somehow, he knew that this revelation would cause many, many bad things to transpire.

A third of the way up the ziggurat stairs Gilgamesh came to the first tier. A wide walkway opened up into a courtyard. It was here that flowering plants were tended to by temple workers, so that their greenery spilled down over the side and created the illusion of a forest trying to burst from the ziggurat's heart. It was here that Ishtar greeted Gilgamesh, with two priestesses flanking Her.

Gilgamesh bowed before Her. Enkidu followed suit.

Ishtar fixed the king and his companion with a bright, hungering stare. "God-King Gilgamesh, son of Lugalbanda and Ninsun! Your quest has been victorious and you have found the Annunaki for Me?"

"We have," Gilgamesh said, daring to look into Her eyes and immediately observing the pained desire of the goddess to possess the statue. Her body, too, was as rigid as an old tree. It may have been this thought, or the angle of sunlight that struck Her face, but he suddenly realized that Ishtar's earthly avatar was not the gloriously young entity he had always thought. Her sparkling makeup failed to entirely conceal the creeping crow's feet at Her eyes, and the wrinkled flesh of Her uncovered throat. Gilgamesh looked at the line of Her mouth (so often during the New Year's Festival yearning to kiss that mouth) and now he perceived its aged condition.

He was also perplexed by the honorific way She was addressing him. Not once had reference to his divine heritage ever been made.

"Produce the statue," the goddess said, "and earn Me as your reward."

Her words provoked two different reactions from the mortals kneeling there. Gilgamesh, and the slaves within earshot, looked stricken. A holy union with Ishtar? Never had such a thing occurred! Not even when Meskiaggaseir, First King of Uruk, first entranced the goddess by building a glorious temple to Her radiance so many years ago!

By contrast, Enkidu's face gave no indication he even comprehended the offer. But behind his eyes, an ironic smile was brewing. He saw Ishtar's plans laid bare, these clever machinations of human politics revealed. Sometimes humanity was so complex; other times, their schemes were like the plotting of cubs!

Gilgamesh met Ishtar's stare. "My reward is a divine marriage?"

Ishtar nodded solemnly. It was the only way, really. During his absence, She had sweated over what to do if the final Annunaki was found. Now there it was! Coral-eyed, holding the last piece to an age-old puzzle in its breast! She needed Gilgamesh on Her side for what was to come.

"As King of Uruk, I would welcome the goddess' love." His mind flew like wind. "But I must ask mighty Ishtar a question before I turn over what She wants."

Not once since Gilgamesh's arrival had Ishtar looked away from the pouch on the king's belt-line, but at this comment Her eyes lifted. As if echoing the brewing clouds overhead, those blue eyes rippled. "Do I hear the Lord of Uruk correctly? He wishes to barter with Heaven?"

"No, Great Ishtar—"

"You have fulfilled your quest and earned My love," Ishtar said hotly. "Do not dig for yourself a grave now!"

"Is a mere question offensive?" Gilgamesh said, breathing rapidly as he considered the ramifications of what he was doing. "You've threatened me once before, Ishtar. Remember? My mother was present, while You claimed to test my courage. I wield the same courage now. Have You changed Your tone?"

Ishtar watched him coldly. "Ask, King Gilgamesh."

"Who were the men sent ahead of us to fetch this thing?" He anticipated her silence, and pressed the matter further. "We found their bodies, pulverized by Humbaba. They were Urukian."

"How do you know that?"

The king smiled. "You don't deny it."

"I need deny nothing. Give me the Annunaki statue—"

"Take it from me!" he roared.

It was then the panic struck him. His voice echoed off the ziggurat steps as clear as a trumpet blast. Everything seemed to freeze in that instant. No! Gilgamesh cried, horrified by the finality in the fading echo. It was the inevitable commitment; the stomp of bandit steeds; the crickets hushing as Humbaba arrived. It was the ruins of a city washed of memory by cold rain. At the same instant, an answering roar swelled in Gilgamesh's heart. *This* is the battle I should fight! Not against an outnumbered animal in the woods but *here*, against this haughty being who commands us about like sheep!

"For this blasphemy you have earned an eternity in hell," Ishtar said bleakly. "Turn over the statue—"

"Why? What is so important about a piece of metal imbued with gems?"

"It is not your place to question the protector of your city—"

"*We* are the protectors of the city!" Gilgamesh roared. "It was Enkidu and myself who sent Agga away like a whipped brat! We brought down Humbaba! You hide like a rat in its hole and consider Yourself worthy of respect? I *denounce* you!" He produced his sword and Ishtar jumped back.

Ishtar's two priestesses threw themselves in front of their patron.

Enkidu rose. "Is goddess afraid of human weapons?"

Ishtar's face transformed into a deformed, fractured mask of livid agony. "I'll raise up the dead! *The dead shall come up to devour the living!*"

But Gilgamesh pressed his advantage, and he saw the panic in her eyes. "Bring them up, then! Let corpses walk the streets! Go ahead!"

The goddess smiled. "Then I summon *death*, Lord Gilgamesh! I summon it to kill you and the beast who hunkers in your shadow!"

Only the rawest instinct saved Gilgamesh's life. A dart of movement out of the corner of his eye made him lean backwards in time to see an arrow fly past his face. A second too late and it would have landed in his neck.

Gilgamesh sprang up in time to see four Death Lords—the *saghulhaza* themselves, rushing at him and Enkidu from both sides of the courtyard's flowing foliage. Rebellion returns to Uruk! the king thought sickly. Rebellion … wearing black-robes and silver masks.

Ishtar sprinted up a dozen steps, cursing, with her priestesses on her heels. "I'll watch you die!"

Enkidu sized up the approaching black-armored assailants. Three were nocking arrows in their bows. The other wielded a black-stained sword.

Gilgamesh handed the Annunaki statue to Enkidu. The archers aimed.

"Throw it!"

Ishtar screamed.

Enkidu chucked the statue at one of the archers the way he had thrown stones at so many animals. The archer was hit in the silver mask with shattering force. The Death Lord was unconscious before his head crashed into the courtyard. His arrow released wildly, hitting the floor, bouncing up, loosing into the city.

The other archers fired at their king.

Gilgamesh felt the arrow pierce his leg below his kilt-hem even as he swiped the other arrow out of the air. There was no pain, not at first, just a warm discomfort that quickly grew white-hot. Blood spurted like a cough, dribbled messily down his calf.

The king turned to the covered caravan he'd brought. "Unleash!"

Many things happened at once. The slaves tossed aside their pale garments to show that they were *not* slaves at all, but armored soldiers. The covered tarps came away to reveal wooden cages, the kinds used to trap animals ... the kinds of cages that Enkidu had wrecked many a time in his younger days. But contained within them was no antelope or gazelle or any other common denizen of the forest.

Gilgamesh's men unlocked the cage gates and gave a sharp prod from their swords. The captured beasts bounded forward.

The three *saghulhaza* never had time to react. The frilled dragons poured forth. For the last few days they had gone without food; Gilgamesh wanted them lean and hungry.

The first *saghulhaza* went down, a dragon snapping his leg with its mighty jaws. The man inside the forbidding armor shrieked, dropping his sword and clawing at the floor as he was dragged away by the beast.

Enkidu saw one of the dragons heading toward him; he hopped off the stairs and would have fallen to his death if not for his remarkable agility. His hands grasped the creeping vines and brush, and he scrambled along the ziggurat's sloping side. Three reptiles surged past him and were upon the remaining two Death Lords.

Amid the screams and desperate slashing, dragons sinking their teeth into leg and belly and arm, Gilgamesh looked up and saw Ishtar watching the fray. Their eyes met, and he thought he heard a voice in his head:

Your life ends today.

She ran for the ziggurat's next tier. He heard her screaming something to her fellow priestesses, in a language unlike any he'd ever heard.

In the courtyard, the dragons had laid claim to all. The *saghulhaza* were being devoured, their armor cracking beneath powerful saurian jaws, their legs or heads or arms torn into ensanguined ribbons. The dragons chewed contentedly and stared lazily at their freedom. It took a moment for Gilgamesh to realize that Enkidu was no longer scrambling up the ziggurat's vegetation.

Panic flooded him. He looked frenziedly around. Another dragon lurched at him. Gilgamesh cut its head off with one swipe ... but the body kept coming at him. He stepped aside to let the headless reptile scamper past, juices spewing from the stump, until it smashed messily into the courtyard wall and died amid flowers.

Something black leapt down the stairs at him.

He barely had time to deflect the Death Lord's blade. The impact was ferocious, knocking him off balance. He fell, rolled over the decapitated dragon, stood, while the Death Lord kept coming, slashing furiously. Its silver mask betrayed no emotion, but if the rapid skill of its swordplay was any indication, the man within was insane with anger.

There are seven Death Lords, Gilgamesh reminded himself. Somewhere close then, two more are lurking.

From below the king, Urukian soldiers raced up in the wake of the dragons. Gilgamesh lost his footing again. He rolled painfully down a few steps.

When next he stood, his soldiers were attacking the fifth Death Lord. The swift confidence of the concealed warrior was chilling. It didn't seem he was fighting at all; rather, his moves had the fluidity of a dream-dance. Eight soldiers against him. His blade whirled, chopped, thrust, whirled again. Four soldiers lay dying on the ziggurat steps.

The last two Death Lords emerged from the next highest tier. If the broken bodies of their brothers dissuaded them, their relentless speed didn't show it.

Gilgamesh leapt up the stairs again. The Death Lord fighting the four remaining soldiers saw him and tried to anticipate his entrance into the fray. It was all the distraction the soldiers needed. The break in concentration saw one, two, three blades stick him in the neck and ribs. His body rolled all the way down the stairs to the roaring crowd below.

For Gilgamesh, all thought vanished. He saw the two Death Lords flying down at him. His legs pushed him to greater speeds. His sword met the nearest attacker, blocking a mortal blow, as he ducked, grabbed the man's boot, and yanked him off his feet. The man fell on his back, sliding partway down the stairs.

The other Death Lord struck. Gilgamesh felt one cold blade lance the meaty part of his shoulder. Pain exploded in his neck. As the Death Lord capered in disorienting onslaught, Gilgamesh knew his life was over. A flood of acceptance rushed his thoughts. Time slowed, allowing him to hear the crowd below, the chomping of the dragons upon their kills, the fallen *saghulhaza* pulling himself up and joining his brother in contest against their king, the moans of wounded soldiers, and the sight of Enkidu crashing into the nearest Death Lord with sufficient force to knock him off the stairs and fall, screaming, to the ground far below.

Enkidu hoisted the other Death Lord into the air and, in the single greatest show of strength Gilgamesh had ever seen, pitched the man into the ziggurat slope off the stairs. To Gilgamesh's eyes, the man looked like a smashed insect, black wings crumpled, silver face ruined.

"Ishtar!" Gilgamesh screamed dizzily. Enkidu caught him as he started to fall.

"My friend? Much blood!" Enkidu looked horrified at the king's wounds.

"She has to die, Enkidu," he managed. "Or else the people will think she really is a goddess and turn against us."

Then he felt the ziggurat tremble.

It was like an earthquake, or the stomp of enormous hooves in a tightly built corridor. Gilgamesh thought it must be the long-awaited thunder. When he looked around, he noticed Shamhat running up the stairs below him, her face pale.

"Ishtar!" she screamed at her goddess. "*No!*"

The goddess' fury at seeing Gilgamesh still alive was obvious, but there was an undeniable glee in her. She raised her hands up to the sky. "Since Uruk rejects Me, I summon the Bull of Heaven to destroy her!"

"Bull of Heaven?" Enkidu asked. The ziggurat shook violently.

Tears spilled from Shamhat's eye. "It's quite real," she said.

The second tier of the ziggurat darkened. Gilgamesh saw a nightmare shape, nearly as large as Humbaba, rush to the edge of the stairs and careen over. Its hooves were thunder. With only seconds to react, Gilgamesh grasped Enkidu's arm and together they leapt off the stairs to the first courtyard, out of the way of the charging monstrosity. It roared past, a black head with protruding horns from the bony carapace of the skull set upon a four-footed, bull-like body. The crowd below shrieked, scattered in every direction.

Gilgamesh's first thought was that Ishtar was truly a goddess, or at least, a sorceress of divine skill who had dredged up a monster not seen since Tiamat laid waste to the surface of the world. He couldn't ignore the reality of his fleeting glimpse; it was a great bull, a black body rippling with muscle. Yet it wasn't simply an ordinary animal grown to gigantic proportions. Two saber-like horns thrust nearly two meters from its skull, while a bony growth from its nose stood straight up like a Y-shaped, stumpy limb. Unlike a bull, the creature was at its highest in the middle of its back so that its hide formed a mountain of flesh. It was then not a true bull at all, but a monster from the forgotten past, herded here in the days of the ziggurat's construction and kept fed by Ishtar and her priestesses.

The sacrifices! Gilgamesh thought. All the goats and cattle and wheat donated to the temple had gone to the feeding of this massive beast. Within the ziggurat its awesome power had been restrained, but now it was out, its pent-up aggression finding sudden freedom.

Below them, the monster stormed onto the Avenue of the Gods and bolted wildly into the adjacent neighborhoods. Gilgamesh pulled the arrow free of his leg at last, leaning on Enkidu for support, and hobbled to the courtyard's edge.

Not even in dreams had he envisioned something like this. The bull was galloping full-force through the southern side of the city, wrecking fences, walls, and homes in a spastic stomp of destruction.

Soldiers hurried up the stairs to their king. "Sire? What do we—"

"Kill it," Gilgamesh said. "It's an animal, understand? Unleash men from the barracks, put them on the wall, fill the thing with arrows! It's an animal and it will die if it loses enough blood."

'So will you," Enkidu said, steadying him. He tore off some of the king's cloak and made a hasty tourniquet for his leg. "Lie back, my friend."

"My city is being destroyed!"

Enkidu nodded. "It just an animal, remember? They kill it soon. You rebuild what it destroys." And then he smiled.

Gilgamesh could have wept, seeing that grin. So much death around them—the air stank of it—and the cacophony below them. Horns sounded in the city. Other horns replied from walls. As Gilgamesh and his friend watched, the wall tops were filling with archers. The Bull of Heaven continued its path of astonishing destruction, kicking up dust and debris. It snorted, tripped over its own feet and crashed through a merchant shop. Then it righted itself, insane with freedom or simply insane ... locked away for so long that its natural instincts were perverted into this wanton apocalypse.

Yet Enkidu was right. They would rebuild whatever the monster destroyed. They would rebuild with the very bricks of the Great Ziggurat itself; in that instant, Gilgamesh resolved to disassemble Ishtar's House piecemeal, abolish the cult, and raid its hidden treasuries to give to the very people who were now suffering at the hands of her pet.

Many things happened in the next moment. The first volley from the wall's archers flew into the monster, sending it squealing for cover. Unlike Humbaba, there was no sadism in its appetites. Gilgamesh could see plainly that it only wished to run; the Bull of Heaven was perhaps even herbivorous, built to be strong and fierce when defending itself from the larger creature who preyed upon it ... perhaps, creatures like Humbaba.

In that same instant, Ibi-Sin emerged from his home, received a quick report of the incredible thing running amok in Uruk, and ordered his war chariot prepared so he could join the hunt.

Ninsun scurried up to the vantage point offered by her temple to get a view of what was happening.

And Enkidu, grinning beside his friend, sucked in a startled gasp as the poisoned arrow hit him from behind.

CHAPTER 33
ERESHKIGAL

The king blinked as Enkidu stood upright and began walking calmly across the courtyard. He saw the arrow sticking from his back but for a moment was frozen with disbelief. He had never seen his friend walk with such unnerving equanimity, nor in such an upright posture … the man Enkidu aspired to be was suddenly *there!* The ape-like hunch gone, Enkidu strode to the edge of the stairs.

But something was wrong. Gilgamesh tore himself from his first impression—that the gods had blessed Enkidu with full humanity for defeating the false goddess Ishtar. He realized that two priestesses above were scurrying up the ziggurat's winding ascent. Then he watched with sick dread as Enkidu, still walking, attempted to descend the stairs, only to fall upon his face.

Gilgamesh rushed to his friend's body. Enkidu looked up at him with a grimace of pain.

"Bad arrow," Enkidu said.

"No!" Gilgamesh screamed for his soldiers. "A physician! Fetch a physician *now!*"

The men raced to comply. Gilgamesh grasped the arrow-shaft and ripped it free.

"Be still Enkidu! I'll return right away!"

Then he ascended the ziggurat stairs three at a time.

Ishtar and her priestesses were drawing themselves into the top temple when the specter of an enraged king was upon them.

The nearest priestess, a bow in her hands, died first. Ishtar screamed dreadfully. Her disciple fell, body cleaved from shoulder to waist. On the temple floor, she looked like some abomination, two torsos sprouting from the same waist.

"**What is the poison you used?**" Gilgamesh screamed, dropping his sword and hauling the goddess off her feet with one arm. He slammed her against the wall.

"Serpent venom!" she screamed wildly. He slammed her again and again, hearing her shoulder give way.

"What's the antidote?"

"There is none!"

Gilgamesh dropped her, collapsing to his knees. The bruised, terrified goddess cowered by the wine fountain. For a moment, she dared to hope for continued life. After all, the king couldn't possibly wish to upset an entire city, slaughtering its patron deity in defiance of history!

Then he looked at her.

Gilgamesh regarded Ishtar with the darkest, sickest, most ferocious eyes she had ever seen on man or beast. She wanted to die then, so horrified she was with this mask of inhumanity.

"If there is no antidote," the king uttered, dragging himself to his feet and coming after her, "then *I'll dress Enkidu's wounds with your blood!*"

Ishtar howled as her king killed her ... with his hands and teeth.

The king leapt down the stairs, four at a time, to where his friend lay. Enkidu heard him coming; he craned his neck to look.

"Be still!" Gilgamesh cried. "Please, Enkidu!"

Enkidu's lips parted in a grimace. "Enkidu can't move."

"The physician will be here any moment!" Gilgamesh ignored what his friend had said; surely it was a mispronunciation, not an accurate report that a poison was paralyzing his body and would next move on to the lungs, heart, brain ...

His friend's eyes rolled back in their sockets.

"*Enkidu!*" Gilgamesh screamed. "Stay awake, by the gods!"

Enkidu's eyes refocused. But there was something wrong. Gilgamesh, powerful ruler of Uruk, was red-faced and sobbing uncontrollably. His eyes squinted with tears. Enkidu had never seen such an expression of pain on anyone. He recalled the bull-like anger of their very first meeting when they fought in the palace. Now, suddenly, he understood that anger. Gilgamesh was a man terrified of things beyond his control. Death, creeping like icy needles through Enkidu's chest, was far beyond his control.

"Enkidu die as a human," he managed.

"*No!*" Gilgamesh's eyes turned wild. "You've been my *only friend!* Do not leave me here!"

In that instant Gilgamesh looked more animalistic than Enkidu ever had; he clutched his friend's hand with fingers as strong as diamonds, as if intending to defy the call of Ereshkigal's Fire Road. Suddenly Shamhat came to Enkidu's other side. She took one look at Gilgamesh's agony and wailed.

"He can't die!" she screamed.

"He *won't* die!" Gilgamesh shrieked.

Please ...

Enkidu smiled. Everyone was around him, and it felt so good. His best friend, the woman he loved, and his tribe beyond them, as shadowy shapes whispering the *lahmu* hymn of death.

"I regret nothing," Enkidu said, and died.

CHAPTER 34
FUNERAL

The Bull of Heaven died as the king's scream rang out over the city. The creature, stuck full of arrows, battered itself madly into the city walls where its neck finally crunched back into its spine. The animal proved a mountain of flesh too heavy to be simply carted off. Soldiers began carving the thing up, chucking cubes of meat and gizzards into the Euphrates, until bones remained. The soldiers discussed how they intended to melt down swords to bronze the creature's bones as a present to their king.

But they never heard from him.

The day after his return from the wilderness, Gilgamesh gathered with his council in the Avenue of the Gods for General Enkidu's funeral service.

The corpse lay on the softest bed of linens and brushed cotton. His thickly muscled body was wrapped in Gilgamesh's own royal robe. He looked like he was sleeping, but as Gilgamesh knelt by his bedside and clutched his cold hand he wondered if he himself was sleeping. Dreams were so peculiar! Unknowable, with imagery that scorched of smells, sounds, touches indistinguishable from real life, until awakening the dream dissolved as sand in an hourglass! Enkidu was too full of life to be dead! He was the champion of the forests! The world would mourn him too much to allow such a thing!

The king didn't know he was crying until the tears had reached his beard.

Ninsun crouched beside her son, looking at the ape-thing he wept over. Surely it had been only an animal, bright and entertaining as it could often be! That thick jaw protruding from a strong-boned face, the low forehead, the lengthy arms! The mere sight of Enkidu had so often unsettled her sense of the cosmos. Shamash the sun god smiled upon the works of men, not beasts!

But Shamash was also Wer.

Ninsun choked on her rising emotions. She cradled her grieving son, pressing his head to her chest like the night when Dumuzi's thugs had attempted to kill him. She rocked him gently.

Then she looked to Enkidu and saw the creature smiling.

Ninsun gasped, startled at this apparition. Her heart squeezed in rapid contortions.

Behind her, a torchbearer moved silently with firebrand in hand, to light the nightly lampposts around Enkidu's corpse. The flickering light played on Enkidu's face, delicately kissing his cheeks, then melted away. The smile was gone.

She breathed deeply to steady her jarred nerves.

Surely it had only been an illusion caused by firelight. Enkidu's lips were a wide line, partly open to show a flash of teeth. She instantly thought of all the times he had flashed that smile at her. "Mother Ninsun!" he would cry. "Good morning!"

Against her chest, Gilgamesh wailed.

"He is at peace, my child," Ninsun whispered, and then her own tears started, slowly at first, then wetting her face as she felt the gravity of the situation. Man or beast, never would she see his smile again.

"He must allow the creature to be buried!" Zariqu whispered to Nedu. Below them, the king and his mother crouched by Enkidu's side.

Nedu nodded. "You go tell him that, Zariqu."

The Religious Minister's single eye was frantic with anxiety, going from the councilman to the king. "It's been four days! The stink is starting! Flies have surely laid their—"

"*Shhh!*"

"If he remains unburied, his soul will be restless in the afterlife!"

Nedu cocked his head. "So you *do* believe that Enkidu had a soul?"

Zariqu pursed his lips. "As surely as I do. Have you ever seen him placing stones over the kill-spots of the dead?"

The councilman gave a surprised look. "Gilgamesh told me of it. I had no idea you watched him so closely."

"I kept my investigation into Enkidu quiet, but always I kept an eye upon him." He grinned at the old joke. "I wanted to assess for myself his nature. Demon, god-hero, or beast of little consequence."

"And what did you conclude?"

Zariqu scratched his beard. "Enkidu was a beast. Gilgamesh a god. Together, they became human."

CHAPTER 35
FAREWELL

"My friend," Gilgamesh started miserably, looking down at Enkidu's corpse. "Breathe the air again."

Gone were the king's long curls, royal beard, and fine clothes. He had shorn these away in grief, clad his body in simple garments like a peasant. By contrast, Enkidu looked the most regal of rulers ever to have walked the world. He even wore his Harappan medallion around his neck. Six days had passed. Each night the torches were lit, the mourners came bearing gifts and prayers.

He closed his eyes and prayed.

His stomach grumbled, his lips trembled as they repeated his endless plea. In his mind, he climbed up to heaven and sat among the gods.

My friend has died, he told them. Bring him back to life.

We cannot do this.

Then what good are you? Uruk's hunters fetch our meat and farmers grow our crops! Our fishermen cast their nets. Our masons build! What good are you? Bring my friend back to me or I'll build a tower to the sky! I'll call on every ally! I'll hail enemies too! King and petty warlord alike will put aside their differences for a taste of heaven's treasures! We'll storm your grandiose halls! We'll take *your* women for our beds! I killed Ishtar! I can bring all of you down!

His eyes squeezed shut.

Bring my friend back to me!

His heart moaned like a throbbing injury.

I promise no more adventures, he told the gods. Enkidu and I shall never again set foot beyond the boundary stones of Uruk. We'll stay here! We'll drink, eat, bathe, laugh, take wives and rule together! If this was punishment for Humbaba, I beg forgiveness!

For six days he had hardly budged from this spot. Slaves brought him water and forced it into his parched lips. Bread was shredded for him to nibble. Sometimes he allowed it; most often he slapped the rations away. The only time he had spoken was yesterday, when he summoned a blacksmith, lapidary, mason, coppersmith, goldsmith, and jeweler. To them he spoke his instructions: Create a statue of my friend. Place it in the palace gardens. Make him the most beautiful construction. Make it for my friend …

Gilgamesh finished his prayer. He opened his eyes.

Enkidu was still there, unmoving. Gilgamesh doubled over with the agony of helplessness.

There must be something I can do! he prayed. Give my any mission!

Enkidu's nose twitched.

The sight froze the king. His heart galloped, stopped, pumped furiously through his head. For a moment, Gilgamesh thought it had been an illusion. Then the nose twitched again, and Gilgamesh cried out in wild laughter. Enkidu was breathing! His friend was smelling the strange smells of Uruk again! The right nostril flared with life.

No!

Gilgamesh's stomach twisted in horror.

In the dark hollow of his nose, a pale bulb was wriggling. It grew in size, bulging, a glob of white snot perhaps, but no ... it was too alive for that, squirming with the desperate energy of something recently hatched from deep in Enkidu's carcass. A tiny head pushed open Enkidu's nostril.

As the king gaped, the maggot fell out of his friend's nose and entangled with the beard. White-bodied, grotesque beyond description, it wiggled in a wild thumping motion to escape this new prison of hair. Gilgamesh reeled back, knowing that his friend was filled with worms now.

Rotting meat.

He turned away, the vomit bubbling in his throat. Behind the potted plants Gilgamesh retched. When he was done, he looked at the half-digested food his body had evacuated and pictured white maggots there in the bile, squirming with horrid parasitic life.

He stumbled, wiping his mouth. Down three steps he went, keeping Enkidu's body in his sights. The beard twitched.

Gilgamesh fell to one knee and retched again. This time it was mostly dry, though his nose filled with an ammoniac reek. Guards rushed to their king's side.

"Bury him," he said, and curled up where he lay. He slept there like a beggar.

The next day, Ninsun climbed the steps of the ziggurat. A column of forty soldiers followed her, while commoners gathered in the streets to watch the procession file into Ishtar's temple.

The din which followed was short-lived. The muffled screams wouldn't have been heard at street-level on any normal day, but the streets were hushed. Then the bodies of the Ishtar cult were thrown out, one at a time, scantily clad and chopped into pieces. Soon the tongue of stairs was stained bright crimson.

Within the mighty structure, Ninsun moved from chamber to chamber, always ahead of the guards. Foolish, she thought. But her icy anger compelled her onward. She found the Gate of Heaven where the giant bull had been kept, and saw four priestess girls cowering there behind one of its dung-heaps. Ninsun merely pointed, and two soldiers rushed in. Ninsun waited until the girls were dead before moving to the next room.

Top to bottom the Ishtar ziggurat was being emptied. The last room she found was the altar for the Annunaki. In the half-dark, their gemstone eyes chastised her for this intrusion and murder.

"Returned to heaven indeed!" she sneered, letting her hand snatch one up. Pearl eyes, pearl heart. A fantastic piece of craftsmanship from an unknown culture, although hardly worth the suffering caused by Ishtar's unprecedented antics these last few months.

Ninsun's fingers ran across the pearl heart.

The Ishtar cult had merely elected members of its own to become the godhead. Who knew what rituals were used? Ishtar must have been a daughter to one of the old priestesses, conceived by a paying customer, birthed in this dank underworld, and raised to service. By bloodline or furtive vote, she was selected to be the next Ishtar when the one Ninsun had known in her youth was too old to portray the fair Goddess of Love and War.

The temptation to smash the idol slithered into her fingers. Ninsun shook her head, refusing to let her swirling emotions dictate the destruction of these relics. In these southern parts of the Fertile Crescent, the Annunaki statues were revered; besides, breaking them wouldn't resurrect her son's friend.

She returned the item to its shelf and turned away. Suddenly her feet rooted to the floor.

With astonished eyes, Ninsun turned back to the row of statues.

In her mind, the image burned: A strange little latch on the statue's hip. When Ninsun inspected the next relic, she discovered a similar latch. They all did.

Ninsun swooped up the pearl statue again, followed by a ruby one. She compared their latches. Her hands worked carefully, finding where the latches clicked into place. Through trial-and-error, she discovered that some statues attached to others. The result was that the statues were face-down (or face-up, as Ninsun flipped it around in her wondering hands) and connected at the hips.

She held her breath, grabbing the amber statue. It clicked against its brethren.

Excitement mounted rapidly in her heart as her hands fluttered to the shelves and plucked one after another, fitting them, snapped them into the ever-growing—

Map! It's a map! Ninsun gasped as she perceived the swirling lines on each relic becoming the etching of rivers, valleys, mountains. Most astonishing of all, cuneiform wedges unnoticeable before were revealing themselves as different seams came together.

Emerald linked to lapis. Onyx, silver, diamond, gold.

Her heartbeat pounded.

Sapphire into opal.

Ninsun finished assembling the map on the temple floor. When the last piece was fitted she stepped back, breathing hard, the hairs on her neck bristling. The entire Mesopotamian valley faced her in miniature. It wasn't the exact world she knew; some familiar cities were curiously missing, whereas others she'd never heard of sat rendered in metal, gemstone, and carven line. But the Tigris and Euphrates rivers cutting mutual swaths across this metallic landscape were unmistakable, and the mountains were all in their rightful spots. So too was the fabled Mouth of the Rivers, sparkling as a coral heart.

Ninsun studied the cuneiform.

CEDAR FOREST. THE RIVER TIGRIS. ARATTA.

She found Uruk on the map and let her fingers glide southward, to the MOUTH OF THE RIVERS.

Chills popped along across Ninsun's arms. Three words greeted the end of the map, there at the place where the rivers entered into the mysterious sea. A name out of legend was scrawled there—*Utnapishtim* the Immortal. Below this, a small island on the sea with three words.

Ninsun exhaled softly.

NEVER

GROW

OLD.

She was so excited by this discovery that she rushed to show her son, hoping it would pull him out of his grief if only for a moment. She never stopped to think of other consequences.

"Look at it," Ninsun demanded gently. "It's a map."

Gilgamesh stared blankly at the linked arrangement of statues. Gone was his royal beard, shorn off like a sheep's fleece. He looked impossibly young without it.

"A map?"

"Enkidu did not die in vain," Ninsun persisted. "He helped you obtain the final piece to this mystery! These are forgotten chapters, my child! And Enkidu helped in finding it! You should be proud of him! This map ..." Her voice trailed off.

Great gods!

Ninsun prided herself on careful planning for everything she did in life. Haste, reckless emotion, were symptoms of weaker women. Now, suddenly, she knew the worst thing she could ever have done was bring this to her son.

Gilgamesh was already hunching over the map, his fingers touching the Mouth of the Rivers and the coral heart glinting there. "Never Grow Old?"

Ninsun's mouth went dry.

"Mother?"

"It's beautiful, isn't it?"

His fingers traced along the cool metallic and gemstone trail. The Red Deserts, Kish, Assyria and Hattusha, all rendered in exquisite craftsmanship. Gilgamesh touched the Mouth of the Rivers as he might dip a fingertip on the surface of a pond; in the gloom, Ninsun fancied she could actually see ripples spreading out through the metal. It was if the Annunaki flesh had transmuted to liquid, reverting without a kiln to the protean matter from which they had first been formed. More cuneiform like dimples in the skin. Etchings of terrible monsters.

But to Gilgamesh, his delicate caressing of the undulating landscape was conjuring very old memories.

"Mother," the king said, strength creeping back into his voice, "Do you remember my childhood studies? Day One was alphabet. Two was Gods. Three … was history."

Ninsun wrapped her arms around him from behind, tucking her head into his shoulder. Hers was a fierce embrace, as she had done when he was so young, and Dumuzi's advisors forever watched them with leering, malevolent stares. "Yes, my son."

"This name here," Gilgamesh tapped his fingernail against the metal. "'Utnapishtim.' Why does that make me think of Day Three?"

Ninsun spoke rapidly, while fear filled her heart like cold water into a pitcher. "It shouldn't. Utnapishtim is a legend related to the gods. It was taught on Day Two. There is *nothing* historical about it."

Gilgamesh's eyes burned steadily in the lamplight. "Really, mother? I suppose Humbaba was just a story! Or that animal which tore up so much of my city! Utnapishtim was the man who survived the Flood! He had the ear of the gods. Somehow … he convinced them to give him the secret of life!"

Several times she tried to drag him away, promising him a hot meal, or to see how the masons were coming along in building Enkidu's statue. He ardently refused, and when she tried to snatch the map away he held fast to it, hands latched onto its edges—

—*the way those statues latched onto each other*—

and refused to let it go.

"A myth!" Ninsun sobbed.

"A hope!" He stood up and brandished the map like the most priceless shield ever forged. It was a cruel barrier erected between them. "Utnapishtim was given the greatest secret in all history! And I'll be *damned* if I let him hoard that power alone!"

The king walked into the courtyard, where a large block of basalt stone now stood. The chalky marks of chisels striated its surface. Uruk's sculptors were more talented than Babylon's; this hunk of rock would be whittled down over the next few months by master hands, the fragments collected into buckets, while masons fashioned arms, legs, a head! Overseers would consult papyrus notes. The king touched his hand to where, one day, a flattish nose would be hammered into being.

This is my friend now, Gilgamesh thought. Cold, lost, shapeless. The world will never know the sound of his laughter. They'll only see this soulless monument.

The temptation to shove against the stone, topple it, watch it crack on the courtyard, seized him with maddened impulsiveness. He knew that even if the masons could render Enkidu's likeness with perfection, it would still only be insensible rock. Citizens would gather around it, recalling deeds, glory, and perhaps a time they saw Enkidu somewhere in the city. But Uruk's youngest children would have no memories of him. To them and their children, he would be like the masked performers on New Year's Festival: loftily disconnected with their own lives. And where would Gilgamesh, his great friend, be to remind them of Enkidu's wit and soul and humanity?

I'll be dead too, he thought. Just another name on the king-lists. There in the land of shades, might not he and his friend meet again? Gilgamesh's heart suffered, feeling the loss with newfound sharpness.

Little comfort was derived from the city-wide mourning, the gifts sent to the palace, the lamenting songs beneath his window. In fact, with bitter irony the only person Gilgamesh had sought to share in his grief was—of all people—Shamhat, whom Enkidu had loved. But Shamhat was no longer in Uruk. No one knew precisely where she'd gone; there were none in her order to question since they were all thoroughly massacred. Only a guard at the East Gate recalled seeing a woman bearing Shamhat's description leaving by that avenue. Visibly grief-stricken, she had gone, so the guard said, off in the direction of the mountains … to die, to pray, or to seek new life, he did not know.

A mason approached the king nervously; Gilgamesh hadn't even known the man was there. "My Lord? Did you want General Enkidu sculpted as he looked before the Kishian war, or after?"

The king pondered this. "I don't know. The decision I leave to you."

The mason nodded glumly, not pleased with this responsibility. "We will do our best to please you, sire. We've just begun."

Gilgamesh nodded. "So have I."

And so it was that King Gilgamesh left Uruk for the wilderness.

It was a full day before his disappearance became known to the City Council, and three months before word finally leaked to the populace that their beloved eccentric ruler had abandoned them. An effort was made by Ibi-Sin to conceal the knowledge, fearing that civil disorder, foreign invasion, or bounties on their king would occur. Ironically, the first two concerns proved illfounded. Upon learning their king had deserted Uruk, the people gathered outside his palace for twelve days with offerings of lament. Singers praised their king and sympathized with his pain, spinning tales of how he had gone into the underworld to wrestle Enkidu back from the abyss. Ibi-Sin doubled the peace-enforcers of the city, but no trouble sprouted on Urukian soil. Instead, the vanishing was treated with empathy that soon grew into full legend.

Nonetheless, the military advisor made a point of conducting massive military exercises on the plains, to discourage any would-be invaders. And in Kish, news reached the ears of King Agga as he lay in bed with his favorite concubine Beletseri.

"He is dead then?" Agga asked the spy.

"The entire city is in mourning," the spy replied, and for dramatic effect hesitated before uttering his next words: "King Gilgamesh has vacated his city, My Lord."

The Kishian king looked to the floor. "Thank you. Leave us now."

The spy bowed, drawing the door shut. Beletseri saw the pensiveness in her lover's enchanting brown eyes. "You think your enemy has gone off in search of the gates of the underworld? To fight for Enkidu's soul?"

Agga kissed her once more. "I'd do the same for you," he said, and they made love for the rest of the night.

But other kings issued bounties for the king's head throughout the valley, dispatching legions of bounty hunters to hunt him. Hearing this, Nedu used one-fourth of Ishtar's treasury to saturate the countryside with disinformation. *Gilgamesh? He went to return Humbaba's head to the North! He went to Egypt to consult with their famed necromancers! He journeyed into the Zagros!*

Gilgamesh himself heeded none of these concerns. He lost himself in the trees and hills to vanish from the maps of humanity.

The months rolled by without him.

TABLET VIII

THE SPIDER AND THE WASP

CHAPTER 36
SIDURI SWEARS ALLEGIANCE

Warad, his hunting bow in hand, crouched by the shield of uprooted trees overlooking the wooded path. A whirling cloud of mosquitoes hovered by his head, attracted to the sweat glistening on his stubbly face. He let them feed.

In the moonlight, Siduri was a fleet-footed leopard moving from boulder, tree, and brush. This last refuge swallowed her whole; she blended in with its skeleton of branches. The leaves danced slightly. Warad studied the forest for any signs of movement, glint, or sound.

The last few weeks had been this and nothing else; a life of hunting and being hunted. Sixteen of Cyaxares' troops had been killed by Siduri and Warad's hunters. Petty retribution, he thought, when one considered that the villages were entirely destroyed. What plague had partly achieved, the torches of Cyaxares' followers had concluded just days ago.

Warad moved away from the wall of roots and ran to a large, split poplar. Through its Y-shaped limbs he watched for signs of patrolling guards or bowmen in the trees. He knew this path, these woods; they were below the great cliff where the warlord's petty kingdom ruled from. Few warriors patrolled this thickly wooded area, mostly because the threat of lions had recently moved into it. Ironically, this too was a recent phenomenon; Cyaxares' many lion hunts were pushing the beasts into newer, safer territories.

Siduri snuck from her refuge, lupine-like in the moonlight. Her hair looked oily black and wild, matted into serpents framing her ash-covered face. The smell of her camouflage alone was enough to ignite old memories. As she ran, thoughts of her quiet tavern sank, bubbling, into a deeper sea of vicious pleasures. She missed these hunts!

Two days after the plague rats were discovered, Lord Cyaxares sent an emissary to the villages.

Ereshkigal has punished your obstinance, the bearded man told her. *But Lord Cyaxares still desires you as his wife, Siduri. His empire must expand. You can be ambassador to the southern peoples who know you. This is our Lord's will.*

It was Warad and his brothers who sent the emissary's body riding back with a hole in his chest, a rat tied into his mouth.

After that she sent Urshanabi and his sister away southeast with the village survivors. Her tavern was now the only stationary target; curiously, it had been spared. She'd retrieved what she needed from it anyway: dried foodstuffs, a waterskin, Taharqa's Nubian blade, and a small leather sack from those early hunting days. Warad had asked to see the items kept in it; he looked, then shook his head, not understanding.

The forest ended sharply at a cliff, atop which Cyaxares' hut overlooked the two rivers. It was possible to scale; vines, jutting rocks, crevices for handholds, provided an agile climber plenty to work with. Ideally, Siduri wanted the ascent timed with rainfall to cover their sounds and movement. But the last few days had been dry, and Cyaxares' men were now openly combing the countryside for her renegade group. The only place to hide was *in* his territory.

Siduri came to the tree-line where the cliff sprouted. Up top, the pointed roof of the hut was visible. So was a line of vigilant archers positioned as lookouts.

Her hands contorted into frustrated claws. By the cursed gods! Nine people could not take them on and live.

So take them on and die, Taharqa would say in these circumstances. Siduri had known her old mentor nurtured an Assyrian-like desire to die in battle against impossible odds. That philosophy had likely encouraged his suicidal impalement on her blade.

The problem with Taharqa (at least, one of many problems with that slayer) was that he was no strategist. A little deceit, some planning, and lots of reckless audacity. Those kinds of tactics typically worked against trade caravans or small encampments. A warlord kingdom of one thousand men was immune.

But there were still options. She needed some rain to cover her sprint to the cliff-feet. The sky was presently missing the required clouds, but patience would reward her. She'd send Warad and the others to the opposite side of Cyaxares' hill. They'd stage a false attack; starting an oil-based fire perhaps in several spots, then shooting dead the warriors who came to investigate. With luck, the cliff-top archers would abandon their posts to be part of the action, giving her enough time to ascend the rocks.

From high above came a voice. "Siduri!"

Her heart stammered. She felt a mosquito land on her cheek and bite.

"Siduri if you're down there!" the voice continued. "We have the boy! He is tied up like a pig and hung from a spit! Lord Cyaxares made some alliances among the southeastern villages! They were very helpful when told the boy carried plague!"

Warad peeked out from the bushes, watching her.

"Siduri if you're down there! The boy confessed where the Immortal lives! The little island! There are monsters protecting him! Great scorpion-things that patrol his forest! The boy told us everything!"

Siduri heard a strange rattling in her head. She realized it was her teeth, clenching with impotent fury and grief.

"Siduri! Lord Cyaxares requests one final time for your hand in marriage. If you fail to answer within two days, this young boy gets roasted and fed to our dogs! We await your—"

She stepped out of the tree-line into moonlight. With the back of her hand she smeared off the coating of ash from her forehead. Behind her, Warad panicked.

"What are you doing?" he cried.

Siduri ignored him. She craned her neck to the unseen orator and shouted, "Is the boy alive?"

"For now!"

"Tell Lord Cyaxares I will surrender."

Warad took two rapid steps to her and grabbed her wrist. "You cannot!"

She hissed violently at him. "I can do whatever I wish! Cyaxares has defeated us! His priest sent plague into the villages, they have killed the few who remained, and now he's captured a child I care for very deeply. What, should we spend the remainder of life hiding in these woods? We've *lost!*" To the cliff-top, she shouted, "I will swear my allegiance!"

A smug murmuring passed among the archers.

"You must do more than that!" the voice persisted. "Our Lord demands that Siduri the Tavern-keeper perform special obsequences to prove her allegiance." And he proceeded to spell out terms of her surrender.

Warad frothed in barely controlled mania. But Siduri only listened patiently while absently tapping her small leather satchel. When the instructions were completely recited, she told the archers that all would be done at sunset. She'd come alone.

So much life thrived near the Mouth of the Rivers. The marshy forests provided home to myriad predators, prey, burrowers, egg-stealers, leaf-cutters, tree-hoppers, branch-nesters, and even some refugees from the deserts in the form of black-tailed scorpions. In her travels she had seen even greater varieties of animals, including rare things few people would believe. Once in her marauding days, she spied a herd of gigantic camels three times larger than the average.

In the burnt-orange glow of a failing afternoon, however, Siduri found the forest preternaturally quiet. She strode on, weaponless, clad only in her leather tunic, a long-necked vase of wine in her hands. Guards spotted her early; they warily searched her for concealed daggers, found none, and waved her onward.

Still there was no life other than man. Siduri approached the warrior-ringed hut longing for a glimpse of gazelle, or even a falcon drawing lazy circles in the sky. The old healers knew a grim rhyme to explain it: the precise words escaped her, but it had something to do with how wherever man's footsteps went, silence followed.

"Welcome, tavern-keeper," a guard murmured.

Denied the company of animals, Siduri looked westward to where the sun was melting down into a brilliant fiery smear. She knew poems regarding sunsets, too.

Four guards flanked each side of the hut's entranceway. Behind them, a drawn curtain prevented her seeing what ceremonies awaited her, but dusky torchlight flickered to the tune of crude jabber.

Siduri halted before the grinning guards.

"You were given specific instructions," one began.

Siduri's lips were set like those of a tranquil statue. She handed the vase over, pulled her tunic over her head, exposing her large breasts to the chilly air. Then she skinned out of her undergarments, letting them crumple around her ankles. Buttocks, legs like slender tree limbs, concave belly, she took back her vase and, with a quick glance at the timbers over her head, entered Cyaxares' hut.

That glimpse satisfied her wanting. Before she passed into the gloomy hut, she'd seen a brown spider tickling its web, strands stretched across the narrow gap between wooden timbers. Something had landed there, blue and winged, a wasp probably, and its frantic fight was a haunting epic all its own. The wasp wrestled for freedom, while the spider tried binding it with ever more silken chains. No one but her noticed.

"Here she is!" Cyaxares exclaimed. He edged forward on his throne, a goblet spilling over in one outstretched hand, and let himself be stirred by her nakedness. Within the red flickering enclosure, his audience of war councilors lustfully shared the view.

The tavern-keeper knelt in front of him.

Great gods! Cyaxares' loins hardened. The sight of her was intoxicating, whetting his appetite like kindling with the knowledge that she would be his. He would break her like a stallion. Sweet Siduri!

In a thick voice, he said, "My lovely Siduri! You swear allegiance to me now?"

"I do," she said.

"You will be my wife?"

"I will."

"What of the rebel hunters? Did you—"

"Kill them all? With ease, and I am prepared to take you to their mass grave."

Cyaxares nodded, wanting to believe her, having his doubts. Nergal had warned him of the shrewdness of Siduri the Wild One. Yet Ereshkigal had spared her; surely even Nergal failed to appreciate this omen. The tavern-keeper was sheltered by destiny; it was surely Ereshkigal's doing.

The warlord's cheeks reddened with heat. "And you've brought me a gift?"

Siduri held up the amphora. "Wine from Nubia."

Standing beside the warlord, Priest Nergal watched her skeptically. "Then we shall test this wine on your young friend. If it kills him, you shall be whipped bloody for months, tavern-keeper."

Cyaxares clapped his hands. A moment later, a lamb was brought in, tied to a pole. Nergal began chanting, Cyaxares circling in the other direction, brandishing his knife. His warlords smiled contentedly. He cut the creature's throat and caught the crimson jet in his cattle-horn goblet. Crazily, Siduri found herself wondering who had won the fight outside: the wasp, or the spider.

"I offer you the first drink, Siduri. Swallow this offering as pledge of your eternal obedience … to me."

Siduri held out her hands to accept the goblet. Cyaxares watched her tilt the cup, draining half. She then gave it back. He scooped the goblet. Gulped the steaming, salty drink. Tossed it away.

"Now give yourself to me!"

Siduri crawled on all fours to the center of the hut. Her rear thrust out, her back dipped seductively, her ribs visible. The audience watched with licking lips.

Cyaxares disrobed his kilt. His prong upturning its head, protruding like a palace pillar. Siduri felt the head of his pillar press crudely against her portals. His hand seized a fistful of her hair and she groaned. That sound was so delightful! He thought she looked remarkably like the lioness he'd speared—he grinned at his own joke. His member, already throbbing by the sight of her crescent-like buttocks, burned.

Siduri felt the invasion of her body. She caught Nergal's disinterested gaze and stared until, visibly uncomfortable with the whole business, the priest turned away, fumbling through old parchment.

The warlord grunted as he pushed all the way in. Dizzy, feverish with lust. For too long he'd desired this warrior-woman. Great gods! It would be shameful if his Final Moment arrived early; he struggled to contain it. His rhythmic thrusts brought him dangerously close to the edge. Siduri wasn't helping; she ground against him until he was forced into staying her hips, teeth clenched, to delay climax. Sweat was breaking out all across his face. His skin itched, impelling him to scratch savagely.

Siduri looked to the war council. They were haughtily mesmerized.

Again came the thought: Had the spider killed the wasp? Did the winged interloper win its freedom?

Cyaxares coughed feverishly, no longer worried with finishing early. He was so hot, burning up. His chest grew heavier as if invisible coils were tightening across it. Then came the pain.

With a small cry, he removed himself from Siduri. The council erupted in cheers, not immediately seeing that something was wrong. When he started convulsing, it was Nergal who flew up from his seat and rushed to his master.

"Sire?"

The warlord hastily strove to form words, to explain that some god or goddess was punishing him for violating Siduri, but his lips wouldn't work. He couldn't breathe. He fell to the ground, twitching and frothing.

Nergal had seen these symptoms before.

"You smuggled *scorpion venom* into the goblet?" he cried, turning to face Siduri.

She was already in mid-lunge, and before he could cry for guards, or utter a spell of protection, or simply scream in fear, she had smashed the vase into his face. He was immediately doused with the putrid wine, sputtering and spitting, realizing with horror that oil was mixed with it.

Siduri's hand came down on his throat. His larynx was pulverized, breath whistling through the passage like wind rustling a shattered flute.

The tavern-keeper stood, spat out the small bladder she'd used to hold the lethal venom beneath her tongue, and strode naked to the hut's wall. The war council's conversations had dissipated. They stared, unbelieving, as Siduri plucked a torch from its holding and returned to Nergal. Seeing her intentions, his eyes bulged.

"Si … du..ri.… Please!"

She bared her teeth. "Walk the Fire Road, Nergal!"

His face immolated the second it was kissed by the flame. She pinned him in place until it was done.

CHAPTER 37
THE LIONS' CRY

She waited for them to kill her.

Unlike Taharqa's glory-in-death philosophy, Siduri realized, facing Cyaxares' councilors, that she wanted to live. The monster was slain; so was his king. There was tremendous life remaining outside the hut; for the third time she found herself wondering if the wasp had succeeded in escaping the spider's web. *Just let me know that!* she asked whatever spirits, phantoms, or gods might be listening.

"Let Urshanabi go," she heard herself utter. Her lips trembled to say more, to barter with these ruffians for the safety of the boy. They might even accept her terms ... but something stayed her voice. Her green eyes lifted to the men watching her.

The bearded, swarthy lot sat transfixed in their furs, goblets in hand, as if stunned by a reenactment of some cosmic drama—Marduk slaying Tiamat perhaps? Or Uruk's first king seducing Ishtar?

Urshanabi was brought before her just a few minutes later. His hands were bound with rope, and his face, arms, and wrists were bruised, but he was otherwise intact. He ran into her arms when he saw her. The temptation to flee the hut possessed Siduri's limbs but she ignored it; determined to play this part to the end for their survival, she boldly walked to the nearest man and plucked his dagger from his beltline. Then she slashed Urshanabi's bonds, tossed the knife to its owner, and calmly—slowly—walked from the hut. Evening's blanket was the only apparel she afforded herself until safely within her tavern again.

The boy slept soundly in one of her guestrooms, once his wrist's abrasions had been treated. Siduri waited until she could hear his rhythmic breathing before she retired to a pantry. Amid the casks of wine, ale, and mead, Warad and eight other hunters were huddled together.

Warad exhaled forcefully. "He is dead, then?"

"Both of them."

"What will happen now?"

"You and your men will leave. Fetch your families and rebuild, or move south with them."

The hunters stood. In the gloom they looked like gatekeepers to the underworld, wrapped in sooty livery, silent, mysterious.

Warad heard the resignation in her voice, however. "Siduri..."

She considered the faceless, black shape from where his voice came. "Yes?"

"What about Cyaxares' men? His sons? What if they come for us?"

By way of answer, Siduri walked to the front door of her tavern and opened the door. "I cannot see into tomorrow. I only know that right now, tonight, I am very tired. My tavern will be open to all in the morning. Observe its rules." Her chest constricted with sharp sadness. It was a familiar feeling. Every time she had bid farewell to a chapter of her life, her soul twisted in silent mourning.

The villages are gone!

The hunters will go with them!

Siduri's face hardened while the men filed past her, heads low. She wondered what they were thinking about. Despite their beards they looked like little children to her, alone with troubled thoughts. She wanted to embrace them all and offer words of undying friendship.

From somewhere close by, a lion roared.

All heads snapped in the sound's direction. They knew the language of beasts, and this roar was one of pain. A second lion answered it. Then abrupt silence fell, a little too swiftly to be natural.

A lion had just been killed in the woods nearby. No rumbling chariot, trumpets, or clashing cacophony linked with royal lion hunts. A lion had been killed without ceremony. Siduri wondered, just as she'd wondered about the wasp in the spider-web, what had taken its life so swiftly in the lightless forest.

It matters not, she thought bitterly. There is nothing constant in life but Ereshkigal's cold seduction.

And constant, merciless, unrelenting change.

Warad was last to go and he turned, understanding what Siduri was feeling and wanting to think of something to say, the proper farewell perhaps, or a promise to see her in the morning, but when he looked back at her the tavern door was already closed.

TABLET IX

THE OLD MAN

CHAPTER 38
STONES FOR THE DEAD

There was no shortage of lions in the Fertile Crescent's wet, diverse country. They had stalked prey, mated, formed prides of playful cubs, in the days far before the ice-walls sheared the forests away. The men-things who once frolicked in high branches were forced into life on the open, raw country of grasslands. It was here that lions ruled supreme. Wooly titans lumbered in the meltwater marshes, but lions had mastered the grassy yellow plains. They melted into the foliage like the very ice which had passed.

For so long, men-things were easy to kill. They knew it, too. From the lonely trees that remained, they ventured forth into lethal grasslands where the supreme predators lurked. Their reddish fur was poor camouflage. All they could do was lean back on their hind legs, propping up their dwarfish bodies, and try to see over the tall plants. Sometimes they spotted the stray hairs of the nightmarish felines and could get away before the pounce. Other times they weren't so fortunate. The lions ate well.

But in a terribly ironic way, this very act of defense turned the tables in the coveted battlefield for top predator, for when men-things took to standing upright they found other uses for their free hands. Stones, jagged and pain-causing. Sticks wielded wildly, to discourage some lions. And in time, the careless rubbing of sticks created fire. Grasslands were set ablaze, while torch-wielding men-things could now venture out even at night and drive lions from caves. It didn't take long for sticks to become spears; tendons plucked from slain beasts were twisted into bowstrings, and the magic of fire soon birthed the first blacksmiths.

The lions' time-tested supremacy was fading fast; so quickly, in fact, that they had precious little time to notice. They went on with what they knew; stalking in the brush, killing what they could, and of course defending their territories from all invaders.

In the country once belonging to a man named Cyaxares, two lions were hunting together. Their alpha had been slain, and the contest to take his place was pitifully brief, for an interloper had bested all contenders and driven them away. The females were his now. So was the land.

So it was that the two lions, both males, were hunting together in the black hours of morning on the periphery of their old grounds. The air was rich with scents. New territorial scents telling them, as surely as boundary stones or yellow-

feathered arrows for the men who lived no so far away, that this region had been claimed and would tolerate no trespassers.

They were hunting gazelle. Gazelle-scent was most heavy on the air.

Blood, too. Something had been killed not far off. The two lions were capable hunters but their flanks were crusted with the scabs of wounds recently received in the contests for dominance. Their bellies yearned for food. Perhaps then, healed and sated, they would together drive off the interloper.

They padded out into the hilly country, tracking the blood. Yes. Something had been killed fresh. Together, they could drive off whatever had slain it and claim the flesh for themselves. It would be easier, in their wounded condition.

One of them stopped, abruptly, as another scent drifted to him. Its companion also halted, seeing confusion and fear in the other's face. The larger of the two sniffed again to be sure. It growled low and derisively.

Man.

The unmistakable musk of man was intermingled with the gazelle's fragrant life. The lions waited, seeking more information from the black morning's breeze. Men often hunted in packs with terrifying wheeled companions and bright metallic fangs. If many men had brought down the gazelle the lions would dare not interrupt them.

The larger male was hungry and curious, though. Men made so much noise and the morning was absent of their usual clamor. He came to a hilltop and crouched, staying low, to peer down the short valley. The gazelle was there. Dead, bleeding, and beside it was the man who had killed it. Only one.

The white moon was gone, but there was enough starlight to illuminate the man's metal fang by his side. Yet he was busy using it to cut away long strips of meat.

The lion's stomach grumbled. His companion slunk beside him, watching.

The wind blew into them. Yes. There was only one man downwind from them, in the dark. There was enough meat between them to justify attacking.

The lions began their stealthy approach. Men were bizarre and frightening, but they didn't have the alertness of other prey animals. The large male enjoyed the ease of this hunt. He dared to edge even closer before he'd pounce. The scent of blood made him salivate.

He watched the dull flash of the metal fang cutting the gazelle.

Then he lunged.

Across the grass he came like a lightning bolt and was upon the man at once. His claw tore open flesh, the man screamed, and, amazingly, didn't try to run off as wounded prey so often did. Splatter was ripe in the air. The lion tried going for the man's throat. The man was still screaming, one arm batting wildly at the lion.

Too late, the lion realized it wasn't just an arm wavering about. It was the metal fang.

What should have been an easy mauling turned into horrendous agony for the lion. The metal fang whirled down on his claw. There was pain and the instinctual realization that the claw had been dismembered. Spurting, made worse when he put weight on it, the lion hesitated, transfixed with the instinct to flee, he proved too angry and unwilling to give up. He lunged again and sank his teeth into the man's leg. By the time he felt the metal fang cutting straight down into his skull, he was already dead.

His companion wasn't as experienced a hunter, but he charged on anyway, seeing that the man was distracted by the first attack. The man heard him coming, though. He glared at the nightshine of his new attacker's eyes and roared himself. The lion leapt. The man crouched behind the dead attacker and avoided the initial lunge. The lion circled, attacked again.

The metal fang pierced his face. The lion howled pitifully. Other cuts of the weapon silenced his further complaint.

The man, staggering drunkenly with all that had transpired, collapsed.

When the vultures came in the morning, it seemed that four corpses—an impossibly wonderful feast—was waiting for them.

At first, he never felt the flies landing on his open wounds.

His mind drifted dreamily, untethered from his body like driftwood on fast-flowing river currents. This image might have been relaxing to another man, but to him it had grotesque parallels. Chunks of driftwood were too much like the body he had found in the Euphrates many months ago. A waterlogged body crawling with maggots.

Gilgamesh awoke in a frenzy. He wasn't aware of pain, not at first, just that his face was sticky and legs were numb. He saw the flies though, looking like black beads on his yawning red wounds. A dozen of them. Sitting in his glistening underskin. He slapped at them in a maniacal panic, and then the pain crackled through him. He screamed in defiance of it, giving a violent start to the vultures. They flapped off, settled a few hops away, and squawked in black-feathered tantrums.

The months had changed the former king of Uruk. Lost in the wilds with only the sun and river guiding his southward trek, he had become a dirt-caked, wild-haired, ragged creature with hunted eyes. He tried to stand again and collapsed. The lion attack seemed a dream. Seeing their pecked, steaming hides around him astonished him.

What he couldn't see disquieted him more. Maggots were all around him, hiding in their invisible eggs, in the steam of coppery-scented flesh. He staggered away from the bodies and tried ascending the hill. He fell again.

A familiar shape hunched over him in the grass.

"You look not good, my friend," Enkidu said.

"I feel not good," Gilgamesh said, hearing the slur in his words. Hunter's shock, it was called. He recognized all the symptoms. He tried to stand again, thought maybe he should use his sword as a walking-staff, then wondered where his sword was. He blinked stupidly, surveying the massacre he'd just left. "I have no stones to put over the dead."

"You must clean wounds," Enkidu suggested.

Gilgamesh tried to make his mouth work. The slurring was so bad he could barely dredge sounds from his throat. He staggered on all fours uphill until he spied the stream on the other side.

Several times he almost passed out. His peripheral vision greyed until he could only see the stream as if through a tunnel. When he reached it he fell, face-first. Pain burst in his nose and turned the water red. But he drank, steadily.

Get up! his mind screamed. *Get up or you'll drown in four inches of water!*

"You must sit up, my friend," Enkidu said.

Gilgamesh lifted his face from the trickling stream. On the water's opposite bank sat a pale green frog watching him with unfazed equanimity.

Pulling himself to his knees took an effort akin to trying to wrench a chariot out from semi-solid mud. Yet somehow, he found himself weaving unsteadily like an enrapt worshiper at the feet of an oracle. His legs felt as if they'd been set afire. Gilgamesh knew enough about open wounds to realize the danger of rot-demons burrowing into his muscle. He had to treat them, scrub the demons out, break through the dried blood, clean them out.

"Find bitter plants," Enkidu suggested, and hopped off into the nearby forest.

Gilgamesh tottered backwards. He wanted to sleep, but he battled the white-hot agony in his legs to stand and push off into the woods. The sun speared his eyes with amber light. The ground shook with every leaden step—

He was in a forest, having already forgotten about the stream. Lapsing again into a dreamlike trance, Gilgamesh zigzagged through the trees as if a rope was pulling him onwards, toward uncertain destinations. Walking was almost like falling. If he encountered another hill, he wasn't sure he'd manage it. If another lion appeared (he hadn't forgotten them) he was done for.

"No more lions here," Enkidu said, appearing again beside him and galloping on all fours in a curious, sideways shuffle so he could face Gilgamesh while moving abreast of him.

"Neeeeither aare yooooou," the king managed. "You diiiiiied."

Enkidu shrugged in a way he had never done. "And I lived," he said, and was gone in a blur of trees. Gilgamesh blinked and stared ahead of him.

He had no idea where he was. Even uninjured, this territory stimulated no familiarity in his memory. The old road to Aratta was long-since overgrown. But there was a smell on the air. Gilgamesh craned his neck so his matted, filthy locks hung lankly down his neck. He sniffed the air.

There was a lake or large body of water nearby. Gilgamesh remembered words from the map his mother had shown him; those words passed, indecipherable, through his feverish mind. And the shouting voices, piping suddenly from the nearby woods, confused him.

"You!" a voice cried. Shapes were moving out of the wilderness.

Gilgamesh trudged forward. His vision was swimming. He might have fallen right then, since black dots were swamping his eyes, but this thought pushed him onward, because maybe the black dots were flies, and he couldn't let them infect him with their eggs.

The worm wriggling in Enkidu's nose.

An arrow flew over Gilgamesh's head. His legs pumped, hands parting tall reeds, and suddenly he was on a shoreline.

Again, angry men were shouting. Gilgamesh looked up and down the beach and saw a lonely cabin interrupting the otherwise bleak landscape.

Just a little further, no? Gilgamesh grimaced and was moving again, kicking sand with each step. He wove off toward the sea, fell into the dirt and rolled onto his injured arm. The pain made him giddy and nauseous by turns, but the water felt so good rushing over his body …

"Wake up!"

Gilgamesh coughed in the water.

Enkidu was over him again, face crinkled in concern. "You want drown, my friend?"

"No." Gilgamesh heard his voice and it was no longer slurred. He stumbled toward the tavern. His feet were unsteady. He wove, trying not to fall. The sea's tide crashed behind him.

Then he saw the woman by the shore.

And she saw him.

A basket of clothes in her arms, Siduri took once look at the bloodied monster crossing the distance to her and knew there would be trouble. The wild-haired, bearded, ensanguined man was clearly in need of help, but his eyes were possessed, forming the most frightful visage she'd ever seen in her life. Not even Taharqa, crusted with battle-gore, could compete with the savage creature hobbling after her.

Siduri was weaponless; she turned her back on the sea and sprinted for her tavern. Before she reached the door she looked to see how much progress the man had made and shouted, for he was *right there*, and she dropped the basket, ducked inside, and slammed the door shut in his face. Shutting and bolting it, she plucked her dagger off the wall.

"Open up!" Gilgamesh cried, falling against the door. His fists hammered it. "*Open the door!*"

The frame shook from his pounding. Siduri backed away, breathing hard, considering her options. He was wounded, feverish, probably close to death anyway. He might be demon-ridden. From the other side of the door, she heard wild laughing. It froze her veins.

"What have you seen, tavern-keeper? What fills you with fear? Open the door or I'll **smash it through!**"

The door bulged as he threw himself against it.

"If you enter here, you die!" Siduri shouted back.

"Then come and kill me!"

Her window exploded. Her basket skittered across the tavern floor, discarding clothes like the slough-off of reptiles.

Siduri tightened her grip on the dagger. "You are only making your wounds worse!"

"I did not come this far to die!" Gilgamesh roared.

"What do you want?"

A place to rest, Gilgamesh thought feverishly. *Then Enkidu and I can continue our quest.* The laughter bubbled up in him, hideous, unstoppable.

"You cannot come in," Siduri repeated.

"*I can do whatever I want!*" Gilgamesh shouted, stumbling back from the door and eying another way in. The world was turning into a tunnel again. "I slew Humbaba and the Bull of Heaven! I defeated Agga of Kish! I killed lions who *dared* to attack me!"

Lions. Siduri thought back to the wounds on his arms and leg. Yes, those were the gouge-marks of a lion attack. She heard a crash outside, but it wasn't against her door. The immediate silence told her what had happened.

Siduri opened the door and saw the stranger on the ground, his eyes rolled back in his head. She went to his scabbard and found it empty. But there was a dagger there. She plucked it from the sheath.

The weapon was remarkably well-fashioned. This was no shoddy work of a second-rate blacksmith. Careful patterns intersected with spirals, and above them was chiseled a high palace. She wondered who he had murdered to obtain it.

He weakly tried to grab her hands. She batted them away and then pressed the dagger to his throat. From up the beach, Warad and two of his hunters came running.

Siduri swallowed hard. She looked back to the stranger. "My name is Siduri, and you must pledge to obey my will. If you attempt to bring me harm, I can end your life as surely as save it."

"Treat me, please," he said brokenly.

The note of desperation moved her. "I shall take that as a yes." She tossed his dagger away and began to drag him inside. The men up the beach were shouting to her.

"I have to save my friend," the stranger said.

She didn't stop pulling him, but grunted a reply. "Where is your friend?"

"On the Fire Road of Ereshkigal."

Her hands froze and released him. His head struck the sand, inches from the doorway. "Are you one of Nergal's servants?" she spat.

"Ereshkigal…"

Siduri almost drew her own dagger and cut his throat. Only the recent tide of death stayed her hand, just for a moment, while she summoned another question to delay succumbing to the instinct.

"Who was your friend?"

"General Enkidu."

"*Who?*"

The stranger's head rolled again, his eyes showing their whites. Siduri struggled to recall the name. It rang with buzzing familiarity. "Who are you?"

"King Gilgamesh of Uruk," he said, and then sleep took him.

CHAPTER 39
CONVERSATIONS

"You made us wait out here for two hours!"

"I had to treat my guest. His wounds were extremely serious."

"He has the plague, Siduri!"

"He does not. And did plague keep me from treating your villagers? What has he done?"

"He's an intruder."

"From Cyaxares' camp? Somehow, I doubt that."

"We saw him leaving a kill-site. Two lions and a gazelle."

"He was alone? He killed two lions *on his own?*"

"I tell you he is an intruder from hell."

"Let me determine what his problem is."

"Siduri ..."

"Since I set up this tavern, I have always treated those who came to me. You want to kill him? Wait until he leaves my house."

"I do not ... I ... Why are you hostile to me, all of a sudden?"

"My apologies."

"We are building fortifications in the south-east, Siduri. Come there with us. We could use someone of your skills."

"I will consider it."

Siduri watched her guest sleep.

Many times, he turned over in his sleep and sobbed. He was one of the tallest men she'd ever seen, with a sculpted body fitting for a crazed brute who survived by strength alone. She approached him, her bare feet silent on the floorboards, and peered at his face. A frown furrowed his brow even in slumber.

Yes, tall. But not quite up to the stupendous dimensions she'd heard attributed to the fabled Urukian king. Nonetheless, he'd have made a powerful addition to her old marauding band.

Though she was certain the lion's claw hadn't punctured the Blood Fountain high in his leg, she checked the limb again anyway. Hours earlier she'd washed it, rubbed healing ointments into the wound, and stitched the flesh closed. The bandages were soaked heavy now. They'd have to be changed tomorrow. Siduri looked at the rest of his naked form. Her eyes noticed other scars, white and faded, on his bare chest.

Then she leaned back against the wall and considered what to do. It was a relief, actually, that he was not involved with the Ereshkigal cult or Cyaxares' kingdom. Siduri had always been fascinated with the world beyond this province's politics (like recent *murderous* politics, she numbly reminded herself) and the stranger clearly hailed from the north. Even slurred, his voice betrayed the fluid, lofty cadence of the northern cities.

Then there was his dagger. After treating his wounds, she had fetched and examined it. Urukian art was unknown to her; but that the blade was fashioned by a royal blacksmith was not hard to believe. Lapis set in a copper hilt with skill and a master artist's confidence. There were no such weapons like that here.

Siduri scratched her neck absently. It embarrassed her that she found herself entertaining the possibility that he might actually be the legendary king. He was likely some madman who, hearing the many tales of Uruk (and there were many tales ... surely, the real Gilgamesh was employing some master bards as of late) had fancied himself to be that ruler.

She looked to his beard. Scraggly, wild, peppered with bits of leaves, dirt, blood. Then she gasped, startled.

His eyes were open, watching her.

"I have no money to pay you for these services."

Siduri nodded, trying to find her voice. There was *no way* he could be conscious after the opium she'd given him; not to mention the sleep his body was surely demanding. On her doorstep he'd been an exhausted, brutalized figure. Many such men had come to her. Some died, others lived to die someplace else.

"Your dagger would fetch me a good price," she said.

For an instant, the stranger's eyes grew sad at the prospect of losing this weapon. Then he nodded.

"Or," Siduri added, "When you are better you could pay your debt through helping the southeastern villages. They need reinforcements built. Walls—"

"Walls?" he laughed bitterly. "Yes, I have some experience building walls!"

Siduri shivered from the cold hate in his laugh. "Yes, I suppose the king of Uruk would."

He looked unsettled. "You recognize me?"

"You told me," she reminded him. Then she realized that, in his delirium, he probably recalled very little of their initial encounter. "I asked your name, and you informed me of ... your royalty." She had meant to keep her skepticism out of her voice, but it filled the words anyway. "I thought you were a murderer."

"I am."

Siduri sat back, coughing slightly on the reek of medicinal oils. She rubbed her hands clean on a fresh towel. "You swore an oath to abide by my rules here."

"And I will."

"My tavern is a neutral place. All respect it."

He considered the room while she studied his face. Finally, he asked, "Who rules these lands?"

"Recently they were claimed by Cyaxares."

He shrugged. "I've never heard the name."

"He's dead now."

The stranger asked for more water. Siduri brought it to his lips, tilted it. He started choking after a few gulps, sputtering, and his eyes became crazed again. She wondered if Warad was right; maybe he was possessed.

But Gilgamesh was only preoccupied with the blackness of the room, the stink of medicinal rags, the black curtain …

The South Tower!

Dear gods!

"Be still!" Siduri exclaimed. Surely he was too weak to harm her! She should be capable of subduing him easily. Then again, it was inconceivable that he could be awake and so vital. He was like a creature ridden by sinister forces of unknowable and unstoppable strength, which would force him to wicked agendas long after he lacked the ability, so he would become as a puppet manhandled into action.

The stranger's lips formed a crooked smile. Coupled with the haunted look in his eyes, he really did look like an intruder from a grotesque underworld. Then the stranger's eyes filled with tears and the illusion vanished.

Siduri came to his side again. "You must be still! I have stitched your wounds. Please try to sleep. You need rest, for …"

Her words dissolved, for just then sleep waylaid him like an expert assassin.

CHAPTER 38
RHYMES

The next morning she returned to the shore with her basket which, along with her clothes, now contained crimson-stained rags, bandages, and empty medicine cups in need of scrubbing. Later she changed his bandages. She methodically sniffed the raw, bubbly scabs for indications of infection. Lion claws were terribly dirty; the stranger had escaped with both his life and health.

He slept through most of it. It wasn't until the last hour of morning that he woke, begging for water. She spooned some fish soup into his mouth. Then he slept soundly for the rest of the day. She tied his hands to the bed-frame; his wounds would start itching as they healed, and few men could resist scratching despite the danger of reopening the stitches.

The following day she entered to find him wide awake. He turned his head and wiggled the fingers of his bound hands.

"I forgot your name," he began.

She reminded him, sat by his bedside, and held out a new cup of hot soup. "You need to drink this."

"I swore an oath to abide by your rules. It is not necessary to bind me like this."

"I did not want you scratching your wounds."

"I won't," he said. "Let me feed myself, please."

Siduri undid the knots. Gilgamesh rubbed his wrists, took the soup, and smelled it. His nose wrinkled.

"Drink," she said.

Gilgamesh looked at the vast amounts of spice barrels and weeds, the crushed powders in medicine drawers. "You manage this place on your own. No guards? No soldiers? How is it you're not robbed?"

Siduri shrugged. "It has happened. Two thieves attacked me one night, and plundered much of what I have. A hunter killed them a league from here and brought back all my stolen items. The locals knew me. I treat the ones who come to me. They pay me how they can. I have no enemies."

Gilgamesh sipped from the soup and retched on its bitter taste.

"A man who kills lions balks at soup?"

Glaring out from his sun-burnt, scabbed face, Gilgamesh brought the bowl to his lips and gulped it all. It steamed and scalded as it went down. Siduri took the empty bowl from him.

She asked, "Why are you in these lands?"

"Utnapishtim. I seek him."

Siduri looked blankly. "I have never heard such a name."

"Yes you have," he said wryly.

"I do *not* take kindly to being branded a liar."

"Then do not lie!" He gave a confident grin, and the expression subdued the glassy coldness in his eyes. "'*All beasts chatter as they can* ...'"

"'*But truth is found in the eyes of man,*'" Siduri finished the rhyme.

Gilgamesh smiled again. He was a handsome vagabond, Siduri decided. Probably insane, but there was something else, too. A dignity tarnished with grief, a cultured soul broken by anguish too great to name. Here was a voluntary exile.

"Your eyes of sea-glass and green fire burned," the stranger continued, "when I spoke his name. The old rhyme is true, Siduri. Utnapishtim lives close. Perhaps he goes by other names. Ziusudra to some. Atrahasis to others."

"Yes," Siduri breathed. "And he is simply an old man who others believe is immortal."

"You believe it."

"No."

"Yes you do."

A gleam came into her eyes. It was as if the tales of a thousand travelers were swirling in her pupils, throwing color like the spices of so many different lands, the painted faces of tribesmen and the dyes of royalty, the words of bards, the eyes and exposed hearts of the Annunaki! In Siduri's eyes radiated the delight of those gems and metals and pearls.

"I believe that others do," she said. "That they would kill a kindly elder to demand such powers for themselves, when in fact he has none to give but compelling tales of bygone days. Do you not understand? The stories of yesterday were collected like rainwater, and passed down many generations to him. So yes, he's an ancient man in the sense that he possesses the collected knowledge of those before him. He is a treasure." She smiled. "You should hear the rhymes *he* knows."

"Tell me."

They were stories she'd heard from the old man's lips, when Urshanabi took her out on his boat to visit the island's forested shore. They never set foot on the island itself; respect for the old man's privacy (and, she had to admit, anxiety over the alleged monsters that guarded him) kept her securely in the boat, but she'd seen him strolling along the beach. From there, he told them shards of old lore, bits of legend, hints of fathomless eons which, even in brief, threatened to reduce her concept of worth to that of a single crab, foraging among the rocks beneath the old man's sandals.

Yet before she could tell her guest any of it, she heard footsteps coming up her stairs. A thin shape appeared in the doorway. Urshanabi stood there, a jug of fresh river-water in hand. She'd told him to leave it downstairs.

Urshanabi deposited the jug in the corner. To the man on the bed, he demanded, "What is your business in these lands?"

Gilgamesh squinted weakly at him. "Who am I answering to?"

"Urshanabi."

"Well Urshanabi," he drew himself into a sitting position. The wound itched terribly beneath his bandages. "I see no reason to confide my quest in you."

The fisherman stepped forward, flooded with aggression, before he realized how unseemly it would be. Confront a wounded, bedridden man? Threaten him? When he caught Siduri's gaze, he apologized.

"Thank you for the water," she told him. He muttered something and left, head down.

Gilgamesh sighed. "A little protective, is he?"

"As I am of him."

"Utnapishtim's rhymes..."

Siduri gleefully related some of the old poems she'd been told. Strange rhymes about how thirsty men should seek the trail of shaggy elephants if they wanted to find water; funny rhymes on how to tie knots; alliterative rhymes teaching methods of reading the sky to glean godly temperaments.

Gilgamesh listened with amusement and growing certainty. He wondered how the rhymes of his own day would fare in the unknowable days ahead. Repeated as jokes by future tavern-keepers and vagabonds, perhaps? And would Utnapishtim be alive in that era too? Cities sprout in the sweat of generations, crumble by conquest or divine will, and he goes on, cackling at his happy twist of fate: to live forever, imbued with antediluvian magic over life and death.

Siduri said, "So unless you want to hear his stories, you have come so far for nothing. You could have sent emissaries here to collect his tales, and spare yourself such an arduous trip!"

"I am not seeking stories." He yawned, feeling sleep collect like rainwater on his eyelids, leadening them. It reminded him of a statuette he had seen once as a sixteen-year-old king. Merchants with royal trading permits often visited the palace; Gilgamesh adored exploring their display carts. Once, an Akkadian coppersmith had sold him an elegant female figurine, wasp-waisted, full-breasted, long-legged. This is Sleep, the old sculptor told him, bearing a surreptitious grin. See why none can resist Her?

Indeed, Gilgamesh thought. And Death Herself must be as dazzling. Crazily, he wondered if this beautiful tavern-keeper in this lonely tavern was in fact one of Death's avatars. There was a terrible logic in the thought. What man could survive the siege of *two* lions? And hadn't he seen Enkidu then, in the gory aftermath? Hadn't flies been laying their eggs in him when Enkidu's shade lured him... across a stream, to this isolated house of gloom?

Sleep lured him deeper, trance-like in its seductions. The tavern-keeper was still talking, pressing her not-so-clever lies to keep him off the trail of Utnapishtim, but Gilgamesh found himself struggling, really struggling, to keep his eyes open.

I'm dead. The thought came unbidden. *I'm dead and my corpse is breeding worms out in the hills.*

"Stop!" Siduri cried, seeing him stagger away suddenly, making for the curtained doorway. She bolted after him, seized one arm, and steered him back to bed. His arm was wet; one of the stitches had popped from his sudden movement.

"I don't ... want to ... sleep."

"You must!"

"Can't," he cried, his voice twisting with fury. "I need to ... I must find Utnapishtim!"

"Then find him in the morning!"

"I—"

She added more pressure to his sweaty chest. His muscles were as hard as a beetle's carapace, arms rigid, cords on his neck like taut bowstrings. His flushed body caused the recent wounds to turn bright red. "Go to sleep, now. Gilgamesh."

The stranger nodded off so quickly it was like he had been slain by invisible spears.

"I dislike him," Urshanabi said.

Siduri walked the shoreline with the young fisherman, lost in a storm of images born from what her guest had told her. Mighty cities, battles, and monsters hatched in her skull, fought, and died in shrieking silence.

"Siduri?"

She tucked her long hair neatly behind her ears. "How can you form an impression of someone you met so briefly?"

"I can see the spell he holds on your mind," he said curtly.

"Is that jealousy I hear?"

Urshanabi winced. "Yes."

Siduri saw Urshanabi's boat on the sand ahead. Abandoned, tilted so that it was nearly overturned, it looked like a sorrowful testament to a lost time. "You should not be in these parts anymore. Everyone who survived the plague relocated to the south. You and your sister will be safer there. Warad already said he'd look after you."

The boy stomped his feet. "You mean the southern villages where they *sold me to that bastard Cyaxares when he found out I was there!*" His face congested with helpless frustration and, to his shame, he began weeping.

Of course, the story wasn't completely accurate. Siduri had questioned both the boy and Warad about that incident. When the boy uprooted with his sister to the south, Cyaxares had him intercepted with a friendly, eager, helpful liar who offered to provide shelter for the boy. It was all to keep him within the warlord's reach. When Siduri and the hunters began resisting in the weeks following the plague, Cyaxares knew exactly where to find Urshanabi.

"That will never happen again," Siduri told him.

Urshanabi scowled, wiped his eyes, and glared at the sea that bound him. "Lots of fishermen want to stay here. It's our home. Why do *you* stay?"

"Because I have no home."

CHAPTER 40
THE THUNDER SHORE

On the fourth day, she entered her guest's room and found him standing in the middle of the chamber, stark naked. He was running his fingertips over the stitches, pressing delicately, leaving pale dimples against the discolored bruising. The scabs looked very black, like crusted oil.

When she entered, Gilgamesh glanced at the wooden tray she carried. Small roasted fish were piled there on a concave slab of bark. "Who supplies your food?"

Siduri considered his nakedness. His bodily stature was incredible, roped with thick muscles and, aside from several recent wounds, relatively unblemished. "I set traps for fish and rabbits. There were hunters, too, who gave me supplies twice a week to pay me for my services. The fishermen still do."

Gilgamesh strode to her, took the tray, and began eating fish with his fingers. He barely glanced at her again, instead pacing gradually through the room while he chewed, letting her examine his body. His flank rippled, ribs like little striated bumps. His rear was as firm as a horseman's, and his sculpted legs boasted the coiled power of a warhorse. The gouge on his thigh still looked scarlet, wet; the claw had very nearly torn away a huge chunk of muscle, requiring her to stuff it back into his leg and then weaving two lines of stitches to seal the fissure. Siduri's eyes explored the rest of him, when a crescent-shaped abrasion beneath one shoulder-blade caught her eye. "Where did you get that mark?"

"A battle."

She crossed her arms beneath the plumes of her breasts. "With Agga of Kish?"

Gilgamesh half-turned at her sarcasm. "No, I emerged from *that* scrape without a scratch. *This* little hieroglyph was earned in battle with a monster."

Siduri smirked. "What monster?"

"Humbaba."

"Humbaba!" She laughed delightedly. "I think *you* are one of the bards Uruk has hired lately! By the end of summer, I wager that people will be shouting how Gilgamesh climbed into Heaven and gave the gods a right good spanking!"

Gilgamesh shrugged.

Siduri's laughter abated. "Oh, come now! You really expect me to believe that you killed the Terror of the North?"

He shrugged again, swallowed the last of the fish, and handed her the empty tray. Then he returned to bed.

Siduri tossed it on the floor so she could sit beside him. She was no longer afraid of him; in fact, his company enlivened the last few bleak months. "Listen Gilgamesh, need I ask why you left your walled city to come *here*?"

"My friend died."

"Would this friend be the famous General Enkidu of—"

His hands were around her throat faster than she'd ever seen someone move. It was quicker than she could draw her concealed dagger, even. "Be *very careful* how you speak of my friend."

She nodded. "Have you forgotten the terms of my tavern?"

He lowered his eyes. "No."

"Good. Because the next time you attack me—" The dagger was at his throat.

Gilgamesh looked at his reflection on Taharqa's polished metal. He nodded, she took the weapon away, while a gentle pink crease widened on his neck.

"Where did you get that dagger?"

"An old enemy."

"It's Nubian."

Siduri smirked. "You have been to Nubia?"

"No. But when I was fourteen I received an entourage of royals from there. Beautiful, black-skinned people who dressed in the colors of the rainbow. They presented me a gift of weapons. Two jeweled spears were among them." His eyes became distant. "A king entertains many visitors, but those same visitors would be delighted to kidnap me for ransom. You could earn quite a price by informing them tavern-keeper."

"I doubt anyone would believe me."

He lay back against his pillow, letting his eyes rest on the sight of her wooden ceiling.

Siduri fingered her dagger. "How did Enkidu die? Tell me that."

"I killed him."

"Why?"

"I'm the one who had him captured, pulled from the forest, dragged to my palace. I brought him to the city, and the city is where he died. So it was me, tavern-keeper. I killed my best friend."

Siduri considered his words. "And what do you think Utnapishtim can do for you?"

"Bring him back." The words, spoken in his broken-timbered tone, seemed less like an answer to her question than a direct plea to the old man on his island. For the moment during which the tavern slowly absorbed his voice, Siduri shared in her guest's fantasy: That the old man was truly the bearer of divine gifts, capable of defeating death through whispered incantations or the touch of his hands.

"It is not possible," she said at last.

"Just like it is not possible that I'm the king of Uruk?"

"Something like that."

His hands moved again, lightning-fast, only this time she was ready for him. Their fingers came together like the collision of armies. Gilgamesh sat upright and stared into her eyes. "'*All beasts chatter as they can.*'"

Much as the incoming tide had so often washed over ankles, the tavern-keeper let herself be engulfed by his eyes.

She almost decided to eat dinner alone.

A hare had wandered into one of her traps; she killed, skinned, roasted it in her kiln while millet bread baked in crisp, flat strips. Her hands did all this on their own; she barely glanced at them. Instead, she kept thinking of Gilgamesh's preposterous quest. Exposure to wild varieties of humanity had honed her skill at reading truth; gifted deceivers might evade her perception, though wouldn't be able to manufacture the broken, hollow, empty, wrathful, fractured soul that burned brighter than her kiln in the man upstairs.

How many people had she lost to death? While she arrayed the food on the tray she tried counting. Confronting and ending Taharqa had been as much about revenge for the healers as it had been to expunge what he'd made her; by killing him, she was ending that tablet of her life. The same with Cyaxares's priest and the warlord himself. Each time she faced death, dancing on the edge of the Fire Road, flirting with that morbid goddess, only to escape into more years of living. But imagine going up against Death Herself!

Lunacy. Yet...

Siduri's hands grasped a long-necked bottle of wine as she went to the stairs. Gilgamesh might be lying about his name (though she was mildly surprised to realize she no longer doubted it.) Unable to deal with loss, he might have adopted a northern legend to better handle his own pain. One thing she was certain of: Her guest was not lying about the loss itself.

Halfway upstairs, she realized another certainty. He really did intend to find Utnapishtim, corner him, demand the secret of life. She knew there was no one in her life she'd ever gotten so close to so that such an irrational obsession could take hold of her soul.

She opened the curtain to his room. Gilgamesh was sitting on the edge of bed, back to her. He had rinsed his body with the water-jug earlier in the day; the room's odor of sweat, medicine, and oils had abated. His untamed hair was also cleaned, drawn back like a horse's mane, and loosely tied with twine. It was astonishing that this was the crazed, defeated creature who had pounded on her door days ago.

Siduri set the tray down on a short table. "Replenish your strength. You shall heal faster."

He stood, wearing only his kilt, and looked at the food. He looked at her.

She tapped the chair for him to sit. "Tell me of Uruk while you eat."

He sat, broke off a piece of bread. "You tell me. What stories leaked down to the Mouth of the Rivers?"

"That the king of Uruk is a haughty, arrogant, ambitious being. He built a wall around his city. He made friends with a *lahmu*. Together, they defeated Agga of Kish."

Gilgamesh nodded, a bitter taste in his mouth. "My life summarized so neatly."

Siduri came to him and grabbed him by the shoulders. "I meant no offense."

He looked wearily at her, and suddenly a remarkable thing happened. Siduri saw in his drawn visage a strange and subtle transformation, as if the boy, the adolescent, the man contained within this masculine frame were striving to rematerialize, to slough off this outer shell of pain like a snake molting the years away.

"Tell me how to find him, Siduri."

She laughed coldly. "Why? So you can defy death? Look around you! Life burns in your chest, Gilgamesh, and you waste it seeking a foolish tale!"

"Like me?" He glared. "Like Enkidu? Like Humbaba of the forest or the Bull of Heaven?"

"Not all stories are true, you foolish man."

"Then you have nothing to gain by hiding his location from me. Tell me where he is. Or perhaps the boy who came to my door knows."

Siduri's face hardened. Reflexively she wanted to warn him to stay away from Urshanabi. She caught the words, stuffed them inside her throat, and started a lie about how the boy was a local braggart who knew nothing … and she stopped again. Gilgamesh was watching her, his sharp eyes trained on hers. Any deception was as plain as sunlight.

"Perhaps he would tell you," she said.

"Good." He stood up. "Keep my dagger for payment."

Siduri frowned. "I did not say you were well enough to leave."

"But I am, and perhaps I was well enough yesterday. Are you so lonely here, Siduri, that you would keep me—"

She moved like a lioness, seizing a tuft of his hair, twisting it. Gilgamesh gazed cruelly at her and suddenly, with speed equal to her own, he had a hand grabbing her by the chin.

Siduri released his hair, slapped his own hand away, and spat. "Utnapishtim lives below the Mouth of the Rivers in the emerald jungles. Go find him! Track through the serpents and monsters ... yes! More monsters for you to kill, Gilgamesh! Perhaps another *lahmu* for you to be friends with!"

The instant the words left her mouth she realized her mistake. She regretted them, saw their barbs, wondered at her own cruelty, begged the gods to take them back, all in the swift and furious instant when Gilgamesh was upon her, shoving her into the wall so hard the breath exploded from her lungs. Black dots swam before her eyes.

"Forgive me!" she cried.

When her vision cleared she was already being flung to the other side of the room. She tripped over the edge of the mattress and crashed painfully to the floor. His footsteps came at her again. Suddenly she was on her feet nimbly, ignoring the pain in her right arm and side, her dagger jumping to her hand.

Gilgamesh trembled with agony, his wounds burning up now. "Are you going to stab me?"

"No," she admitted. She had been threatened before, and strangely—for all the brutalizing he had just inflicted on her—she knew she was in no real danger.

A blur of movement. The knife was knocked from her hands with one firm, open-handed slap. It landed with undue gentleness onto the mattress.

"I apologize for offending you about Enkidu," she said.

"I accept your apology," he said, and turned to leave.

Suddenly her weight was against him, forcibly throwing him to the wall. She had twisted his good arm behind him in a sudden jerk; Gilgamesh slowly rotated into the attack so that the two were facing. His kilt fell away, his stitches burst. One! Two! Three! It took a moment before the wound wept, but when it did, the tears were scarlet and steady.

Gilgamesh pushed her away from him. He touched the leaking gash. He descended the stairs, crossed the main room, went through the door and marched naked to the shoreline. Siduri followed him to the doorstep, watching as he splashed freshwater onto the injury.

Gilgamesh stood tall, feeling how cold the sea was on his body. He gazed across the water at the misty horizon. The sky looked like jagged overlapping pieces of shale, grinding against each other and tearing each other to pieces.

By his foot, a drop of rain made a perfectly round dimple in the sand.

Gilgamesh craned his neck. The rain washed over him, while he held out his arms, legs slightly apart. He closed his eyes.

It was so unfair! He thought of all the beasts sharing the rain with him, the dry head of crocodiles turning glassy wet, the monkeys scampering for shelter, various birds and creatures darting for dryness. None of them knew they were going to die. They lived heartbeat to heartbeat, breathing in one sweet gulp of life only to exhale and be gone, with only fear! impulse! hunger! as companions of the mind.

Quiet thunder growled behind the clouds. Gilgamesh's eyes snapped open and he growled back, his lips pulled back from his teeth. *I live!* His thoughts shrieked it. *God or man or beast ... I exist!* The unspoken statement energized him like never before, filling his veins with blazing ichor, alerting him to his bodily sensations like never before. All the women who shared his bed or the men he killed in battle seemed like panoramas of someone else's life—the illustrious bas reliefs of some king from some city with a name time worn away by wind, by sun, and yes, by rain.

Gilgamesh stepped away from the shore. He looked at Siduri where she waited for him. He walked toward her and the tide melted his footprints.

Siduri breathed hard, the flush of their fight still tingling her skin. There was a special ferocity in his gait; his manhood stirred with each step, thickening like a serpent. Gilgamesh had almost reached the doorway when she undid a hasty knot from her garment, and the tavern-keeper raiment dropped like a disused skin to the floor.

His legs didn't stop when they reached her; Gilgamesh merely wrapped his arms around her wasp-like waist and held her to his chest. Siduri cried out, intoxicated with the paradoxes of the cold rainwater on his impossibly warm body. His chest hair tickled her; she buried her nose in it. Siduri grunted and kissed his mouth, the scruff of his beard scratching her skin in delightful violence. Her teeth clasped his neck as a wolf might during mating. Not hard enough to break the skin; rather, to feel the flesh beneath her panting breaths, and to press teeth-marks into it like a savage scribe carving words into wet clay. He ate along her neck, too, miming the same murderous impulse. She seized his hand and pressed it between her legs and he panted, his tool as rigid as bronze.

"Inside me," Siduri grunted. The words seemed to take forever to form. Gilgamesh pressed the smooth head of his shaft against her portals and began a slow entry, teasing her portals, plunging deeper with every thrust. Siduri felt her eyes leaking with incredible delight. The tavern was filled with fog or gone, forever, just a construction of wood anyway, lost to wind and time and water. For Gilgamesh, however, Uruk seemed to sprout up around him as they mated. It wasn't that all the women he'd had returned to his memory; instead, the other ambient sounds he'd barely noticed during lovemaking now filled his ears. He remembered the scrape of worker tools at Uruk's walls, noisy festivals below his bedroom window, palace slaves clattering pots in the hallway, flutes of street-side musicians.

Siduri and Gilgamesh moved like an organism trying to tear itself to pieces. They thrust together and apart; grinding for their own indulgent satisfaction and to enhance each other's; hands turned to claws to scratch red trails on their backs and necks; moans a mutual battle-cry, both musical and tumultuous. Siduri climaxed in hard succession; Gilgamesh felt his own Final Moment approaching and the noise of Uruk became unbearable to his ears—

The gods drowned humanity because of all the noise we made, he remembered explaining to Enkidu.

—and he ignored the rain pouring outside turning the beach to muddy slush, concentrating only on Siduri's eager wetness. He thrust furiously. Her kisses turned softer, lovingly gentle now, soothing the same spots on his neck she had bit earlier, licking a new wound she had caused in her frenzy of passion. Gilgamesh felt his orgasm rush past the unstoppable threshold and then a powerful release that felt like he was turning inside out, losing everything into her saturated depths.

When he came to his senses he was looking into her eyes. Green glass and sea-fire.

"And yours are amber trapped in crystal," she said.

The rain assailed the cabin.

Time flowed by unmeasured. They held each other in the cabin's gloom that was now absolute, given the premature loss of daylight. Reduced to voices and breathing and thudding hearts, they clutched each other, pawing the invisible. Gilgamesh fancied they could be anywhere in the world right now. Or nowhere at all.

Siduri disturbed the perfect quiet. "You are leaving tomorrow?"

"Yes."

She felt the stab of sadness in her heart. Instantly, she captured the feeling with an unseen net and put it away. "Utnapishtim lives across the water. On a very small island."

"Good."

"If you set foot on its shore, you will die."

Gilgamesh pressed his nose into her hair and kissed her forehead. "Why?"

"Because monsters live there."

"Indeed."

Siduri tried to sit up, but he held her fast. She twisted, straddled him, and faced his warm, sweetened breath. "I do not jest. No one here would ever dare to step onto Utnapishtim's island. A very ancient race guards him."

The king grinned blandly in the darkness. "Of course. What better way to keep trespassers off your land? Invent monsters …"

"There are things in this world still, Gilgamesh. When I was younger I rode out … I lived a wilder life. One day my group and I encountered gigantic camels with heads that stretched taller than three men balanced on each other's shoulders."

"And camels are certainly terrifying."

She gripped his hair in mock severity. "My point—"

"Yes, yes," he said, gently massaging her wrists. "We are not alone in this world."

His choice of words stirred her. Throughout her whole life it seemed that, in the end, she was always alone. The episodes of her life passed across her thoughts as a Babylonian mural might. There was no better reminder of that than the obliterated villages, their timbers prowled by wind.

Or Utnapishtim. She swallowed hard, thinking of the island she had only seen from Urshanabi's boat. A forested tuft of land floating on the water, hilly and mysterious and host to something that rustled the trees. Every so often, too, harrowing choruses of howls floated off the island and carried itself to her ears. Something *was* there … along with the old man.

When she repeated this last sentiment to Gilgamesh, he laughed coldly. "Do you really think monsters frighten me? Even if something crawls this earth more vicious than Humbaba, I shall always remember that he is dead. Everything in this world can be cut. Even a goddess' flesh!"

Siduri sighed angrily. "The future is not for you to have! Return to Uruk and let your scribes write down the twelve tablet story of your life for tomorrow's generation to read!"

"Twelve tablets would be a complete story. I have more to do yet."

"Did you truly kill Humbaba of the North?"

She felt him nod in the oily blackness.

"And the Bull of Heaven?"

Again he nodded.

"And those accomplishments are not enough?"

"No."

"Eternal life is not possible."

"There are things that can grant death as quickly as a scorpion's kiss. There must be something that can grant life too. Utnapishtim has that answer. I shall use it to bring Enkidu back. And give it to my mother, too, so she can be young again. And to my friends … and to myself when I begin to tarnish." He tried to catch sight of her eyes, but there was only a shuffling, swirling shadow and so he pictured her eyes, like gemstones at midnight. "To you as well."

"I do not want immortality."

"Yes you do. You just can't imagine it, so you cowardly hide from the concept."

"We live *now*, Gilgamesh. Fill your belly, take a wife and make children. This life you seek you cannot find." She laughed scornfully, then softened. "And yes, I fear the idea of eternity. Life has been hard."

"But it needn't always be! Perhaps the gods never intended us to comprehend our own mortality. I care not! They say that before cities people lived in caves. Perhaps the gods wanted us to live there, too. But we have built cities, and tamed rivers, and brought animals under our sway. Why not death too? If death is a god let me tear its throat out. If it's a great monster like Tiamat, let me war with Her like my patron deity once did. A great clash! My dagger against her heart."

"I own your dagger now."

"You would lend it to me if Tiamat was threatening your door."

In the morning they made love again, and again. In the waters of the Mouth of the Rivers, they bathed. In her tavern, they dried each other off without a word.

Siduri didn't watch him go.

TABLET X

NEVER GROW OLD

CHAPTER 41
ISLAND

At dawn Urshanabi was kneeling beside his boat, his neatly folded net piled near the footboard, the oars balanced across the hollow, reciting urgent prayers to Nammu the Birthgiver when he first heard the interloper nearing him along the beach. It was a quiet approach, but outsiders possessed acuities unknown to city-dwellers; Urshanabi sensed the clumsy, injured steps of Siduri's tavern-guest long before he appeared in the wakening sunlight.

From a distance, the man looked neither so tall nor fierce. The fisherman's heart stuttered, elated to see him away from the tavern, for surely this meant he was leaving their lands forever. Good! Let him march onward to certain death!

Urshanabi immediately pounded a fist into the sand, furious at his mistake. Nammu wouldn't stand for it. From Her womb sprouted life in the form of flowers, birds, or fish; She had peopled the dead universe fashioned from Tiamat's cloven corpse. Naturally then, Her worshipers included trackers, hunters, and fishermen. And they could appeal to Her, provided their wishes were made without thinking of Death, speaking of Death, or especially *wishing* Death upon someone. The young boy sighed, frustrated with himself. An hour of prayers were ruined because of one careless mistake!

From across the distance, Gilgamesh called to him. "Urshanabi, is it?"

The boy sighed again. He wasn't comfortable with confrontation and knew, instinctively, that this older man was quite adept at it. The stranger came to the boat, smiling but not *really* smiling, not smiling in his eyes, which was where a true smile resided. He rudely peered into the boat. In particular, his attention fell to the half dozen stone statues lining the vessel's upper lip. They were humanoid in shape, chiseled from sandstone, with perfectly round heads. Some were male, others female, sitting comfortably in their deep nook like miniature passengers on a gargantuan ferry.

"I seek an old man who lives on the island," the stranger said. "You know him."

Urshanabi nodded, new anxiety drowning his hopes. "I thought you were leaving."

Gilgamesh laughed, amused at the boy's tactlessness. It was the same with Gudea back north. He wondered when children learned the art of real deception.

"Soon enough, boy. I just require Utnapishtim's advice, and I'll be on my way."

"Who?"

"He is known as Atrahasis in these parts."

The boy swallowed. "All visitors to the island die."

"Thank you for such concern."

Angry, remembering where the man's wounds were and entertaining, however briefly, whacking the man with an oar, Urshanabi said sullenly, "I am forbidden to approach his island. Find someone else to help you."

"Forbidden? Then how did you and Siduri hear all his stories?"

The boy was stricken at hearing Siduri's name pour off his lips. Had they coupled? The thought sickened his heart.

Gilgamesh picked up one of the little stone statues from the boat. It depicted a male god or local hero, arms straight against its sides, eyes wide and set with flecks of pearl.

"There's a young boy about your age in my city," the king continued, absently fingering the statue, aware that Urshanabi was uncomfortable with having the figurine handled. "He is a hunter named Gudea. You remind me of him." The king's eyes turned unkindly. "Take me to Utnapishtim. Siduri herself endorsed the meeting."

"She did not!" Urshanabi shouted.

"Ask her," Gilgamesh said, perceiving the boy's desire for the tavern-keeper. It touched him, actually, reminding him of his own infatuations at a similar age while living under Dumuzi's rule. There were servants in the palace Gilgamesh wished to bed. Dumuzi had forbid it, of course. No point in risking a new royal heir from the line of Lugalbanda.

Suddenly Gilgamesh understood why the boy was so nervous at having the stone statues manhandled. "Siduri gave you these?"

The boy reddened at the knowing tone in the stranger's voice. "Atrahasis made them for me. They are protectors of …" He stopped.

"Protectors of …" Gilgamesh cocked his head. "You, your sister, her family?"

"How do you know all this?"

"Take me to Utnapishtim."

Urshanabi felt his mouth going dry with fear. Still, his lips twitched a reply. "No."

Gilgamesh braced one finger behind the statue's head, then pushed with his thumb. The head popped off, dropping inelegantly to the beach, and with a wild cry the boy dove for it, sobbing hysterically.

The king calmly took another statue. "Someone you care for won't be protected anymore, is that it? What about this one? This one with breasts and long hair. Is this the sister you care for? Or is it the tavern-keeper?"

The boy trembled terribly. "I will take you. Just please … give the statue back. *Please.*"

Gilgamesh tucked it into the belt-line of his kilt. "Get me to Utnapishtim's island and you shall get it back."

Urshanabi's lips shivered. It would have been comical if not for the helpless rage in his eyes. He understood how ineffective any resistance against this warrior-killer would be. Terrible comprehension washed over his thoughts: His life was akin to the long-legged birds that speared fish daily with their saber-like beaks, whereas this interloper was the lion which the birds fled before. He looked yearningly at the nearest oar, wondering if he had time to grab it, wield it, knock this stranger unconscious.

Then he saw Gilgamesh's eyes, and realized how transparent his schemes were.

"I will take you," he whispered.

"Give the statue back to him, Gilgamesh."

The voice came from behind them both. They turned.

Siduri stood just four paces away, but something was different about her. Gilgamesh secretly gaped at the green tunic cladding her, the leather satchel tied at her beltline where her Nubian dagger was tucked, and the aggressive stance of her feet … a classic warrior's pose. In one hand she gripped a spear. The king of Uruk grinned, swiftly seized with the knowledge that if she had been with him during the lion attack, things would have gone much, much smoother.

He returned the statue to Urshanabi without looking away from her.

"Let us go," she said.

Light rain sprinkled them with liquid diamonds, as Urshanabi rowed into the miasma at an oblique angle from the shoreline. They were silent for most of the journey; watching each other turn silver in the shower, the cloudy sunrise glittering in every raindrop on their clothes or hair. Siduri enjoyed a peculiar clairvoyance, seeing the effect this rendered upon her former guest. Whether king or liar, he seemed the most regal creature she'd ever encountered. The scraggly hair hanging from his chin, lips, cheeks, *glowed*.

When the mist ahead darkened around a jutting shape, Siduri broke the silence. "It would be nice if you had a sword," she observed.

"I lost it near the lions."

"So it's probably still there. You didn't bother to fetch it before heading out to this island? Stop and consider, Lord Gilgamesh. You move as a possessed man bent on his own destruction."

"I am still here, no?"

With a sigh, Siduri handed him the spear. He slid it through the back of his tunic so the shaft rested across his spine.

Urshanabi squinted at him. "You are *King Gilgamesh* from Uruk?"

"Once."

The rain fell more forcefully, no longer content to sit idly on their clothes and hair but to weigh them down, staining dark. The sea's surface frothed and jittered as if the water had transformed into noxious poisons. The thought was disturbing. Gilgamesh fancied that the next dip of the oars would see them dissolved, stranding them out here forever amid bubbling acid.

Urshanabi said, "They have spoken of you in the fishing villages."

"Have they?"

"They said that Uruk's king lost a friend, so he went searching for the entrance to the underworld to fetch him back."

Siduri stiffened. Her guest's eyes became very distant; suddenly, she was pierced by her soul's deep aesthete. Trapped between shoreline and island, wreathed in misty rain, her heart rapidly increased. She remembered old stories of glorious adventures again. To her sensibilities, Utnapishtim's island had only been a chunk of rock inhabited by an old man; now it became steeped in magic, promise, purpose.

She smiled at Gilgamesh. He didn't see the expression; his attention was entirely arrested now by the island they approached with each oar-stroke. But she knew now. It was the same when she'd peered into his eyes in her tavern, seeking truth, finding it, like spying the glint of treasure beneath tenebrous waters.

"I have heard the island's monsters myself," she said.

Gilgamesh looked at her. "The braying of mighty camels?"

She related the howls that carried across the sea to her ears. Low, hollow ululations suggesting hulking creatures quite unlike any dog, wolf, or jackal. They weren't horns, either, or any instrument of mankind. Flesh-and-blood animals prowled the immortal's island. Perhaps they were familiars he had conjured to protect his sanctuary; whatever they were, their ominous cries stalked the floating forest. Sometimes local fishermen dredged corpses from the sea, and it was assumed these were intruders who had chanced to visit. Chanced ... and failed.

Gilgamesh listened without reaction. *I'm no longer afraid of anything*, he thought. The tavern-keeper was a grim, practical being; she wasn't the type to believe wild hearsay. Part of his mind fixated on her story, in fact, envisioning all kinds of chimeras. Maybe Utnapishtim was a sorcerer, or herdsmen of forgotten beasts, or shrewd employer of entities like the *saghulhaza* who once guarded the House of Uruk. Gilgamesh no longer doubted the existence of monsters. He just wasn't afraid of them.

Much of life was fear. Amorphous, unseen devils hiding in corners, denizens of outsider lands, fear took many forms. The worst kind, though, was when it was *formless*. Gilgamesh remembered that nightmarish night of childhood. *Twelve years old. Wrapped in sheets, asleep. Suddenly waking. The footsteps stalking him. Closer. The convergence of malignant beings around his bed while he secretly fingered the copper dagger beneath his pillow.* Hadn't that been the worst part? When his desperate instinct galvanized him to leap from bed to thrust the dagger into the first protean shadow, he was still afraid, yes. But the certainty of that first kill, and the panicked flocking of the assassins to tear down the drapes for want of starlight, was more than a blow against Dumuzi's thugs. It was a strike into fear's formless shape. The same was true of Humbaba in the forest. Oh! Gilgamesh doubted any artist on Earth could paint an abomination more disturbing than what he faced in the Cedar Forest, but the real terror was in *waiting* for it. The first glimpse, obscured, tree-shrouded. Humbaba brought insane carnage to his assailants but when Gilgamesh saw him, in the light, he ceased being the devil-god of legend and became an animal to be slaughtered.

Utnapishtim's island might be crawling with broods of Tiamat. Gilgamesh didn't fear them.

The rain fell around him, bubbling the water, churning it, as if a million slavering mouths were chomping at the boat. The island's rocky coast materialized from the mist.

Staring at it, Gilgamesh realized he was wrong. Formless fear might not trouble him any longer, but tangible fear, possessing definite form, did. He thought of Uruk filled with corpses, vultures pecking bloodily at his mother's silver scalp. Nedu dead, Ibi-Sin chalky with corpse hue, Gudea's reckless passion buried in the earth …

Enkidu's smile stolen from him. Those childlike eyes brimming with wonder. Ripped away, eaten by worms.

Gilgamesh watched the beach with steely determination. If Utnapishtim was real, if he truly harbored dominion over life and death, the king resolved to receive it from him. Given freely as a magical amulet would be preferable, but if the power was contained solely in the old man's heart Gilgamesh had no qualms with ripping the organ from his chest to possess it.

Urshanabi's boat glided beneath low-lying branches into a small inlet, from which his passengers stepped out into waist-deep water. "Come back for us in the morning," Siduri told him.

The boy's eyes filled with bitter tears. "If you're still alive!"

"Shhh!" she warned. "We will be, I promise. Just be back here by first light."

As the boy rowed away from them with evident reluctance, Gilgamesh rested his spear upon his shoulder and studied the tree-line. Siduri trudged forward, her green kilt clinging wetly to her as she emerged to the beach.

"Do you know how to track?" she asked.

He kissed her lips. "I know how to kill."

"Then we are meant for each other," she said, and was glad the forests were shadow-drenched because it hid the blush which crept into her cheeks.

Gilgamesh watched the woods while she scanned the ground. There were tracks, she reported. Pigs, four different kinds of birds. Other depressions in the soft soil of uncertain origin.

"There," she said, pointing.

"A trail," he agreed.

Siduri bristled, seized with a sudden chill. Instinctively, she lowered herself and held her dagger taut, ready to impale anything that came charging out from the trees. Gilgamesh hunkered with her, a questioning look on his face. They waited.

Wind rustled the branches above.

Gilgamesh craned his neck, to make sure it was only the wind.

Then he heard the sound. Siduri's description had been accurate, yet couldn't embrace the full texture of the cry he now heard. It started as a dull vibration at first, then swelled into a bloated howl sweeping through the trees, ungainly, menacing, alive.

Yes, alive, he thought grimly. His fingers clenched the spear-shaft.

They crept on their bellies uphill until reaching white, rocky outcroppings, at which point they climbed wherever handholds allowed. Rain spilled awkwardly among the trees.

Two hours later, they reached the pond.

The pond was not passable by either side; a dissuasive alliance of tightly gathered trees and thorny bushes crammed this low country for as far as Gilgamesh dared see. Slashing the foliage was impossible; too much noise would result, and besides, neither he nor Siduri had the equipment to accomplish this. When they attempted to bypass the region entirely, intending to cut outward to the beach to attempt a different path to ingress, they discovered fallen trees, beyond which was—

"Bad ground," Gilgamesh whispered, using Enkidu's phrase. Immense pits were strewn beyond the logs. Reeds covered them well, but not well enough. Gilgamesh could almost feel the ghostly impact of Enkidu's arm against his chest, warning him from proceeding any further.

"So we cross the pond," Siduri ventured.

As with the sea that morning, a low steamy vapor drifted like an incorporeal, carnivorous creature that had laid claim to this spot on the island.

Gilgamesh stepped into the water. Siduri's boot was beside him in the very same moment.

"You've killed before," he said. It wasn't a question; no one could fake the predatory way the tavern-keeper moved, or how her lupine eyes watched every leaf for signs of ambush.

Siduri squatted in the water, edging forward so that her head seemed to glide on its own across the surface. Noiselessly. Gilgamesh followed, smiling broadly. When he was beside her ear, the water was deep enough for them to kick out in an anxious swim.

She'd make a great Assyrian, he thought in admiration. Rimush was fond of relating how Assyrians were known to cross large bodies of water without boats. They simply swam the distance, often while breathing through hollow reeds.

"You realize we are not the first people to come seeking him," she whispered in his ear.

He nodded.

"What do you think happened to them?"

"I don't care."

Another howl erupted through the trees—much closer than before. Gilgamesh stared into the fog, stricken by panic.

Entering the pond had been a terrible mistake.

The certainty of this twisted his stomach. Some hideous *thing* nested here, as crocodiles selected places to deposit their eggs. Why else would Utnapishtim have made it so the only way into the island was to come this way? Perhaps the pond was bottomless, and tentacles were even now uncoiling in the murk, questing for their feet ...

Formless fear, Gilgamesh reminded himself. He struggled to rein in his panic.

Up ahead, he could discern the opposite shore. Peculiar, thorny, short-stalked plants nestled there in tight, shriveled bunches. Gilgamesh didn't recognize them; this didn't surprise him too much, since new lands would understandably possess flora unique to the region. But the condition of the plants intrigued him. They were clearly dying; the leaves brown like Egyptian parchment, the stalks thin as bird bones. There were black clusters beneath each leaf too.

Gilgamesh let his eyes wander further up where two enormous shadows breached the mist.

The shadows howled at him.

Though the fog blurred much detail, the king couldn't deny what he plainly saw: Two scorpions as large as transport caravans, pincers bent to the water, their bodies pinning the vegetation. From behind them, two columns of shadow indicated where their deadly tails arched. Their black carapaces glistened wetly in the morning dew. Siduri saw them an instant later and she reversed her kick, bobbing in the water only a meter from the nearest claw.

Gilgamesh's mouth went dry. He retrieved the spear from his tunic, spreading his legs in outward strokes to keep above the water.

The fear isn't formless.

Another thought invaded his mind: No, but these are *giant scorpions* in front of me. Tough to remain placid when confronted with *this*.

More to the point, he grimly calculated, how do we get past them? His spear suddenly seemed as helpful as a soggy twig against that arachnid armor.

Siduri's eyes were bulging. She lowered her head so only her eyes showed above the water, ready to submerge entirely should the creatures scurry into the water. *Could* they survive on the water? Wouldn't they drown as most insects did?

Gilgamesh blinked, bobbing up and down.

The pond was silent. But for the lapping of water against his ears, there was no movement. Fog closed in around the monsters.

Gilgamesh looked at Siduri. She raised an eyebrow quizzically.

Without a word, he returned the spear to its makeshift sheath. His fingers found his pocketed dagger, and he lobbed it toward the nearest monster. It wept a trail of droplets as it fell toward one of the threatening shapes.

Clang!

The sound was unmistakable. Neither shadow moved. They couldn't.

Siduri spat, chuckling. Feeling very sheepish, the king paddled toward the statues—for that's all they were. He grabbed one of the pincers and used it to hoist out of the water. When Siduri came in range, he took her hand and drew her ashore. She was still laughing when he picked his dagger from the soil.

"Glad you think it's funny," he said.

"A couple of great hunters we are!"

"How could we expect … these ungainly things?"

Siduri held her sides, laughing so heartily that she nearly fell over. Her rump rested against the backside of the nearest scorpion-carving and this inspired even more guffaws.

"Come now!" she cried. "Have you forgotten how to laugh?"

He didn't answer her. Laughter bubbled in his stomach but he tried to extinguish it. He didn't want to be feeling good here. He didn't want Utnapishtim to detect any gentleness in them. If it came to it, he intended to pulverize that selfish hoarder of life—

Siduri kissed him.

Her warm lips pressed demandingly, offering no chance of refusal. They felt softer than any girl he'd kissed, exuding confidence and skill. She broke the kiss only to laugh again. This time he couldn't help but join in.

"We do not have to do this," she whispered.

Gilgamesh's eyes changed.

Pulling sharply away from her, he said, "Is the old man your ward, Siduri? Is that it?"

"No."

"Did you come along to *stop* me?"

She said nothing. At that very moment, wind shook the trees and new howls erupted around them. They both looked to the statues. The source of the sound.

"There are holes here, in the backs of their heads," Siduri said. "It channels the wind." She pressed her hand over the orifice, shushing the creature.

Gilgamesh stepped toward her. "If you try to stop me ..."

"I understand."

CHAPTER 42
UTNAPISHTIM

The cabin was just beyond the woods, at the bottom of a valley that must have dipped below sea-level. It was modest, built of wooden beams, with a thatched roof. A small enclosure kept some two dozen pigs contained; they squirmed like pinkish maggots in the mud. Strangest of all, a fence girdled the property, as if to keep invisible neighbors at bay.

"Dogs." Siduri pointed with her dagger in the direction of three scampering animals on the outside of the fence.

"Utnapishtim," Gilgamesh said. The old man himself—he could be none other—emerged just then from behind the house. Three planks of wood were tucked under his arm while he walked, knelt at the holding pen, and began replacing the support beams.

Gilgamesh stood. The old man looked very slight at this range, even with the cabin as a point of reference.

"What are you doing?" Siduri asked, pulling at him. He shook her off and began a deliberate walk downhill toward his objective.

The dogs saw him immediately. They barked, kicking dirt as they raced at him. Gilgamesh eyed their speed, adjusted his position, held his spear with two hands the way Gimil-Sin had trained him.

Neither scorpions, nor dogs, can stop me today old man, he thought hatefully.

Siduri burst from her hiding place. The dogs barked furiously, wisely separating to attack from front and flank.

"*Here!*"

The single word stopped the dogs in mid-run. They frothed, purely honed aggression in their eyes, but before the echoes of the word had faded they were trotting rapidly in the direction of the voice. Gilgamesh grinned coldly, continuing his walk to the old man who stood at the fence, watching him.

His first impression of the old man was of a shriveled, brown-skinned, peasant. Worn, grey clothes attired him. His skin was hard, pebbly, like a lizard's. His eyes squinted at the two intruders as they stood before his gate.

"Utnapishtim," Gilgamesh said.

The old man opened the gate's latch. The planks of wood were still in his hand; Gilgamesh realized they could be easily used as a weapon. This understanding came along with another: The old man wasn't that old, at least not in physical appearance. He might have been Nedu's age, though years—

—*centuries?*

—of outsider life had rendered him this sun-battered creature.

Inside the fence, Gilgamesh and Siduri put some distance between themselves and their host. The dogs sat in the doorway, chillingly alert to their master's every move.

The old man moved to the side of the holding pen where the wooden beams had become cracked. "Help me with this," he commanded.

Gilgamesh kicked out the rotting planks. They skittered across the yard. Two pigs ran free, their hind legs slipping in the mud, then righting themselves to escape into the countryside, for the outer fence was too high to withhold them. Three more pigs followed them, grunting excitedly.

Utnapishtim placed his hands on his hips. "That wasn't very helpful."

"I have a friend who died."

The old man watched the free pigs cavorting. They had reached clustered reed bushes and stopped there, at the base of a tree, sniffing the roots. Gilgamesh's unexpected defiance had imbued the man's face with stronger color. He glanced past the strangers to see his dogs at the cabin's corner, watching him, tails straight up, ears flat.

Gilgamesh didn't need to turn to know they were there. "If you call them ..."

Utnapishtim glared. "I can see that. You are not the first haughty man I've encountered in my years." He turned his radiant brown eyes on Siduri. "Nor are you the first woman."

"Perhaps you prefer us to be the last?" the king said.

Utnapishtim approached him, letting the spear-tip press into his chest. "Drive it in, stranger. You will not get my knowledge by drinking my blood. Neither will it make very good war-paint for your face."

Siduri watched the old man's face, seeking signs of bluffing. Usually a lie was betrayed by creases in the forehead, an indefinable tic of the skin around the eyes, and of course the eyes themselves as the old rhyme so succinctly noted. No indications were there ... but after so long a life, who wouldn't learn to master the art of deception?

Do I believe it? she wondered. Is he truly immortal?

Gilgamesh didn't withdraw his spear. "I don't want your knowledge. I have a friend who died."

"So you said."

"You know how to fetch him back from the underworld."

Utnapishtim blinked. "I do?"

Gilgamesh swallowed anxiously. "You must. You possess the gift of life ..."

"But not of resurrection."

"Nonsense!" The king swallowed again. He turned, paced once. "Some think you're only an elderly man stuffed with legends of bygone eons, passed down from lip to ear, for thousands of years. I do not believe that. I look at you and see the one who toiled on these shores before the Flood."

"Not these particular shores," Utnapishtim muttered. Gilgamesh froze, his eyes flashing. The old man sighed and attempted to see where his escaped pigs had gone to, but there was no sign of them now. His weary face wrinkled into a grudging smile.

The king nearly shrank before those eyes. They glimmered like hot oil, full of mischief and danger.

"How did you find me here?" asked the old old man.

"The locals know you."

"Not by the name of Utnapishtim."

Gilgamesh nodded. "A map of Annunaki statues."

Utnapishtim looked surprised at this. "You found all the pieces?"

"You know of them?"

"I made them."

In the cabin, Utnapishtim drew a chair out from behind a pile of firewood, placed it alongside an elegantly carved table. There were four people in the house: the king, the huntress, the old man, and a woman. Gilgamesh was only slightly surprised to see her. She clearly came from the same race as her companion. He marveled at their faces ... visages which a difficult world had shaped, chiseling them as if from oak. Yes, she was a woman like the many he had known, with long black hair, swollen breasts, pinched waist and flaring hips. But her brown countenance, like that of her mate, was so unlike anything Gilgamesh had seen, as if here was the mother and father of all humanity. The high forehead of Hittites, the Assyrian nose, the flat cheeks of Nubia, the almond-eyes of Egypt. Here was the parent face, wrinkled and worn. And yes! there was Humbaba in those wrinkles and Enkidu ... dearest Enkidu!

The woman offered them a loaf of bread. Neither Siduri nor Gilgamesh moved to take it.

Utnapishtim dismissed her without a word, just a nod of his head. She returned the bread to a counter, glanced worriedly at her husband, but left the room. The three dogs trotted after her.

The old man looked into Gilgamesh's eyes. "Who did you lose?"

"A friend."

"Life does that."

Gilgamesh moved threateningly at him; Siduri grasped him by the tunic to stop him. To the old man, she said, "We know about life, Atrahasis."

"Do you?" he asked, staring hard at them both. "I would say you know about death."

"But you don't," Gilgamesh said, unable to keep still. He didn't come this far to listen to the philosophical ramblings of an oracle. But Siduri's hand kept him from manhandling the immortal.

"I knew of death once," Utnapishtim said.

Siduri felt the contest of gaze between Gilgamesh and their unwilling host. She turned to the latter. "Some of us feel death more than others. You understand that people like us would seek you out."

The old man sighed. He folded his arms across his chest. "The ice was retreating when I was a boy. Great walls of white-blue, sundering the land, splitting around mountains. In their place, the world awoke in its first spring. Brush, grass, and trees greeted the sky." He hesitated, perceiving the coiled violence in Gilgamesh.

"How long ago?" Siduri asked.

"You wouldn't understand."

Angered by the impish, haughty demeanor, Gilgamesh hissed, "Try us."

"I meant no offense," the man stated. "What I mean to say is, how would you describe your era to future peoples?"

"The fifth generation of Uruk, eighth year of King Gilgamesh."

Utnapishtim nodded, visibly attuned to every inflection of his guests. "And that may mean something if your king-lists survive the conquests to come. We measured life differently when I was young. Warm seasons, cold seasons. The years of the Dark Sky which killed so many tribes. The Bird-Kings. The Floods. Does it mean anything to you? Of course not! You are children of the modern world." He trailed off, sized Gilgamesh up, asked, "How old are you, stranger?"

"Twenty."

The old man's eyes brightened. "Twenty!" The number seemed to puzzle and delight him, confuse and stir him. His mouth twitched, eyes shifting to watch some inner scene that his guests weren't privy to. His lids drew shut.

Gilgamesh and Siduri watched him; indeed, it was impossible not to watch. Utnapishtim barely moved, though it wasn't precisely a lack of activity. Standing, arms folded, legs crossed, he seemed a casual wanderer prone to sleepiness. But no ... his lips continued moving, his eyes rolled like eggs beneath thin fabric. The lean muscles in his arms bunched, flexed, twisted the way a dreamer might practice his life's activities if he were an archer, a swordsman, a mason.

Utnapishtim's eyes swiveled open with new hardness. "I could tell you how we settled down in the newly opened regions when the ice had peeled off the land. Horses as small as children ran before us. Rats bigger than that, vicious critters, and if they caught you out in the open—" He smiled malevolently. "We named Earth's regions after the creatures we encountered there. When I was *twenty*, these things still lived."

In spite of himself, Gilgamesh felt his rage cooled as by the frost of that forgotten spring. "And the *lahmu*? Did you meet them?"

The old man looked at him knowingly. "You knew one, eh? Is he the friend you've lost?"

"His name was Enkidu," the king said defensively.

"I am not surprised some broadbacks survived to your days. In a way, that makes me glad. We knew them. Ignored them at times. Other times ..."

Siduri didn't need to press for elaborations on this point; she hoped Gilgamesh wouldn't either. The old man's playful eyes danced with cruel memories.

"And the Flood?" Gilgamesh asked.

"The Great Flood was preceded by thunder unlike anything I have heard since." The playfulness was gone; the old man seemed a destitute beggar again recounting life's hardship for want of charity. "The waters were always rising, you understand. Routes available to us one year would be swallowed by ocean the next. But this thunder, more like the sound a mountain would make if it cracked off and came tumbling down, it sent the waters into our villages in just days. We had boats, loaded them with what we could. So many died again, like when the Dark Sky came. There's so much I don't remember, but I shall never forget the blue coils of ocean snaking into our valley. Like a great dragon, eh?" The mischief returned.

Gilgamesh grinned humorlessly. "The gods warned you of the Flood?"

Utnapishtim's broad face grinned. "I don't remember."

"Liar! If you remember flood waters and black skies or whatever you refer to, you would recall the voice of Ea or Shamash!"

Utnapishtim was unmoved. "I remember the first time we pressed our mud-caked hands to a cave wall and saw the impression left there. A hand! How we captured animals in our paint, and fought for fire and water with … the other tribes."

"But," Gilgamesh cried, "The gods *must* have given you the eternal life you enjoy! How did you earn such a blessing? Which one spoke to you?"

"In the days before the Great Flood I found a plant that no longer grows," the ancient spoke. "Studded with thorns, with yellow berries bunched beneath its leaves. All animals avoided it. But some of us tried those berries. I remember how it warmed our stomach. How it changed us."

Gilgamesh bolted upright. "A *plant?*"

"We called it Never Grow Old."

The king blinked, his legs trembling until he could no longer sit and so stood and began pacing again through the small room. The plant's description unsettled him. Siduri followed him with her eyes. She had heard similar stories, in her many travels, of a plant whose berries granted exotic powers.

Again, he said, "A plant?"

"When the waters receded, some of searched for the plant again. Some bushes survived on high mountains. We brought them back into the valley, nurtured them. People came to barter for the berries but, once eaten, they took many decades to grow back. Parents wanted those berries for their children.

Chieftains wanted it for their wives. Soon, tribes were not asking; they were coming in force to get it. That is the curse of Never Grow Old."

"Can it revive the dead?"

Utnapishtim cracked his knuckles, one at a time. "No."

Pain exploded in Gilgamesh's heart. He sagged forward. The table, foodstuffs, and room wavered under his tears. How can so much hope be destroyed by such a simple word?

"Are you certain?" he heard himself ask.

Utnapishtim face had thus far been like a wood sculpture, showing little reaction and less emotion to anything his guest had said. Now, however, there was a subtle twist of anguish near his mouth, a glimmer in his eyes, as old memories shuffled like beasts of his childhood from their caves of slumber. He fought to wrangle them, to push them back where they had come.

"I am."

Gilgamesh stood upright so fast he knocked the chair backwards. He paced around the room wildly.

Utnapishtim said, "It cannot bring your friend back from the dead."

Gilgamesh sobbed once, striding back and forth like a caged beast. He remembered a story from his childhood about a man who had lost a lover to death, and so went into the underworld itself to rescue her. There, he encountered Ereshkigal. They fought. The years rolled around them, yet their battle raged on. Thunder, earthquakes, and at last victory! Ereshkigal cried surrender at long last, and released the lover from Her decaying halls. Gilgamesh thought of the old stories that had proven to be true—the Wildman of the forest, the Guardian Humbaba, and now Utnapishtim himself—and he prayed that this fourth legend might be true as well. Ereshkigal would be no match for me! he screamed inwardly. I'd take Her with my bare hands! I'd beat Her, rip Her apart! After all, is not Ereshkigal the sister of Ishtar?

He looked with last desperate hope to the ancient man who studied him. "Can Never Grow Old preserve the living?"

Utnapishtim sighed. "Yes."

"Then give it to me."

"For whom?"

The king blinked. "For my mother Ninsun, who approaches Ereshkigal's halls daily."

"We all approach those halls—"

"Then perhaps it is time for change!" Gilgamesh leapt and flung aside the table. It flew across the small room and cracked messily on the wall. Siduri gasped. "You've seen so much, Atrahasis! You have seen the world change! A people coming out of ice's shadow to tame the land! Villages swelling to cities!

The wooly titans you speak of, the beasts you saw each day on the horizon, these things have departed the stage of my world! *My own sword has helped in that!* Newer metals, grander pottery, pyramids which stab the sky! When you were a boy, how few men went out to hunt? To raid? To defend? There were *eight thousand men* in Agga's army when it came to lay siege at Uruk. In my city, seventy thousand sleep each night! This world is a tree rooted in change!"

"Who besides your mother?"

Gilgamesh halted, his lips trembling. "What?"

"You wish to preserve your mother against death. Who else?"

Gilgamesh laughed. "Who else indeed! *Me*, mighty ancient! And the sons I have yet to have! And their wives!" His thoughts whirled violently. "And my trusted councilman Nedu, if he wished it. And my other councilors. And Gudea, a brave boy who fought a monster and earned victory with his king! And his father!" The king looked sharply to Siduri. "And to her, who contains mysteries as lofty as your own. Would you have all that she learned perish in a mere few decades?"

Utnapishtim had been threatened before. Back in the days when he founded villages, watched the first cities grow, even ruled from citadels, he had faced death. Each time it thundered along bearing different forms: flint-axes, the beaks of wingless bird-kings, the arrows of tribes, the clubs of *lahmu* or other devils, nearly drowning when fallen overboard during a storm, escaping from the fiery cataclysm of cities far older than Uruk, of illnesses which tried rotting his stomach, of amber blades, bronze blades, copper blades swung for his neck. He looked to the spear slung behind Gilgamesh.

Fear, boiling into panic, wrapped icy tendrils around his heart as he realized suddenly that this stranger had every intention of burying that spear in his heart.

He did not want to die.

"The world could never survive a race of eternal people," Utnapishtim managed.

"Then we shall remake the world! These cold years you speak of … were they tolerant of your people? Did the winters threaten to freeze your bones? Did you allow it to? No! You cut down beasts and stole their fur! You took their bones and made homes! You ripped out their tendons and fitted them to bows! Why not? Where was the evil in that? When the sun is in my eyes I can create shade, and if a loved one of mine were cold I'd spear the sun itself, pull it down, force its golden rays to warm us! I do not accept death! *I do not accept mortality!* Give me a good sword and map, and I'll walk the Fire Road to set free all the shades of all people! My father! The ones we've lost! It is *my* will that changes the world!"

In a blur, Gilgamesh grabbed Utnapishtim and threw him against the wall, twisted the man's tunic, and leered murderously at him.

"You will take me to Never Grow Old or I end the legend of Utnapishtim."

Siduri stood, licking her lips frenetically, wondering what to do. She had no doubt that the Urukian king meant what he said. Her fingers touched her concealed dagger. She saw Utnapishtim look at her for help.

The brown man stared mute as Gilgamesh's fingers closed on his throat. Black dots scampered in front of Utnapishtim's eyes. The room's edges faded.

"I will take you," Utnapishtim said. "But you won't like it."

CHAPTER 43
THE POND

"There," the immortal man said.

Gilgamesh didn't need to look. But he did anyway.

He had noticed the plants when first crossing the pond. Frail, withered, dying, their berries black with death. The water should have nourished them as it did the trees and bushes.

Siduri felt Gilgamesh's pain as surely as it was her own. She crouched, letting her fingers explore the leaves. "Why are they like this?"

"I don't know," Utnapishtim said. "They were rare enough in my own day, but now they're dying off entirely."

Gilgamesh fell on his knees. He gaped and wondered, not for the first time in the last two years, if his life was simply a nightmare from which he might awaken in his silken bed, with a nubile girl resting her sweet head on his chest.

Brown plants. Shriveled leaves.

"This is the only place in all the world where they grow, but they aren't the first plants to be killed off by time and wind and gods. Neither will they be the last."

"*You* are killing them!" Gilgamesh cried. "You have your gift and want none other to possess it!"

Utnapishtim shook his head sadly. "Not so. My survival, and my wife's, is all that concerns me now. These plants died of their own accord. I have tried planting them many places. This pond is their final home. They lived here before your city was built. Budded every twenty or thirty springs, then fifty or sixty, and now not at all."

Gilgamesh could summon no further tears. He knelt, staring the blackened berries. Siduri's arm cradled him.

He looked one final time to the old man. "Then this is my answer?"

Utnapishtim's face turned both grim and mischievous. "Perhaps."

And he walked away.

TABLET XI

URUK

CHAPTER 44
HOMECOMING

The guards in the southern watchtower had seen him coming, and they were at the gate by the time he reached it. Copper-helmeted, looking fine in their livery, they indulged lengthy stares at the strange visitors who were coming to Uruk.

Siduri saw their skeptical eyes from fifty yards off. "Are you truly the king?"

Silence had been her companion through the entire northward quest. It wasn't a cruel silence. Neither was it cold. Wrapped in antelope-skin blankets she slept with it, made love to it, embraced it fiercely, wiped away its tears.

"Yes, Siduri."

Her heart thrilled to hear him say her name after so much time. She hadn't known what to expect, coming to these unknown lands. Seeing Uruk's incredible walls astonished her, pierced her heart with its beauty in the afternoon sun.

The guard-captain glowered with distaste when they came to the gate. "You have business here?"

Gilgamesh nodded.

"State it then!"

"I came to see your regent." Pain blossomed suddenly in his heart, and he wondered how his mother had fared during his absence. Surely no new Dumuzi had tried to supplant her. The possibility tormented him, though, until the guard spoke his next words.

"It's a hot day, beggar. If you have legitimate business, make it known or be on your way."

Gilgamesh smiled at him through the bars without humor. "Regent Ninsun has lost her son on a mission to the Mouth of the Rivers. Look at my eyes, gatekeeper. Tell the priestess her son has returned."

He expected the palace would torture him with memories, and it did. Enkidu's ghost flitted through halls and chambers, along with living bodies like bald Tirigan, dark-faced Rimush, fat Kazallu, one-eyed Zariqu, and Ibi-Sin.

And Ninsun. She ran through the labyrinthine corridors of the palace with a sobbing desperation, and when she saw her long lost child she cried his name aloud, rushing into his embrace.

Siduri looked on, her lips set in a tight lock. So much history pulsated from this place. It moved her to tears that were difficult, so difficult, to withhold.

From far behind her, a white-robed figure came running.

"That nervous gait is unmistakable," said the king.

Nedu panted as he halted beside Ninsun. "Yes, well, it's good your eyes are as well! That gatekeeper was within his rights to slay you for making such a preposterous claim!"

In the most playful, affectionate, and endearing way, Gilgamesh took the councilman by the tunic and drew him close in mock threat. "Do you think that could have happened, my friend?"

Nedu laughed heartily. It felt good to.

The king released him and looked at his mother and Siduri. Yes, he thought, it was time for an introduction.

Nedu watched the three of them leave the hallway. It was then that a most peculiar thing happened. Before King Gilgamesh disappeared out of sight around the corner, Nedu felt his heart and mind grasped with overwhelming portent. It may have been the way the sunlight caught Uruk's master and the tavern-keeper from the south, shimmering on them just the right way. Or perhaps it was the Kishian mead Nedu had gulped upon hearing that king was returned from exile.

Whatever the truth, Nedu believed his wish had been granted: he had indeed been granted a look into Uruk's future.

When summer came there were problems with the canals overflowing, bringing a storm of mosquitoes into the crop fields. The dismantling of Ishtar's ziggurat had been complete for weeks, but there was an abundance of brick piled in city corners and disused avenues and no one knew what to do with it, except that a heavy rainy season was expected and the brick would turn to mud if something wasn't done soon.

Change, Gilgamesh thought. It comes without conscience or mercy.

One evening, Gilgamesh went out into the courtyard where a shapeless block of stone once stood. By moonlight, the canals were milky white and the dragon pools, now possessing scarce few of the magnificent creatures, glowed in magical opalescence. He walked listening to the crickets in the bushes.

"Hello, Enkidu," he said.

The statue watched him blankly. Rendered in the stone, gold, ruby, emerald, amber, Enkidu was larger than in life. The sculptors' chisels had forged the curls of his beard and flowing hair. Silver had been added to his armor, studded with lapis. His eyes were pearl. Onyx glittered on the greaves he wore. His jaw and mouthful of teeth, his eyes smooth as egg-shells. His tawny belly, barrel-chest, ropy arms. It was Enkidu.

The figure stood on a pedestal on which words had been grafted. The king's moistening eyes found the golden placard.

MY FRIEND

"As long as you're in my thoughts," he told the memorial. "You always will be."

For long after he returned to Uruk, Gilgamesh rarely went to sleep early. Instead, he walked through most of the night until, tiring, he retired to his bedchamber. Beneath the covers, Queen Siduri slept peacefully.

Down the hall from the bedchamber, Gilgamesh rarely walked. Enkidu's old room was the source of far too much pain to let it stand as it was. It had been converted into a royal storage room with a secret vault. The night after he visited Enkidu's statue for the first time, Gilgamesh went into this room. His bare feet padded on the cool stone. The ornate door to the secret vault faced him like an emerald serpent's eye.

He stared at it.

There was no need to open it. The vault was sealed by ingenius locking mechanisms allowing no air or moisture. A copper dish lay there. A yellowish berry rested upon it with all the patience of millennia.

Gilgamesh closed his eyes.

At last he understood that final expression on Utnapishtim's face by the pond's edge, when they saw the withered plants. That glint of mischief. For there was only *one* berry left alive on *one* plant, hidden beneath a curling leaf. Gilgamesh had uprooted the entire thing, tried desperately with the help of Uruk's finest gardeners, to get it to proliferate, but it had died long before arriving in the city. The berry didn't.

King Gilgamesh returned to his bedroom. As he slid beneath the covers, Queen Siduri rolled over onto his chest. His lips touched her cheek and she smiled dreamily.

"Hold me forever," she said.

NOTES

The Epic of Gilgamesh is one of the first stories ever written. As such, it provides a spectacular view into the hearts and minds of the people living in civilization's early days. It also demonstrates how little humanity changes; the bond of friendship, the thrill of adventure, and the fear of death (as well as the thirst for immortality) remain dominant in the modern appetite. A lesser theme—that of the friction between man and nature—is also far from irrelevant.

The oft-described Epic of Gilgamesh is actually several distinct stories surrounding the ancient Sumerian king. Like the Bible, some tales were subtracted from the final version—most notably, "Gilgamesh and Agga," which relates the brief confrontation between these two warrior-kings. It was my intent to weave all stories of the Gilgamesh tradition into a single narrative.

To this end I've remained as faithful as possible to the source material. The king, his mother, his friend, as well as Ishtar and Shamhat, Siduri and Utnapishtim, are each featured in the original epic.

Enkidu

Enkidu was a *lahmu* hero, a recurring tradition in Mesopotamian literature. Primitive, hairy, a being of the wilderness, he is Gilgamesh's equal and opposite. Tales of such primal creatures are not, however, the exclusive domain of Mesopotamia.

In 325 BCE while on march through Gedrosia, Alexander the Great encountered a tribe of uncouth, beast-like people. Shaggy, without any understandable language, these primitive beings were called by the Greeks the ichthyophagi—"fish-eaters," a reference to their preferred diet. Alexander attempted to enlist their services, but quickly found attempts to communicate beyond his grasp.

A full list of the historical encounters with such wildmen could well fill an entire book, even before we add folklore to the mix. Time and again in virtually every culture, we find references to this creature, whether he is called an ogre, troll, goblin, knoll, troglodyte, imp, gremlin, dwarf, gnome, bogeyman, kobold, or outright devil. Whether to add the claims of cryptozoology to the mix is a deeper debate. But it does seem unlikely that such a specific report would find universal telling if it was entirely fiction.

Neanderthal Man lived as recently as 30,000 years ago. He was not an ancestor of ours; rather, he was a genetic cousin and contemporary. The two tribes dwelt in the same general regions of the Earth, and at times shared the very same valley. Both hominid, both tool-users and fire-tamers. Both buried their dead with flowers and personal affects.

If stumbling upon a Neanderthal camp, though, you wouldn't think these were just a different bunch of people. Neanderthal was physically far stronger than Cro-Magnon, with a compact muscle density that would make him a terror against the fiercest boxing champion or ultimate fighter. His tolerance for cold was also superior, and he had 150,000 years of survival in some of the most hideous winters this planet has ever seen to prove it. When Cro-Magnon first began its Great Diaspora from Africa into other parts of the world, they encountered these ogre-like beings and, for whatever reason (and we might entertain several) Neanderthal Man and a great deal of other species disappeared into the ether.

However, the notion that scattered tribes may have persisted into historical time hardly seems unreasonable, particularly when we consider that so much of the ancient world remained unexplored; a nifty haven for outsider species. When encountered, they might have given a fright. Stories would be told, of the hairy monsters dwelling in the woods.

Enkidu, Humbaba, and the Bull of Heaven may be pure inventions, or possibly "living fossil" varieties of Neanderthal, Gigantopithicus, or brontothere, respectively. It is also worth noting that many more species likely lived and died on this world than we've found fossils to show, and this was the approach I elected to take when dealing with some of the entities in these pages.

Whatever the truth, it makes for an interesting discussion.

Brian Trent
Prospect, CT
June, 2007

978-0-595-42983-7
0-595-42983-1

Lightning Source UK Ltd.
Milton Keynes UK
UKOW051139140113

204838UK00002B/416/A